FIVE STEPS TO HAPPY

FIVE STEPS
TO HAPPY

Ella Dove

First published in Great Britain in 2019 by Trapeze,
an imprint of The Orion Publishing Group Ltd
Carmelite House, 50 Victoria Embankment,
London EC4Y 0DZ

An Hachette UK company

3 5 7 9 10 8 6 4

A CIP catalogue record for this book is
available from the British Library.

ISBN (Paperback) 9781 4091 8458 4

Typeset by Born Group

Printed and bound in Great Britain by Clays Ltd, Elcograf S.p.A.

www.orionbooks.co.uk

For Althea,
Who has always been there to catch me
Even before I fell.

Note from the author....

On May 29 2016, I woke early on a Sunday morning to go for a jog with my sister, Althea. Bleary-eyed, we pulled on our gym gear and trainers, and headed for the canal path in Stratford, East London, our usual running route. But halfway home, I tripped – and then everything changed.

There was a man on the path that day. He came along as I lay on the ground, a pain like nothing I've ever felt before searing through my right leg. Through tears and panic, Althea and I begged him to phone an ambulance. He did – but then he hung up and told us he had to go. 'I've got a train to catch,' I remember him saying. And then he was gone.

I don't know how long I lay there until the girl appeared; the girl who waited with us and flagged down the ambulance, who helped rather than abandoned. And to this day, neither Althea or I remember anything about the man's physical appearance – only that he was there, and then he wasn't.

For a long time, I was fixated on this stranger. Where was he going that was so crucial? Did he just panic and flee? And, most haunting of all, would things have been different if he'd stayed? This faceless man eventually became Alexander Mitchell. It was the beginning of Five Steps To Happy.

I've been an amputee for a few years now. I won't lie, there have been dark times; times when the outside world seemed so frightening that I wanted to shrivel in my wheelchair and disappear. For a naturally upbeat and positive person, it wasn't a welcome feeling – and psychological recovery from any kind of trauma is an ever-shifting process.

But one thing's for certain – the good times hugely outweigh the bad. The people I've met and the experiences I've had since my accident are amazing and far reaching. I've taken part in a triathlon, told my story on stage in front of a packed theatre and danced with Jonnie Peacock for a *Good Housekeeping* feature (we literally have two left feet, and who could resist that pun?!). I've become an ambassador for the Limbless Association and Barts Health's Transform Trauma campaign, two causes now incredibly close to my heart. And to top it all off, I've achieved a long-held childhood dream that still gives me a little thrill every time I say the words out loud. I, Ella Dove, am an author.

I wonder, readers, if the man from the canal path will pick up this book. And to the faceless stranger on the day that changed my life: if you're out there, know that you're forgiven. Because without you, my own path would never have changed direction.

Thank you all so much for picking up this book.

Ella Dove, January 2019.

Part One

Part One

Chapter One

It took three and a half seconds for me to fall. And yet it felt like slow motion. I landed awkwardly on the canal path. Stones rough against my back. Blood wet on my forearm. My heart pounding.

'Are you all right?'

I opened my eyes and looked up. I'd forgotten that the man was still here. He had the whitest blond hair I'd ever seen. His pale blue eyes darted nervously left and right. He looked as dazed as I felt.

'Heidi,' he asked. 'Are you OK?'

I touched a hand to my head. Had I hit it? My hair smelt of stale smoke and dry shampoo – last night had been my fourth bar shift in a row, penance for yet another failed audition. Three years out of drama school, and still no luck. These days, I was more of a barmaid than an actress. Stale-smelling hair and a sore throat from shouting drink orders over music had become my life. I'd planned to wash my hair post-run. Now, tiny pieces of gravel were caught in the loose lilac strands that were stuck to my cheek. I was flustered and embarrassed.

'Fine, yes . . . I think,' I gabbled. Trust me to trip over in the midst of flirtation. Smooth, as ever. There was something wrong with my leg. I scrabbled up onto my elbows, wincing

3

as pain shot through my knee. My face was hot. I felt drops of cold sweat on my forehead.

I had the urge to get up, to jog home to Dougie, who was back in our flat, sleeping off his hangover after joining me on a riotous post-shift night out with my work friends from Bar Conscience. His door had been closed when I'd left, blissfully unaware of my morning jogging ritual. He never understood why or how I chose to get rid of the toxins with a run. But when I was jogging, I felt free and at peace. My thoughts aligned with my feet on the pavement. The world made sense again.

'Are you sure?' The man, Alexander, looked worried, blond eyebrows knitted together.

'Yeah, yeah.' I waved away his pity. Embarrassment stabbed at my gut. I tensed my stomach muscles and tried to sit up. But the pain in my leg had intensified. There was a rushing in my ears. I collapsed back to the ground. Alexander was staring down at me. I fought the urge to cry.

'My leg . . .' I managed.

I felt sick. The sounds of the birds and the canal water against its banks now seemed loud and unnerving. What was happening?

'That doesn't look good,' Alexander said, uncertain. 'It might be broken.'

'Broken?'

I screwed up my eyes. I thought about my plans for the day – a lazy brunch with Dougie, a Netflix marathon. I'd planned to learn my monologue for next week's audition – not that I was feeling very hopeful about it. That night, I was due to meet Olly Burton-Powell from Tinder, a thirty-four-year-old chef from Hackney with a full beard and a mildly worrying taxidermy hobby. He was to be my third date this week – after sushi with a sales manager named Jeff who'd dropped a spicy tuna roll into his man bag, and non-alcoholic cocktails with

Martin from Brixton (note: teetotal) who'd had his two front teeth knocked out by a BB gun during a re-enactment of the Battle of Waterloo in an East London warehouse. Dating in your thirties was hideous. Let's face it, all the best men had been snapped up already, stowed away with brides and babies, leaving people like me doomed to meet the same rotation of weirdos and narcissists online or else stuck on the 'single' table at weddings.

'You need a hospital,' Alexander said. His voice brought me back to the present. He reached into the pocket of his jeans and pulled out his phone.

'Really?' I lifted my head, attempting to survey the damage. But the world whooshed in and out of focus, forcing me back down against the gravel. Fear began to set in.

'Ambulance, please,' I heard Alexander say.

I blinked once, twice. Nausea rose. My vision blurred. I knew I couldn't try and move again. My body felt rigid with shock, frozen to the ground.

'Yes, hello, there's a girl here by the canal in Stratford, she's tripped over and hurt her leg. We're on the towpath that runs towards Hackney – near Three Mills Studios.

'Yes, she's conscious. Yes, she's breathing, she's responding. OK great, thank you.'

He shoved the phone back into his pocket. I vaguely remembered a first-aid lesson from school. Wasn't it better to stay on the phone to an ambulance?

'It won't be long,' he said.

His body language was twitchy. I remembered the way I'd seen him hurrying along the path, large black headphones blocking out the sound of my approach.

'How are you feeling?'

Hot tears sprang to my eyes.

'So painful.'

5

'Help is on the way, I promise.'

He squinted down at me through the morning sun. His shadow fell across my body.

'Hold tight. Won't be long.'

The pain made everything hazy. Practical thoughts floated through the panic. Would Dougie be awake yet? When would he realise something had happened? Should I cancel my date? Why the hell had I left my phone at home?

Alexander crouched down beside me. He stared anxiously at my leg, his mouth set into a tight line. I could no longer feel my foot. My eyelids flickered. I tried to fight it.

'You'll be OK. Just hold on. The ambulance will be here soon.'

Was he reassuring me, or himself? From inside his pocket, I heard a shrill, old-style ringtone. Alexander retrieved his phone and answered it.

'I know,' he said. 'She told me. I'm coming.'

He ended the call and straightened up. He pressed the screen again, checking the time.

'Look, Heidi, I'm so sorry. I've really got to go.'

'What?' I craned my neck to look at him. I was sure I'd misheard.

Alexander began to pace. Dust from the ground rose up and into the air.

'I need to go,' he said again. His tone was tortured. 'I am so sorry.'

His phone was still in his hand. Every couple of seconds, he checked it. I heard a series of beeps as a flurry of messages came through in quick succession.

'Why?'

Alexander didn't respond. His attention was glued to his screen. Fear jabbed in my stomach. What about the ambulance? Surely he didn't mean it?

'Please,' my voice was rasping and hoarse. 'Don't leave.'

There was no holding back now. Tears ran down the side of my face and dripped into my hair. I pleaded with him, his features blurring in front of me.

'You can't . . .'

How could anyone be so heartless?

'I really have to. I have a train to catch. Please understand . . .'

With every ounce of energy I had left, I tried one last time to force myself upright. Below my knee, I felt a slicing, tearing sensation. I held my breath when I saw my leg, twisted at a horrifying angle in my new green gym leggings. I felt a sound escape my throat. I realised I was screaming.

'Is everything OK?'

Another voice now, high-pitched and urgent. My world swam in and out of focus. A blur of pink with black clothing.

But I didn't hear any more. I took one last look at Alexander before he turned and strode rapidly away. The last thing I remembered was the cloud of conflict behind his eyes. It was the sad smile of a man who had tried to stop me from falling. It was the regret of a man who had missed.

Chapter Two

Two hours later, I was in a curtained cubicle. The drapes were blue, the walls and ceiling white and clinical. A continuous beeping noise entered my consciousness, high-pitched and urgent. I inhaled deeply. There was a hard tube caught in my nostrils. The pain hit me. I started to scream.

'It's OK.' An unfamiliar voice. A blurred face in front of me. 'We'll make it better, promise.' I felt a warm sensation through my wrist and up my arm. And then I was no longer there.

There was a buzzing in my ears. I was swaying on choppy seas. Up and down, up and down. I felt blissfully numb. A night sky with pink stars glittered in front of me. A purple-tinged haze like smoke. I was caught between worlds; a life in motion, floating, but not unpleasant.

'Where am I?' I asked. Was I alone? Could anyone hear me? I tried to open my eyes. I could feel my heart thrumming.

'Heidi?'

Voices saying my name. Lots of them, over and over, urgent and insistent. Inside or outside my mind? Impossible to tell. I shook my head. I didn't want to listen.

'No . . .' I mumbled. Don't shake me from this euphoria. Don't wake me up. Don't break the spell.

'Heidi, can you hear us?'

'She's totally out of it.'

Hands on my shoulders. I gulped in a lungful of air. The hospital room was shrinking. Strange faces began to appear; sudden horror overtaking the bliss. A face in the bed sheets; gurning and terrible. Then others on the wall, in the curtains, in the clock, among the lights. They grinned with menacing eyes and wide mouths, moving closer, ever closer. They were going to suffocate me. The walls were closing in. I tried to scream, but they were pressing on my chest. I couldn't catch my breath.

'Her heart rate's dropped.'

'Heidi, breathe.'

A sharp tap near my collarbone. I gasped; a terrible, screeching sound. Then a different face. A man. A nurse. Dark eyes, kind face.

'Come on. Breathe.'

The oxygen filled my lungs. The pink fog grew thinner.

'Heidi?' My dad's voice, almost a whisper.

I reached towards him, noticing a collection of tubes dangling from the inside of my right wrist. A sharp pain shot up my arm.

'Is she OK?' he asked. His thick eyebrows were furrowed in concern, almost meeting in the middle of his leathery forehead. As children, we used to pretend they were caterpillars.

'It's wearing off,' the male nurse said. His eyes were like chocolate buttons. I squinted to read his yellow name badge; Joaquim.

'Thank God,' my mum answered. 'Her breathing was so shallow. I thought she could have . . . Oh , I don't know what I think any more.'

'It's the shock.' Joaquim soothed. 'She will be very tired now, but she's over the worst. We never know exactly how patients will be with ketamine. It is the strongest painkiller we have – but sometimes it has this effect.'

'Horse tranquiliser,' I murmured. Some of the drama school gang took it. I'd been tempted, in the past. But now, I couldn't stop shaking. A sense of blackness and doom obscured everything.

'Well, it can also be used for that, yes,' Joaquim answered.

'It's . . . it's cruel. For the horses.' My mouth was so dry. Every word was an effort. My head flopped, doll-like against the lumpy pillows. None of this felt real.

'Shhh, love,' Mum said. Normally immaculate, her long grey hair was clipped into a messy ponytail. She wore a creased blue linen dress and a coral cardigan that didn't match. She'd usually hate being out in public like this. She must have left the house in a rush.

'Do you know where you are, Heidi?' Dad asked. His eyes were pink and puffy, ringed with exhaustion. His receding, badger-like hair stuck up at odd angles.

'Hospital,' I said.

That much I could tell. There was a digital clock on the wall. I strained to read it. It was out of focus. My bed was by the window. The London skyline was black against a backdrop of heavy grey clouds, obscuring an early morning sun. What time was it exactly?

'That's right,' Dad said. His voice was low and hushed. He seemed to have shrunk from the capable man I grew up with, knobbly shoulders slumped in his tatty indoor cardigan. 'You . . . well, you had an accident.'

'I fell.'

He nodded sadly. 'You did.'

'Oh, it's all so ridiculous,' Mum said through her tears. 'A flat path! This shouldn't be happening. Tim, it shouldn't be like this.' She buried her face in his cardigan. He brought a hand up to stroke her head.

'I know, love,' he murmured. 'Trust me, if I could turn back time, I would.'

A fractured memory came back to me then; the path, the fall, the man walking away.

'The date . . .' I said out loud. There was no way I'd make it now.

'I hate this,' Dad said to Mum. 'I hate that there's nothing I can do. I just want to fix it, Sandy.' They clung to each other.

A damp patch had appeared on Dad's cardigan, Mum's tears soaking into the sleeve. I felt confused – why was I in hospital? I realised then that I was no longer wearing my gym clothes. A loose hospital gown covered my body, layered with a sheet and a scratchy blue blanket. Cold, synthetic air hit my skin and I shivered. There was an open carton of apple juice next to my bed. The contents had spilt, sticky and shining on the table. The sickly sweet smell made me retch.

The nurse, Joaquim, leant over me and wrapped something around my upper arm. A gold link chain dangled from his neck above my head. His forearms were tanned and hairy, a white watch mark around his wrist. A machine bleeped and the cuff tightened. Panic swelled in my chest. I couldn't breathe. No. No, not again. I screamed out.

'No, get off!'

'Shhh,' he said, his tone kind but professional. 'It's only the blood pressure machine. No problem, see?'

And then it was over. Joaquim released me, placing a cool hand on my clammy forehead. I waited for my heart to slow down.

'It's OK, Heidi,' Dad said. 'Just breathe. It's OK.'

'Why am I here?' I asked. Nothing made sense. 'What's happening?'

'You're in intensive care,' Mum replied.

'What?' No. I tried to sit up. Looming blackness pushed me back. 'Why?'

'How do we explain?' Mum said. She squeezed Dad's hand. His eyes were rimmed with red. I'd never seen him cry before.

'I can't . . . I don't know,' he answered. He tripped over his words. 'I just, I'm sorry.' He bent over, face in his hands. His shoulders were shaking.

Mum looked to Joaquim. 'Help us,' she whispered. 'Please.' Joaquim nodded. He took a breath, his thick lips set into a tight line.

'Heidi, you had a very bad accident,' he began.

'My leg . . . it hurts so much.' I tried to wiggle my toes. I couldn't. Dad scraped his plastic chair closer.

'When you fell, you dislocated your knee badly, love,' he said quietly. 'The blood supply was cut off.'

'What?'

'They tried so hard.' Mum was wracked with sobs now. 'You were in there for over twelve hours.'

'We stayed here the whole time,' Dad said. 'Just sitting, waiting. And when you came out, when they brought you back, it was . . . we didn't expect . . .'

'Wait, what? I don't understand,' I said. I tried to focus, but they were speaking too fast. I couldn't follow them. The cubicle felt like it was shrinking.

'The surgeons,' Joaquim said. 'They had to act fast. Mr Rhys Jones is one of the best vascular consultants in the business, Heidi. Believe me, he and the team did everything they could. But in the end, it was too dangerous to leave it.'

He gestured towards my leg. Fresh jolts of pain surged through my body. With huge effort, I raised my head as much as I could manage. And then I saw it.

As I lifted the sheets, a strangled gasp escaped my throat. I wanted to scream, but I didn't have the energy. I threw the covers back down again. If I didn't look, maybe it wouldn't be real. It couldn't be real. Shock consumed me. I was going to be sick.

Because where my right leg should have been, the blue blanket lay completely flat.

*

Somehow, the day had disappeared. All around, tiny red and green lights glowed and flickered in the dark ward. The whirring and beeping of machines provided a constant reminder of activity, as though the brightness had been turned down on the bustling daytime routine. Next to me, a man called out for Allah. His voice was cracked and heavy with pain.

I pressed my morphine button continuously, desperate for even the merest hint of relief. I remembered I'd been told that it was on a timer; that it was a deliberate technique used to stop an accidental overdose. Yet still my finger found the button, my knuckles turning white with the effort.

Sleep came in fits and starts, momentarily dulling my senses with the sweetness of oblivion. But every time I woke up, I remembered the hideous truth. I was living in a nightmare.

Every movement was agony. I was sure I could still feel my right foot, that it was trapped beneath the short, bulky bandage now encasing my amputated leg. I could even wiggle my toes beneath the skin. The firing of nerves felt like pins and needles, electric jolts that made my whole body convulse.

I felt suddenly hot. The pillow beneath me was soaked with sweat, droplets trickling through my scalp, making me itch. Just moments ago I'd been cold, teeth chattering almost painfully, sheets and blankets pulled up to my neck. The night nurses floated ethereally past, skilled at their noiseless care. It seemed as though they moved in slow motion, communicating with a series of nods and gestures, their smiles casting a warming reassurance over the patients they surveyed.

'Hot,' I croaked. In the bed opposite, a woman was crying. I couldn't see her but I heard the sobs, deep and rasping, echoing across the room.

I was scared, but I was also angry. Angry at the world; at the man who had left me, at myself. I'd taken everything for granted. All the times when I'd forced my body to cope with pinching and blisters, the times when my feet were cracked in winter and I hadn't bothered with foot cream. Why hadn't I looked after them better? Now, it was too late. Now, everyone else had more control of my body than I did.

'Hot,' I said again; louder this time.

My nurse for the night switched on the fan next to my bed. The breeze dried my forehead. I turned my face towards it and the cool air hit my skin. The relief was sweet. But I knew it was temporary.

'Heidi, we need to move your position,' she said.

Her badge read 'Natalia'. Her olive skin was flawless and she wore a tiny silver 'N' around her neck.

I forced myself to focus on the clock on the wall. It was 3.26 a.m. A continuing current ran down my right leg, right to the ends of my toes, even though they were no longer there. I took an obscure comfort in the sensation. My brain still remembered how things should be. Maybe, in that case, there was hope.

'I can feel my foot,' I told Natalia.

'Is normal,' she nodded. 'Phantom pain. We move your position now. Press your pain button before we start.'

I followed her advice and felt the buzz of morphine enter my arm. Natalia and two others placed their hands beneath me, counted to three and slowly, gently, rolled me onto one side, cushioning my back with pillows. I was shouting. I couldn't help it. The noise escaped from within me, a deep, animalistic screech.

'Shhh,' Natalia soothed, her smooth accent like cool, flowing water. 'Is OK. We are done.'

I felt out of breath, sick and dizzy. I pressed the morphine button again and again, frustrated when no more relief would come. Natalia placed a hand on my head, smoothing back the damp lilac strands from my forehead.

I felt like the pain would never leave me. The nurses retreated; floating towards their next patients, fading into the darkness. The oxygen tube was hard and uncomfortable as I tried to regain my breath.

I remembered the last time I saw my foot – the bright red toenails, the mottled hue of the cold skin beneath. The foot that had helped me learn to walk, to run, to jog up stairs or run down beaches into clear blue waters. The foot that had worn toe rings, anklets and henna when I'd visited India before university. The foot I'd shoved into all kinds of painful and inappropriate shoes: glittery jellies, platform trainers and precarious stilettos. I'd already got my bridesmaid shoes for my sister Jenny's wedding; nude-coloured heels with tiny decorative pearls. I'd been planning a pearl pedicure to match. The foot I'd jogged on, just hours ago.

I imagined the nerve endings in my leg firing desperate signals, working in overdrive to replace my missing piece. The thought filled me with sadness. Tears fell into my pillow, the salty tang of memories and heartbreak. Even now, my body was fighting for me. But it was a fight I'd never win.

Chapter Three

After four days in the high dependency unit, I'd been moved to the trauma ward. I should have been relieved to have my own room after the non-stop activity of Intensive Care. But all I felt was sadness. The move had hugely unsettled me, a small change with what seemed like a monumental psychological impact. I missed Natalia and all my nurses from HDU. I hated that they'd already moved on from me to look after someone else.

I shivered beneath the air vent above me, fighting fever, my forehead soaked with cold sweat. My stump was encased in a huge bandage. Yellowish brown discharge had leaked from the wound and spread across the plaster. An acrid smell of iodine and flesh buried itself in my nostrils. It revolted me. I pulled the blue hospital blanket up to my nose. The walls in this room were stark and cracked, soaked in the anguish of patients who'd lain here before me.

'Hello, my little sunshine!'

Uma, one of the healthcare assistants, barged into the room and wrenched back the curtains without warning. I squinted and groaned in the sudden, piercing sunlight.

Uma raised her arms heavenwards. 'Why you lay in dark? It is beautiful today!'

My mouth was dry and my leg was throbbing. My view from the twelfth floor looked out to the other side of the hospital, rows of curtained windows with fears and unknown futures beyond. I didn't want the curtains open. I wanted to shut out the world.

'Don't,' I protested. She ignored me.

'What time is it?' I asked. I had no concept of the days passing. Not that it mattered. Nothing mattered any more.

'Visiting time!' she chirruped. 'And someone is here!'

'What? No . . .'

I didn't want to see anyone. Especially not today. If life had gone to plan, I'd be on my way to my audition right now, nerves fluttering in my stomach. It was set to be my biggest opportunity since I'd finished drama school three years ago. Everyone kept asking me when I'd 'make it', when I'd get my so-called 'big break'. Jade had been signed to a top agency and had already done three TV adverts, with several more in the pipeline. Jonno was doing *An Inspector Calls* in Ealing, while Emily had landed a UK tour of *Starlight Express* and was currently travelling the length of the country – it helped that she could roller-skate. After countless futile auditions, I'd had a good feeling about this one. But now it had been ripped away; all the hard work and preparation falling into an ever-deepening pit of darkness.

'It's your sister!' Uma announced. Her high-pitched cheerfulness was grating. 'She outside! I get her . . .'

'Uma, no, I don't want . . .' But she'd gone.

A few minutes later, Jenny appeared. Tall and deer-like, her head almost brushed the doorway as she came in. Hiding behind her was my five-year old niece, Evie. She wore her school summer dress and was clutching a cluster of Barbie dolls.

Jenny swept into my room, threw her bags and camel trench-coat on a plastic chair and planted a kiss on my head. She wrinkled her pointy nose.

'Lord, have you showered today?'

I shook my head.

Jenny tutted and threw me my cosmetics bag from my bedside table. It landed with a thump on my stomach.

'Well, at least use some body spray, will you? For my sake if nothing else.' Reluctantly, I did as she asked. It was easier not to argue with Jenny.

'Mummy, what is this for?' Evie was pointing to the hand sanitiser by the door.

'It's for cleaning our hands, darling,' Jenny answered. 'We can have some when we go home.' She turned back to me. 'Sorry, Mark's away at a conference and the after-school club's off – Mrs Mayhew had to take her cat for emergency dental treatment. I had no choice – I had to bring her with me.'

She dumped a canvas tote on top of the sheets in front of me. 'Now, I've brought you a few bits. Just little things that might be useful.'

'Thanks, Jen.'

I rummaged in the bag. More face wipes, hand cream, some cooling skin spray, a cherry lip balm and several packets of tissues. I pulled out an adult colouring book and stared dubiously at the tiny geometric patterns. The black lines blurred. My head ached.

'Good for mindfulness,' Jenny said. She waved a hand demonstrably. The diamond of her engagement ring flashed in the light. 'The latest wellness trend.'

'OK . . .' I snapped the book shut and placed it on my bedside table along with the set of sparkly gel pens. When it came to art, I had limited patience at the best of times. In school textiles lessons, I'd once bought a T-shirt, cut the label out and tie-dyed it. Amazingly, I'd got an A – but then our teacher, Miss Grayson, had been distracted due to her not-so-secret fling with Mr Single (real name) from Woodwork.

'Well, do you like your gifts, Heidi?' Jenny asked as if speaking to Evie. I nodded wordlessly. My bones ached with exhaustion. She cast a glance at my niece, now cross-legged with her Barbies on the floor. 'We chose them together, didn't we? Evie?' No response.

'Jenny, it's OK, she doesn't have to . . .'

'Evie,' Jenny said again, sterner now. I recognised her Teacher Voice coming out. 'Come over here and say hello to Auntie Heidi.'

Evie stood up and crept slowly closer, Barbies held out like a weapon. She looked dishevelled, as she always did after a day at school, her meticulously tied pigtails now loose and drooping, one of her knee-length school socks halfway down her leg. Unlike Jenny and Mark, she was a dreamer, the sort of little girl who sat for hours surrounded by toys and imagination, who didn't fold her clothes before PE and who frequently misplaced her possessions, much to Jenny's annoyance.

'Hi, Evie,' I said.

At first, she didn't look at me. Her eyes darted nervously around the room, taking in the clinical surroundings; the sticky plastic chairs, the wires and tubes, the yellow hazardous waste bin. But then she noticed my leg. I saw the moment she clocked it; her little face pale, her expression more uncertain than ever. She poked out her bottom lip and stepped quickly backwards. Watching her reaction, a new and awful pain stabbed at my heart.

'Evie . . . it's OK,' I said, as gently as I could. 'It's only me.' But my niece had scooted back towards Jenny. She clamoured at my big sister, wide-eyed with fear.

'Mummy, I don't like it,' she said. It was a whisper, but I heard. The tremor in her voice ripped through me. I was a monster.

'Don't be silly, darling.' Jenny said in a singsong tone. 'Auntie Heidi had a very bad accident. Remember what I told you? We need to be kind.'

'But I don't like this place.' A pale pink blush had spread across her cheeks. She looked like she was going to cry. 'It smells funny. I want to go home.'

Jenny cast me a concerned glance, her businesslike demeanour now vanished. My fingers gripped the sheets, knuckles turning white as I tried to control my own tears.

'She doesn't mean it, Heidi,' she said quietly. 'She doesn't understand.'

'I know,' I said, though it felt like my world was broken. 'I don't like it either.'

The door was flung open and Uma came in.

'Your tablets,' she announced.

The tiny paper pot rattled as she set it down beside me. She eyed my lunch left untouched on the tray; two bites taken out of my tuna sandwich, a bruised banana still in its skin.

'You must eat,' she said.

'I don't feel like it.'

'Oh, come on, my sunshine.' Uma fixed Jenny with an enormous smile. 'This is your sister?'

'Hi, I'm Jenny,' she said.

'Well, hello! So nice to meet you. You tell your sister, she needs to eat, OK?'

'She's right, Heidi.' Jenny's face was creased with sincerity. 'You need to look after yourself.' Uma nodded, satisfied at the backup.

'You listen to your sister, darling,' she said. 'And cheer up, OK?'

Cheer up? Seriously? When my entire life was in tatters? I wanted to punch the insensitive cow. My fingers gripped the sheets even harder, balling them up into fists.

'Heidi . . .' Jenny warned. I knew she'd picked up on my mood. As little girls, I was the hot-headed one, the one most likely to brawl in the playground or turn a bickering session

20

into a full-on fight. Over the years, I'd got better at controlling it. But now it flared inside me, white hot and dangerous. I exhaled deeply through my nose, counting to ten in my head like Dad had always taught me. It was only Evie, cowering behind Jenny, who stopped me from letting rip completely.

'Now, temperature and blood pressure time!' Uma sang.

She squeaked across the room in her regulation shoes. She raised the thermometer aloft.

'Mummy, what is that lady doing?' Evie asked quietly. I saw Jenny look to me, then back to her frightened daughter. A brief nod of understanding passed between us.

'Evie, why don't we go and get a snack from the café?' she said. 'We'll come back a bit later.' Evie's expression brightened immediately.

'Is there chocolate?' she asked hopefully.

'Probably.'

'OK!' Evie jumped up and skipped towards the door. She didn't look back at me.

Once they'd gone, Uma jammed the thermometer into my ear. I winced, but the pain was nothing compared to my emotional torment. I couldn't get Evie's terrified expression out of my head.

'Is good,' Uma said approvingly. 'Now, we do blood pressure.'

She turned on the machine and it woke up with its usual series of five staccato beeps, the sound of them now imprinted on my mind. Robotically, I held out my arm, feeling the Velcro cuff tighten as the measurement was taken.

'Oh,' Uma took a clipboard from the end of the bed and scribbled furiously. 'Blood pressure is low. You need to drink more.'

'Of course it is. I've been lying down.' I couldn't hide my frustration.

'You drink big glass of water, yes sunshine?' Uma said, unperturbed. Her enthusiasm was having the opposite effect on me. I was tired of being nice to infuriating healthcare staff. I was tired of everything.

'Please,' I said as calmly as I could. Rage boiled within me. The woman was infuriating. 'Please go.'

'What?'

'Get out of my room.' I took a breath and lowered my voice. 'Please. I want to be alone.'

'OK . . .' Uma retreated uncertainly, her hands held high. 'I pray for you.'

The door closed. I pulled the sheets over my head. The air beneath smelt stale and tangy, a tomb of my own making. My whole body was quivering. Encased in futility, smothered by fear, I began to sob.

Chapter Four

From the moment Dougie walked in, I could tell Jenny had told him about my outburst. His soft voice had an unfamiliar lilt; a tone of forced positivity, his smile just a little too wide.

'There she is,' he said.

He stooped to give me a hug. He smelt like Issey Miyake and coffee. At six foot six, he seemed to fill the room, a hulk of a man with broad shoulders, large features and long dreadlocks tied back in a low ponytail. The top two buttons of his shirt were undone and he'd rolled his sleeves up as he always did at the end of a working day. A royal blue tie poked out from his pocket. An IT consultant for a financial services company in Canary Wharf, he had to dress smartly, although he'd live in his extensive array of active wear if he had the chance; branded vests and T-shirts and fitted track-suit bottoms. I glanced over to the window – was it evening already? Sure enough, dusk had descended outside, the sky a moody shade of orange. I blinked, recalibrating. The stark hospital lighting hurt my eyes.

'Jenny called you, didn't she?' I sighed. My run-in with Uma and subsequent breakdown had left me utterly exhausted. I felt like my tear ducts had dried up.

'Well, yeah.' Dougie eyed me sheepishly. 'I was planning on

coming anyway. But she wanted to warn me you'd had a bad day. She's only being protective.'

'Dougie, every day here is a bad day.'

'I know.' His black-brown eyes were wide and earnest. 'What happened to you is just . . . well, it's the worst thing, H. It's shit, it's unfair, and to be honest, you're entitled to react however you bloody well want.'

'Thanks, Dougie.' I took in the creases on his shirt, the deep shadows under his eyes. He looked as shattered as I felt.

'I brought you something,' he said. He passed me a large carrier bag. 'Sorry it's not wrapped. I meant to buy wrapping paper, but time just kind of disappeared . . .'

'It's fine.'

I managed a smile. Dougie Oyinola was one of the most scatterbrained people I'd ever met. He'd lost more wallets, phones and sets of keys than I could count. In fact, we often joked that his disorganised nature was how we'd become friends. On our very first day at primary school, he was distraught to discover that he'd left his new pencil case in his mum's car. Seeing him upset, I'd lent him my crayons, and we'd spent the afternoon drawing together. We'd made a pact then and there to become best friends. Amazingly, we'd stuck to it. We separated to go to different secondary schools and universities, but we'd been in contact every day, both eventually gravitating towards the twinkling lights of London, where we'd decided to move in together. He was the brother I'd never had. And despite his job in IT, he still had a passion for art.

'I hope you like it,' he said. Despite his imposing physique, he'd always been a gentle giant; shy, sensitive and thoughtful.

I reached into the bag and pulled out a large grey throw. My fingers ran across the soft fur, the sensation instantly reassuring.

'Dougie, it's perfect.'

'Hal tried to convince me to buy one of those fancy hand-woven Moroccan ones, but well, I thought you needed something a bit more comforting.'

'Course he did.'

Hal was Dougie's partner. Ten years older and a manager at the same company, they'd met just over six months ago when Dougie had been summoned from IT's basement lair to fix Hal's computer. As it turned out, there was nothing wrong with it – Hal had unplugged several wires in a ruse to ask Dougie for a drink. In fact, that pretty much summed up Hal Wesley-Fogg; confident to the point of ridiculous. He would do anything to get what he wanted, a trait I personally found very off-putting. But Dougie had agreed to move in with him after just six months together – he owned a flat in Canary Wharf which he shared with his ragdoll house cat, Princess Diana. Even before this, I'd hated the idea of Dougie leaving our cosy if chaotic rented flat. Now, the thought struck terror in my heart. What if he left me alone?

'Glad you like it,' Dougie said of the blanket.

I managed a weak smile in return.

'Definitely nicer than those hideous blue things, anyway.' He gestured at the bobbly hospital blanket draped across my bed. 'I just thought, well, anything I can do to make this whole experience a little bit more bearable, y'know? It must be hell staring at these same four walls every day.' He surveyed the sparse space. The only sign of personalisation were my 'get well' cards that Mum had lined up along the windowsill, which grew in number every day. The nurses always knocked them over. They didn't always pick them up. Dougie let out a low whistle.

'Wow, someone's popular.' He pointed at the largest card which displayed a sad cartoon puppy and the words *Sorry to hear you're feeling ruff*. Definitely not an appropriate choice, Jenny and I had agreed.

'Who's that big one from?'

'The bar gang.'

I'd worked at Bar Conscience for over two years now. It had started as a stopgap to bring in some cash while I awaited my big acting break. It had since become near enough full-time. I hadn't found fame – but I had found a great group of friends. In fact, they'd taken over from my drama school pals, who were largely too busy seeking their respective fortunes to even try and stay in touch. Though the staff turnover was high and a few of them had moved on, we always stayed in touch, meeting up for drink-fuelled birthdays and raucous celebrations.

They'd all scrawled over-the-top and inappropriate messages in the card. 'Can't wait to do shots again soon,' party-girl Ally had written. 'You're beautiful and strong – and I cry every time I think about what happened,' sensitive Laura added. 'Get the fuck back here now,' tough-as-nails Caitlin had kindly contributed. My heart skipped when I spotted Ben Grady's loopy scrawl in the corner.

'Chin up, Jackson,' he'd written, with a winking smile. 'B.' There were two kisses beneath the letter. Ben was an Australian cocktail expert with chiselled cheekbones and a glint in his eye. We'd been sleeping together for about three months on and off, a very casual arrangement that Dougie wholly disapproved of. Ben was a famed womaniser full of two-dimensional charm, and I knew that too. I just kept coming back because I didn't have anything else going on in my love life. It didn't help that he was gorgeous.

However, despite these messages in the card, not one of my colleagues had asked to visit. I was disappointed in them, but I was also a tiny bit glad. I didn't want anyone to see me so vulnerable, least of all Ben. I wasn't strong enough to cope with their 'banter.'

'Look, H,' Dougie said, 'I had an idea on my way here. How do you feel about a trip to the café downstairs?'

'What?' While I'd been disconnected from the drain and catheter, I was still reliant on occasional morphine to soften the pain. I stared at the tubes in my wrist. The idea of being so far away from potential relief sparked panic in my gut. 'Like, now?'

'No time like the present.'

I hesitated.

'I don't think I can.' I'd only transferred to the wheelchair a few times – on each occasion with two nurses and a physio on hand. They'd shown me how to manoeuvre myself to the toilet, but the furthest I'd wheeled myself was to the end of the ward and back. I wasn't ready for this. I felt a tightening in my chest. This room was safe. Outside, there was only fear.

'It might do you good.' Dougie lent forward and put his big hand on my arm. It was warm and reassuring against my pale, goosebumped skin.

'But what if people stare? I couldn't bear it, Dougie. I don't want to be a freak show.'

'I won't let them.' He raised a three-finger salute to his forehead. 'Scout's honour.'

'You hated Scouts.' He grinned at me then, a flash of mischief twinkling through the worry.

'I know. And I still can't tie a reef knot. So, are we going then?'

I nodded, defeated. I didn't want to. But as with so many aspects of life since the accident, it seemed like I didn't have a choice.

'Excellent.' He handed me the men's oversized Nike sweat-shirt that hung from the back of the chair. 'I don't mean to sound like Jenny, but pop this on. You might get chilly. Wait, hang on a second, isn't this mine?'

'Maybe.' I pulled it over my pyjamas. 'It's been in my room for ages. And anyway, you packed the clothes bag for me. You could have taken it back, but you put it in there . . .' I was gabbling now, compensating for the extreme, irrational nerves that flowed and pulsed through my body. Dougie rolled his eyes in faux-annoyance.

'Bloody cheek. Honestly.'

Next to my bed, the wheelchair was waiting. Dougie put his hands beneath my armpits and I slowly rose, shuffling to the edge of the bed the way I'd been shown a few days before by the physios. Pain followed my every movement. I felt fragile, like paper. I placed my left foot on the ground and he helped me to stand, my toes clenching as my hospital-issue slipper socks gripped the floor. I wobbled dramatically. My muscles tensed. I felt like I was on a tightrope.

'That's it, almost there,' Dougie said.

Using him for balance, I pivoted on one foot, performing a half turn before toppling inelegantly into the wheelchair. The cushion sighed. I'd made it. Slowly and cautiously, I lifted my amputated leg up and onto the stump board that was attached to the front of the chair. I hated the way it poked out in front of me, like the leg was screaming for unwanted attention.

'Can you pass my blanket?'

'Course.'

He tossed it over and I spread it across my legs, grateful for the cover. I unclipped my brakes, ready for the off. I could do this, I told myself. There was no need to feel panicked. But the tight feeling in my chest continued.

'Shotgun driver!' Dougie said.

'What the . . . ?'

But before I could finish my sentence, he jerked the ancient wheelchair into motion. It gave a loud creak of surprise as we turned sharply from the room. Out in the corridor, he started to jog. I gripped the arms of the chair so hard that my knuckles turned white.

'Dougie!' I screeched.

All at once, I was powerless, totally in his control. It was terrifying flying so fast along the corridor. But it was also weirdly exhilarating.

'Freedom!' he yelled. 'Escaped patient on the loose!'

He ran faster. With chipped maroon paint and rusting wheels, the wheelchair was unused to such breakneck speed. It squealed and groaned in protest. It reminded me of all the times we'd taken our bikes to the woods as children. Dougie was the one who'd egged me on to freewheel down the steepest muddy slopes, or to try tricks and wheelies across ditches, much to Jenny's irritation. We'd returned home with dirt covered knees and leaves in our hair, while Jenny and her bike remained pristine.

Several nurses tutted as we careered past. My heart was in my mouth. At the lifts, Dougie came to a sudden stop. He swept a hand across his shining brow. He was panting.

'How was that?'

'Bloody terrifying.'

He began to laugh. Seeing the light returning to his eyes sparked something within me. For the first time since the accident, I realised I was laughing too. It felt so good to release it, hiccupping convulsions as powerful as sobs. Once I'd started, I couldn't stop. It was almost manic. I breathed deeply, struggling to regain my composure.

'It's good to see you smile, H,' Dougie said. 'And now I know how to make it happen, well, there are plenty more high thrill rides where that came from.'

'You better not.'

Yet to my surprise, I didn't actually mind. Over the past few days, everyone had approached me like I was a china doll; delicate, fragile, breakable. Granted, I was all of those things, but I was also still me, still the same person I was before. Dougie was the first of my family and friends to recognise that. He was the first to treat me normally. And no one but me could fully understand just how important that was.

Peak post-work visiting time, and the hospital café was buzzing. Families and friends huddled around cappuccinos and mochas, deep in conversation. It was easy to distinguish the visitors from the patients, the patients with their dressing gowns and machinery, or else in their own clothes, looking too pale for the time of year. A long queue snaked from the counter, surgical staff in blue scrubs and brightly coloured crocs waiting patiently behind anxious relatives, too stressed to decide what to drink. Floor-to-ceiling windows bathed the foyer in a garish glow that made me blink. My head was still pounding. I realised it was the first time I'd seen real sunlight in almost two weeks.

Dougie bought us cappuccinos and wheeled me over to a table in the far corner, parking me facing the window. Outside the main entrance to the hospital, I could see a gang of incredibly sick looking patients, all smoking. One of them had an oxygen tank. Dougie saw me looking.

'Makes you wonder, doesn't it?' he said.

I looked around, taking in my surroundings. I wasn't the only one in a wheelchair. In fact, there were loads of us. The world hadn't collapsed when I left my room. And no one was staring at me.

'It was the audition today,' I told Dougie, shivering but emboldened. '*The Curious Incident of the Dog in the Night-Time*. The only West End audition I've ever had.'

'Oh man.' His eyes filled with pity. 'That's rough. You'll get back to it though. I know you will.'

'I'm not sure.' The idea of standing on a stage, all eyes on me, was currently too much to bear. 'I can't really think about it right now.'

'Completely understandable.'

I stared beyond him, out of the window, where a steady stream of people flowed to and fro. A middle-aged woman helped her elderly mother into a taxi. A teenage boy hopped towards the entrance on crutches. Two hospital transport drivers in dark green uniforms sat on a low wall, sharing a large bag of crisps.

'You OK there, buddy?' Dougie asked. I blinked, turning my focus back to him.

'Yeah . . . Sorry. I was miles away.'

'Do you think about it much?' he asked. 'The accident, I mean.'

I looked down at what was left of my leg, my stump blotched with scars and blue and purple bruises. It was a horrible word, stump. So harsh, so hard; so final. I pulled my blanket closer.

'It's all I think about,' I said quietly. 'Even when I try not to, it's there.'

'Course it is.' His expression was tortured. 'Honestly, H, it kills me to imagine you lying there.'

'Oh, Dougie!' I reached across the table and placed my hand on top of his. It was like of a game we used to play at school, piling our hands up and pulling the bottom one out as quickly as we could.

'Thank God someone found you. You could have been there for hours.'

'It felt like I was.' I still had no idea how long I'd been on the path. My memory had veiled the incident, casting shadows of uncertainty over timescales and order. 'Dougie, the guy who was with me when it happened, Alexander. I'd just asked him out when I fell.'

He raised his eyebrows, a new lightness covering his worry. 'Tell me more. . .'

'Yeah.' I shrugged. 'I bumped into him. Literally. We got chatting for a good five minutes. I thought he was attractive, so I decided to go for it and ask if he fancied a coffee.

'You did what?' Dougie's eyes were wide. 'That's bold, H.'

'I know.' How I wished I could turn back time. Why hadn't I ignored him like people usually did in London? I could have just kept to my plan, jogged home for breakfast and returned unscathed. I shook my head, the regret overwhelming. 'Anyway, it was pointless. He said no; waved the idea away with some vague excuse about needing to go. And then I fell.'

'Oh, Heidi.' Dougie stared at me, his eyes glinting with a mix of sadness and amusement. 'Only you.'

'Don't.' I pushed the thought of Alexander firmly aside. I didn't want to think about him any more. 'So, how is everyone?' I asked, trying to change the subject. I needed a distraction. 'I mean, really. How are they doing?'

'Coping as well as we can, I guess.' He fiddled with his ponytail, undoing and retying the elastic band around his dreadlocks as he often did when he felt awkward. 'Your mum cries a lot – when she's not hoovering, apparently. She told me on the phone the other day that she can't stop cleaning. And your dad's finding all kinds of things to fix. Says he's in the garage for hours.'

'Oh, Dad.' Dad was a newly retired building surveyor. Never an emotional man, he always channelled his feelings into practical matters. It was probably where Jenny got it from.

'I know. But you know it's his way of coping.' Dougie took a sip of his cappuccino. 'Jenny's gone into manic wedding organisation mode, which won't surprise you. Poor old Mark's bearing the brunt of that as usual.'

'And you? How are you doing?'

Dougie paused, considering. When he spoke again, he didn't meet my eyes.

'I've decided to take some time off work,' he said quietly. 'I got signed off today.' At this admission, his big frame seemed to crumple, shoulders hunching in his creased white shirt. The worry in his eyes suddenly made sense.

'Oh no, Dougie, why?'

'I just can't deal with it at the moment. It's too much. Hal's not happy about that, of course – he says I need to go back and use it as a distraction. But I can't, H. Not just yet. I don't want to argue with him but I need some time to sort my head out. All I can think about is you. Oh, actually, that reminds me.'

He reached into his pocket and took out a piece of paper, folded into a tiny square. He unfolded it and handed it to me.

'I drew this on the night of your accident. We had so long to wait while you were in theatre. I had to do something. Anyway, I thought . . . well, I thought you might want to have it.'

It was a cityscape of the view beneath my hospital room, the pencil smudged like London smog across tall, intrusive buildings.

'Dougie, it's so good,' I said. I felt suddenly choked. 'Thank you.'

'Bleak is what it is.' He leaned over my shoulder and surveyed his work. 'But I felt like it was important you have it. It's how I felt. How I still feel. Why did this have to happen to you, H? You're the best person I know.'

'Don't . . .' I was trying not to cry. 'Please.'

'I'm sorry.' He cleared his throat. 'You're right. We need to try and look forward – hard as it is.'

'Feels impossible at the moment.' I stowed the drawing safely inside my dressing-gown pocket. 'But one day at a time, right?'

'Right.'

'They say I'll start physio soon. If it all goes well, I could be out of here in a few more weeks.'

'Well, that's great news.' I could tell he was trying to sound enthusiastic. 'So then you'll come home?'

'I'm not sure. They want to send me to an amputee rehab place. Apparently it's the quickest way to get me up and walking again.'

The thought of this caused my breath to catch in my throat. I'd seen running blades on the Paralympics and the occasional soldier at an awards ceremony on TV, but apart from that, I didn't really know anything about amputees. Would it be hard to walk with a prosthetic leg? Would I even be able to learn? Thoughts tumbled and spiralled. The noises of the café felt distant. I struggled to calm my breathing.

'You'll be jogging again in no time, H,' Dougie said. 'Don't ever think that this is going to stop you from living your life. Because it won't. I won't let it.'

I turned away. My chest was tight. I needed to compose myself. And then I saw it.

It was only a matter of seconds. But the flash of white-blond hair made my heart jolt against my ribcage. Here, in this hospital? What was he doing? He rounded the corner. Then he was gone. I gasped aloud, unable to suppress my shock. Because I couldn't be certain, but I thought it was Alexander Mitchell.

Chapter Five

Arriving at the Amputee Rehabilitation Unit was not dissimilar to becoming an unwilling extra in a remake of *One Flew Over the Cuckoo's Nest* – only with a lot more wheelchairs. As my dad pushed me out of the lift and onto the second-floor ward, I could see them lined up along the wall; looming, bulky contraptions of differing sizes, from the average model to the bariatric, which looked like it could fit three of me across its vast seat. It was a very depressing sight.

A brisk lady in a navy ward sister's uniform strode along the corridor. She had a long grey ponytail and the tired air of someone who'd done the same job for slightly too long.

'You must be Heidi,' she said. Her puckered lips formed into something vaguely resembling a smile. 'I'm Sharon, the ward manager. Welcome to the ARU.'

'Thank you,' I replied.

I shivered in Dougie's big sweatshirt. I didn't feel very welcome. The long corridor around us was stark and cold, with industrial white handrails everywhere and tiny circular windows reminiscent of portholes in a ship. The strip lighting on the ceiling bathed everything in a crisp, harsh brightness. Even Sharon's tone was clipped and severe. It felt like the warmth had been sucked out of everything.

'OK, Heidi?' Dad asked. He put his big hand on my shoulder. The gentle touch almost made me cry. I nodded stiffly. I couldn't speak. I couldn't show my emotion – it would make me look babyish and pathetic.

'Follow me,' Sharon half-barked.

She turned abruptly on her heel, chunky lace-up shoes squeaking as she strode away. I took the brakes off the wheelchair and Dad followed, almost crashing into a very large old man. The man was wearing baggy elasticated shorts and had no legs beyond his thighs. An enormous woman in a blue and white floral dress was pushing him, waddling behind the wheelchair.

'Wotcha!' he yelled. I inhaled sharply as we narrowly avoided a headlong collision.

'Sorry,' Dad said. 'Didn't see you there.'

'New arrival is it, Sharon?' the man asked.

'Yes, George,' she answered over her shoulder.

'Oh, lovely,' the woman puffed. They both had East London cockney accents. 'I'm Bessie. George's wife.'

George gave a gummy smile as our paths crossed. I tried weakly to reciprocate. In truth, I felt completely overwhelmed.

There were six bays in total, each made up of two beds. Mine was at the far end, a large, airy room dominated by two hospital beds and the sudden and strong smell of Chanel's Coco Mademoiselle. The aroma caught in my nostrils, sickly sweet and cloying.

'OK, so this is Ward 4,' Sharon said. She spoke as if from a script; lines she'd delivered many times before. 'It's a twelve-patient unit in total, two people per room. Balcony is out there, bathroom across the corridor, TV to share. You're free to explore the garden and we have gardening therapy on Fridays. Crutches are forbidden unless the physios give you permission. Always use the wheelchair for moving around. Breakfast is at 8 a.m., lunch at twelve and dinner is at five.'

Dinner at 5 p.m.? That was worse than the hospital. I'd always been a night owl, susceptible to insomnia if stress or anxiety got the better of me. Now, it was a thousand times worse. The thought of those twilight hours stretching ahead each night felt like being marooned alone in the driest, most torturous of deserts. I glanced over at Dad, who shrugged sympathetically. Meanwhile, Sharon continued her monotone recital.

'One day each week, the patients take it in turns to attend breakfast club, where you'll be cooking in your wheelchair and later navigating the kitchen with your prosthetic leg. The therapy team will make you an activity timetable in the next couple of days. It's important you're not late to their sessions. They'll schedule your therapy around your own individual goals, so make sure you think about what you want to achieve.'

'Oh, they'll push you hard, that they will.'

From the bed opposite mine, an elderly lady grinned. She was so tiny that I hadn't noticed her before, the hospital bed dwarfing her meagre frame. Her pale pink T-shirt was tucked into navy tracksuit bottoms pulled high above her waist, giving the air of someone unused to such casual attire. She sat back against the pillows with poise, silver bangles jingling on both arms and a pale sheen of gloss across her lips.

Like me, she was a below-knee amputee. I couldn't help noticing the way her right trouser leg fell flat against the sheets. I looked down at my own leg. That was how people saw me now, too. From now on, everyone I met would know me as disabled. The thought landed heavily on my heart.

'I'm Maud,' the old woman said. She had a soft Irish accent and a kind glint in her sea-green eyes. 'You must be my new roomie.'

'I'm Heidi,' I answered.

'And I'm Tim,' Dad added.

'I'll leave you to get acquainted,' Sharon said. 'The nurses will come and do your initial health checks shortly, but if you have any questions or if you need a staff member in the meantime, there's a call button by your bed.'

She swept from the room, pumping a dollop of hand sanitiser from the dispenser by the door as she left.

'You have lovely hair, Heidi.' Maud patted her own blue-tinged perm. 'Wish mine would go that colour. I did have pink streaks years ago, but the dye just doesn't take to it these days.'

'Thank you,' I said. My brain wasn't functioning. I couldn't think of what to say.

'So, how did you lose yours, then?' Maud asked. She gestured to her leg.

The question took me by surprise. I looked at Dad, aghast. How could she ask so bluntly? But instead of the encouraging nod I wanted, Dad simply looked confused. He rubbed his greying chin stubble and gave a shrug, his bony shoulders poking out from his zip-up Saturday gilet. He'd never been the best with emotion.

'I, well, I had an accident,' I said.

'Oh?' Maud cocked her head to one side, listening. Her curly white hair was out of control, strands sticking up at various different angles.

I explained as briefly as I could. As I ran through the story, I thought about Alexander Mitchell. He'd seen I was in pain – and he'd just left me lying there. What kind of person did that? His face loomed in my mind, eyes large and unblinking, projecting a coldness that made me shudder.

'Jogging? Ah Christ, you poor thing,' Maud said. Her tone was soft and consolidatory. 'It's the smallest things sometimes, isn't it? Must have been a real shock – for all of you.'

I couldn't shift the lump in my throat. I simply nodded. I didn't trust myself to speak.

'It was,' Dad replied. His voice had a gravelly edge. 'It was the biggest shock of our lives.'

'Ah listen, I get it,' Maud said. 'It hits the family hard. And you're obviously close.'

I nodded. I was close to both my parents, but Dad and I had always had a bond, an unspoken connection that had formed even when I was little. In many ways we were similar, more outgoing than Jenny or Mum, calm to a certain point and yet prone to sudden volatility when provoked. We relished our own company, which strangely made us perfect companions. Some of my fondest childhood memories were times we spent in silence, heads bent together as we built Airfix planes together, or muddy hikes lost in our thoughts. Dad didn't know how to manage emotional overload, but he did understand me. He always had done.

I watched him nod too, clearing his throat, recovering from his earlier swell of sadness. He swallowed.

'We're very close,' he agreed. 'And what about you then, Maud? What happened?'

'Me?' Maud rubbed her stump. It was large and swollen, covered with a stretchy compression sock. 'Oh, I was on my way to an Age UK meeting when I was run over by the bin lorry. Bloody great thing too – I just didn't see it coming round the corner.'

'What?' I snorted, then quickly covered my mouth. I didn't want to offend her.

'It's OK – you can laugh,' Maud said. She was grinning herself. 'I know it's ridiculous. Irony was, I was wheeling my bin down the path at the time. I always forget when it's bin day, and the one time I actually remember, it backfires on me in the worst possible way.'

'Christ,' said Dad. I heard his arthritic knees click as he sat down on a clinical plastic chair. The years of walking around vast building sites and navigating flights of stairs had taken their toll on his joints. 'That's . . . well, that's awful.'

'Oh, no.' Maud waved away the sympathy. 'I'm lucky really, that I am. I'm eighty-two and I'm doing all right. Plus I've got a great family. It's not to be underestimated, that at times like this when you really need to keep your loved ones close.'

Instinctively, I reached for Dad. He closed his big hand around mine. I didn't want to let go.

'So, Maud, where do you live?' Dad asked. I was grateful at his attempt to make conversation I was too overwhelmed to even try.

'Watford. Been there for over fifty years now, so I have. I was a seamstress, see. Thought I'd try my luck in London. I had big dreams about this city – and I wasn't disappointed.' Her face crinkled at the corners when she smiled. 'I fell in love here – with the place, the people, and later, with my Pete. He's at peace now, Lord bless his heart. Sure, there's a piece of my heart in Dublin. But I wouldn't live anywhere else.'

'Do you have children?'

'Just the one. My Billy. He's a London boy with an Irish heart, so he is.' She pointed at a framed photo by her bed; a smart silver-haired man with laughter lines and a weathered tan, and a tall, lithe woman in a long black dress. In between them was a boy about my age. He had vibrant ginger hair that matched his mum's.

'That's them,' Maud said proudly. 'Billy and Aurelie. Beautiful pair, aren't they? She used to be a model. He's a journalist – met her on a trip in Paris. And that's my grandson, Jack.'

'Lovely,' Dad said.

I didn't speak. I felt distant; there in body, yet my mind was far away. There was too much to process, too many assaults on my senses. The air in the room felt thick and heavy. I could taste Maud's perfume on my tongue, a bittersweet sharpness that made me feel faintly sick. A sudden, confusing nostalgia passed over me. I wanted to be back in hospital. There, a predictable familiarity of routine had comforted me in the worst of times. It had been an airlock between the past and my uncertain future.

'Nice here, isn't it, H?' Dad said. He gave my hand a squeeze, a silent signal between us to show he knew how I was feeling. 'So light and bright.'

I gazed around the space that was to be my home for the next six weeks. It bore more resemblance to the hospital than I'd imagined, with a locked drugs cabinet next to each bed and an adjustable bedside table on wheels. In the corner of the room were three hospital-type armchairs, covered in a bright blue industrial plastic fabric, the type that stuck to bare skin and caused unnecessary sweating. There were windows all around, from the door that led out to the balcony to a row of skylights by the ceiling. The beds themselves were hospital beds, complete with buttons to raise or lower them, and the bobbly blue blankets I'd come to loathe. I felt a flash of gratitude for my soft throw from Dougie. A touch of comfort amid the institutional impersonality.

I was shell-shocked, my brain whirring with new information. There was doubt, confusion and fear; a lot of fear. What kind of world had I been thrust into? I dreaded being left here.

'Sure I get it, love, it's weird to start with, right?' Maud said. 'But you'll soon get used to the routine. Anyway, I'm pleased to see another woman. I've been here a week and it's been all men so far. It'll be good to have some girl time.'

I tried to smile. Dad was still holding my hand. Nice as Maud seemed, I wished I had my own room. At least then there'd be no need to keep up the pretence of strength. Then I could pull the sheets over my head and cry.

'Right, Heidi,' Dad said. 'Shall we go and look at the garden? Before the nurses come and see you?'

'Yeah, OK.'

I was fast running out of positivity. To be honest, I just wanted to go back to Mum and Dad's house. I wanted to be held, looked after, even smothered by their love and attention. I never normally craved my parents' company, and yet I felt a strong, visceral pull towards them. I didn't want to be left alone.

'See you later, Maud,' I said.

'See you in a bit, love,' she replied cheerily, reaching for the *Woman's Weekly* on her bedside table. 'I'll save you a place at lunch!'

Dad wheeled me back down the corridor and through the communal dining room, where twelve trays with cutlery and paper napkins were already set out on the table. A Jamaican lady in a chef's hairnet was loading foil trays reminiscent of airline food into a large serving trolley. It didn't look appetising.

The dining room led out onto a large garden, with slopes designed for wheelchairs and rails along every path. Despite a few grey clouds, it was a mild and pleasant day. I relished the fresh air that filled my lungs.

'Someone takes good care of this garden,' Dad said.

He loved a garden. He was forever taking on outdoor projects, water features, coloured lighting or exotic plants that would never survive an English winter. Last year he'd even installed mirrors to make the garden look bigger – until Mum walked into them one too many times and insisted the 'bloody things' be removed immediately.

'Yeah. It's nice,' I said.

It was hard to believe that this was central London. Aside from the distant rush of traffic, the only noises were a gentle rustling breeze and the twittering of birds as they chattered in the trees overhead. The scene was the picture of serenity. But my mind was wild and frantic.

We sat together in silence, Dad on a wooden bench beside the wheelchair. I wondered if he was soaking in ideas for our own family home's back lawn. Without really meaning to, I let out a long sigh.

'You're going to be fine here, H,' Dad said. 'Trust me.'

'Six weeks,' I murmured.

It was six weeks without work; no bar shifts meant no money. I knew Dougie couldn't really help – he was channelling every spare penny into his savings, ready for the imminent move-in with Hal. We both knew Hal was loaded, but I understood that Dougie didn't want to be a leech. Anyway, I didn't want my best friend's money. It was a totally unfair demand.

'My rent,' I said. 'How am I going to manage?'

'We'll find the money,' Dad assured.

'But you're retired . . .'

'Heidi, trust me, that's the least of your problems. You concentrate on recovering, OK?'

I sniffed. 'OK. Oh, Dad, I don't want you to leave me.' I was aware I sounded pathetic; a grown woman crying out for her father. And yet, the idea of abandonment filled me with dread. I closed my eyes for a moment and I was back on the path, alone. I couldn't stand being left again.

'I know.' Dad said. His voice cracked as he spoke. 'This is hard for me too, Heidi. Do you think I want to leave you here?' I saw the worry across his face, the lines on his forehead, the sadness in his eyes. Suddenly, I felt very guilty.

'I'm sorry, Dad.' My eyes mirrored his; grey blue like the rest of our family, now red rimmed and full of pain. 'I don't want to put you through this. Any of you.'

'Heidi, you have nothing to apologise for,' he said softly. 'We just have to try and carry on. It's all we can do.'

I rested my head on his shoulder. He put an arm around me and pulled me to his chest. I cuddled into him, the gilet's padded fabric cushioning my cheek. It smelt like the coat cupboard of our family home; sweet, musty and comforting. He planted a kiss on my hair.

'You're going to be OK,' he told me. 'This will become your new normal, promise.'

'But I want the old normal,' I whispered.

Chapter Six

At university, I used to do a circuits class, moving from station to station around the room, attempting wall squats, planks, burpees and various other forms of exercise-related torture. Day Two in the amputee physio gym felt a bit like that – except this time the participants were all missing limbs.

I sat in my wheelchair, a weight in each hand. They were only 2kg, nothing compared to what I used to lift in the gym. And yet, my unused muscles quivered with the strain. Chart hits crackled from an ancient ghetto blaster in the corner. It was hard to concentrate. There was too much going on around me.

'George, are you actually doing anything?' Tara, the lead physiotherapist called. She wore a whistle around her neck and her dark hair was tied into a severe ponytail like a highly-strung PE teacher. She wasn't much older than me – and yet her air was of someone far more mature. 'I can see you, you know.'

'Yeah, yeah, all right darlin',' George answered. I recognised him as the man I'd seen in the corridor with his wife the day before. He had a strong East End accent, husky with a touch of phlegm. 'Just tired.'

George was lying on one of the therapy beds that lined the far wall. All I could see was his stomach, which protruded like a mountain from his tracksuit-clad body. Sighing heavily, he raised his head a few inches off the bed, before replacing it on the pillow.

'All right, all right,' he said, 'I'm not as young as I used to be. She always picks on me, don't she, Shahid?'

'She picks on everyone, mate.' Next to George was a slightly younger man in a West Ham football shirt. He had one leg and was also missing an arm. He was sitting in his wheelchair, a hand weight on his lap.

'And you, Shahid,' Tara said. 'You're supposed to lift that weight, you know.'

'See?' Shahid gave George a conspiratorial grin. 'You ain't so special.'

I finished my third rep of weights, before moving to the next 'station'. As I eased myself onto the plinth next to George's, my arms were burning. I winced as they shook under my body weight. I hated how weak I'd become; how the smallest of tasks seemed to require the greatest of efforts. I felt completely pathetic. George turned his head and gave me a knowing wink.

'All right, new girl?'

I tried to smile, then attempted to do some sit-ups. Beads of sweat formed on my brow and upper lip. I tried four or five times before I collapsed; defeated.

'What's yer name then?' Shahid chipped in. The weight was still in his lap. He hadn't even tried to move it since Tara's warning.

'Oh, I'm Heidi.' I wiped my face with the back of my hand, ashamed at my obvious decrease in fitness. I felt useless; hopeless. I couldn't even manage a simple sit-up.

'Aye, don't you worry about that,' George said, noticing my struggle. 'None of us want to do physio. I'm gagging for a fag.'

'Same,' Shahid added. 'More tricky since I lost me arm though. Do you smoke, Heidi?'

'No,' I said. I didn't feel like chatting. But they didn't seem to notice.

'You're missing out,' George said. 'See, years ago, Heidi, I used to work in the Tate and Lyle factory down in Silvertown. And let me tell you, after a day of hard graft, there's few things better than a proper pork pie and a fag.'

'Totally agree, mate,' Shahid added. 'I mean, I don't exactly have a job at the minute, but when I did, I used to love fag breaks on the building site with the lads. Bonding, innit?'

'Oh, it is.' George paused to cough; a hacking, deep-throated sound that suggested the very opposite. 'We've met here before, y'see, Heidi. Both lost a leg around the same time. Few years ago now, wasn't it, Shahid?'

'About four, I reckon.'

'That's it, yeah.' He gave a throaty chuckle. 'And what are the odds, eh? Reunited back here again.'

'We always have a fag break together,' Shahid explained.

'And you both have Type 2 diabetes,' added Tara.

I couldn't believe what I was hearing. I felt a sudden anger towards them both, behaving like this was some kind of old boys' club. How could they be so jovial when it turned out that their amputations were entirely preventable? Stop smoking, eat a bit better; job done. I hadn't asked for this to happen. I didn't deserve it. It was unfair and cruel.

'Nothing to do with it.' George rolled his eyes. 'Give over, will you?'

Tara's eyes flashed. She took a breath. When she next spoke, it was with clipped professionalism.

'Right, carry on, both of you.' She gave a short toot on her whistle. 'Heidi, why don't you try some planks?'

I rolled onto my front and heaved myself into a one-legged plank position. I was aiming to hold it for a minute as I always used to in the gym, but I caved after just fifteen seconds, my good leg collapsing beneath me. I was shaking with effort and rage.

'Good try,' said Tara. 'Again?'

I didn't want to. I lay on my front and pressed my forehead to the mat. It smelt like feet – or perhaps more accurately, foot.

When had I become so weak? I thought about the day of my accident, that rush of endorphins as I pounded the pavement, my heart beating; fit and capable. To me, running hadn't just meant fitness. It had brought me serenity and joy, the knowledge that I could achieve, pushing me on as the future stretched ahead. But the positive memory was short-lived, eclipsed as it always was by my fall. I craved that sensation of strength again. My tired body yearned for that familiar burst of energy. But it didn't come. What if that day had been the last time I'd ever feel so strong? I closed my eyes, wishing I could turn back time. My forehead stuck to the mat.

'Have another go, Heidi,' Tara urged.

Sighing heavily, I pushed myself back up on to my elbows. My muscles began shaking almost immediately. This time, I only managed ten seconds before the burning became too much to bear. It was hopeless. I pounded the mat with my fist, angry at my body

When 10 a.m. struck, George and The Diabetics were back in their wheelchairs immediately. Session over, their wheels creaked as they each tried to be the first to the dining room for coffee and biscuits. Bending my knee and pushing up on the wheelchair with my aching arms, I heaved myself back to sitting. Bleakness had settled in my heart. I felt like a failure.

'Still here, Heidi?' Tara was sitting at the desk, folders of notes spread out in front of her. 'All OK?'

'Fine, yep.' But my voice shook. Tara looked up, concerned.

'It's going to be tough, you know.' Her tone was gentler now, professionalism laced with compassion. 'It must be pretty weird here for you.'

'Yeah.' Emotion swelled in my throat. I tried to control it, but someone being nice to me was sure to make it worse.

'Look, what have you got on now?' Tara asked.

'I think I have a free session.'

In truth, I was planning to go back to bed. My body and mind were exhausted. Sleep was my only escape. Tara put down her pen. Her eyes locked with mine. They were a total contrast to her otherwise plain appearance; clear amber and very pretty, with impossibly long eyelashes.

'Look, we have a counsellor in twice a week here. Bryony. I know she's free this morning – why don't you pop along? It might be useful.'

'I don't know . . .'

The idea of baring my soul to a stranger made me feel sick and shaky. She'd ask me about the accident. And I was trying my best to forget it.

I had never had counselling. I'd known people at drama school have sessions throughout drama school but my inner sceptic had always reigned supreme.

'Just go and say hello.' Tara was insistent. 'It can't hurt.'

I hesitated. In hospital, someone had told me that psychological recovery from trauma was like a heap of dirty laundry. Very often, it was shoved to the bottom of the basket and left, thoughts tangled and stained with memory. It needed to be sorted, made sense of and restored to order again. I was trying to shove it all down and close the lid. But my worries and fears were rising, threatening to overflow.

'You may as well try it,' Tara persisted. 'What have you got to lose?'

'Nothing,' I said under my breath. And it was true.

The counselling room was sparsely decorated. The sum total of its contents was three chairs, a desk and a sad looking houseplant which languished in the corner with drooping leaves and a vague sense of defeat. The walls were painted in a pale, cracked green, which was probably designed to be calming but in fact resembled an unhealthy shade of vomit.

'I'm Bryony,' a woman said. Her voice was rippling and soft, like a stone dropped into shining still waters. She had large eyes, a wrinkled, sun-dappled complexion and a flower pinned into the side of an enormous mass of grey corkscrew curls. I guessed she was around the same age as Mum. 'You must be Heidi. Please, make yourself comfortable.'

I took the chair by the window. My legs were shaky, my mouth dry. I felt nervous and defeated. I wanted to run and hide.

'So, how are you feeling today?' Bryony asked.

Angry? Upset? Confused? None of these words came close to explaining the cocktail of emotions swirling around my head. I stared at the novelty mug on her desk: there was a *novelty mug*, was all I could think. 'Keep calm and hug a clinical psychologist', it said. I'd rather not.

'Not bad,' I replied woodenly. Even to me, the words were robotic and fake. My stump gave a jolt of phantom pain, like extreme pins and needles. It felt like a reprimand.

Bryony gazed at me intently. Her eyes were deep brown, verging on black, full of understanding and stories.

'Heidi, it's important you know that these sessions are completely for you,' she said. 'We can discuss anything you want, however you feel. And I want you to remember, nothing leaves this room. OK?'

I nodded, although my heart had sped up. I didn't want to be here with this woman I'd never met. How could I tell her how I felt when I could barely understand it myself?

'Good.' Bryony sat back in her hair and folded her arms across her large bosom. 'So, Heidi, your accident. Can you talk me through what happened?'

'Erm . . . OK.' Anxiety pounded in my stomach. The room smelt of carpet cleaner and coffee, bitter and pungent.

'Set the scene for me. What was the weather like that day?'

I stared at her blankly. Why did she need to know that?

'Sunny,' I said quietly.

'OK, good.' Her huge head of hair bounced as she nodded. 'What we're trying to do here, Heidi, is to create an overall picture. Little details will help to take you back there. They make the memories more vivid. So, it was sunny. And I know you were out jogging. What time of day?'

'Morning. I can't remember. Early.'

'No problem. Talk me through what happened next.'

I paused. The room was boiling, heat pumping from a plug-in radiator in the corner. Sweat pricked my spine. The air was dense and suffocating. I massaged my temples. I didn't want to remember.

'There was a man coming towards me,' I said carefully. 'I tripped over and he tried to grab me, but . . .'

'But?'

'Well, he missed.'

I didn't want to tell her the full story. What would she think of me, trying to chat up a total stranger mid-jog? A sudden shot of embarrassment swirled into the cocktail of nerves and fear in my stomach. I wiped my hands on my leggings. They were shaking.

'And what was the pain like when you fell?' Bryony asked.

In an instant, I was back on the path, lying on my back, the branches from the overhanging trees silhouetted against a cloudless sky. I still remembered my exact position, the way my left knee was bent upwards, the right at a sickening angle. But I couldn't truly recall the pain.

'It was awful,' I said eventually. 'The worst pain I've ever had.'

'But you're struggling to imagine it now, right?' I nodded, confused.

'That's normal. When we experience trauma, our brains often block out the sensation of pain. It's taken over by the adrenaline. Fight or flight. Now, you mentioned a man was there on the path.' She sat back in her chair, fixing me with an intense expression. 'Do you remember much about him?'

Everything.

'No, not really,' I said. I didn't want to talk about him. The guilt and the burden was too much to bear. If I hadn't stopped, if I hadn't spoken to him – then maybe this wouldn't have happened.

'Any physical details? Hair colour? Eyes?'

'Nope.'

I stared at the carpet; insipid beige, scuffed and stained by years of wheelchairs and coffee spillages. The sight of my one white trainer there against the floor triggered a sudden, overwhelming sadness.

'Are you sure?' Bryony said. I could feel her eyes on me. She didn't believe me. 'I understand this is difficult, but it would really help you to . . .'

The room was shrinking. I was struggling to breathe. I needed to escape.

'Sorry but I need to go,' I gabbled. 'It'll be lunchtime soon.'

And then I made the mistake of looking up. The counsellor stared at me, her kind, wise gaze boring into mine. As our eyes connected, I knew that she was reading my thoughts. But I no longer cared. It wasn't working; I wasn't feeling better. If anything, I was feeling worse. I didn't want to analyse my accident or unpick my feelings. I didn't want to remember. I just wanted to get out.

Chapter Seven

Mealtimes at the rehab unit were an interesting experience. The cook, if you could call her that, was a formidable Jamaican lady called Fajah, as strict on portion control as she was about the nurses wearing hairnets to serve the meals.

'Late,' she barked as I came in. It was only five past twelve.

I wheeled over to what had become my place by the window. Maud was there already, but the table was otherwise empty. The Diabetics always took up residence at the larger table nearest the TV. There, they could turn on *Flog It* or Magic FM up as loudly as they saw fit. Today, it was Magic – Spandau Ballet's *Gold*. George shouted the chorus, merrily displaying the contents of his mouth to the room.

'Disgusting,' Maud said. I couldn't have agreed more.

I began to tackle my watery vegetable soup starter. It wasn't clear what kind of vegetables were in it – or even if there were any. George was already on pudding. He had custard caught in his beard, and he shouted gaily at the nurses for seconds. Familiar anger flared up again. Type 2 diabetes, and he wasn't even trying to help himself.

'No, George,' Fajah said as though telling off a disobedient dog.

Outside the dining room his wife, Bessie, was lurking. I'd noticed she was a frequent visitor, never far from her husband's side. Today she was wearing an orange and brown dress, and took up almost the entire doorway.

'Sure I can't come in?' she called.

'No,' Fajah scowled. 'Is not allowed.'

'Ah, c'mon . . .'

'No.' There was a strict 'no visitors in the dining room at mealtimes' policy.

'Honestly, some of the rules in this place . . .' Maud raised her eyebrows at me. 'Makes you wonder, doesn't it? Anyway Heidi, what have you got on this afternoon?'

Her trademark silver bangles jangled tunefully each time she raised her cutlery to her mouth. She wore them even with her sportswear. In the midst of the chaos, I was grateful for her attempt to form a normal conversation. I swallowed my anger with the lukewarm soup, both beginning to cool in my stomach.

'Occupational therapy at 3.00 a.m.,' I told her, in as normal a tone as I could muster. 'That's it, I think. How about you?'

'Fall prevention.' Her face creased into a smile. She held out her arm to me, displaying an orange band around her wrist amidst the bangles. 'I'm a mild hazard, apparently. May need assistance with transfers.'

My own band was green, meaning I was trusted to move in and out of the wheelchair independently. Over on the other table, most of them had red.

'Any visitors today?' Maud asked. She took a swig of her powdery orange squash and grimaced. 'Horrible stuff.'

'My parents, but not until this evening.'

Mum and Dad were insistent that someone come every day. I was always glad to see them, but I hated it when they left.

'Smashing. I'm having visitors too,' Maud said.

Unable to stomach any more watery veg, I pushed my soup bowl aside. Fajah glared at me, before slamming down the next course; a brown mush that vaguely resembled shepherd's pie. I sniffed it doubtfully and reached for the ketchup.

'Oh? Who's visiting?' I asked.

'My grandson, Jack.' Maud's crinkled face lit up as she said his name.

'Lovely.' I smiled back.

'He's thirty-four now, though I can barely believe it. Actually Heidi, it might be nice for you to chat to someone your own age after being cooped up in here with me.'

'Yeah. . .' I said.

But the thought made me anxious. It would be the first time I'd met someone my own age as an amputee; someone from the outside world who would surely look and judge. I gazed down at myself; at the baggy jumper hanging off my frame, at my old gym leggings and my pale skin, starved of sunlight for so many weeks. I knew the purple dye in my hair was growing out, dark brown roots now clearly visible. My stump was huge and swollen, laid out on the stump board with livid bruising and jagged scars, like something from a horror movie. I'd never felt less attractive.

'Oh, right. Yeah, I'm sure I will,' I replied, unconvincingly.

A moment later, there was more raucous laughter and the slamming of hands and stumps on tables. George's false teeth had fallen into his custard.

'Poor old bugger,' Maud said. I shook my head and pushed my plate away. I wasn't hungry any more.

After lunch, Maud and I retired to our room. The beds had been laundered with fresh, crisp sheets, which we sat on top of. All of us had been given a stretchy airline-like compression sock called a Juzo, which we had to wear on our stumps when at rest to combat any swelling. Looking over at Maud, I could make out the outline of a dressing beneath hers.

'Have you got a sore?' I asked. Maud rubbed her leg.

'Aye, skin breakdown, apparently. Means I have to wait even longer before they let me try a leg. It has to heal first.'

'That's a pain.'

I pulled my blanket from Dougie over my lap. My bare leg felt chilly in the breeze from our open terrace door.

'I know,' Maud answered. 'I just want to get moving now, you know?'

'I don't blame you.'

'So, when are you being cast for your leg then?' She reached for her Chanel, spritzing it liberally across her neck, arms and wrists.

'The prosthetist's coming tomorrow,' I answered.

The thought provoked a cocktail of emotions. There was excitement naturally, the tingling anticipation of taking the first – literal and metaphorical – step forward. Yet lurking beneath that was trepidation. How would people react to seeing me with a prosthetic leg? What if I couldn't manage? And most frightening of all, what if I fell? Logically, I knew I'd had a freak accident and that it wouldn't happen again. But that didn't stop the terror.

'Oooh, bet you can't wait!' Maud said excitedly. 'You'll be strolling out of here in no time!'

'I hope so. But Maud, what if I can't do it?'

'Sure, you're young and fit, girl.' She held up a hand mirror and spread pale pink gloss across her lips. 'You can't think like that. If all these old boys manage, you sure as hell can. You're doing so well.'

But I didn't feel like I was. The feeling of hopelessness persisted, weighing heavily on my heart. My emotions were torn. I wanted to be alone, but I was terrified of my thoughts. I knew everyone around me would recommend more counselling, but I couldn't speak to Bryony again. The fear, guilt and shame was simply too much to face.

'I can't cope,' I said. And I really meant it.

Before she could answer me, there was a knock at our door.

'Jack!' she screeched delightedly.

'Hi, Nanna.'

He wore loose jeans and a faded shirt with cartoon hedge-hogs all over it. It looked like it needed a wash. His ears stuck out from his head like a curious baby elephant. He smiled in a way that didn't quite meet his eyes.

'Jack, my darling, come over here and give your Nanna a hug.'

He did so obediently. Maud cupped his face in her hands.

'Jack, it's so lovely to see you.' She was bursting with happi-ness. 'This is my room-mate, Heidi.'

'Oh.' He cast a glance towards me. 'Right. I didn't know you had a room-mate.'

'Good to meet you,' I said.

'Yeah, and you.' He spoke in a near-monotone, like someone going through the motions of politeness.

'Oh, Jack, I'm sure you did know,' Maud said. 'Did your dad not tell you about Heidi? She's been keeping me sane.'

'I'm sure.' He positioned himself in the chair nearest the balcony door. Outside, two fat pigeons perched on the back fence, sizing each other up. 'I thought I'd be speaking to you . . . alone,' he said, pointedly.

'Don't be silly, Jack.' Maud waved away his bluntness. He yawned theatrically.

'Oh dear, are we keeping you up?' Maud teased. His eyebrows dipped into a scowl.

'Couldn't sleep last night,' he muttered darkly. He stared out across the garden, fiddling with a packet of cigarettes that protruded from his pocket.

'Do you like his shirt, Heidi?' Maud asked. 'You should see the rest of his collection. Honestly, there are some real stunners.'

'It's . . . colourful,' I said. I saw Jack stiffen.

'Nanna, stop getting at me, OK?' He folded his arms like a moody teenager.

'I'm sorry.' She smiled hopefully, eager to please. 'Anything you want to talk about? Anything I can do?'

'No.' He slumped further in his chair, adding grudgingly, 'but thanks.'

'OK. So, how are you then, my boy? Busy at work?'

Maud looked intently at her grandson. It was as though she was drinking him in, fixing this moment deep in her memory. Jack chewed his lip.

'Always,' he answered.

'Jack's a journalist,' Maud informed me.

'Nice.'

'Just like his dad. See, my Billy was something of a legend on Fleet Street. Billy's retired now, of course. Well, he's writing a book actually; a memoir. Tales of the glory days, he says . . .'

As Maud launched in to tales of 'her Billy,' I looked over at Jack. His eyes were feline green, his hair a rich burnt orange, thick and unruly against a pale, freckled face.

I glanced down at myself. My leggings were thinning in places and my ancient Nike T-shirt was several sizes too big, probably another one of Dougie's. I looked a mess.

'I don't want to talk about Dad.' Jack cut through Maud's monologue. 'Or his legacy.'

'Oh. OK. Sorry, love.' She turned her attention to me instead. 'Heidi's an actress, Jack.'

'Well, I was.' I baulked at the sudden attention. I didn't want to be the focus. Besides, 'actress' was a stretch. Three years and I had only had TV extra work, one pub play and two badly paid commercials to show for it.

'Right,' Jack said.

It wasn't a reaction I was used to. Most men I met were curious, even impressed, by my career choice. They followed up with questions, asking me what shows I liked, often showing an engagement akin to flirtation. And yet Jack didn't sound the slightest bit interested. In fact, his coldness made me feel dull and overlooked.

'Life can change so quickly, can't it?' Maud said.

'Tell me about it,' Jack muttered.

His words were so quiet that at first I thought I'd imagined them. I turned my head, sensing his gaze, my skin prickling with his scrutiny. For a few seconds, he looked straight into my face, his large green eyes locking onto mine, as though he was searching for my innermost thoughts. I lowered my head, embarrassed by his intensity. But when I looked up again, he'd moved on. Shoulders hunched and arms crossed, he'd turned back towards the window. Sitting there on my bed, a cloud of sadness passed over me. I wasn't even worth speaking to, let alone flirting with.

Chapter Eight

Peter the prosthetist had very small hands. He folded them around my stump, creating a thick plaster cast mould. His delicate fingers were incongruent with his otherwise weathered appearance; creased brow, unkempt brown eyebrows and peppered-grey stubble.

'Should harden up soon,' he smiled. There was a gap between his front teeth.

I watched him work, my skin warm as he shaped and smoothed the plaster. The cast made my skin tingle, a strange but not unpleasant sensation. Yet sitting there on the physio bench, I felt disconnected, as though watching the action happen from outside myself. This wasn't the body I knew, with red scars and staple marks; weak, battered and shrouded in uncertainty. Any anticipation of my new leg, my new start, was overruled by fear.

My right leg twitched beneath the warm, hardening plaster. It felt trapped, encased, as though if I pushed against it enough, I could break out and set it free. I clenched my calf muscles, going through the motion of pointing my toes. It felt like I could do it; they were still there, still responding. My muscle memory was as strong as ever. Except nothing happened.

'Keep still,' said Peter.

I looked down at my stump. An acute sadness came over me, so strong I had to pinch my thigh hard, deferring the pain, distracting myself from tears. My brain remembered what my body could no longer achieve. It was heartbreaking.

Peter rubbed his hands together, surveying his work. The back of his knuckles were hairy, the skin dry and flaked with a career's worth of plaster and paint. His left fourth finger bore the pale ghost of a wedding ring.

'I'll just mark this up . . .'

He was speaking, but not to me. Pulling a pencil from his lab coat pocket, he began to draw shapes around my knee.

'What's that for?' My voice sounded strange – faraway and faint. I was asking the right questions, but the answers remained unclear. To be honest, I was struggling to concentrate. It was all too much to take in.

'Weight-bearing surfaces.' He placed the pencil between his teeth, leaned back and squinted over the top of his glasses. 'The areas where your leg will tolerate more pressure. Does that make sense?'

'OK.'

It didn't, not really. I realised I had next to no knowledge of prosthetics. Everything I thought I knew about amputees now seemed contradictory: young, strong athletes with blades, shooting down tracks at lightning-fast speed, versus the dishevelled man who sat in his wheelchair outside Stratford Tube station, stumps dangling dramatically as he held out his hands and begged. I didn't know which camp I belonged in. Both? Neither? How would I find that in-between?

I watched as the cast, now solid, was pulled from my leg; a perfect replica. Peter put it to one side with a nod and flexed his tiny fingers.

'Bloody carpal tunnel,' he muttered. Then, addressing me. 'It should be done in a few days' time. I'll come back to fit it.'

'Oi, Peter!' George shouted. Bessie wheeled her husband and his odour of smoke and unwashed man into the room. 'When are my legs gonna be ready, eh?'

'Yeah,' Bessie added. 'When do I have to stop pushing this thing around? And by that, I mean George, ha!' She gave a throaty cackle. Sweat gleamed on her brow. Peter raised his fuzzy eyebrows ever so slightly.

'I told you, George,' he said with visibly forced patience. 'It takes three to five days, depending how busy the centre is.'

'Christ. This chair's so inconvenient, Pete. Can't even pop to the offie for a packet of fags. It's too hard.'

'And it hurts my arms something chronic when I push,' Bessie said.

'Ah, sorry Bess. It's frustrating, being held prisoner in me own body like this. Relying on you for everything.'

He reached back to take her hand. For the first time, I saw a glimmer of a softer, more sensitive side. Then he glanced at the clock and let out a trumpeting cry.

'Christ, it's almost lunchtime! Bloody hell!'

He span suddenly in his chair, causing Bessie to let go of the handles in alarm.

'George!' she cried.

He bashed into the wall several times as he performed a twenty-three-point turn. Flecks of white paint crumbled from the already chipped door frame. Peter curled his tiny fingers into fists.

'Erm, what was that all about?' I said.

'Don't.' Peter's fuzzy eyebrows had almost reached his hairline. 'It's very hard to stay professional at times.'

'I bet.'

His patience was astonishing. I wanted to give George a shake. More than that – perhaps an affectionate slap. His sheer lack of common sense was ridiculous.

'So, anyway, as I was saying before, well, before whatever *that* was, when the check socket's done I'll come back and fit it. OK?'

'OK. Thanks, Peter.'

There was a sucking, squelching noise as the prosthetist slid the hard cast off my stump. Cold air hit my skin. Phantom pain jarred through my leg. I held my breath, willing it to calm down. My stump jerked involuntarily before settling again, the initial agony replaced by a dull throbbing, the now-familiar pins and needles deep inside, pricking like the tears in my eyes.

Jenny, Mark and Evie were waiting in my room after lunch. Jenny scribbled in a ringbound folder marked 'wedding' and Mark flicked through the latest issue of *Step Forward*, the amputee magazine that was dotted all over the centre. It was an accurate picture of their relationship, my sister throwing everything into their forthcoming nuptials while Mark took his usual three steps back. Jenny was going big for the wedding; 120 guests and a huge elaborately decorated barn after the service in the Kent church of our childhoods. I knew Mark would have preferred a simpler ceremony; fewer people and less celebratory fuss. Although he was laid back enough to let Jenny do what she wanted, his way of coping tended to be withdrawal, much to Jenny's irritation.

Evie was wearing fairy wings over her school uniform. She jumped up as I came in, throwing herself at me with such force that I had to put my foot on the floor to prevent the wheelchair toppling.

'Auntie Heidi!' she yelled. She looked down, staring at my leg. I turned away, my face flushing. I knew she was only curious, but I didn't know how to react to her scrutiny.

'Evie,' Jenny said. 'Be calm. Remember, Auntie Heidi had an accident. She needs to relax.'

'But I want to know about what happened.'

I looked into my niece's wide, hazel eyes; more like Mark's than Jenny's. I took a deep breath. 'Evie, you know when you fall over in the playground?' Evie nodded emphatically.

'Yes, I do it all the time. The big boys chase me and Abbie and we can't run fast enough and the other day Abbie fell over and she had a big cut on her knee and she needed to have a bright blue plaster.'

'Exactly. Well, that's kind of what happened to me. Except my falling over was really, really bad.'

I felt a rush of pins and needles in my stump. Whenever I thought about the accident, the phantom pain seemed to get worse.

'Did it hurt lots?'

'Quite a lot, yes.' I was surprised to find my voice came out choked.

'I thought so,' Evie said. 'Because then the doctor had to take your leg away.'

Holding my emotion inside, I could only nod. Everything was so simple to a child. I tried to summon Evie's perspective, hoping it might help. At first I had a leg. Now, I didn't. But the black-and-white thought pattern only made me feel worse.

'So, how did the prosthetic casting go this morning?' Jenny asked.

'Oh yes, the casting!' Mark echoed. He was forever echoing his soon-to-be wife. 'I'm sorry, Heidi, work's been so hectic. I haven't kept up with you as much as I should have done. It seems to be one conference after another at the moment . . .'

'Yes, it does, doesn't it?' Jenny said. There was a note of sarcasm to her voice. 'Manchester last weekend, Birmingham this weekend, and what is it, Newcastle next week?'

'Cumbria.' He shrugged. 'These things often happen around the same time.'

'Do your colleagues realise you're getting married soon?' Jenny was pink in the face; a sure sign of impending anger.

'Jen, of course they do . . .'

'Right,' she said dryly. She crossed her arms and looked towards the window. The tension was palpable.

'So, I'll get my leg in a few days,' I announced, trying to resume normality.

'That's great!' Mark answered with a little too much enthusiasm. He stole a glance at Jenny, but she was studiously ignoring him.

I knew Mark had looked up the process of prosthetics on the internet. He'd also watched all my operations on YouTube. Thorough and disciplined, Mark was a man who liked to be well-informed, often to the point of irritation.

'So you'll be walking soon?' he asked. His round tortoiseshell glasses bounced on his pointy nose.

'Well, it's not quite as easy as that . . .'

At that moment, Maud returned from lunch. At the sight of a little girl in the room, she beamed, throwing her arms out widely.

'And who is this little love?'

Evie jumped away from me and ran to Jenny, leaping up onto her lap.

'I'm Heidi's sister,' said Jenny, with inherent politeness despite her strop. As she spoke, I saw Mark's shoulders drop. He was as relieved as I was. 'This is Mark, and this is Evie. And you must be Maud. We've heard all about you.'

'All good I hope?'

'Of course.'

Maud wheeled over to her bed and heaved herself out of her chair with a grunt. Evie watched with wide eyes, captivated by the sight of yet another limbless lady.

'We were just talking about the recovery process,' said Mark. 'Heidi tells us she'll get her prosthetic leg in a few days.'

'Wonderful, isn't it?' Maud beamed. Seeing her obvious joy, I felt a rush of fondness. 'Mine will take a few more weeks, I think. It's this wound,' she pointed to her stump, 'old skin doesn't spring back so quickly, unfortunately.'

'So how long until you're walking then, Heidi?' Jenny asked. She clutched her wedding folder more tightly, brandishing it as though about to take notes.

'It doesn't just happen, Jen,' I said. 'You start with crutches, then sticks, then eventually move to nothing. But it's different speeds for everyone. There's no set pattern.'

'Right.' On her lap, Evie squirmed. Jenny released her. 'But how long until you leave here? I know it's a six-week stay, but will you be here that whole time? I mean, you must have a rough idea, surely . . .'

I gritted my teeth, speaking slowly and carefully. Now it was my turn to be angry.

'I don't know yet, Jenny.' There was a silence between us. She really didn't get it.

'I think what Jenny is asking is will you be walking at the wedding?' Mark asked. He pointed to Jenny's folder, clearly desperate to be back on her side. 'We're onto the final count-down, you see.'

'It would just be good to know, that's all.' Jenny shrugged. 'Obviously, in an ideal world you'll be walking down the aisle, and we'd prefer it if you were able to . . .'

'Jenny!' The volume of my shout surprised me. My anger had risen like fizzy bubbles in a bottle. 'I'm an amputee! I've just experienced the biggest trauma of my entire life and you're seriously asking me when I'll be walking again?'

From the floor, Evie stared up at us, her eyes wide with alarm.

'All right, calm down,' Jenny said. 'Honestly, you're always so *dramatic*.' She rolled her eyes at me – a red rag to a bull.

Heat seeped from every pore. I was quivering with rage. And still Jenny continued.

'I just need to know,' she said, her tone infuriatingly matter-of-fact. 'Because obviously if you are going to be in a wheelchair, there are certain access requirements we need to sort out—'

'Jen . . .' Mark said. Everyone ignored him.

'Really, Jenny? Really?' I'd lost it now. 'Jesus Christ, give me a bloody break will you? I barely know how to dress myself without help!'

'Heidi's right,' Maud said loudly. I'd forgotten she was there. 'Look, I'm sorry to be an interfering old woman, but please, don't put too much pressure on the poor girl.' She heaved herself upright and stared at my sister. 'It's bloody hard, this amputee stuff. We need small goals, not huge things. Otherwise, it's just too daunting, right, Heidi?'

I nodded, unable to speak.

'Personally, I just want to be able to make a cup of tea in my own home again.'

A frosty silence descended. It was like Jenny and I were little girls again, each trying to out-stare the other. My big sister wasn't used to being answered back. She was used to being top dog. In the end, it was Mark who broke the tension.

'Evie,' he said, 'why don't you show Auntie Heidi what you brought her?'

'Oh, yes!' She rummaged in Jenny's bag and pulled something out, holding it behind her back. 'Auntie Heidi, I found you a friend.'

The curvy Barbie had long crimped hair and a tiny silver crop top. She wore a green mermaid skirt complete with glittery fins. Her tanned plastic skin was shiny and flawless – but there was something that wasn't quite right. The Barbie only had one leg.

'Her name is Sophie,' Evie said. 'She's like you.'

Mark eyed me apologetically. 'Evie's idea,' he mouthed.

Jenny poked her chin into the air and ignored me. She was clearly still in a huff.

I didn't know what to say. Evie put a hand on top of mine.

'Sophie has one leg too but she can still swim really well,' she said. 'She can still be a mermaid.'

'She found her in her toy box the other day,' Mark explained. 'We're not quite sure where her leg went . . .'

'Oh, Evie.' I held the doll to my chest. 'She's lovely.'

'She can be your friend,' Evie said. 'She has magic powers.'

I stroked Sophie's perfect hair. I could do with a bit of mermaid magic.

'I hope you don't think it's offensive,' Mark said.

'Of course not.' I looked into Evie's earnest little face. 'I think it's adorable.'

'What a lovely thought,' Maud said to Evie. She was speaking slowly and softly, as though careful not to startle her. My niece rewarded her efforts with a shy smile. Maud looked thrilled. 'I think your auntie is just as pretty as a mermaid, don't you?'

'Me too,' Evie nodded.

'Thanks, Maud,' I said.

'Oh, you're welcome, love,' came the reply. 'Now, please don't fall out with your sister.' She looked from Jenny to me. She was taking on the wise grandmother role, and I was grateful. 'It's not worth it, girls. Life's too short. Surely we of all people know that?'

'I guess so,' I answered.

I was still stung by Jenny's insensitive comments. I couldn't believe how clueless she could be. Wrapped up in her own life, drowning in wedding admin, she hadn't even thought about the scale of my predicament. Clutching Sophie tighter, I addressed my sister.

'Sorry I shouted, Jenny,' I said. It was the way it had always been – me backing down first, keen to restore the peace. Jenny was much more of a sulker. From the corner of the room, she gave an almighty sigh.

'Yeah. Sorry, Heidi,' she mumbled back.

It was grudging, but I knew it was the best I was going to get. Jenny wasn't the type to ever admit her failings. Maud nodded, satisfied at our truce. It was at that moment that I realised: not everyone I encountered would understand. This was a battle I'd fight for the rest of my life – confusion, explanations and sadness.

Chapter Nine

Breakfast the next day, and Maud was in a mood. She stared miserably into her Corn Flakes, bracelets jangling against the plastic bowl as she stirred the cereal around and around. It was the first time I'd seen her anything but upbeat. I didn't like it at all.

'Hi, Maud.' I parked my wheelchair up opposite her, taking my usual position.

'What? Oh, morning, Heidi.'

She barely glanced at me. Her eyes were hooded with tiredness. I knew how she felt. After my argument with Jenny, my thoughts hadn't settled. Thanks to Maud's intervention, my sister and I had parted on a civil note, but once I'd said goodnight to Maud and we'd pulled our cubicle curtains around our beds, the darkness had taken over my mind. Unwanted yet uncontrollable, the film of my accident played on repeat. I'd watched myself over and over on the path, two feet pounding, jogging towards an unknown horizon. Smothered by worry, shrouded in fear, insomnia and nightmares had once again haunted the night. I was exhausted.

'What's up?' I asked Maud. I tried to sound casual, but worry gnawed in my stomach. It was the first morning since I'd got here that she hadn't changed out of her pyjamas. For the first time, I noticed her spindly wrists rather than just her bangles;

her slender, arthritic fingers curled around the spoon. She was so tiny, so frail. Since becoming friends, I'd stopped thinking of her as an old lady. It was a shock to see her vulnerability.

'Ah, nothing really, love. I'm grand. I'm just a bit fed up, that's all.'

'Why's that?'

She put the spoon down and pushed her bowl away. Across the room, Fajah glared.

'I'm just bored. Bored of the wheelchair. Bored of being bed-bound. Bored of this place. I know they warned me it'd take a while to heal, but I just want to get up and get on with it now, y'know?' I nodded.

'It must be tough, especially when you hear I'm collecting my leg soon.'

'Oh no, love, I'm so happy for you.' She looked at me, sincerity etched across her face. 'Really. Don't ever think anything else. I know it sounds pathetic, but I just want to go home now.'

'No. It's not pathetic at all,' I said. 'I feel exactly the same.' I put a hand on her arm. As I did so, I noticed my biceps. Toned and prominent, they definitely hadn't been so defined before. I felt faintly pleased. The wheelchair was a good arm workout if nothing else.

'Come on you two, it's almost physio time.' Tara had arrived. Her hair was wet from the shower and scraped back into her usual high ponytail. She was holding a home-made protein shake. 'I want you down in the garden in five minutes.'

She turned on her heel and jogged downstairs, taking the steps two at a time. Maud and I stared at each other.

'Look, I don't think I can do it today, Heidi.' She sounded different to her usual self; drained of all lightness. 'I slept badly. I'm in too much pain.'

'But it's group physio . . .'

'I know.' She sighed deeply. 'I'm sorry, love.'

'Is there anything I can do?' I took in her lined face, strands of un-coiffed bed hair sticking up at strange angles. I hated seeing her like this.

'No, no.' She gave me a weary smile. 'All I need is oral morphine and a long nap. I'll be right as rain after that, promise. Apologise to Tara for me, will you?'

'Course.'

'Thanks, love.' She took a half-hearted sip of coffee before releasing the brakes on her wheelchair. 'Fajah,' she called, 'be a doll and take me back to my room, will you? I don't have the energy to push today.'

I watched from the table as my room-mate and confidante was wheeled away, thin shoulders hunched over, gaze fixed firmly on the floor. Of course, I recognised that everyone had bad days, that recovery was a rocky road. But in that moment, I realised how much I'd come to rely on Maud's stability and wisdom. Seeing a crack in her courage shook me far more than I expected. I needed her to stay strong; for both of us.

After breakfast, I duly headed out to the garden. I wasn't really in the mood for physio either. And I was even less in the mood when I saw Jack McNally.

He was chatting to Tara, hands in the pockets of his jeans, red hair bright against the grey blue sky. When he noticed me, he lowered his gaze, tilting his head downwards to meet mine. I hated the barely concealed pity in his eyes as he looked down at me. It made me feel disabled and worthless.

'She's not coming,' I said, more bluntly than intended.

'What?' Tara spun around to face me, eyebrows raised.

'Maud.' I shrugged, relishing the way Jack's expression instantly clouded. Served him right for his attitude. 'She had a bad night and her wound's hurting. She doesn't feel like she can face it.'

'Is she OK?' Jack was looking at me properly now, suddenly attentive.

'She said she just needs to sleep.'

'OK, well, I suppose we'll have to manage.' Tara pursed her lips. 'But that does kind of ruin my plans for the session. Unless . . .' Her gaze fell on Jack. 'What are you doing for the next hour?'

'No,' I cut in. 'Bad idea.' The thought of spending an entire session under his patronising gaze filled me with horror.

'Well, I only popped by to see Nanna.' Jack hesitated. He looked from me to Tara, biting his lip. 'I guess now she's sleeping I'll just sit and read my book.'

'Right,' I said.

'Wrong,' said Tara. She clicked her fingers, indicating an idea. 'You're going to be the second participant for wheelchair time trials.'

'What?' We both said it at once.

'But he's able-bodied!' I protested. 'How's that fair? Really, can't I just do it on my own?'

'Without another person there's no competition.' Tara smiled, visibly relieved to be back in control. 'Go on, Jack, it'll be fun.'

'Well . . .' he floundered, biting his lip. 'I suppose I'm not doing anything else . . .'

'But—' I tried. I could not believe this was happening.

'Excellent!' Tara crowed.

'What's wrong, Heidi?' His green eyes flashed with challenge. 'Worried I'll beat you?'

'No,' I shot back. 'More worried that you'll embarrass yourself. Again.'

'Fighting talk, that's what I like!' Tara was bouncing on her heels, clearly thrilled with herself. 'Right, I'll go and grab you a wheelchair, Jack!'

She dashed off and we stared at each other, neither quite sure of what had just happened. I was not looking forward to it at all.

'Right, so it's up the hill there, around the back of the garden, twice round the fountain and then back down to me. Got it?' Tara asked. She held a stopwatch in her hand.

'Yep.' We both nodded.

It was weird seeing Jack in a wheelchair. One of the special bariatric designs, it was far too big, almost room for another person to sit beside him in the seat. His knees stuck out comically and his pale face was brushed with pink. He looked incredibly awkward – and I couldn't help feeling smug. Now we'd see how he liked it.

'Not gonna lie, I didn't expect this to happen,' he said.

'You're telling me,' I replied. I wanted to add that I hadn't expected any of this to happen, ever. But I held my tongue. Sarcasm wouldn't help me win.

Jack experimented with releasing the ancient chair's brakes. They let out a tremendous creaking sound, as though protesting against any movement. Much like many of their occupants, I thought.

'You start on my whistle,' Tara said. 'Jack, you're up first. Ready?'

'I think so.' He craned his neck, tilting his chin up to address Tara. At least now he saw what it was like to be stuck on this level; looking up to everyone, whether they deserved it or not.

'Good luck,' I said, dryly.

'I need it,' he replied.

'Go!'

Tara blew the whistle and he was off, hands on the wheels, head and chest thrust forwards. He was surprisingly fast for a novice, his arm muscles bulging as he put in the maximum effort. Adrenaline surged through me as I watched his progress. I'd never be able to beat him. But then he hit the hill. His arms quivered as he fought the steep gradient. He began to roll backwards.

'Bloody hell!' he cried. He put a foot down on the ground to control the movement.

'Penalty!' yelled Tara. 'Ten seconds added on!'

I stifled a laugh. I don't know what had got into me; I wasn't normally this competitive. In the past, I'd been used to losing on purpose, allowing Jenny to win everything as children to avoid the inevitable sulks of my bossy big sister. But this was different. Somehow, this was personal. And I desperately wanted to win.

Jack completed the course in seven minutes and twenty-three seconds; thirty-three if you counted the extra time (which I very much did). By the time he returned to the patio he was redder than ever and panting, sweat running from his forehead and down his neck, pooling in patches beneath his armpits.

'Phew. That is harder than it looks.' He wiped a hand across his brow.

'I know.' I kept my tone cool, but my insides were jittering with the anticipation of imminent competition. 'Try being in a wheelchair full-time.'

'I honestly don't know how you do it.' I watched as a new-found respect crossed his expression. He sat next to me, face shining with sweat and sincerity. For the first time, he was on my level. 'You all make it look so easy.'

'Well, I don't know about that . . .'

'Ready, Heidi?' Tara reset the stopwatch and put her whistle between her teeth.

'As I'll ever be.'

'Good luck,' Jack said. He held out a hand. 'May the best man win.' We shook. His palm was warm against mine.

Tara gave a short sharp blast on her whistle. The first few pushes were easy, a burst of speed as I propelled myself swiftly across the patio. Inevitably, the hill proved more challenging. My left foot twitched as I heaved myself up, desperate to root me to the ground. But remembering Jack's penalty, a stubborn streak I hadn't even realised I had took hold. I wouldn't give in. I wouldn't let him have the satisfaction. I wouldn't lose.

By the top of the slope, my breathing was laboured. I huffed and panted, my heart dancing against my ribcage. And yet the adrenaline surged on, forcing me forwards, refusing to slow my pace. I rounded the fountain at such a pace that I almost tipped over my wheelchair.

'Careful!' I heard Tara call.

Thank God for stabilisers. The back path was gravelled and rough, the bumpy surface slowing my speed. By now, a fiery ache had spread through my arms, my muscles protesting with every turn of the wheels. Despite my gloves, my fingers felt raw. Almost there. Approaching the downhill slope, I freewheeled as fast as I dared, hands grazing the wheels as I controlled my direction, careful not to career into the flower beds on either side. I launched myself across the patio, almost crashing into Tara's legs.

'Seven minutes, seventeen seconds,' she said. 'Heidi wins.'

'Yes!' I punched the air, though my arms were like lead. They felt like they didn't belong to me any more.

'Congratulations,' Jack said. 'Although in fairness, you have had more practice.'

What? Riding high on a rush of adrenaline and victory, I opened my mouth to snap at him. But then I saw he was grinning.

'Relax, I'm joking!' He held his hands up in a surrendering gesture. When he smiled, deep dimples appeared on both his cheeks. They lit up his whole face. 'You're the worthy winner, Heidi. No arguments from me.'

'Well, thanks . . . I think.'

'And thank you, Jack, for being such a good sport,' Tara added.

'You're welcome. It was surprisingly more fun than I expected.'

'That's great to hear.'

'But I better go and check on Nanna. Are you coming, Heidi?'

'Yep.' I watched as he released the brakes on his wheelchair and began to move away. I called out after him.

'Err, Jack?'

'Yes?'

'You're not actually disabled, remember?'

'Oh my God, yeah!' He stood up and began to laugh, a hearty, infectious chuckle. And when he caught my eye, I found I was laughing, too.

Chapter Ten

I sat on a chair in the middle of the gym's parallel bars, watching as Peter the Prosthetist adjusted my new foot's alignment. Tongue poking out, he tightened the bolts with a silver Allen key, his long fingers deft and nimble.

The prosthetic leg was much heavier than I'd expected. Bolstered by two thick stump socks, it was held up by a rubber suspension sleeve that stretched up over my thigh. It smelt like the AstroTurf of Evie's school playground.

'That should do it,' he murmured – more to himself than to me.

It felt very odd to have weight at the end of my leg again. In fact, the only reminder that I'd ever had anything there was the phantom sensation, which hummed through my nerves like electricity each time the accident crossed my mind.

To be honest, I'd expected to feel happier. I'd been waiting for this day for two months. I'd even ordered new trainers for the occasion. And yet, when I looked down at the huge, bulbous socket, emotion rose in my throat. I'd been told over and over that the first leg wouldn't be pretty, but nothing had prepared me for the reality. The flesh-coloured plastic atop a crude metal pole was so basic, so stark and so bleak. It looked nothing like the streamlined prosthetics I'd seen on TV. My sleek Nike trainers wedged onto the clunky, doll-like foot did nothing to soften the sadness. Disappointment weighed as heavy as the leg.

'Right, I think you can try standing on that now,' Peter said. He rubbed his peppery stubble with a tiny hand. 'Just mind you keep hold of the bars.'

Slowly, tentatively, I rose from my seat. The prosthesis was cumbersome to lift and I felt a squashing sensation in my socket, as though an invisible pair of hands held my stump tightly in their grasp; clutching, squeezing and crunching.

'That's it,' Tara said. She came over to survey me, whistle between her teeth.

Across the room, Shahid was attempting a one-handed press-up. He wore tracksuit bottoms tucked into ankle socks and his usual West Ham shirt.

'Check this out, Tara,' he called. I watched as he puffed out his chest with bravado, before dipping down with one arm towards the mat. His elbow gave way and he collapsed heavily onto his stomach.

'Nice try,' Tara said dryly.

'Nah man, wait. That wasn't it. I'm gonna go again. And this time it's gonna be *proper* good.'

'OK, Shahid.' A brief but clear sign of agitation crossed Tara's expression. 'Keep trying. I'm just watching Heidi.'

She sighed and turned back towards me. The lines in Peter's forehead had deepened. I felt very conscious of their eyes on me. Taking a deep breath, I lifted my prosthetic leg and began to move. And then, for the first time, I was walking.

Unused to the sudden pressure, my stump felt bruised and swollen, the prosthesis pushing and rubbing in places I never knew could hurt.

'Is it supposed to be this painful?' I asked through gritted teeth.

'It won't be when you're used to it,' Tara replied. 'It's natural to have a bit of pain at the start.'

I clung on to the bars and pushed all my weight through my arms, anything to offset the pressure.

'You're doing great,' Peter assured.

Gingerly, I took another step, only to bring my good leg through to take the weight again as quickly as possible. I couldn't linger on the prosthesis side for more than a few seconds.

'Try to be a bit more even,' Tara said. 'I know it's hard, but it's good to establish the right habits early on.'

'I don't trust it,' I answered, blinking back tears. 'I feel like it's going to give way.'

'You will feel like that. Honestly, everyone does.

For the next ten minutes, I walked up and down. By the end of it, I was exhausted. My knuckles turned white from the effort of clinging to the bars. My palms were wet and slippery. The repetitive limping motion made me feel like a lame tiger in a zoo. I was on the verge of tears and I blinked them away, desperate not to let my weakness show. The session marked a new waypoint, a step forward in my recovery – so why did I feel so hopeless?

Steph, the occupational therapist, was a conscientious and anxious sort of woman. She wore dark lip liner with pale lipstick, and while most of the rehab staff opted for trainers, Steph favoured a sturdy lace-up shoe. As my mum would have put it, she was an old head on young shoulders. She was also a rigorous timekeeper.

I was three minutes late to my session. After the drama and agony of my prosthetics session, I hadn't wanted to go at all. As I wheeled myself into the rehab kitchen, Steph tutted and clucked, stabbing pointedly at her watch.

'Sorry,' I mumbled.

She nodded curtly. 'You're here now, so let's get on with it. Right, so when we're moving around the kitchen, we need to be *very* careful.' She spoke loudly and slowly, careful to enunciate every syllable.

'Right.' She looked down at me in the wheelchair and I felt five years old again.

'We'll weigh the pasta out first. So when you're ready, you can stand up.'

I rose from the chair obediently and grabbed the work surface for balance. On instinct, I shifted my weight to my good side.

'The pasta's in the top cupboard,' Steph said. 'So try and tense your core when you stretch.'

'OK.' I did so, surprised to find the motion easier than expected. I held the packet aloft. 'Got it.'

'Good work.' Steph sounded like she was talking to a small dog.

I tried to ignore her patronising and looked around for the scales. No doubt deliberately, they were on the other side of the kitchen. It was only a few steps away, but to me it seemed like a marathon. I took a tentative step forward, wincing as the prosthesis pinched at my stump.

'No, no,' Steph said. 'You could fall. Remember, the best way for an amputee to move around the kitchen is by side-stepping. That way, you can grab onto the work surface if you feel wobbly.'

She leant against the work surface in her OT uniform; green trousers and a pristine white tunic. She had a habit of fiddling with the lanyard around her neck. I'd noticed that she never let it flip over. Instead, she always ensured it was turned to the side with her picture and title: Senior Occupational Therapist.

'Got it,' I said.

Facing the counter, I held onto it like a rail and began a slow shuffle, pushing the pasta along with me to save an extra trip. I'd learnt by now that amputee recovery was all about problem solving; forward thinking and minimising the amount of necessary movement.

She was right that side-stepping was easier. But I felt ridiculous. Each time I placed weight on the prosthetic foot, I stifled a grimace. It made me angry to think that just weeks ago, I could have reached the other side in just a couple of strides or a jump. With each small movement, pain fuelled my frustration.

Finally, I made it. I weighed out 150g of pasta and tipped it into the saucepan that was waiting on the hob. In spite of myself, I felt a small spark of pride. Ridiculous.

'Great job,' Steph said. 'High five.' She held her palm up. Now that was going too far. I really didn't want to high five her. But I did it anyway. I felt like I couldn't refuse.

'Love it!' she said – and my face flushed warm with embarrassment. Thank God no one else was watching. Keen to get away from her, I began to move towards the kettle. But Steph jumped towards me and blocked my way.

'No, no,' she cried out, somewhat dramatically I thought. 'I'll do that bit!'

'What?'

'The boiling water,' she said slowly and patiently, as though it were the most obvious thing in the world. 'It's *far* too dangerous.'

I grit my teeth at her tone. I wanted to scream at her for treating me like an idiot. Yes, I had one leg, but there was nothing wrong with my brain.

'Steph, it's pasta.' I said, as calmly as I could manage. 'Seriously?'

'It's the rules.' She smiled sweetly. 'Now, you stand well back while I pour.'

I gripped the counter until my knuckles turned white, suppressing the sudden urge to lash out. As the days and weeks went on, I was seeing disability in a new and sharp light. Why did people feel it was OK to talk down to us as though we were lesser, lower somehow; as though we couldn't understand. And why did they use that ridiculous baby voice? Steph was a professional. She of all people should know better.

'Right,' Steph said. She seemed completely oblivious to my anger. 'We'll just wait for that to bubble up. Now, can you reach the pesto, Heidi? It's down in the bottom cupboard.'

'Fine.' I almost spat my response. In a violent, jerking motion, I moved my hands from the counter and stepped backwards to open the cupboard. But as I did so, I tripped. My prosthetic leg gave way beneath me. And then I was on the floor.

'Heidi, are you OK?' Steph rushed over and crouched down next to me. I put a hand to my face. It surprised me to find that I was crying. I gave myself a quick mental check. No damage done, although my whole body was shaking. My heart pounded against my ribcage.

'I'm fine,' I told her. I rolled quickly over onto my knees. Steph held out her hands to help me up but I ignored her, heaving myself back to standing with my aching arms instead. I didn't want her pity. Not now; not ever.

'Are you sure?' Her eyes were wide. No doubt she was thinking about the paperwork.

'Fine,' I said again. I plopped down into the wheelchair and brought my T-shirt to my face, rubbing angrily at my eyes. 'It's not a big deal.'

I sat on my hands, willing the shaking to stop. I was worthless. I couldn't even perform the simplest of tasks. I wished I was somewhere, anywhere else. My face was warm and my heart was racing; embarrassment coated by fear.

'Of course it's not.' Her faux-soothing tone felt like drowning in whipped cream. 'All new amputees have falls. It's a natural part of the rehab process. If you don't fall, you'll never learn to get up again.'

The terrible irony of this statement seemed lost on her. I took some deep breaths. I was struggling to control the tears. If I couldn't even make pasta, how the hell would I go back to a normal life? How could I go jogging, or even walking? How would I ever manage auditions, and how could I go food shopping when I couldn't carry the bags? How would I ever live independently again? The questions ducked and dodged around my brain, too many for me to cling to. I screwed up my eyes, trying to block them out.

'No harm done anyway,' said Steph, 'and do you want to know the good news?"

I didn't respond.

'We can take some deep breaths and have a big soothing bowl of pesto pasta together.' She beamed at me. 'Isn't that nice?'

I shook my head, staring down at the floor. I wasn't hungry at all.

Chapter Eleven

A strong summer sun peeked through the lush garden greenery, casting dancing shadows onto the perfectly manicured grass. Birds chattered and danced around the branches, ducking into birdbaths and perching on the sundial in the centre of the lawn.

Behind the main lawn was a little courtyard, secluded in the corner and surrounded by wild flowers. The air smelt sweet and fresh. I parked myself among a circle of carved stone statues. I flexed my arms, aching from the effort of pushing, noticing again as I did so the definition in my biceps. In fact, I was more toned all over. I looked considerably less gaunt, my stomach no longer concave, my left thigh hard with muscle. I felt stronger. Leaning backwards to feel the sun's warmth on my face, I breathed.

'We've got to stop meeting like this.'

The voice made me jump. Across the courtyard, I saw a flash of orange hair, beneath it a vibrant lime green shirt. My heart sank slightly as he approached. Despite my new truce with Jack, I'd been looking forward to some time on my own.

'Jack,' I said. 'What are you doing?'

'I could ask you the same question.' There was a lit cigarette in his hand, tendrils of smoke rising into the air.

'You can't smoke out here,' I said.

Jack's lips curled into a smile. After one more deep drag, he threw his cigarette onto the floor, stubbing it out pointedly.

'There.' He stood in front of me with folded arms, his round figure and sticking-out ears casting a cartoon-like shadow. 'Better?'

'Thanks.' I was aware I sounded petulant, when really, I had nothing against smokers. On nights out, both Dougie and I were partial to the smoking area gossip. But in an environment where the majority of patients had lost limbs due to their lifestyles causing diabetes, I had to defend the rules.

Jack took out some Extra Strong Mints and popped one into his mouth. He offered me the packet.

'Want one?'

'I'm OK, thanks.'

I tugged my exercise shorts further down my thighs. They'd ridden up in the wheelchair. The way he looked down at me made me feel uncomfortable and exposed.

'I came out here to get some peace,' I said. It was a hint, but he didn't take it.

'So did I,' he shrugged. The top two buttons of his slightly too tight shirt were undone, revealing wiry orange chest hairs beneath. It wasn't a great look.

In the distance, I could still hear music coming from the centre, faint but distinguishable nonetheless. It was 'Take a Chance on Me' by ABBA. Never, I thought. Jack squinted in the sunlight. It gave him crows' feet in the corners of his eyes.

'I'm a bit early to see Nanna,' he said.

'She's at physio.'

'Yeah. I know.'

He moved out of my path and sat down on one of the wooden benches across from me. I stared at the nearest bed of wild flowers, yellows and oranges, nodding their heads in the light breeze. We sat in silence. I wished he'd leave. Somewhere behind me, ABBA continued to play.

86

'Sounds like someone's having a morning rave.' Jack motioned towards the building.

'Yep. It's why I came out here. To be alone.'

He ignored my bluntness. He really wasn't getting the message.

'Well, I hope it's not Nanna raving and misbehaving in there,' he said. There was a sudden glint in his cat-like green eyes. 'I brought her up better than that.' Despite my irritation, the comment made me smile.

'My money's on George.'

Most of the inmates didn't know how to work the dining room TV, and Shahid was more of a rap man. Besides, George was the deafest of the lot. If we could hear it out here, that was a telltale sign.

'They're a funny bunch, aren't they?' he said.

'They sure are.'

Jack pressed a hand against his bare arm, then shuffled to the shady side of the bench. 'I don't have my factor fifty with me,' he explained.

His face was so earnest that I couldn't help laughing.

'What?' he said. 'It's not easy being ginger, you know.'

'I'm sure it's not.'

I sensed the cloud of tension between us beginning to dissipate. I inhaled deeply, the summer air filling my lungs. It really was a beautiful day. The sky was cloudless, a lone plane casting a trail across the blue as it escaped to a faraway location.

'Look, Heidi,' he lowered his voice. All traces of amusement vanished. 'I'm aware I probably haven't made the best impression.'

'No.'

'Thing is, I've been going through a bit of a difficult time.'

I waited, anger stirring inside me. Difficult? Was he for real? What did he know about difficult?

'I . . . well . . . I'm not a journalist. I mean, not any more. I was made redundant.'

He averted his gaze. His pale face had reddened and a blotchy flush crept over his cheeks and neck.

'When I came to see Nanna that first day I met you, no one knew,' he explained. 'It had only just happened. I was going to tell Nanna, but she seemed so happy to see me, and then you were there. I just couldn't bring myself to say it. That coupled with . . . other problems.'

'What do you mean?'

He ran a hand through his unruly russet hair. I noticed that his bushy eyebrows were the same colour.

'Oh, let's not go there. We barely know each other, Heidi. The last thing I want to do is burden you with my own worries.'

'OK . . .' I frowned. Something about his expression told me this was about more than just a job. I decided not to push it. After all, he was right. I didn't know him at all. I reached for safer territory.

'So, do they know about your redundancy now?' I asked. 'Your family, I mean.'

Jack nodded. For the first time, I noticed the creases in his vibrant shirt, the dark circles beneath his eyes.

'How did they take it?'

'My dad didn't react well. He doesn't understand the state of the business any more. To be honest, I think he sees it as some sort of personal failure. It's not easy when you're Billy McNally's son.'

'I can imagine.'

In an instant, I saw it. The generational legacy, the display of male pride; the son who couldn't quite match up to his father.

'It'll be OK though, right?' I said. 'I mean, you can get another job?'

'I hope so. I'm looking. But it's not easy out there at the moment. The industry's shrinking, so many job losses, publications shutting down . . . there are far more job-seeking journalists than there are roles to fill.'

'Surely your dad can help?' I ventured. 'He must know people.'

'No.' His tone was sharp. I flinched slightly. 'I'm not doing that.'

'Why not?' I didn't understand. Jack's eyes had clouded, a storm brewing across a misty green sea.

'I don't want his pity. Heidi, do you know what it's like being in the same industry as your successful parent?'

'No . . .'

'Exactly. People judge you. They assume you're only there because of contacts. You have to fight, Heidi. Every single goddamn day you have to prove your worth, prove you're there on your own merit. I've worked so hard to build up my own reputation, stand on my own two feet. I am not caving in and running back to Daddy. Not now, not ever.'

He finished his speech and sat back, pulling another cigarette and a lighter from his pocket. He took a long, slow drag and turned his head away from me to exhale, the smoke coiling upwards towards the clouds.

'So you see, I'm sorry if I wasn't myself the other day. There's a lot on my mind. It's no excuse, really.'

A haze of smoke lingered between us. It wasn't unpleasant. Actually, neither was Jack.

'It's OK. I get it,' I said.

'Thanks.' He gave me a small, grateful smile. The dimples in his cheeks appeared.

I looked out across the garden. At the bottom of the slope, I could see Shahid on the patio. Tara threw a tennis ball, and he stretched up from his wheelchair to catch it with his one remaining hand. He held it aloft and whooped. Meanwhile, the unknown DJ of the ABBA disco had moved on to 'Thank You for the Music'.

'Another classic,' I remarked. Jack chuckled, before growing serious once more.

'So, Heidi, how are you getting on? I'm sorry I didn't ask you that before. It should have been the first question. Nanna told me what happened to you. It must have been such a shock.'

'It was.'

I paused, unsure how much of myself to reveal. Jack was looking straight at me now, his gaze fixed on mine. There was a new honesty in his face that hadn't been there before.

'To be frank, I don't know what's going to happen,' I said, realising as I spoke that I hadn't yet admitted that to anyone but myself. 'Some days I think I'm fine, but sometimes it gets on top of me.'

'In what way?'

'Well, the outside world just has too many obstacles – I mean, I can't even go up and down stairs without feeling like I'm about to fall. How am I going to manage being a bridesmaid for my sister?'

'When's the wedding?'

'Autumn.' Despite the heat, my body shivered involuntarily. 'But I don't know if I'll be ready. The whole learning to walk again thing . . .' I trailed off. My heart was beating in double time at the thought. Jack bit his lip.

'Man, you make my problems seem trivial. I shouldn't be banging on about my job. You have enough to cope with.'

'We all have our own stuff going on.'

'I know. But still. What happened to you was so bloody unlucky.'

I felt tears behind my eyes. I blinked them away, hoping he wouldn't notice. These days, it seemed to happen every time someone was nice to me.

'I just want to get back to normal. To feel like I've achieved something, you know?'

For a while, Jack was silent. I wondered if I'd said too much. I could feel myself blushing. The ABBA music had faded, replaced instead with the low hum of a passing plane and the rustling of the trees above. Sunlight streamed through the bushes around the tiny courtyard, casting a golden light on the intricate stone statues around us.

'OK,' he said eventually, 'so, feel free to say it's stupid. But I think I might have an idea.'

'What do you mean?' I sat back in the wheelchair. The cushion was hot against my thighs.

'Well, it's all about completing tasks here. But how about if you write some goals of your own?'

Goals. The word reminded me of Tara and her whistle; the way rehab life was measured in a series of time trials and tick lists. Just this week, I'd seen George stand from his wheelchair to flick the kettle on and make a cup of tea in occupational therapy. His subsequent elation had been almost irrational. He'd been so thrilled he'd be able to make a morning cuppa again for Bessie. And yet, I got it. Yes, I could be scathing outwardly, but I couldn't deny the feeling of happiness that swept over me when I achieved even the smallest of tasks. Jack was talking faster now, excited by his thoughts.

'You could write a list of things you want to achieve. Challenges, if you like.'

'We do that already here. It doesn't help much.' I still felt confused.

'But Heidi, you need to think beyond these four walls.' He gestured around the garden. 'Forget all the nurses and the bloody timetables. Focus on your future. Do that, and you're setting yourself up in the best way. We both know there's more to life than here.'

'Thankfully.'

But he was right. There was a whole world out there, beyond these safe, rail-lined corridors and wheelchair-friendly garden. There were real situations, real obstacles, real worries. I needed to face my fears.

'So, what do you think?' He blinked nervously, his eyes wide and expectant.

'Do you know what, Jack McNally? That's not a bad idea.'

'I'd be happy to give you a hand. Really, just say the word. It's not like I have much else going on at the moment. I'd like to help.'

'Only if you don't wear that shirt.'

Jack grinned. 'Oh, there's plenty more where this came from. Right, where is that Nanna of mine? She must be free by now . . .'

After he'd left, I stayed in the courtyard for a while, listening to the birds and digesting our conversation. Under the healing glow of the sun, the pale freckles on my arms were beginning to appear. But it wasn't just my skin that had warmed. I felt more energised than I had done in weeks. I had a focus. I had a purpose. And I had a list to write.

FIVE STEPS TO HAPPY

1) Independence. Conquer public transport (and escalators).
2) Body. Go shopping – try skinny jeans again? Build up muscle, find body confidence.
3) Career. Try a shift at the bar/work out what I want to do next.
4) Challenge. Learn to dance?
5) Closure. Walk down the path where I fell.

Part Two

Chapter Twelve

Lunchtime, and I arrived in the dining room to the sound of George bellowing a painful rendition of 'Light My Fire'. Even worse, he'd put the subtitles on the TV so all the men could sing along. I parked myself in my usual spot and tried to ignore the raucous chorus behind me. I supposed it made a change from the ABBA tunes he'd been belting out last week. I was quickly learning that there was no such thing as a peaceful meal.

Maud had gone out for lunch with Billy, so I'd assumed I'd be alone. However, sitting at our table in a wheelchair miles too big for her was a girl I didn't recognise. She stared down into her soup, long and thick blonde hair covering her face. She was a new arrival.

'Hi,' I said. 'I'm Heidi.'

The girl looked up.

'I'm Skye.'

She was very young, no more than seventeen, with a doll-like face; large blue eyes, long eyelashes and naturally blushed cheeks. She wore leggings and a black T-shirt several sizes too big for her and her nails were painted in rainbow colours. As she raised her spoon to her mouth, I spotted a small tattoo on her right wrist, three clouds with the hint of a sun peeking through.

'I like your tattoo,' I said.

'Thanks.' She ran a finger across it. 'It reminds me stuff will get better, y'know?' She spoke in a mild, well-mannered voice, yet there was a hard edge to her tone, a grittiness I hadn't expected.

'It will,' I answered.

'Well, it can't get much worse. God, this place is a shithole.'

She seemed so tiny, her petite frame dwarfed by the enormous chair. And yet, as she spoke, her eyes shone with defiance, as though daring me to contradict her. I didn't.

'Yeah . . . I've been in better situations,' I said.

Skye raised an eyebrow. She let out a humourless laugh. 'Understatement.'

Across the room, The Diabetics had begun to sing. As Fajah ripped the plastic sleeves from the ready-meal trays, they pounded hands, spoons and stumps on the table.

'Why are we waiting . . .' they chanted. 'We are suffocating . . .'

'I'll suffocate them if they don't shut up,' Skye said. 'Honestly, is it always like this here?'

I shrugged. 'Pretty much. Is it your first day then?'

'Yeah. Fresh from hospital. Thrust from one shit show to the next. My parents said they'd take me home, but my surgeon insisted this was the quickest recovery route.' She pushed her soup away and shuddered. 'That's if I don't starve first. They don't seem to understand the concept of veganism.'

'Doesn't surprise me.'

'What happened to you, then?' She fixed me with that stare again, curiosity edged with challenge.

'I fell over, jogging.' It still sounded ridiculous when I said it out loud. Skye pursed her heart-shaped lips. She let out a low whistle.

'Shit. Talk about a freak accident.'

I nodded. 'Yeah.'

'I borrowed my mate's motorbike. Turns out they're not as easy to control as I'd expected.'

She glanced down at her leg, stretched out on the wheelchair's stump board. Like me, she was a below-knee amputee. Her stump was noticeably larger than mine, the swelling still fresh and prominent.

'We've lost the same leg,' I said.

'Well, would you look at that. Two left feet, right?' That mirthless smile again.

Her sarcasm unnerved me slightly. I wasn't sure how to react to it.

'Fucking hell, I can't wait to get out of here. It's only day one and I'm already losing my mind.'

'It does get a bit better . . .' I offered. 'When you get used to the routine.'

'Fuck the routine!' She spat the words so sharply that they seemed to ricochet around the room. Fajah scowled at her.

'Now, now,' George called. 'Young girlie like you shouldn't be using words like that.'

'Oh, piss off, old man.' In a sudden, dramatic movement, Skye pushed her wheelchair away from the table, her manner reminiscent of a toddler having a temper tantrum. 'Ugh. I can't deal with this any more.'

'Skye . . .' I said. But I'd already lost her.

She spun herself violently in the chair, long blonde waves flying behind her as she sped from the room. Fajah watched, open-mouthed. Pink custard dripped steadily from the ladle in her hand.

'Teenagers,' George said. 'Makes you realise how far we've come, right Heidi?'

'Do you know what, George? I think you're right.'

The old man gave me a broad false-teeth smile. And then he turned back to his pudding.

Chapter Thirteen

I was watching *Homes Under the Hammer* when Jack next turned up. It was mid-morning and I sat by the open window in our room, prosthetic leg on, a cup of lukewarm instant coffee cooling on the table beside me. Strangely, Maud didn't seem at all surprised to see him. She usually waxed lyrical for days and hours beforehand when he was due a visit. She hadn't said anything this time.

'Hello, my boy,' she called. He moved towards her outstretched arms.

'Morning, Nanna.'

He wore a denim jacket over a tangerine orange shirt, a couple of shades brighter than his hair. He didn't move to sit down or take off his jacket.

'Heidi, I'm taking you out,' he announced.

'What?' I turned my attention away from the two-bedroom house in Catford that filled the TV screen. 'What do you mean?'

'We're going out for the day.'

My heart thrummed against my ribcage. Opposite me, Maud was grinning.

'But . . .' I floundered. I couldn't leave. There was too much danger out there; too many opportunities for shame and embarrassment.

'It's all arranged, love,' Maud chipped in. 'Jack's got permission and he's happy to look after you. Don't you worry about anything. Your challenge for today is just to have fun!"

A flurry of nerves caught in my stomach. Go out, for a full day? Writing the list had been one thing, but doing it? Well, that was an entirely different matter. Every time my family or Dougie had tried to take me out so far, I'd fobbed them off, usually with some excuse about my hectic rehab timetable. Up until now I'd got away with it, the truth being I was simply too scared to leave the safety of the rehab centre. But now, there was no time to think. I had been caught completely off guard. I couldn't see a way out.

'So, are you ready then?' Jack asked. He stood in the middle of the room, expectant.

Was I ready? I stared down at my prosthetic leg with my sparkling white trainer on the end of it. These shoes were unsullied, safe, a reflection of my own clinical existence. They'd barely been out of the rehab grounds. They bore no trace of dirt or difficulty.

'I don't know,' I said.

'Great.' He tossed me a sweatshirt. 'Then let's go.'

Waterloo station was quieter than usual. It was that rare time of day between the morning and evening commutes when you could see the entirety of the long-suffering, scuffed floor, where coffee cups rolled and pigeons pottered in search of leftover McDonalds.

Jack pushed my wheelchair across the concourse. He was a surprisingly confident driver, weaving through the steady trickle of daytrippers with ease.

'Good to be out?' he asked from behind me.

'I think so,' I replied.

Truth be told, I was in a bit of a daze. Yes, I'd written the list – but had I really intended to carry it out? If I was honest

99

with myself, I wasn't sure. I'd thought about it, sure; it had been a welcome distraction. However, actually fulfilling the challenges was another thing entirely. Now, thanks to a near-stranger and a scheming old lady, I'd been galvanised into action, whether I liked it or not. Around us, the reassuring bustle displayed the city's constant hum, lives crisscrossing but never quite meeting. It reminded me that for us all, life simply goes on. Maud was right; I'd needed a push.

'Right, let's start over there,' Jack said.

He pushed me towards the far side of the concourse. A home-less man laid his sleeping bag across some seats, his head flicking anxiously towards two balding security guards at the barriers. The two men didn't take any notice. They were deep in chat and sharing a jumbo sausage roll, crispy crumbs dropping from their mouths and gathering in the folds of their navy regulation coats.

'Jack, what are we actually doing here?' I asked.

'You'll see. Ta dah!'

I was staring up at an escalator. The silver-grey steps seemed to resemble a set of jagged teeth; a racing metal monster waiting to pull me into its never-ending jaws. I shuddered at the sight. Fear pumped through my body.

'Jack . . .'

'Look, don't freak out, OK? This is an easy one, promise.'

But I could already feel my chest tightening. In the past, I'd never paid much attention to escalators. I jogged up or down them without thinking, forever in a rush and grateful for the extra speed. I'd even been known to join in with fellow commuters when they tutted at tourists who stood casually on the right-hand side, unaware of the unspoken rule to keep it clear. Jenny had been frightened of escalators as a child, but it had never been an issue for me. So why couldn't I breathe?

'Heidi, it's OK.' Jack looked concerned. 'If it's too much too soon, tell me. I just thought that . . .'

'No. I'm doing it.'

And just like it had that day with the wheelchair racing, a firm resolution took hold. I would not look stupid in front of Jack. I couldn't give up.

Steadying myself with my crutches, I stood up from the wheelchair. The prosthesis was already pinching.

'Did escalators always move this fast?' I asked. I tried to sound breezy. My voice shook.

I rocked from foot to foot, trying to even out my weight distribution. I hadn't quite shaken the bad habit of leaning only on my good side – even though I knew it might cause hip and knee problems in future. Jack glanced around, considering.

'This one's much slower than the others. And shorter.'

'OK, if you say so.'

My heart was thumping. My wet palms slipped and slid against the crutches. Jack put a hand on my shoulder.

'Look, are you sure you're ready for this?'

'Born ready.' I wasn't sure my fighting talk was convincing. 'But what should I do with the crutches?'

'Well, you could keep them both in one hand as you go up. Or you can use one and give the other to me. That way, you'll be able to hold the handrail.'

I eyed the rail. I'd forgotten that moved, too.

'If I give you a crutch, it's one less thing to think about, right?' I said.

'Exactly.' He gave a reassuring smile. 'We'll leave the wheelchair down here. I'll be right behind you.'

A train delay announcement boomed in the background. The 15.32 to Alton was running seven minutes behind schedule, following an electrical fault, apparently. I reminded myself to focus.

'OK,' I said. 'Let's do it.'

Fear lurching in my stomach, I moved towards the escalator. I paused at the bottom to let a few people ascend. A dumpy man in a straining suit brushed my side with his McDonalds bag. Two middle-aged ladies with matching bleached-blonde hair offered maternal smiles as they passed in a cloud of perfume.

'All clear,' said Jack. 'Remember, good leg first.'

I just needed to go for it. I watched the stairs roll by, choosing one and keeping my eye on it as it drew closer, counting down the seconds – three, two, one. Left foot first, I lurched onto the escalator and gripped hold of the moving rail. My heartbeat whirred faster.

'I'm here,' Jack said. He was one stair behind me. 'You're doing great.'

As the stairs levelled out, I took a breath and stepped off, wobbling as the sudden change in surface threw me forwards. Jack jumped and grabbed me. For a split second, his arms were around my waist. He smelt sweet and musty, like old cigarettes and aftershave.

'I'm sorry, I just . . . you were falling,' he stammered, releasing his grip immediately. His pale cheeks had coloured. I could feel my own reddening in response.

'It's fine, honestly. Thanks.'

'No worries.' He cleared his throat. 'And hey, look – you did it!'

I turned back to look at the escalator and felt a rush of pride.

'I did.' I wiped my palms on my leggings. Jack grinned.

'Now, let's get back down there, soldier. No time like the present.'

Although I hadn't realised before, it turned out that down was a lot scarier than up. I eyed the steep drop. I imagined myself falling and felt suddenly sick. I gripped my crutches closer.

'I can't do it,' I said. In an instant, I forgot all bravado. Panic caught in my chest. My breathing was shallow.

'You can.' Jack placed a hand on my shoulder. 'Look, let me tell you something that might help. Promise not to laugh?'

'I'll try not to.'

'OK, so when I was little, I was terrified of going to school.'

'Right . . .' Where was he going with this? My hands trembled against the crutches as he spoke. I tried to hold them steady.

'There was no reason for it really, but honestly, for months I'd cry every day in the car – and when we actually got there, I was a nightmare for at least an hour before I calmed down.'

We were interrupted by a station cleaner in a hi-vis jacket and headphones barging past us with his rubbish sack. I jumped in alarm.

'Mate, watch out,' Jack shouted.

The cleaner ignored him, striding down the steps, his head nodding to a private rhythm. He had no concept of the people around him. It was the kind of thing I would have done, before.

'Are you OK?" Jack asked.

'Yep, fine,' I answered. 'Thanks. So how old were you when all this school business was going on?' Jack looked away.

'Too old. Probably about eleven. Definitely secondary school.'

'Wow.'

'Told you it was ridiculous.' The pale pink flush had spread across his neck, down beneath the collar of his orange shirt. 'But look, the reason I'm telling you this is because it was my grandad who stopped it in the end.'

'Maud's husband?'

'Pete, yeah.' He smiled wistfully, his green eyes shining with memory. 'He was a great man. Anyway, one day he gave me this tiny piece of paper. He told me to keep it in my pocket, to read it any time I got scared or worried.' He shrugged. 'Sounds stupid. But it worked.'

'It's not stupid. What did it say?'

'Two words – stay brave.' He smiled. 'And whenever times get tough, I still think about that piece of paper. Holding it in my mind, kind of like in my pocket back then, well, it makes me feel better somehow.'

'That's really lovely, Jack.'

I imagined him as a little boy, with sticking-out ears and an oversized school uniform, the precious paper tucked into his pocket. I realised my breathing had normalised. He looked at me, his expression earnest.

'I'm telling you this because it applies to you, too,' he said. 'And you can do this. You can bloody conquer these escalators. I know it.' His tone was bold, impassioned. It sparked a new fire of determination in my belly.

'OK,' I said. 'Let's do it.'

With renewed purpose, I stepped onto the escalator. I felt fiery and powerful. Nothing would stop me now. But I was also distracted. Fixated on Jack's words, I wasn't concentrating enough. Somehow, I forgot to move my prosthetic side. As my left leg moved downwards, the right remained at the top of the stairs. Slowly, I was forced into the splits.

'Jack!' I screeched. Sudden panic knotted in my stomach. I was powerless to stop the movement.

'Stop the escalator!' he yelled.

The security guards were with us in an instant. Someone jammed down on the emergency stop button. With a low screeching sound, the escalator ground to a halt.

'Heidi, are you OK?'

I froze, bewildered. My legs were so far apart that I couldn't right myself without falling. I paused. Was I hurt? My inner thigh muscles felt strained – but I could tell it was nothing serious. My cheeks burned. So much for not making a fool of myself. I didn't know whether to laugh or cry.

Jack hauled me upright from under my armpits. With his hands on my arms, I walked my way slowly down the stationary staircase. My legs were quivering.

'Heidi?' he said again. His face had drained of colour. He looked terrible.

I collapsed into the wheelchair. I felt ungainly and inelegant, like Bambi on ice.

'All right, love?' A big bald security man came over; the one who'd pressed the stop button.

'Yes, yes . . .' I shooed him away, anxious to avoid any more attention. A policeman gawped but was clearly trying not to. A group of ladies laden with shopping bags were staring. They made no move to help, simply watched and whispered to each other. I felt like some kind of circus act. A freak show. Tears pricked my eyes.

'I'm fine. Really,' I told Jack. I was, technically. But my pride was wounded. My confidence was crumbling.

'Sure?' Jack looked dubious. He bit his lip. I nodded.

'It's a good job I'm flexible.'

'I must say it was impressive . . .' He smiled weakly.

I swallowed my emotion and cleared my throat. 'OK, time for round two.'

'Really?'

'Definitely. Stay brave, right?'

I stood up again and readied myself for action. I refused to let these metal beasts beat me. And I refused to let Jack see me cry.

'Let me take you for lunch,' Jack said.

We were sitting in the centre of the concourse, he on the row of metal chairs by the ticket machines, me in my wheelchair beside him. My muscles ached and my stomach growled.

'Will we be allowed?' I asked.

'Oh, yeah.' He waved away my doubt. 'I have permission to take you out for the whole day. Besides, I already know where we're going. I've had the idea in my head for a while.'

He looked so animated, the dimples in his cheeks deep and mischievous. He was a different person to the Jack I'd met before. It was as though the challenge had rejuvenated him. And slowly, his insistence that I face the world was restoring me, too.

'OK, you're on,' I said. He grinned.

'Great.'

'Where are we going?'

'Down there.'

He pointed to the Tube entrance and my stomach lurched. Was I imagining, it, or did it seem busier than before? Passengers scuttled in and out, a never-ending stream of brief-cases, bags and purpose. Heads down and elbows out, they jostled for position. Some were meandering and chatting, in the way of others, who strode in irritated silence. Many were plugged into headphones, their journey their only goal. I glanced at my watch. Of course; – lunchtime. That would explain it. I looked back towards Jack. Head to one side, he waited.

'OK,' I said. 'If you think I can do it.'

'I know you can.' He smiled. 'And just think – another thing to tick off your list.'

'Independence. The first step to happiness.'

'Exactly.' He stood up and brushed down his jeans. 'So let's get going. I don't know about you but I'm ravenous.'

An acrid smell of mingled fumes and body odour filled my nostrils as I descended towards the Tube, down into the belly of London, my pulse racing. I was keen to avoid another acro-batics display. My inner thighs ached from the splits, but I was otherwise unharmed.

'Sure you're OK with this?' Jack asked.

Since the splits, he'd become slightly clingy, walking behind me with his arms outstretched, as though fielding a football goal or protecting a diplomat from snipers. It was sweet, if slightly suffocating. I tried to stay calm.

'I'm positive,' I replied. I wouldn't be beaten.

'That's the spirit. Right, this way.'

Jack pushing the chair behind me, we made our way slowly to the entrance. Waterloo was one of the few underground stations with a lift. Naturally, today it wasn't working. Jack frowned at the large Tube map poster.

'That's annoying. We need the Northern line. I'm not sure how else we can . . .'

'Jack, it's fine. I'll do the escalator.' In some ways, I thought, it was probably a good thing. It avoided the formation of a mental block. It forced me back into action. But it didn't stop the nerves.

'God, hardly any of these stops are accessible,' Jack said. He traced the Tube lines with his finger. 'That's so bad.'

'I'll manage,' I answered. I could just about do stairs these days. However, I was ashamed to realise that the accessibility of Tube stations had never even crossed my mind before. The tiny wheelchair symbol was distinctly lacking from much of the map. On some lines, it wasn't there at all.

When we got to the escalator, I clung to the handrail and tried not to look down. The rail moved at a different speed to the stairs, forcing me to readjust my grip every few seconds as it jerked beneath my fingers. This escalator was longer, steeper and busier than the one in the station concourse. Jack lugged the wheelchair with him, turning his head every few seconds to ensure I was managing to stay upright. His round face was red with effort.

A stream of people passed me, jogging confidently down the stairs. They weren't even holding on. I shrank to the farthest side, trying to distract myself from my nerves by counting the theatre ads on the walls. Seen that, I thought to myself. Seen that, haven't seen that. It was a game I'd always played on family daytrips to London as a child. *The Phantom of the Opera* poster made me smile. It was the first musical my Nanna Vera had taken me to as a birthday treat. I'd been about seven at the time, and I was completely entranced by the theatrical world. It had been the start of a lifelong love.

At the bottom of the escalator, Jack held out his arms again, as though preparing to break my inevitable fall. He moved from side to side like a goalie – much to the annoyance of other passengers, who barged past him, their tutting audible. But this time, I didn't wobble.

'Amazing!' Jack looked as surprised as I felt. 'That was seamless!' His happiness was infectious.

'I reckon it's because I didn't think about it.'

'Well, whatever you did, it worked.'

Down in the ticket hall, I swiped my Oyster on the card reader and the gates sprang open. They didn't quite give me enough time, and bashed into my hip as they closed again. I cursed. Jack looked concerned.

'Sorry,' I said, 'everything just moves so quickly.'

Another battle wound, but I wouldn't let him think I was weak. Jack swiped in behind me, hauling the folded wheelchair quickly through the gates before they snapped shut.

'Do you know, I haven't done this for three months,' I remarked. 'Been on the Tube, I mean.'

'Big moment,' Jack said. I thought he was joking, but his expression remained sincere. 'We're not going far – just to Tottenham Court Road. There's step-free access there, I checked.' I smiled, touched at his thoughtfulness.

'Thank you.'

Three minutes until the next train. We stood on the platform and I leaned further into my crutches, giving the aching prosthetic a rest. He was right about the tiredness.

It was an odd feeling to be here. The surroundings were so familiar; the well-trodden floors, the people scuttling like ants underground and the robotic announcements reminding passengers to 'mind the gap' or 'always travel with a bottle of water in hot weather'. Yet in such a short space of time, so much had changed. I looked up at the display board and felt my stomach lurch. Two minutes to go.

'I don't know about you, but I wouldn't miss the Tube,' Jack said. 'Being continually whacked by backpacks and sniffing someone's armpit every morning. It's not the most pleasant way to start your day.'

'I used to cycle, mostly,' I said. I thought about my trusty bicycle, Emily. Bought second-hand when I first moved to London, she had a basket at the front and a bell that didn't quite work. I wondered if I'd ever ride her again.

'Me too.' He looked up and down the platform, largely empty save for a few groups of shoppers and the odd stray businessman. One minute to go. Down on the track, a solitary mouse washed its whiskers, unconcerned with the oncoming potential peril.

There was a sudden rush of wind, and a loud clanking, rattling noise as the train approached the platform. My hair blew into my eyes. The winking headlights drew closer. The little mouse looked up and froze, before disappearing into a tiny crack. Instinctively, I stepped backwards, as far away from the yellow line as possible.

The doors sprang open and the carriage released its contents; business people, ladies who lunched and a hoard of day trippers in bright mackintoshes, jostling and laughing as they made their way along the platform.

'Ready?' Jack asked.

'As I'll ever be.'

Thinking everyone had alighted, I moved to step onto the train. But then a large man shoved me backwards. I nearly toppled.

'Let the passengers off first,' he shouted in my face. I teetered backwards, Jack supporting me from behind. 'Don't you know the rules? Seriously, no fucking patience, some people.'

'I've got one leg,' I shot back. I resisted the urge to stamp down on his toes. After all, it would hurt him far more than me.

'I don't care.' He pushed out and onto the platform, still ranting and raving. 'Bloody rude.'

I made it to a seat just as the doors closed. I smiled reassuringly at Jack, but deep down, I was seriously shaken. What kind of person didn't care that someone was disabled? I knew it was a spur-of-the-moment comment, but it felt like a slap in the face. Londoners could be self-centred, intolerant and ruthless. They could also be seriously cruel.

The train lurched off into the darkness. The carriage was packed and the air smelt of a hundred different coat cupboards, musty jackets rubbing together in the dark, airless tunnels. The collective body heat felt oppressive, personal boundaries crossed beyond return. A woman sneezed loudly without covering her face. Instinctively, I wrinkled my nose. At the next stop, a heavily pregnant woman got on.

'Give up your seat, will ya, love?' a man in a tweed jacket said. He looked down at me, expectant. 'This lady's pregnant.'

'I . . . I can't,' I said, too quietly. 'I'm an amputee.'

'You're what?' He hadn't heard. His eyes narrowed. 'Look, love, this poor woman's about to drop. You're young and fit. It's only fair that you stand up and let her sit down.'

Around him, his fellow passengers nodded and murmured their agreement. All they saw was a selfish girl stubbornly holding her ground. No one looked down at my leg.

'I have one leg,' I said. This time, I'd spoken too loudly. The clattering of the train on the tracks grew quieter. The man in the tweed looked horrified.

'Oh. I didn't see.'

Opposite me, an immaculate woman in a pale pink hijab noticed the situation. She leapt up immediately. Crisis averted.

The man in tweed didn't bother to apologise. Instead, he simply shoved his earphones back in and looked away. Suddenly, it felt like everyone in the carriage was staring. Their cold eyes and unsympathetic expressions frightened me. Instinctively, Jack moved closer, standing in front of my prosthetic leg to block it from view.

'Keep calm,' he mouthed. I tried. But I was struggling.

The station came around much more quickly than I remembered. As we pulled into the platform, I felt fresh panic tighten in my chest. Did I stand up now? Later? When? I felt everyone's eyes on me. I couldn't catch my breath.

'This is Tottenham Court Road,' a well-spoken voice announced to the carriage. 'Change here for the Central line.'

'Jack . . .'

I floundered, my crutches slipping through my sweaty palms. The doors were already whooshing open. The platform was packed. Passengers flooded in and out.

'Come on,' Jack urged. But I couldn't find a gap. I wasn't ready.

''Scuse me!' A tall woman hollered. She had bright red lipstick and very sharp elbows, and pulled three small boys through the crowd. 'We're getting off here!' She barged past, pulling her first boy's arm so hard that he cried out in pain. 'Have you got your brothers, Leo? That's it, come on, quick!'

The family spilled out onto the platform. Jack and I tried to push through behind them. But then the doors closed.

'Shit.'

My body jerked backwards as the train pulled off. I tensed my muscles, struggling to stay upright. I wanted to cry.

'I'm so sorry, Jack.' The tears invaded my eyes. This time, I was powerless to stop them. They rolled down my cheeks. I couldn't let go of the handrail to wipe them away.

'It's OK, it's fine.' He held onto my arm, steadying me. The folded wheelchair banged precariously against his legs. 'Let's get you a seat.'

Using the wheelchair like a shield, he forged a path back through the passengers. 'Could my friend sit down, please? She has a prosthetic leg.' A man stood up and I threw myself into the seat. My leg was throbbing.

'But Jack, your lunch plan . . .' I trailed off. I felt useless, hopeless. I'd ruined everything.

'Look, we'll just get off at the next stop with wheelchair access, OK?' He squeezed my arm. 'It's not a big deal. Euston's the next accessible station – it's only a few stops away. Think of it as a mystery tour. We'll find somewhere else to eat.'

'I think . . . I think I might just want to go back.'

For a moment, his face fell. He tried to cover his disappointment with a smile, but it was too late. I'd seen it.

'OK.' He nodded. 'If that's what you want. But let's think of the positives here. You've completed the challenge.'

Had I? The train creaked and whirred through the tunnels, its passengers bobbing up and down with the movement. I'd felt so triumphant after the escalators, but maybe I'd done too much too soon.

'This is Euston,' Emma the Tube woman announced. 'Change here for the Victoria line and National Rail services.'

'Let's go, Heidi,' Jack said.

Thankfully, the carriage had emptied out slightly. With Jack leading the way, I made my way to the door. I forced myself to concentrate, to regulate my breathing, to stay calm. My stump gave a jolt of phantom pain. I winced. But I moved. And then we were on the platform.

'Right, let's find the lift.' Jack glanced up and down. Gingerly, I took a hand off my crutches and tapped his arms.

'Actually, I want to do the escalator.'

'What?' He stared at me. 'Seriously?'

'Yep.' I refused to end the day on a low.

'Well, OK. If you're sure.'

It was longer than I'd ever done before. My knuckles turned white as I gripped my crutches. My stump ached down to the bone. But I was going to do it.

Buoyed by bravado, I stepped onto the escalator, this time without any hesitation. I could hear Jack whooping behind me. I loosened my hand on the rail, now holding instead of gripping as I soared upwards towards the daylight. I was bold, I was brave – and I was back in control.

But then it happened. We were halfway up when I saw a sight that made my breath catch in my chest. An icy fear clasped hold of my heart. I wanted to run, to hide, to scream. A tall man with pale blond hair and a strong physique was passing down the other side of the escalator. Alexander Mitchell? The moment passed in a flash, dissolving before I properly registered what was going on. I hadn't seen his face, but gut instinct told me I was right. I tried to turn and look but I wobbled, gripping more tightly to the rail. Jack held out his arms like a spotter.

'OK?' he asked. I nodded. But I wasn't.

Meanwhile, the figure had been instantly lost in the crowd. Gone again.

Chapter Fourteen

'Are you sure it was him?' Dougie asked.

In the rehab dining room, we spooned egg fried rice onto mismatching plates. A splash of black bean sauce flicked onto his old teal Adidas T-shirt, already flecked with white paint from an art session.

'As sure as I can be,' I answered.

'And he saw you?'

'I don't know.'

I remembered the man's white-blond hair against the steel grey surroundings and felt a shiver run through me.

'Did you tell Jack?' Dougie reached across the table for a spring roll. I shook my head.

'He doesn't know about any of it. Anyway, he was freaked out enough after my escalator splits.'

'Good,' he said through a mouthful of food. 'You need to be careful there, H.'

'What do you mean?'

'Well, you don't know this Jack character. You don't want to be pouring your heart out. You have no idea who he really is . . .'

'Dougie!' His jealousy was obvious. 'He's a nice guy.'

'I'm just saying. You trust people too easily sometimes, that's all.'

'Right.'

He sucked up his chow mein with a loud, smacking noise. I nibbled at a prawn cracker. Chinese was normally my favourite, but my stomach was churning, anxiety overtaking my hunger.

'I suppose in a way I blame him,' I said.

'Jack?'

'No, of course not. Alexander.' I shook my head. 'Honestly, stop being so suspicious. Jack's a friend.'

'Mmm.'

Dougie began to untie and retie the elastic around his dread-locked ponytail.

'That's why seeing him there was so awful,' I continued. I decided to strategically ignore his spikey comments. 'That's twice, Dougie! In hospital, and now on the Tube! What do you think it means?'

Dougie swallowed. He stared beyond me, out through the window. Outside, the garden was dark, tall trees silhouetted against a purple cloudy sky.

'Look, H . . .' he said eventually. 'Don't take this the wrong way, but are you absolutely certain it was him?'

'What do you mean?' My fork slipped from my fingers and clattered against the plate.

'Well, it's just I've been reading up a bit on trauma.'

'Oh God, you sound like Jenny and Mark.'

'No really – hear me out.' He leant forward, fixing me with a look of sincerity I knew all too well. It was the look he'd developed from a young age; the one that had always made teachers and parents alike sit up and listen.

'Right . . .' I folded my arms and sat back in the plastic chair. I forgot my walking sticks propped up beside me. They crashed to the floor.

'Trauma can do funny things to the mind.' He gestured towards his head, a forkful of crispy beef held aloft. 'It can cause delusion, like a form of post-traumatic stress. People see things, have flashbacks. They can find reminders of the trauma almost anywhere.'

'You . . . you think I'm making it up?' While normally appealing, the glutinous shine of the crispy beef was beginning to make me feel nauseous. 'Seriously?'

'Not making it up, no.' He put the fork down and lent closer towards me. 'I just think, well, you've been through a hell of a lot. And this man, this Alexander, he saw it happen. It's natural he'll be on your mind.'

'He left me there, Dougie. He bloody abandoned me.'

'I know, H.' But his gentle voice did nothing to soothe me. I felt choked with anger and disappointment.

'Why don't you believe me?'

'I believe that's what you think you saw.' He ran a hand over his head and sighed. 'Look, I'm just saying, it's equally likely it might not have been him.'

'Right, well let's find out then, shall we?' I snatched up my phone from the table and opened up Facebook. I typed in his name. I had to know.

'Heidi, is this really a good idea?' he asked.

I didn't respond. I had a point to prove.

There were thirty-four Alexander Mitchells on Facebook in London. The list of results popped up on my screen, a line-up of smiling faces in tiny, colourful squares. Heart thumping against my ribcage, I began to scroll through them. There was an Alexander doing yoga on a beach, an Alexander with a pug under each arm and an Alexander with biceps bigger than his head posing for a black-and-white selfie in the gym. One man called himself Xander and was dressed up as a giant tomato in the middle of a nightclub, arms spread wide as his mates pretended to eat him. And then, I saw him.

As usual, it was the hair I noticed first. It stood out, white-blond and distinct against a clear and cloudless sky, just as it had on that day. He stood on the top of a lush green mountain, smiling at the photographer in triumph. He looked younger, more carefree. The profile photo dated back to 2014. Annoyingly, his privacy settings were tight.

'Heidi . . .' Dougie said again. There was a note of caution in his tone. Of the two of us, he'd always been the more careful; the one less likely to chat in class, the one who thought things through. He was a daredevil in his way, always willing to push himself to the limit. But he only climbed a tree if he knew he'd be able to get down.

I clicked on the 'About' section of Alexander's profile. I felt perversely curious now, like a wounded victim stalking their attacker for closure. According to his profile, Alexander Mitchell liked darts and Radio 4. He grew up in Surrey, and he had one brother. He was a management consultant at a firm called Waterhouse Taylor. Other than that, the information I could see was limited. In 2011, a friend checked him in to St Pancras International station. Last year, he'd set up a group to sell his bike. Then I saw his relationship status. I gasped involuntarily, clapping my hands to my mouth.

'What?' Dougie leaned forward. 'What is it?'

'He's married.'

'So?'

'So, I asked him for coffee that day, remember? No wonder he wanted to get away. I wonder what his wife's like.'

'Heidi, I don't think this is helping anyone. . .'

But I was already too deep down the rabbit hole.

'Found her!'

Kate Mitchell was a pretty but plain sort of woman, with chocolate brown hair to her chin and a full, unkempt fringe. She was attractive, although her dress sense seemed fairly dull; jeans and nondescript T-shirts. Alexander was there in her profile picture, their heads thrown back with laughter in a black-and-white shot of their wedding day. The picture was dated two years ago. It had almost 200 likes.

So that could explain why he'd left. But was embarrassment really enough reason to leave an injured person on the ground and walk away? Why was he at the hospital, just days later? And had I really seen him at Euston?

'Heidi,' Dougie said again.

I looked up, realising as I did so that I was halfway through an album of Kate Mitchell's holiday snaps. What was I doing? Stalking her girly trip to Spain in 2015 wasn't going to help anything.

'Sorry.'

Dougie sighed. His kind face was etched with worry, big dark eyes full of pain. It broke my heart to know it was my pain. I hated that I was the cause.

'Look, H, I really think it'd do you good to speak to someone about all this.'

'Like a counsellor?' I baulked at the suggestion. A familiar fear caught in my throat. I hadn't been back to Bryony since our first session. To everyone around me, I'd passed my hesitance off as scepticism, but in truth, I was terrified. I didn't want to revisit those memories. 'No, no way. Not again.'

'It can help, you know.' A strange expression had crossed his face; pensive and pained. 'It's helping me.' I stared at him, stunned.

'You?' The takeaway congealed in my stomach as endless questions rose up.

Dougie looked down at his plate, the image of the shy little boy I'd known when we were five.

'What? For how long?'

'A couple of months now.' He turned his fork over and over in his hands. 'I didn't know if I should say anything. But honestly, H, it helps.' I stared at him. He didn't look at me.

'Why didn't you tell me before?'

'Because I didn't want to make things worse for you.'

I faltered, processing his words, 'I still don't understand . . .'

'Secondary traumatic stress.' He looked up and I saw the pain in his big, gentle eyes. 'It's quite common, apparently, when something sudden happens to someone you love.'

'Oh, Dougie,' I reached out to him. Beneath my touch, he seemed to crumple, his big shoulders collapsing as he lent into my hug.

'I'm sorry,' he mumbled. His voice was thick. 'I shouldn't have said anything. Hal told me not to as well. He just wants me to move on from my mental load and go back to work. He doesn't want me to voice my feelings to you. We've been arguing about it for weeks.'

'It's really nothing to do with Hal.' I felt suddenly irritated. The ten-year age gap between them meant Hal could be such a bloody know-it-all. I forced myself to stay calm. Although I wasn't Hal's biggest fan, Dougie didn't always rate my taste in men either. He was especially wary of my very casual arrangement with Ben from Conscience, who was renowned for his womanising exploits.

'This is about you, Dougie,' I said as patiently as I could.

'I know, but Hal's only trying to help. He's not the best with emotional stuff.'

'He's not the best with anything that doesn't involve him.'

My words came out before I could censor them. Dougie only shrugged in response. I was surprised to see that he didn't try and correct me.

'Anyway, look,' he said. 'Let's not talk about me and Hal right now. You have enough going on in your own head.'

'Don't be ridiculous.' I felt guilty. I'd been so caught up in my own emotions and all this time he'd been struggling too. 'I should be the one apologising. I had no idea.'

'I didn't want you to worry about me,' he said sadly. I caught another flash of that little boy; sensitive, emotional, vulnerable. 'To be honest, I thought I could deal with it, to start with anyway. I was able to kind of ignore it. But I tried to go back to work the other day and I just couldn't do it. Not yet. I'm not ready.'

'Hang on, you went back?'

'Yeah.' He sighed heavily, suddenly seeming more fragile than ever. I hugged him closer. 'Hal nagged me so much that I thought I may as well give it a go. But I had to walk out after a couple of hours. It all just seemed so trivial, y'know?'

'I know that feeling,' I said. He was looking at his plate again, pushing the food around. My heart ached to see him so vulnerable.

'I will go back, soon. I have to. But at the moment, work, the house move, Hal, you . . . well, it's too much.'

'I get it,' I answered. The thought of him moving out continued to fill me with horror. However, I knew I couldn't tell Dougie. He was going through enough turmoil already; I didn't want to heap more worry onto his shoulders. Even though the idea of living in our flat without him felt daunting and impossible. Even though I didn't know how I'd cope alone.

'There are certain triggers that set me off,' Dougie told me. 'I can't even look at people jogging. I'll walk the other way to avoid them.' He gave a sad smile. 'Means I've been lost in Epping Forest several times.'

'But the counselling's helping?' I ventured.

'For sure. It's got loads better.' He sniffed, regaining composure. I realised he'd been close to tears.

'I'm glad. You need to be kind to yourself.'

'So do you, H.' His eyes met mine. 'Just promise me you'll think about this Alexander Mitchell thing, OK? Remember, trauma can do funny things to us all.'

'OK.'

I gave him a weak smile. He returned it, relief in his eyes having set down his burden.

But his words seemed to echo around the empty room, pressing in on me, casting doubt on my conviction. What if it really had been my imagination? Maybe I was going mad. With a heaving sigh, I pushed my plate away.

Chapter Fifteen

I hadn't wanted to come back to counselling. Every ounce of my being had rejected it, my feet slowing as I approached Bryony's door, chest swelling with anxiety. And yet Dougie had sparked a new resolution in my mind. Maybe I hadn't given it enough of a chance before. Maybe I should try again.

Bryony, of course, was delighted. She was beaming, her front teeth crossing into a snaggle-toothed smile. As I sat down, she tried her best to return to professionalism; that sincere serenity so central to the therapist's image that I wondered if it was a taught skill.

'Good to see you, Heidi,' she said. The room smelt of coffee and vanilla air freshener. A sports bag and tennis racket were propped in the corner; a reminder of her life beyond these walls.

'Hi, Bryony.'

I thought back to our last encounter. She'd been perfectly pleasant, and yet I was abrupt to the point of rudeness. I gave her a small, sheepish smile, which she returned with professional dignity. I felt guilty about that, too.

'I'm glad you came back,' she said. Today, the flower in her hair was an enormous purple rose, flecked with glitter. It matched her purple tights. 'When it comes to therapy, you need to be ready. It needs to be your decision.'

'Yeah.' I thought again about Dougie; my poor, conflicted pal. Bloody Hal needed to butt out of his emotions and let him find his own way forwards. 'I can see that.'

'So, what would you like to talk about?' She leaned back in her chair. 'Remember, these sessions are completely dictated by you.'

'Well,' I hesitated, unsure where to begin. 'The thing is, I keep seeing the man from the accident. The one who was there that day.'

'How do you mean?' Bryony's face remained neutral. I had no way of knowing what she was thinking.

'He was at the hospital a few days later. He was in the café. And then I saw him again the other day – he was at Euston station.'

Bryony paused. Her silence filled the room.

'How sure are you?'

'Well, I don't know now,' I answered honestly. 'I mean, one of my friends said it could be my imagination . . .'

Bryony twisted the flower around and around in her hair. Her grey corkscrews twisted around the petals like vines. The flower was in danger of getting lost amongst them.

'Mmm,' she said. 'Well, that's possible. I've certainly encountered that kind of projection before. Although of course, there's no way for me to tell you one way or the other.'

'I guess.' I felt suddenly disappointed. I'd expected her to have all the answers.

'It was hard for you to talk about him when we last met, wasn't it?' she said. It was more of a statement than a question. 'You didn't want to remember. Perhaps you blame him for what happened?'

'Well, yeah.' I stared at the carpet. I could feel tears behind my eyes. 'I mean, he just left me lying there. And if he'd stayed, if the ambulance had been faster, maybe then this wouldn't have happened.'

'I imagine you must want to see this man again. You must want answers.'

'I just want to know why.' I wiped my eyes roughly with the back of my hand. Bryony held out a box of tissues. I took one gratefully. 'Why did he do that?'

'Heidi, you need to realise something,' Bryony said, her tone even more gentle now. 'The blood supply to your foot could have been cut off within a matter of minutes. Even if the ambulance had come faster, chances are it would have led to the same result.'

'Are you sure?' I stared at her.

'Yes.'

I looked away, trying to digest this new information. Outside, an elderly double amputee negotiated the pathways towards the building in his wheelchair, face lined with concentration as he attempted to mount the kerb. Three tiny sparrows fluttered and played, hovering above the lawn.

'I still want him to know,' I said finally. 'I still want him to realise what's happened.'

'That's understandable,' Bryony replied. 'We all need closure. It's a human impulse. It seems to me like you blame this man – and that's natural. It might even help psychologically. But the thing is, Heidi, you need to focus on the future. Don't you think that's where the real answers lie?' I sniffed.

'Maybe.'

'Definitely.' She adjusted her hairclip and fixed me with an intense, imploring gaze. A single grey curl wound its way down her face. She blew it out of her eyeline. 'It might have been this man you saw. It may not have been. But whichever, you shouldn't dwell on it. Coincidences happen. You need to look forward. Do things that make you happy.'

'It's hard,' I said.

'It will be,' she nodded. 'But you can do it, if you really set your mind to it. Remember, I'm here whenever you want to talk – about anything.'

'Thank you.'

I blew my nose. Somehow, this unlikely woman with her red-freckled chest and garish flower hair clip made a lot of sense. I just hoped she was right.

Chapter Sixteen

The crowds surged as Mum pushed me down Oxford Street, elbows barging, copious bags hanging off their arms, banging into the side of my chair. I flinched and ducked, convinced every few seconds that I was about to be hit in the face. From her illustrious position above, Mum was oblivious.

'Lovely afternoon, isn't it?' she commented. She was looking at the window displays as we passed, several of them too high for me to see. 'Thank you for inviting me, love. It's nice to get out for a bit.'

'Yeah.' I gritted my teeth, trying to ignore the palpitations in my chest. I felt penned in and claustrophobic. 'Mum, can we – can we go into a shop now?'

'So eager,' Mum laughed. 'Of course. Topshop?' She pointed across the road and I nodded.

'Great.' Anything to get me out of the tide.

Inside wasn't much better. While the crowds had thinned, the shop was filled with the banter and arguments of teenage girls, fighting over the only crop top left in a certain size or debating which belt should pass as a skirt. The lighting was lurid and artificial, and the air smelt like cherry Bakewells, no doubt from some awful body spray. For some reason, there was an actual DJ on the shop floor, pop hit remixes blaring from giant speakers. Having grown used to the relative serenity and order of hospital, the chaos made me feel about eighty years old.

'How about these?' Mum held up a pair of trousers. They were wide-legged, cropped and made of thin, pleated material. 'They've got different colours, too.'

'They're perfect.' One thing about Mum that was different to many of my friends' parents: she did have an eye for style. 'I'll definitely try those on.'

With Mum's help, I picked out several loose dresses, a couple of skirts and a pair of flared dungarees. I also picked up a pair of black skinny jeans – although I remained unsure if they'd fit over my prosthetic foot. However, many of the rails were too high to reach, forcing me to rely on Mum or stand up on one leg to retrieve the items of clothing.

In the changing rooms, my mood worsened.

'Really sorry,' a girl in black denim hot pants said, without sounding sorry at all. 'Our disabled fitting room is out of action – the pull-down seat broke.'

'I don't think that's good enough,' Mum replied. Behind us in the queue, I heard a teenager complaining to her mum.

'How long does it take to try on a few outfits?' she whinged. 'Seriously, move along, people.'

I shrank down in my chair. I didn't want her to see the true source of the delay.

'Yeah,' the salesgirl said with a shrug. She had the horrible habit of bending her back slightly as she addressed me. 'Sorry. Do you need me to call my manager for assistance?'

'No. We'll have to just manage, I suppose.' Mum was tight-lipped. Too mortified to answer, I stayed silent. Let her think I was mentally disabled too. After all, that's how she was treating me.

The wheelchair only just fitted into the cubicle. Mum insisted on coming in with me, the two of us rammed behind a thick velour curtain. It was hot and bright, the atmosphere suffo-cating. There was a distinct aroma of sweaty feet.

I tried the dresses first. They were at least easy to put on, slipping over my head while Mum acted as personal stylist, smoothing them around my legs. Gingerly, I stood up to look in the mirror. I wasn't used to the longer length. In the past, I'd always gone for above the knee. Of course, I knew it was there, and yet seeing the pole of my prosthetic leg poking out from beneath the fabric still made me stop and stare. It was disconcerting and alien. It made me feel hideous.

'It looks stupid,' I said, gesturing at a red floral boho dress. There were ruffles everywhere. 'I look like a buttoned-up Sunday School teacher.'

'I think it looks lovely,' Mum said. 'The colour suits you.'

'No.'

I knew I sounded like one of the irritating teenagers – but I couldn't help myself. My mood had darkened suddenly, making me tense and fractious. It wasn't Mum's fault. It wasn't even the insensitive salesgirl, although her long, tanned legs and athletic figure definitely didn't help. It was me and my mind; battling to feel normal when in fact I felt anything but. How could I have assumed this would seem like a normal activity, that it would make me happy to sit in this cheesy-smelling changing room and stare at myself in a mirror? I hadn't even massively enjoyed shopping before the accident. Now, it was only making my body image worse.

In the end, I decided on the simpler styles; plain-coloured and straight-shaped dresses that would work with any shirt or jacket. I felt more comfortable, less conspicuous, less like a circus act on a day off. The wide-legged trousers Mum found were the only item that made me feel halfway human. And then we came to the jeans.

As predicted, getting them over my prosthetic foot was a complete nightmare. Mum and I hauled and wiggled, both of us by now boiling hot, sweat tickling our foreheads and upper lips. I tensed my stump, the muscle memory reminding me how to point my foot. And yet, of course, when I tried, nothing happened. The plastic foot remained rigid and stubborn, the hard denim straining as we pulled and manoeuvred the best we could.

'Let's just not bother,' I said, after at least five minutes. The salesgirl was probably out there listening to our groans, wondering what on earth we were doing. 'I need to get out of here, Mum.'

'Heidi, we've come this far.' I could see the veins in her temples throbbing. 'I am not giving up.'

With one more almighty pull, the jeans slid past the foot.

'Got it!' Mum crowed.

Exhausted, I fastened them up. My left leg looked great, the denim clinging to and highlighting my new-found muscles. However, the prosthetic side told a different story. The material flapped redundantly around the pole, making the top of the prosthesis seem wider and more bulky than ever. I rolled up the jeans, but it didn't make much difference. I'd already made up my mind that I looked awful.

'Nice, right?' Mum said. Her tone was encouraging and hopeful. I shook my head and collapsed back into the wheelchair. The cushion let out a surprised rush of air.

'Horrible.'

'Oh, Heidi, come on. You were so keen to try some skinny jeans.'

'That was before.'

'Before what?' She fiddled with the dresses on their hangers, ensuring they were hung just right.

'Before I realised how ugly I am.'

'Oh, Heidi, never say that.' She stood in front of me, her hands on my shoulders. 'I don't ever want you to think that.'

I shrugged. She had to be nice to me. After all, she was my mum. Swallowing my tears, I unbuttoned and unzipped the jeans, sliding them back down my legs. I couldn't bear wearing them any longer.

'Come on, let's think positive,' Mum said. 'We'll get the dresses, and the wide-legged trousers. And I'm going to buy you those jeans, Heidi.'

'But Mum . . .'

'Nope, no buts. You will feel better about yourself soon, Heidi. I promise. And when you do, you're going to put those jeans on, and you're going to stride out into the world. OK?'

'OK,' I said.

I knew arguing with her would only prolong the experience. But beneath the shop's bright lights, I'd never felt more exposed. Recovery was a marathon, not a sprint. And I was only at the starting line.

The day had drained me of energy. I lay in bed, unending thoughts dancing through my mind. Across the room, Maud snored gently behind her curtain, oblivious to my internal conflict. I wished my own sleep could be that easy and peaceful. Sighing, I reached to turn off the bedside light above me. But then I heard the noise.

The crashing sound seemed to come from next door. Straining my ears, I could hear a muffled shriek, a female voice cursing. Skye. I sat up and pulled on my prosthetic leg.

Outside, the corridor was dingy, a strip of industrial lighting in the ceiling guiding my path. Silently cursing my clicking crutches, I made my way to the next-door room; a private room usually reserved for MRSA patients. It had been the only one left when Skye was admitted – I was sure she was secretly pleased that she didn't have to share.

'Skye?' I knocked at the door. 'Are you in there?'

'Heidi.' Her voice sounded strange, slurred and inarticulate. 'Fucking get in here now.'

'OK . . .'

Tentatively, I pushed open the door. The room was a complete mess. There were clothes thrown everywhere, spilling from a large suitcase in the corner. Empty crisp packets and crushed-up coke cans littered the floor. The overpowering aroma of alcohol made me reel.

Skye was on the floor, her back propped against the side of her hospital bed. Her wheelchair was on its side, the spokes still gently spinning.

'Fell out of my fucking chair, didn't I,' she said. 'Whoops.' She hiccupped violently.

'Skye, are you drunk?'

'What's it look like, Heidi?' She gestured wildly around the room. 'A couple of mates took me to the pub. And what?'

'Oh, Christ.' Carefully, I set my crutches aside and moved to pick up her wheelchair. It was heavier than I'd expected. My arm muscles quivered in protest, but thankfully, the hours of weights in the physio gym had paid off. Skye remained where she was on the floor. She was staring at the tattoo on her wrist, tracing the sun beneath the clouds.

'The sun will come out tomorrow,' she slurred. 'What a load of shit.'

'Listen,' I told her, 'you need to sober up right now – before the nurses see. You realise you could get kicked out for this.'

'Ohhh.' She stuck out her bottom lip, her tone laden with alcohol-fuelled sarcasm. 'And what a fucking shame that would be.'

'Skye, seriously.' I put my hands beneath her armpits and pulled. 'Get up.'

'All right, all right.' She reached to hold the bed behind her, hauling herself up with surprisingly little effort. 'No need to be so bossy. You're just like my dad. Go to uni, Skye, get a proper job, Skye, stop partying, Skye . . . Jesus. Give it a break.'

'OK, point taken.' I raised my hands in surrender. 'At least drink some water.'

She rolled her eyes at me but she did as she was told, swigging from a water bottle beside her bed.

'There. Happy?'

'I think you need to try and get some sleep. You'll feel better tomorrow.'

'Mate, I guarantee I'll feel ten times worse tomorrow.'

She pushed her cloud of hair from her face. The long waves were tangled and matted, giving her a wild-eyed, feral look. I felt the sudden urge to brush it. Since when had I become so maternal?

'How do you do it, Heidi?' she asked. 'How do you cope?'

I stared at her, floored. Had she not noticed my struggles, my constant battle for happiness? I'd clearly been hiding it well.

'Well, I—'

'It's awful.' She looked down at her stump, still swollen despite its compression sock. 'And I swear, if one more person tells me that I'm a fucking inspiration, I'm gonna knock them out.'

Angry tears were rolling down her cheeks. I perched on the edge of her bed, unsure what to say. The stench of alcohol and cigarettes was strong on her breath. I handed her the water bottle again.

'Stay brave, Skye,' I murmured.

'What?'

'Just something a friend told me once. You'll probably think it's stupid though, right?'

I waited for the inevitable eye roll, the put down or snide retort. And yet, amazingly, it didn't come. Skye looked up at me from her pillows, her pupils large, eyes not quite focusing on my face. Despite her heavy make-up and fighting talk, in that moment I saw a young girl. A young girl who was very afraid.

'Nah.' She wiped her nose on the back of her hand. 'You're right I'm not usually one for all that "Live, Laugh, Love" fridge-magnet shit, but I guess stuff's different now.'

'You're telling me,' I answered. 'And for the record - I hate all that too.'

Skye tried to smile. But seconds later, she let out a low groan.

'Ugh, the room's moving, Heidi.' Her voice was thin and fragile, all bravado evaporated. 'It's all spinning.'

'Maybe drink some more water.'

'Fucking motorbikes,' she mumbled, ignoring my suggestion – or seeming not to hear it. 'I wasn't even supposed to be riding it, you know. My mate dared me.'

'Have your friends visited yet?' I asked.

'Nope.' She lay back against her pillows, defeated. 'Georgie, whose bike it was, says she's too scared of hospitals. How does she think I feel? I've hated these places since the whole thing with Mum.'

'Your mum?'

'Oh, right, yeah, you don't know.' Her tone was flat, almost matter-of-fact. 'She died two years ago. Cancer.' She didn't look at me.

'Oh Skye, I'm sorry . . .'

'Don't, Heidi.' She brought her hand to her mouth, a gesture somewhere between nibbling her nail and sucking her thumb. 'I don't need fucking apologies.'

'Sorry,' I said automatically, immediately regretting it. 'But look, Skye, you're doing amazingly. You're going to get through this, you know. You are one strong girl.'

'Not as strong as you.' She gave an enormous yawn. 'But yeah. I'll try.'

'That's the spirit.'

In that moment, I saw her in a new light. She wasn't just a rebellious teenager, angry for anger's sake. She was a damaged soul, struggling beneath a monumental burden. But as I sat there in the alcohol-infused air, I felt a small spark of hope. For the first time since she'd arrived, I really felt like I'd got through.

'Skye?'

I wanted to tell her how much I admired her, that she should keep going, never give up, push for what she wanted to achieve. I wanted to tell her she was brilliant.

But she was asleep.

Chapter Seventeen

I had an audience for physio the next day. I didn't want it, but Mum and Dad had insisted, keen to witness at first-hand (or foot?) how my recovery journey was going. Tara seemed a bit peeved to see them perching on her disinfected plinth. She banged the equipment around, unsmiling and unspeaking. Then again, her ponytail was pulled so tight that it was impossible to deduce her exact emotions. It acted as a natural facelift, raising her eyebrows in an expression of permanent disapproval.

'Impressive set-up.' Dad surveyed the room. I watched him take in the arm bike, the treadmill, the Wii Fit in the corner locked into the transparent TV cabinet and half-covered with a dust sheet. 'Do you use that?'

'Sometimes,' I answered. 'They've had problems with stealing in the past.'

'Buggers tried to flog it on the World Wide Web, apparently,' Maud added. This morning, her timetable had summoned her to the gym at the same time as me. Having originally thought I had a one-to-one session, I was slightly confused as to why.

'Sad.' Mum shook her head. 'The lengths people will go to.'

'Oh I know, love,' Maud said. She was wearing her eighties headband, grey and white bed hair sticking up from her scalp. She reached to adjust it and saw me watching. 'Really makes me feel the part, this does,' she grinned, pointing at her head. 'Just call me Jane Fonda.'

Mum smiled politely. Dad let out a guffaw. They'd both made an effort too; Mum in her long white denim dress and favourite pearlescent lipstick, Dad in his non-ripped, non-gardening jeans and a pale blue polo shirt. I could tell they'd both lost weight over the past few weeks; Dad's stomach was significantly less rotund than usual. Mum had never been a large lady, but her cheekbones were definitely more pronounced. Their legs dangled from the physio plinth like they were a pair of expectant toddlers.

'Right, what are we doing today then, Tara?' Maud asked.

'Something a bit different,' Tara replied. She strung a net up between two poles, lowering it to a wheelchair-friendly height. 'Volleyball.'

'Christ,' said Shahid from the doorway. 'Mate, I've got one arm . . .'

'It'll be fun.' Tara clapped her hands together. 'We're just waiting for one more. Ah, here she comes.'

Skye whizzed into the room; noticeably more lithe in the wheelchair than the others. She was wearing high-waisted gym leggings and a neon pink sports bra. Mum's eyebrows rose at the sight of her.

'Sorry I'm late,' she said half-heartedly. Tara tutted at her.

'Skye, you're with Shahid.'

'Oh, you're kidding me!' Skye eyed her partner. He saluted with his remaining arm. 'He's gonna be rubbish!'

'Thought you didn't care?' I said.

'Whatever.'

'Right, are we going to do this or not?' Maud asked. She pinged her headband impatiently. 'I'm not getting any younger.'

Tara blew her whistle and we all jumped. 'Let's start.'

'Go team!' shouted Dad.

We moved into position. Between us, we had three legs and seven arms. Inevitably, there were several near-capsizes as we dodged and weaved, wheelchairs rocking back and forth each time we leaned to catch the ball. I was grateful for my stabilisers. For a man who constantly reminded us of his one-armed handicap, Shahid was surprisingly competitive.

'C'mon, Skye, bloody concentrate will ya?' he barked. Skye cursed under her breath. Her co-ordination was terrible. Maud wasn't much better.

'That's it, Heidi, my girl, let's take them down!'

My parents were enraptured. Mum was quite literally on the edge of her seat, her buttocks dangerously close to slipping off the plinth.

'Ahh, so close,' Dad lamented with each of my many near-misses. His investment in my progress was akin to watching a World Cup free kick. Phone held aloft, Mum snapped a stream of photos and videos of my (consistently poor) attempts at catching.

'Do you have to do that?' I asked as the ball sailed past my ear for the umpteenth time.

'Of course I do, I'm your mother.' She peeked out briefly from behind the camera. 'And anyway, it's good to document the journey.'

Personally, I was with Skye. I'd rather have been anywhere else than batting a ball over a makeshift net in front of my over-enthusiastic parents.

By the time Tara released us, my breathing was laboured. The physical exertion, combined with my anxiety, had left me in a hot and cold sweat, perspiration prickling my spine and my scalp, the hairs on my arms on end.

'Well, thank God that's over,' said Skye.

'How about we pop outside, Heidi?' Dad suggested. 'You look a bit hot.'

The sun hid behind grey skies, glowing within the clouds. I manoeuvred out and parked on the patio, angling myself in the direction of the most warming rays, hoping my goosebumps would vanish. I still felt short of breath – and it wasn't just the volleyball. I concentrated on inhaling and exhaling, forcing a regular rhythm. My parents took a seat at one of the wooden picnic benches across from me. They were both smiling broadly.

'Heidi, you're doing so well,' Mum said. Her eyes glittered with barely suppressed emotion. 'Honestly, we're so amazed by your progress.'

'We are.' Dad rubbed Mum's shoulder. 'Your mother tells everyone about you!'

'Not everyone, Tim,' she chastised. 'Only people I bump into when they ask – and maybe the odd stranger. Anyway, Heidi, the point is, we're very proud of you.'

'You're so brave,' Dad said.

'Thanks,' I replied.

I didn't feel it. My head was aching with worry. I felt weak and helpless, like something was about to crack. But I knew I couldn't show it; not in front of them. I mustered a smile and took another deep breath.

'I'm trying my best.'

'It's incredible.' Mum took a scrubby tissue from her dress pocket and dabbed at her eyes. Dad took her hand.

'You daft old thing,' he said. 'Heidi, I'm sure six weeks feels like forever, but you really will be waltzing out of here in no time, love.'

'I know.'

'All ready for the wedding!' Mum practically sang. 'I bet you're excited!'

'Of course.'

But discharge meant I'd be on my own. And then what would happen? I decided to change the subject.

'Mum, Dad, how are you both doing?' I asked. They glanced at each other.

'Oh, we're fine,' Dad assured. 'Ticking along; the usual. Your mother's started volunteering at the hospice shop.'

'Heidi, it's brilliant.' She grinned at me. 'I'm really loving it. And I'm doing a few more shifts for the next few weeks, now that Val's away on her Greek Islands trip with Pedro. You remember Pedro, she met him in Puerto Banus.'

I nodded.

'Well anyway, yesterday a lady brought in the loveliest little porcelain donkey. I just had to have him for the collection.'

'Mum, you don't need any more. We've talked about this.'

In recent years, she'd developed an obscure fondness for animal ornaments, much to the rest of the family's confusion. They lined the mantelpiece – dogs and ducks and a tiny grey squirrel climbing a tree. The dusting was becoming increasingly high maintenance.

'But darling, they make me so happy,' she trilled. 'And what's wrong with that?'

She had a point. To be honest, I was beginning to wonder if I should invest in my own menagerie of porcelain creatures. Happiness was all any of us wanted. Next to her, Dad had gone quiet.

'And Dad?' I ventured. 'What about you?'

'Oh, fine, yes,' he said. 'I've been doing a few extra jobs here and there, you know, just to keep the money trickling in.'

'But what about your retirement?' I frowned. Dad looked sheepish.

'Well, there's a lot of building work going on in London at the moment,' he replied. 'All these new developments and whatnot. They're in need of experienced surveyors—'

'But Dad, you said months ago that enough was enough. Look at you, you look shattered!'

'I do wonder if you're taking on too much, love,' Mum added.

'Sandy, don't start.' Dad sighed heavily. He did look distinctly more haggard, the corners of his mouth turned down with the weight of his worry. 'Not in front of Heidi.'

'Dad, I'm an adult.'

'I know, love. It's just there's a lot going on, so your Mum and I . . .' He shot her a pointed glance. 'Well, we thought it might be handy to have some extra money.'

'You mean for me, don't you?' I felt a stab of sorrow as the force of his words hit home. 'It's for my rent, isn't it?'

The silent flicker of recognition between my parents confirmed my suspicion.

'No, Dad,' I said. 'You can't go back to work because of me.'

'I'd do anything for you, Heidi.' His eyes glistened. 'You know that. And anyway, with the wedding to pay for, it's good to have a nest egg.'

'Exactly,' Mum jumped in. 'Weddings are an expensive business.'

But they weren't fooling me. I'd seen the fleeting panic cross Dad's lined face; the worry that he'd revealed too much. At a time when both of them should be slowing down, he was forsaking his retirement to support me. The realisation sealed a fresh layer of grief across my heart. We sat there for a time, each unsure of what to say. The wind had got up, and the goosebumps reappeared on my skin.

'Shall we head inside?' Mum said eventually. 'It looks like there's a storm on the horizon.'

'Good plan,' Dad replied.

I nodded wordlessly and took the brakes off my wheelchair. Worries roared through my head like thunder and lightning. My own storm had long since begun.

*

Post-volleyball, I was relieved to say goodbye to my parents; Mum rushing off for another shift at the hospice shop back home, Dad her chauffeur as usual. I longed for some quiet time, the space to free my emotions.

With an hour to go before lunch, I decided to take a shower. In the ward's shared bathroom, a faint smell of mildew and plastic lingered in the air. Orange emergency cords hung down from three areas of the ceiling. On the far wall, someone had stuck a laminated poster. Water marked and curling at the edges, it depicted a clip-art stick man mid-stumble. 'STOP. THINK. REMEMBER – MISSING LEG!' the bold red words above proclaimed. I couldn't help but notice the pedal bin beneath it. Not the easiest for someone with no legs. Just a couple of weeks ago, I wouldn't even have thought about these details. Now, the smallest of obstacles required the greatest of efforts.

I sat on the shower stool and raised my face to the water. A steady stream ran into my eyes and mouth. Hidden and protected by the flow, I allowed myself to cry. Keeping up the pretence was hard. Really hard. I had a prosthetic leg, I could almost walk. But it didn't end there. The psychological impact ran deeper; seeping, unrelenting through my mind like the teardrops and water on my face. I didn't want to tell my family I was struggling. Not when they were so pleased with my progress. I didn't want to admit it, least of all to myself. Better to cower behind the physical progress, hoping it would outweigh the fear.

I rinsed off my conditioner and massaged my head, digging my fingernails into my scalp, a satisfying sensation somewhere between pleasure and pain. I closed my eyes and took some breaths, trying to calm the tightness in my chest.

I was about to turn the water off when the fire alarm started. Shrill and insistent, the sound was like a klaxon, echoing in the wet room. In the corner, a beam of red light began to flash. Someone knocked on the door.

'Who's in there?' A nurse's voice. 'Do you need help getting out?'

'It's Heidi,' I yelled above the noise. 'No, I'm fine. I'm coming.'

Buoyed by urgency, I grabbed my towel and half-slid, half-fell into the wheelchair, my one-legged pivot distinctly less controlled than usual. The door was wrenched open. I shrieked and held the towel across my body. An agency nurse I didn't recognise stood there looking at me.

'I said I didn't need help!' I cried.

Without even acknowledging me, the girl began to manhandle my wheelchair. I held my towels close, too stunned to argue.

Out in the corridor, pandemonium ensued. The alarm was even louder here, screeching like a wounded fox. The girl pushed me towards the fire exit. Most of the rooms were already empty, although George was arguing with ward manager, Sharon.

'I just need to find me fags,' he shouted above the din. 'Won't be two ticks.'

'George, this is a FIRE alarm,' she yelled back.

'And I'm stressed! I need a fag!'

'No, you don't.'

In a sudden, authoritative gesture, she tucked her large folder of notes under her arm and grabbed the handles of his wheelchair, propelling him away from his search. The noise of the alarm drowned out his resulting stream of obscenities.

There was a fire engine outside. All twelve patients were lined up along the street, parked in our wheelchairs, surrounded by confused and bustling nurses. My hair was still wet, droplets of water running down my neck and body. I was shivering. I was handed a foil blanket and I wrapped it around my shoulders.

'Reminds me of the time I accidentally set my chemistry classroom on fire,' Skye said. I couldn't even look at her. I was in no mood to joke.

In the row of terraced houses opposite the rehab centre, a number of faces had appeared at windows, curious to discover the source of the commotion in their quiet, residential street. An elderly couple peered around their lace curtains. Two doors down, a little boy of no more than seven waved happily at us all, as though watching some kind of parade. I felt vulnerable and exposed. It was hideous.

'Are you OK, Heidi?' Maud wheeled over and put a hand on my bare thigh. 'That must have been a shock, being in the shower.'

I gave a small nod. Her kindness made me want to cry.

Sharon marched along the line of patients, calling out names and ticking us off her list. She wore a yellow hi-vis tabard with 'Fire Marshall' in bright red letters on the back. She was walking even taller than usual as she headed over to speak to the three young firemen. Inadvertently, I caught the nearest man's gaze and his eyes travelled briefly over me. He gave me a sympathetic smile.

I shrank down in the wheelchair, hunching my body to try and combat the shaking. I could tell it was more than just the chill. Shock had set in and my adrenaline was on high alert. The alarm itself had stopped, but commotion of flapping nurses and the men's booming voices jarred in my skull. I clamped my jaw to stop my teeth chattering. And then it got even worse.

A figure was coming down the street, the half-bouncing, half-lumbering gait all too familiar. I saw a flash of orange hair and a checked gingham shirt and the remainder of my strength crumbled to dust. Why him? Why now?

'Jack!' Maud called out delightedly.

I wrapped the foil blanket closer. Despite my chill, I was sweating now, the wheelchair cushion sticky and uncomfortable against my thighs.

'What's happening here then, Nanna?'

'Someone set the fire alarm off.'

Jack looked around, taking in the scene. Then he spotted me.

'Christ, what's going on, Heidi?' Amusement glittered in his eyes. 'Naked wheelchair race, is it?' I shook my head.

'Don't.' I couldn't bear it.

'She was in the shower,' Maud explained. There was a note of grandmotherly warning in her tone. 'She had quite a fright.' Jack's expression softened immediately.

'Oh my God, sorry, that's horrible.'

'Yeah.'

I kept my head bowed, unable to look him in the eye. I wanted to disappear, to crumble and fade out of the picture, to forget it had ever happened. Jack seemed suddenly very interested in his hands, picking at a loose bit of skin on his thumb.

'Stop that,' Maud chastised. She reached to slap him on the wrist.

'Sorry.'

'OK, all clear!' Sharon shouted. 'False alarm!' She nodded to Tara, who gave a blast of her whistle.

'Everybody back inside!'

'Took bloody long enough,' George grumbled. He was lisping slightly, a sign he didn't have his teeth in. 'Thank Christ me fags haven't burnt.'

'Go on up and put something warm on, Heidi,' Maud said. 'We'll stay down here for a bit, give you some privacy.'

I nodded gratefully. The embarrassment had spread down my neck and body, tingling even at the end of my stump. I suppressed the urge to cry. When I turned to leave, Jack was lighting a cigarette, studiously avoiding my eyeline.

'Oi, laddie,' George called. 'Give us one of those, will ya?'

Back inside, I'd never got dressed so quickly. I pulled on Dougie's big jumper and my ancient tracksuit bottoms, worn and bobbly but the most comforting thing I owned. My skin had dried but still felt clammy, the remnants of anxiety clinging to my pores. In front of the mirror in our room I held my head upside down and dried my hair, closing my eyes as the rush of warmth hit my scalp.

When Maud knocked on the door, I was sitting on my bed, trousers rolled up, rubbing Bio-Oil into my scars.

'Feeling better?' Her tyres squeaked across the floor as she made her way to her bed.

'Much better,' I answered. I noticed Jack was loitering in the doorway.

'Do you mind if I come in?' he asked. His expression was uncertain.

'Course not.'

I popped the Bio-Oil on the table and rolled my trousers back down. He took a seat by the window. The scent of freshly smoked cigarettes followed him. Maud sniffed the air and frowned.

'Oh Jack, do you really have to smoke?'

He shrugged. 'For now. Helps me de-stress.'

She tutted. 'Look, I know you've got a lot on. But you just be careful, my lad. Otherwise you might end up in here.' She lifted her stump demonstrably. 'And believe you me, you don't want that. Does he, Heidi?'

'Absolutely not.'

In principle, I agreed with Maud. And yet strangely, the smell seemed to suit him. Combined with notes of citrus and musk, it was a distinctive aroma, one that I'd begun to notice as soon as he walked into a room. Even after he'd left, I could capture it in my memories, the sort of scent that couldn't belong to anyone else. Strangely, I quite liked it. Across from me, Jack let out a sigh.

'Nanna, I didn't come here to be lectured.' He sounded weary, a man with the world on his shoulders. I knew what that was like. Maud reached for her Chanel and spritzed herself liberally.

'Why did you come here, then?' she asked Jack.

'I just wanted to drop in.'

'Well, that's lovely of you, I'm sure.' Maud grinned at him, her dressing down now completely forgotten. It was so easy to make her happy.

Had I imagined it, or did Jack's gaze flick briefly towards me? I cast the thought from my mind.

'I must say though, I wasn't expecting so much drama,' he said.

'Neither were we.' I tried to keep my tone light, covering the discomfort that lay beneath.

'It was quite a palaver,' Maud agreed. 'Listen, Jack, why don't you take Heidi for a coffee or something. Maybe get a bite to eat. Lord knows the lunch here isn't worth waiting around for.'

'Do you think?' he raised his ginger eyebrows. 'It depends if Heidi wants to.' He turned to me. 'What do you reckon?'

I paused, considering. In some ways, I felt like I'd had quite enough adventure. And yet, the alternative was to sit here on my own, trying to control my thoughts, a feat I already knew was impossible. The prospect of getting away, of doing something normal, was very tempting.

'Don't say I don't treat you,' Jack said as he placed the tray in front of me.

'Would I ever say that?'

Two iced coffees sat between us, gooey slabs of home-made chocolate cake on mismatching green and blue clay plates. Jack pushed the bigger slice towards me.

'Go on, you deserve it.'

I didn't argue, taking the fork from his hand and spearing the slice. It had been hours since breakfast. The morning physio session with my parents seemed like a lifetime ago. I realised I was hungry.

'Good?' Jack raised his eyebrows, awaiting my reaction.

'Mmmhmm.' The texture was perfect, crunchy pieces of milk and white chocolate and a gooey caramel filling. It was immediately comforting.

Nestled between an off-licence and a dry-cleaners' on the leafy Kennington road, the Kennington Coffee Shop was a tiny, nondescript building. I'd seen it many times from taxis and occupational therapy outings, but I'd scarcely glanced in its direction. And yet inside, the atmosphere was wholly different; characterful and lively with low jazz music playing in the background and the scent of good coffee in the air. Low sofas lined the walls; the sort that sighed when you sat on them. There was a stack of newspapers in one corner, a stack of board games in the other. The owner's little sausage dog snored gently in a basket by the counter. For a weekday, it was surprisingly busy.

'It's lovely here,' I said. With every mouthful of caffeine and chocolate, I could feel the tension draining from my body. Jack sipped his iced latte and smiled.

'Glad you like it. I come here sometimes. You know, when I can't concentrate at home.'

'How is the job hunt going?'

'Slowly.' He looked down at his coffee, swirling the long spoon around and around in the glass. 'I've had a lot of rejections. Sometimes, they don't even bother to reply. And Dad's getting far too involved.'

'In what way?' I licked chocolate cream from my fingers. 'I thought you didn't want his help?'

'Seems like he's not giving me a choice.' Jack took a big gulp of coffee. A line of frothy milk appeared on his upper lip. He wiped it with the back of his hand. 'He thinks it's embarrassing, me being unemployed. He says he's trying to help. But he's only really thinking about himself.'

'And your mum?'

'She tries not to interfere,' he said. 'Knows that my dad's too strong-willed to change his mind. When he settles on a project, he'll keep on going. And this time, the project's me.'

'It must be tough.'

'Yeah.' He ran a hand through his hair. 'And what with the other stuff, too . . .' he trailed off.

Intrigued, I opened my mouth to dig deeper, but he cut me off.

'Heidi, have you ever felt betrayed by anyone?' His gaze was intense now, eyes boring into mine.

I thought about it. Alexander Mitchell was the first person who came to mind. I nodded slowly.

'It's the worst, isn't it?' A lost, faraway expression crossed his features, a hidden sadness I hadn't seen before. 'Especially when it's by someone you care about. Someone you never expected to hurt you.'

'Jack . . .' I leaned closer across the table. He flinched and moved away, the hurt evident on his face.

'I'd prefer not to talk about it any more, if that's OK.'

'Of course.'

I wondered what 'it' was, but I didn't push him. I knew about complicated. Sometimes, you just didn't want to explain; and I understood that better than anyone. I brushed cake crumbs from my lap. The little dog opened one eye, sniffed the air and promptly resumed his slumber.

'Have you thought much about your job?' Jack asked. His green eyes bored into mine, flecked with bronze and gold.

'A bit.'

He'd hit upon another difficult conversation. No way was I ready to I stand on a stage again. Being stared at in the street made me feel exposed enough, and the tiniest of misaligned comments from a passing stranger held the power to dissolve my composure. The idea of an audience scrutinising my every move filled me with horror.

'And?' Jack leant forwards, as though attempting to read my thoughts. I let out a sigh.

'It's a scary prospect, you know? The acting world is tough. And it's so image-focused. What if no one wants me?'

'Mmm.' He swallowed a mouthful of cake. 'I mean, I guess you have to own it.'

'You mean apply for disabled theatre companies?' I shuddered involuntarily. I didn't want to be labelled. I didn't want my leg to define me. And yet, sometimes, I felt like it was all people saw.

'No!' He stared at me. 'Heidi, you're not disabled.' His dimples became straight lines of sincerity.

'Jack, I am.' I pointed at my prosthetic leg. 'One leg. In case you'd forgotten.'

'You're not disabled,' he repeated, leaning closer. 'You're temporarily incapacitated.'

His expression was so earnest that I snorted with laughter. I couldn't help it. The tops of his sticking-out ears reddened at my response.

'Well, that's one way of putting it!' I said. He looked wounded.

'I just don't think you should look at it as a disability,' he said. 'It's too negative. You need to focus on your ability.'

'Now you sound like a TED talk.'

'Whatever. But honestly, you can do anything you set your mind to. You wrote that list for a reason.'

'I wrote that list because you told me to.'

'Well, yeah, OK,' he sighed. 'But they're also the steps you need to feel confident again. To go back to your old self or make your new self even better. Stay brave, remember?'

At this, I smiled. There was no need for my petulance. I shouldn't be taking out my moods on him.

'I remember,' I replied. 'Sorry, Jack. It's been a tough day.'

'We all have them.'

I finished my last bite of cake. Jack smiled, squinting in the sunlight that streamed through the cafe windows. His hair shone copper and gold.

Chapter Eighteen

The reception area of Forever Yours Bridal felt like the worst kind of purgatory. On Saturday morning after physio, I found myself on a cream chaise longue, awaiting my final bridesmaid dress fitting with Mum and Jenny.

Upon reflection, wearing tracksuit bottoms to a wedding boutique was probably a bad idea. Sipping prosecco and snacking on rose-flavoured popcorn, I couldn't have felt more out of place. The constant adjustments needed for my prosthetic leg meant that once again, I'd opted for convenience over fashion. A looser fit tended to make things easier when I needed to hitch up my trousers.

The signs on the walls made me feel faintly nauseous. *'You are my today, and all of my tomorrows,'* one said in loopy writing, below a photo of a young, beautiful couple on a beach at sunset. *'Every love story is beautiful, but our's is my favourite,'* another proclaimed, showing a black-and-white image of two hands intertwined, golden wedding bands sparkling. The misplaced apostrophe made me wince.

'Aren't those lovely?' Mum said, pointing. It wasn't the kind of decor she'd usually favour, but she was on her second prosecco and slightly emotional.

'Six minutes late already,' Jenny said. 'Really? I mean come on, what am I paying these people for?'

'Technically, it's me and your dad paying, love,' Mum pointed out.

'Yeah, can you calm down a bit, Jen?' I said. I couldn't help it. Her snappiness was irritating. 'It's a lot of money for Mum and Dad.'

'Calm down?' Jenny's eyes flashed. 'You try planning a big wedding like this.'

'It doesn't have to be quite so big,' I shot back. And then, without really thinking about what I was saying, 'Mark doesn't think so anyway.'

'Oh, that is so not fair, Heidi. You know how much tension that's causing.'

'Yeah, I know.' I felt a bit guilty then. I'd seen the snide comments and the scornful glances between Mark and Jenny, the unspoken strain and weight of organisation. The closer the wedding grew, the further apart they seemed to be drifting. 'I just wish it didn't make you so moody, that's all.'

'Girls,' Mum reasoned. 'Come on. This is supposed to be a fun day.'

'You're right,' I said. 'Sorry, Mum.'

But true to form, Jenny persisted. She wasn't one to give up easily on an argument.

'I just think Heidi needs to be a bit more understanding,' she said. 'There's a lot going on right now – for all of us. Her recovery, the wedding stuff, Dad . . .'

'Dad?' I turned to face her square on. 'What's he got to do with this?'

'Jenny . . .' Mum warned.

'He won't stop work,' Jenny said. I stared at her.

'What?'

'Jenny, we agreed not to talk about this,' Mum said. 'Your dad and I both think it's the best thing for now.' Her eyes flicked towards me. It was only a split second, but I saw it.

'I knew it,' I said.

Mum tried her best to look vacant. 'What do you mean?'

'The money thing. It's because of me, isn't it?' I felt a surge of guilt. 'It's not the wedding at all. You're using that as an excuse. You're worried about supporting me.'

'Heidi, no, it's not like that . . .'

'It is, Mum. Of course it is. I'm an out-of-work actress, I have one leg and I need to pay rent. I know you're worried about it.'

For the first time, I was seeing my new self through my parents' eyes. I knew they only wanted to help, and yet their good intentions made me feel completely incapable, more a hopeless child than a thirty-two-year-old woman.

'We just want to take the pressure off you, love,' Mum said. 'You've got enough to think about.'

'But Dad . . .'

'It's his decision.' She finished her prosecco and slammed the glass down a little too hard on the table. Across the room, a snooty mother and daughter with matching poodle hairstyles pretended to flinch. 'Look, I don't want to discuss this any more. When you're well enough, you can work again. But until then, just let us help you. Help you both. It's what parents do.'

'I still think that—'

'Heidi,' she said sharply. 'Enough now.'

I sat back on the chaise longue, chastised. The news still hadn't fully sunk in. I thought about Dad. He'd been so thrilled to retire, full of plans for travel and new DIY projects. But now that excitement had been torn away from him – and all because of me. Guilt swirled in my stomach.

My own job was also still very much on my mind. I knew it would be a while before I felt able to go back to acting, not that it had exactly taken off in the first place. I thought about the list, about the final challenge I'd set myself – learn to dance. Maybe that was the next step? I looked down at my leg and my stump twinged in its tight-fitting socket. Maybe not, then. It was a crazy idea.

'Holly Summers?' A tall woman in a tight black pencil dress called. She appeared to be all legs. Poodle Daughter stood up.

'That's me.'

'You can go through to Dressing Room Two now.'

She swept past us, Poodle Mother taking a long, uninhibited glance at my leg as they passed. I pretended I hadn't noticed, but the unwanted scrutiny made me feel like a freakshow.

'Seriously, why is this taking so long?' Jenny said. 'I do have other stuff to do today.' Her prosecco was untouched on the glass coffee table.

'Have a drink, Jen?' I suggested.

'You know I'm off alcohol until the wedding, Heidi,' she barked. I raised my hands in a surrendering gesture.

'All right, sorry, I'd forgotten.'

'Alcohol, sugar, carbs, dairy and meat,' she said. She pinched the almost non-existent layer of skin around her hips. 'I never lost this baby weight after Evie.'

'You're going to look gorgeous, Jenny,' Mum assured. 'Do try not to worry.'

'At least you have two legs . . .'

'Heidi.' Mum looked at me sternly. 'Let's not start again.'

'Sorry.'

But it was true. I felt so out of place. Across the room, two more sets of mothers and daughters waited on identical chaise longues. The first pair both wore kimonos and talked in loud, shrill voices as though to an audience, calling each other names like Petal and Honeypot. The second had folded arms and pinched faces, the daughter dressed all in black. They looked more like they were arranging a funeral than a wedding. I sent a quick message to Jack.

'In wedding shop hell. Send help xx'

'Haha!' Came the reply. 'Sounds like someone needs a drink x'

I snapped a quick shot of my glass and pressed send.

'Cheers!' he answered. I smiled at my phone screen.

'What are you grinning at?' Jenny asked. Having flicked through every bridal magazine on the table, she'd resorted to twisting her engagement ring around and around her finger.

'Oh, just a text,' I said. She gave me a knowing, big sister look. 'I see.'

'Jenny Jackson?' The receptionist called. 'Truly's ready for you. Dressing Room One.'

'Finally,' Jenny muttered.

'Where's my beautiful bride?'

Truly Forever – let's be honest, probably not her real name – was an enormous woman with the loudest laugh I'd ever heard. Swathed in colourful fabric, her thick black hair was crimped and piled up on her head, topped with a tiny silver crown. She wore a giant lock and key locket around her neck.

'There she is!' Truly pulled Jenny into huge hug – everything about her was huge. 'And my bridesmaid! And Mummy, too! So wonderful, you're all here! Come in, come in . . .'

Truly beckoned us into an airy room, complete with several more cream chaise longues. At one end was a large changing cubicle with a glittery curtain. Mirrors surrounded the walls. The thick caramel carpet sank beneath my prosthetic as I walked.

'OK, let's get you into this dress!' Truly clapped her hands and gestured towards the cubicle. 'Really, you're going to look like a princess.'

'I'm not sure about that,' I murmured.

I still found it hard to understand why straight-laced Jenny had chosen this crazy woman. Apparently, it was the only bridesmaid dress she'd found that she liked. The style was simple; straight cut with a tasteful V shape at the back – a surprise given that everything about Truly Forever herself was larger than life and frankly, a bit too much.

I stood there, taking in the beautiful dress that was already hanging from the wall of the large, airy fitting room. The dress was a pale lilac, a few shades lighter than my hair. I stared down at my leg in my grey tracksuit bottoms as a stark, bleak reality took hold. The idea of walking down the aisle in front of an entire church full of people made me shiver. I really wasn't sure if I could do it.

'Go on,' urged Mum. 'In you go, Heidi. We haven't got all day.' She gave me a little push.

'Oh, you are going to look so precious!' Truly bounced up and down, bracelets jangling, her enormous bosom in danger of thwacking her in the chin.

I pulled the changing room curtains around me. The luxurious ivory carpet was soft and plush beneath the toes of my remaining foot. I slid the dress over my head and took in my reflection. The top half wasn't bad. My collarbone peeked out from the wide neckline, the fabric sweeping delicately across my shoulders. The dress nipped in at my waist at exactly the right point, flattering my bust and hips.

Yet where the chiffon flowed down towards my feet, the outline of my prosthetic leg was visible, bulky and unflattering. I stared, squinting my eyes up to pretend it wasn't there. For any other girl with my average-sized physique, this was the perfect, feminine bridesmaid dress. But not for me. The fabric was light and airy, making the prosthetic feel heavier than ever. As I stood there, a violent jerk of phantom pain hit me. I tottered backwards, practically falling onto the velour stool behind. When I stretched my legs out in front of me, the chiffon flopped hopelessly around the pole. I buried my head in my hands. I felt suddenly, desperately sad.

'Heidi? Everything OK in there?' Jenny called.

I didn't answer. Sobs constricted in my chest. I couldn't catch my breath. 'You're ugly,' a voice in my head chastised. 'You're ugly and you have one leg. You'll never get married. Who could ever want you now?'

'Heidi?' Mum said.

I tried to fill my lungs, wheezing as I forced the air down my ever-tightening throat. The depth of my emotions smothered me. I wanted to cry. I couldn't.

'Oh, do let us see you, darling.' Truly Forever joined in the tirade, her tone shrill and excitable.

The floral smell of the changing room was nauseating, clogging my nostrils with its sweet, overwhelming aroma. My pulse was racing. My palms were sweating. A sense of impending doom occupied every part of my brain. Why couldn't I breathe?

Devoid of the energy to stand, I collapsed to the floor. My back against the wall, I curled my knees up and hugged them. I can't breathe, I thought. I can't breathe. This is it. I closed my eyes. Sparks of light danced in the blackness. I heard a faint voice say my name again. I couldn't force enough air into my lungs to respond.

'Right, I'm coming in.'

The curtains were wrenched back and Jenny stood in front of me. Immediately, her face softened.

'Oh, Heidi.' She crouched down and took my hands in hers. 'You're shaking.'

'I'm . . . sorry, can't . . . breathe . . .' I tried to form a coherent sentence, my mouth slurring the words. I didn't understand what was happening. All I could feel was fear.

'It's all right,' she soothed. 'It's fine. You're OK.'

'Just sit there and relax.' Mum was by my side too now, crouching despite her bad knees. 'Try to count to ten.'

I tried, murmuring the numbers under my breath. Slowly, torturously, my breathing began to return to normal. I smoothed the bridesmaid dress with the palms of my hands. The chiffon was creased where I'd been clutching it in my fists.

'I'm sorry,' I said again. 'I just . . . it was all just . . .'

'Shhh,' Jenny answered. 'I think it was a panic attack.'

'But I thought . . . I thought I was fine. It came from nowhere.'

'You're bound to have times like this,' Mum assured. 'Given what you've been through.'

'Darling, you look absolutely beautiful,' Truly announced. She lingered outside the cubicle, fiddling self-consciously with her long, false eyelashes. 'So stunning. My beautiful bridesmaid princess.' Jenny and Mum exchanged a look.

'Truly, can you get us some water?' Jenny asked.

'Oh yes, yes, of course.'

She backed away, two hands raised as though in surrender. As she turned to leave the room, I saw her lipstick smile waning, uncertain tears at the corners of her large, glitter-dusted eyes. Because in Truly Forever's world, everything was happily ever afters. And I was still waiting for mine.

'Heidi, am I putting too much pressure on you?' Jenny asked.

We were back in the waiting room, my prosecco now replaced by a large glass of icy water. I took a gulp and winced at the coldness. Brain freeze, we used to call it. I massaged my temples.

'No . . .' I replied. It sounded unconvincing, even to me.

Jenny raised her eyebrows and I looked around, checking Mum couldn't hear me. I could see her through the open door of the dressing room, deep in conversation with Truly. I didn't want her to know how I really felt; not after the finances conversation. She was worried enough already.

'OK, well yes, maybe a bit,' I admitted. Post-panic attack, I felt weak and nauseous. My lungs craved fresh air.

'You have to tell me these things, Heidi.' Jenny sounded weary. 'This wedding's all I can think about at the moment. It's taking up all my energy.'

'I know.'

Jenny glanced around the reception area. The Poodle family had long since left, and the two women in kimonos had disappeared into a dressing room. Only the pinched-face mother and daughter remained, side by side yet not talking, their expressions sombre. The daughter had heavy kohl eyeliner and black streaks in her sawdust-coloured hair. She was staring, open-mouthed, at my leg. Her curiosity both unnerved and irritated me.

'I guess, in some ways, I'm using it as a shield,' Jenny said. She glanced towards Mum, then lowered her voice, obviously thinking the same as me. 'I need something to channel my emotions into.'

'What do you mean, Jen?'

I was unused to her being so honest. After all, I was the volatile, emotional one. My big sister was the one people relied on. She very rarely showed any kind of weakness. She stared down at the floor, clearly as uncomfortable with the admission as I was.

'People deal with things in different ways, right?' she said. I nodded.

'Of course.'

'Heidi, when you had your accident, it was . . . well, it tore me apart.' Her voice cracked slightly and I instantly felt alarmed. Was she crying? Across the room, kohl-eyed girl was still staring.

'I didn't know how to process it,' Jenny told the carpet. 'I had to be in control at work, a good mum to Evie, an almost-wife organising every part of this bloody wedding on my own. And then, well, this massive thing happened to you. This thing that threw all our lives into the air. I had to cling onto something. I knew otherwise I'd fall apart.'

'Oh, Jenny . . .' I reached out and took her hand. She blinked back her tears, still brave in spite of her pain, refusing to let them fall. 'I had no idea.'

'Mark and I have been arguing a lot,' she said. 'When Evie goes to bed, it feels like all we do is get at each other. He's just not pulling his weight, and he's been away so much, I've never known him to go to so many conferences.'

I looked at my big sister, emotions laid bare. And I felt really bad.

'I'm sorry if I touched a nerve earlier,' I said.

'You did. But I shouldn't have snapped like I did. We're just rowing constantly about the scale of the wedding. He's accusing me of being showy, like I just want to put on this massive performance for everyone.'

'But that's not you, Jen.'

'I know.' She sniffed loudly. 'He doesn't get that it's helping me cope. I've tried to explain, Heidi, I really have. But he just brushes me off, says I'm making excuses. I just want a day where we're all there and we're all united, you know? I want to put us back together.'

Suddenly, I felt guilty for resenting Jenny's demands. My accident wasn't just about me. There were ripple effects, rings of worry sinking and spreading right across the pool of my life. I squeezed my sister's hand tighter. She gripped mine back, her palm damp.

'I just don't know what's going to happen,' she said in a small voice. 'I thought we were unwavering. I mean, we always have been. But the way things are now . . . I don't know what I think about anything any more.'

The weight of her words bore down on me. Rowing was one thing – but was she really suggesting their relationship could be under threat?

'Mark adores you, Jen,' I said as firmly as I could manage,

though I felt choked now too. 'He loves you, and he loves Evie. Everything's going to be fine.'

'I know. I sound insane.' She let out a mirthless laugh. 'But I'm paranoid. In the past couple of months, the unexpected has become the normal, you know? I can't rationalise anything properly any more.'

'I know how you feel,' I replied. Jenny took a tissue from her pocket and blew her nose.

'It's so shit,' she said. I couldn't help but smile as the word came out of her mouth. My sister never, ever swore.

'Collette Nichols?' The receptionist called. The girl all in black stood up. As she passed us, she stopped.

'Can I just ask, what happened to your leg?' she said. Jenny and I looked at each other.

'I was attacked by a gang of sharks,' I snapped. Next to me, Jenny snorted. We were still holding hands and then we were laughing; sisters reunited.

Chapter Nineteen

'So, challenge three then.' Jack slid into the back seat of the patient transport van beside me. His hair was damp and a thin sheen of sweat shone on his forehead. 'How are we feeling this morning?'

'Good, I think.'

Butterflies flickered in my stomach. I was going home. I couldn't wait to see Dougie; to show off my progress and be back in my flat, even if just for a day. Tara had insisted I move on from my trusty crutches, and I sat with my two walking sticks balanced against the seat between us. They made my walking distinctly wobblier, and I was forced to bear more weight on my prosthesis, which pinched and burnt in places. However, my stump was hardening, and I was starting to get used to the feeling. It wasn't nearly as painful as it had been in the beginning.

Jack popped an Extra Strong Mint into his mouth. He smelt like shampoo and cigarettes.

'Do you think you'll ever stop smoking?' I asked.

'I want to.' He shrugged. 'But now's not the best time.'

'Because of the job stress?'

'Something like that,' he said vaguely. He dabbed his brow with the back of his hand and switched tack. 'You look nice.'

'Thank you.' I blushed, flattered in spite of the swift subject change. 'I was beginning to think I'd be in gym leggings for the rest of my life.'

I wore one of my new wide-legged summer jumpsuits, pale denim with a big bow at the front. I'd tied my favourite silk scarf in my hair. While I still didn't have the energy for eye make-up, I'd applied a hint of pale pink lip gloss and bronzer, hoping it would cover my paleness. It was the most like myself I'd dressed in weeks – although I still hadn't quite found the courage to try on the skinny jeans again.

'We match,' Jack said, indicating his own denim shirt. It was demure compared to his others.

'OK, you two?' Steph the OT asked from the front seat. We nodded.

'Now, remember, today is not just for fun. The main purpose is to assess your needs, to find out if your home is suitable to live in as an amputee and make adjustments accordingly.'

'Got it,' I said. I refused to let her kill my excitement.

'Will it involve side-stepping?' Jack muttered. I nudged him in the ribs. Thankfully, Steph didn't hear.

On home visits, Steph insisted on wearing the type of plastic apron usually sported for treating patients with MRSA. I could see it poking out from the top of her handbag, a distinctly unsanitary environment – although I decided not to point this out.

'You can never be too careful,' she said when she saw me looking.

'Should we sing a coach song?' Jack murmured.

'Oh, definitely,' I replied. I felt like we were rebellious kids on a school trip. 'Want to take the lead?'

'What was that?' Steph said sharply.

'Nothing.' Jack smiled sweetly at her and I snorted. 'Just chatting.' He turned to face me. 'You seem happier,' he said, more seriously.

'I am,' I answered. He was right. I did feel much brighter. 'I think the list must be working.'

'That's great.'

The journey passed quickly. Fuelled by anticipation, I gazed out of the window, seeking familiar landmarks and pointing out every finding to Jack. He was immensely patient, given my unprecedented levels of enthusiasm for restaurants I'd eaten at, nail salons I'd frequented and the bar in Shoreditch where I once thought I'd seen Kit Harrington from *Game of Thrones* but it turned out to be a greasy long-haired hipster who lived on a Bethnal Green barge.

However, I wasn't prepared for seeing the canal path again. Sitting on the right-hand side of the back seat, I was the closest to it. The traffic was denser as we drove down the high street. My heart jumped when I saw the track's narrow entrance. Reflections of trees danced off the water. My breath caught in my throat. I didn't want to look, and yet I couldn't tear my eyes away. I craned my neck, searching for the spot that changed my life.

'Is that it?' Jack asked quietly. I didn't realise I'd made a noise. I nodded wordlessly, turning my head to watch it through the back window as we passed.

However, I was soon comforted by the familiar sight of my building, the red-brick ex-council block with its 'no ball games' signs and little jutting balconies. I pointed to the last sixth floor balcony on the left.

'That's mine,' I told Jack.

'The one with the fairy lights?'

'Of course.'

Our balcony was our pride and joy. Over the past two years, it had played host to many a laundry session, lazy weekend brunch and house party dance. I'd tried to grow a few herbs there at one point – although I'd somehow managed to kill the apparently resilient mint plant my dad had potted for the purpose. I hadn't inherited my parents' green fingers.

We pulled into a free space on the road outside the building, parallel parking between a battered Clio and an Asda delivery van. Intent on walking, I wobbled to the entrance with my sticks, while Jack unfolded the wheelchair to push behind me, a precaution insisted upon by Steph. I fumbled for the key in my bumbag, struggling to remain upright. Even taking one hand off the stick remained a difficult, fear-filled prospect.

'Everything OK?' Steph asked.

'Yep, totally fine.'

After a couple more attempts at balance, I retrieved the key with a flourish. There was no way I was letting Steph think I couldn't cope.

By the time the rickety lift reached the sixth floor, my leg was throbbing. Beads of perspiration had appeared on my forehead. Several more ran down my back. I wiped them away and slid my key into the lock. I'd made it.

'What time do you call this, then?'

Dougie threw open the door. He was dressed for the occasion, black jeans and a plain white T-shirt replacing his usual tracksuit bottoms. His long dreads were tied back, his face freshly shaven. His smile was enormous.

'Right on time, I'd say.'

I opened my arms to hug him. I couldn't quite believe I was here. A sudden memory of the last time I'd left returned to me with bittersweet emotion. I pushed it away. I refused to let it tarnish the moment.

'H, you're looking so great,' Dougie said. His eyes travelled upwards from mine, spotting Jack behind the wheelchair. A slight frown creased his forehead. 'Oh. To what do I owe this pleasure?'

'Jack McNally,' he said. 'My Nanna is Heidi's room-mate.'

'I know who you are,' Dougie said. He spoke through a smile but I caught an edge to his tone. His initial enthusiasm seemed to waver in front of my eyes. 'I must admit, I wasn't expecting Heidi to have a chaperone.'

'He's come to help out,' I explained.

'Qualified occupational therapist too, is he?'

'Certainly not,' Steph said. She brushed down her uniform pointedly.

'Stop it,' I told Dougie. 'Be nice.'

Jack pushed the wheelchair inside, then held out a hand to Dougie. Hesitantly, Dougie took it.

'It's a pleasure to finally meet you,' Jack said.

'Oh, honestly, the pleasure is all mine.'

'May we come in?' Steph's tone had changed. She spoke in a formal phone voice; a woman doing her job.

'Oh, yeah, sure.' Dougie stood back to let us pass. He was avoiding my gaze. 'Excuse the clutter.'

The hallway was full of half-packed boxes. Some of them were labelled; 'crockery' and 'bedroom' and 'art stuff.' Others were more haphazard, a glass cafetière sandwiched between coffee table books, Delia Smith's classic recipes and an illustrated history of birds. A selection of Dougie's canvasses were propped against the wall. There was a gorgeous carpet of bluebells, several cityscapes and a close up of a large oak tree, the sunlight peeking through its branches.

'These could be a hazard,' Steph said.

'They're not always there.' I leapt to Dougie's defence – although truth be told, it looked like the packing hadn't much progressed since the day of my accident.

'I'm moving,' Dougie said. 'At least, I think I am. At some point.'

'Huh?'

I frowned at his hesitance. I was pretty sure Hal wouldn't be able to handle this waiting around for much longer. He was a man of action: make a decision and follow through without qualm. It was what made him so cut-throat in his job. He'd never understood Dougie's tendency to mull and dream – Hal said he was over-sensitive. He even laughed at how much Dougie enjoyed solitude in nature. I hadn't known him to ever accept an invitation to join Dougie on his weekend art sessions in Epping Forest, however many times he'd been asked.

'I just mean it's a bit up in the air at the moment,' Dougie clarified.

'You mean to say Heidi will be living in this flat by herself?' Steph pulled a pen from her pocket and scribbled something onto her clipboard. 'Well, that might change things when it comes to my assessment.'

Dougie and I looked at each other in alarm.

'No, no,' he said quickly. 'Not for a long time. As I say, it's up in the air. I'd never leave until she was settled. I'd make sure she was completely capable.'

'He would,' I agreed. 'It's why he hasn't gone already.'

I spoke confidently, but I felt very nervous. The boxes in the hallway were a glaring reminder of my unknown future. I fought the urge to tip out their contents, to start putting everything back in its rightful place. I wanted to grab Dougie, to shake him by the shoulders and tell him he was making a mistake. I reined in my feelings, settling instead for a weak, well-meaning smile. Hal may not be my favourite person, but ultimately it was Dougie's decision. I was being selfish, I knew that. He'd already put this off for weeks because of me. He shouldn't have to put his life on hold.

Apart from the hallway, the flat was spotless. Wheeling myself into our lounge-kitchen, I couldn't believe what I was seeing. The surfaces were so shiny that I could practically see my face in them. There wasn't a used coffee cup in sight. There were no stray takeaway flyers, bills or out-of-date vouchers for the latest gym opening or beauty salon anywhere. The usual corner of drying and un-ironed laundry was clear, the racks neatly folded by the wall. Our ever-growing line of wine bottles along the windowsill had been removed. On the far wall of the living room, Dougie's largest canvas, a gorgeous oil painting of Epping Forest at sunrise, had been dusted off and straightened. There was even a vase of daffodils on the kitchen table, their yellow faces smiling amidst the fresh rays of sunlight that swept in through the open balcony door.

'Wow,' I breathed.

In all the time I'd lived with Dougie, he'd never once washed the floors. In fact, as flatmates, we tended to reside in thickening dust and creeping clutter until one of us eventually cracked.

'What d'ya reckon?' Dougie said. 'Not bad, right? I can't say I did it all myself though. When your parents stayed here your mum insisted we hired a cleaner. Her name's Maria and well, what can I say – the woman's a dab hand with a duster.'

'Right, well, must get on,' Steph said. She pulled out a tape measure and glanced around, her steely gaze reminiscent of an Ofsted inspector at a school. 'We have a lot to do. I'll start by measuring the door frames. If they're not wide enough for a wheelchair, we could have a problem.'

'Sorry, what?' I said. Her words were so casual that at first I thought I'd misheard. 'What kind of problem?'

'Well, Heidi,' she spoke slowly, the same infuriating tone she'd used in the rehab kitchen. 'Today's all about making sure you'll be capable of living here. And that means your home has to meet certain requirements . . .'

'And if it doesn't?' I leant against the kitchen worktop. My leg felt suddenly heavy.

'Then we'll have to talk about alternative arrangements.'

'No.' Dougie jumped in. 'She's coming back here. This is her home. End of.'

Steph sighed heavily as she tied on her plastic apron.

'I quite understand. But let's see how we get on before we all start clucking unnecessarily, shall we? Right, enough chit-chat now. I'll go and make a start.'

Tape measure held aloft, she swept from the room. Dougie, Jack and I were left staring at each other, in shock at Steph's offhand revelation. Suddenly, my good mood wasn't quite so bright. Until that moment, the prospect of not being able to go home hadn't even entered my head.

'It'll be fine, H,' Dougie said, breaking the silence. 'Don't worry. I'm sure it's just routine.'

'It's all bloody box-ticking,' Jack agreed.

'I hope you're right.'

We retired to the living room with our coffee. Dougie assumed his usual position, back against the side of the sofa, legs curled up beneath him.

'So, Jack, what do you do then?' he asked. His tone oozed brightness. I eyed him with suspicion. He already knew the answer; I'd told him it myself.

Jack's gaze flicked momentarily to the floor. It was a split-second movement, but I noticed it.

'I'm, well, I was a journalist,' he said. His voice wavered. 'I got made redundant.'

'Ah, sorry to hear that, mate.' His pity sounded genuine enough. I assumed he was trying to be polite.

'It's OK,' Jack answered. 'I mean, it was pretty rubbish at the time. I keep getting rejections for jobs – or even worse, total silence. But y'know, I'm sure I'll sort something out.'

'Course you will,' I said.

His eyes looked haunted. He smiled vaguely, studying the sofa cushions, which were white and red to match our red microwave and coffee machine. He pulled one onto his lap and crossed his arms over it. Conflict clouded his face.

'So you've been visiting Heidi,' Dougie said. Jack blinked a few times, as though pulling himself back to the present. His distracted expression cleared.

'Yeah. Well, and my Nanna too, of course.'

He smiled at me and I felt a rush of warmth. In recent weeks, I'd begun to notice tiny details about him – the flower-shaped mole on his neckline and his bounding gait like a skip. He always bit his lip while he was thinking, something he seemed to do a lot.

'How on earth do you put up with this one, eh?' Dougie's tone was strange again, casual yet somehow aloof. He put an arm around my shoulders protectively. 'I have to live with it 24/7.'

Jack continued to smile politely, although his eyes told a different story. They flicked between us, uncertain. He hugged the cushion on his lap.

'We've been having a great time,' he said. 'Right, Heidi?'

'Right.' I nodded.

'I've missed all your little habits, H,' Dougie said. 'Especially your shower singing. Did you know she did that, Jack? Like a bloody opera in there sometimes.'

'I miss you too, Dougie.' I tried to shrug his arm off, but he wasn't finished.

'Oh my God – and the way you always put the toilet roll on the holder the wrong way round. I'd forgotten about that! You see, Jack, we have a private ongoing war, us two. She likes the paper coming over the front of the roll, but I've always preferred it round the back . . .'

'Dougie,' I said sharply. His eyes gleamed.

'Sorry.'

'Well, I'm sure you'll be back home in no time,' Jack said smoothly.

'She will.' Dougie gave me a wide smile. 'Anyway, Jack, thanks for hanging out with H. I'm sure she appreciates it.'

'It's helped us both, I think,' Jack said.

'Oh?' Dougie took a big gulp of coffee. 'How so?'

'I don't know,' he shrugged, gripping the cushion tighter. 'I guess it gives me purpose. My dad's giving me grief; constantly trying to put me in touch with his old hack friends on the off-chance they'll have some work. I don't think he realises that they're pretty much all retired.'

'Something will come along, Jack,' I said. 'I'm sure of it.'

'Heidi!' Steph called from the corridor. 'I need to watch you getting in the bath.'

'Oh, bloody hell,' I muttered.

I grabbed the walking sticks and rose to standing, wincing at the pressure on my stump. At the sound of Steph's voice, a familiar fear crept into my heart. I'd been so focused on coming home that I hadn't even considered the possibility that my flat might not be fit for me. And where would I go if it wasn't? I thought about my parents; my mum fussing and pandering while my dad worked harder than ever, driving himself into the ground for the sake of my financial support. The thought of it killed me, yet another thing to feel guilty about. I couldn't let them do that. I was disrupting everyone's lives enough already.

'Heidi!' Steph yelled again.

'Yes, OK, coming!'

I needed to ace this challenge; to prove to Steph and to myself that I was ready. Steadying myself, hands on the sticks, I put my best foot forward.

The visit came to a close too quickly. I'd proved I could clamber in and out of the bath. I'd braved the balcony. I'd side-stepped around the kitchen. I'd even managed the toilet without a toilet frame – with the door closed, I hasten to add, although I was sure that if Steph had her way, she would have watched my technique closely, and probably made notes too.

I sat on top of my pale grey duvet, my prosthetic leg discarded on the carpet. The familiarity of my surroundings cast a spell of calm over me; from the yellow cushions that matched my curtains to my world map pinboard on the wall, brightly coloured tacks marking the independence and adventures of me before the accident. I yearned to sink into the memory foam mattress, to curl under the covers and succumb to the comforts of home. Relief flowed through me knowing I'd passed the test; I'd be able to come back here after all. Unfortunately, there was no time for celebration. Outside in the hallway was an angry occupational therapist on a tight schedule.

'The driver's waiting, Heidi,' she barked.

'Coming.'

I moved to the edge of the bed and laced up my left trainer, pushing my right leg into the prosthesis. The shoe was still on the foot where I'd left it. My stump gave a jolt of protest. I grit my teeth as I stood up. The first few steps were always the worst.

'Heidi?' Jack appeared in the doorway. 'You good to go? Steph's gone down to reception.'

'Almost.' I took out a sports jacket from my wardrobe. It was a men's one I'd bought in Broadway Market, maroon and navy with faded green cuffs. Jack eyed it with amusement.

'Very East London.'

'Always.'

He hovered in the doorway, one foot tentatively across the threshold. His big toe poked through a large hole in his striped sock.

'Jack . . .'

'Yes?' He leant against the door frame and turned towards me, his green eyes alert and expectant.

'Did you mean what you said earlier? About the challenges helping you, too?'

'Yeah. I really did.' He paused, the creases in his brows deepening. He spoke with a quiet hesitance I hadn't heard before. 'I won't lie, Heidi, this job thing's knocked my confidence a lot. It's good to feel worthwhile again, to have a purpose, you know?'

'Oh trust me, I know. You've helped me so much, Jack.' As I spoke, I felt myself blushing.

'You've helped me too, Heidi,' he said softly.

Dougie padded barefoot into the hallway.

'Guys, just to say, I think that Steph woman's going to explode soon . . .'

'Oh, let her,' I said.

Jack grinned. Then he looked at Dougie and a strange expression passed between them; a note of warning thinly veiled by politeness. My bedroom felt suddenly suffocating. Silently, Dougie sat down on my bed and folded his arms, waiting for a reaction. Jack gave a barely perceptible nod and began to reverse from my room.

'I'll wait in the corridor,' he said. 'Give you two a chance to say bye.'

'Thanks, mate,' Dougie answered. But his tone suggested anything other than friendliness.

'What was that all about?' I asked as soon as Jack had gone.

'Oh, not much. We had a little chat earlier, that's all.' Dougie crossed his legs and leaned back against the wall. It felt like he was marking his territory. 'I just told him to be careful.'

'Careful?' I felt a pang of worry. I knew his behaviour was off. 'About what?'

Dougie simply shrugged.

'What did you say to him?'

'Look, I just think it's weird he's become so invested in your recovery. The man barely knows you, H. I wanted him to know I'm looking out for you. I'm not going to let him mess with your head.'

He looked at me, his expression sincere and concerned; which he was, of course. But I knew him better than that.

'Dougie, are you jealous?'

'Of Jack?' He raised an eyebrow. 'Seriously?'

'I know I've been spending a lot of time with him. But it's different, Dougie. It's a different kind of connection.'

'Because you fancy him.'

'I never said that,' I snapped.

However, I was beginning to wonder. In recent weeks, I'd started to really look forward to Jack's visits; more so than I'd ever envisaged. When he walked into the room, adrenaline leapt like a jack-in-a-box within me, popping up and refusing to be pushed back down. When we were apart, I found myself wondering what he was doing, who he was with, whether he ever thought about me. Whenever I had a mental wobble or a funny story, it was Jack I wanted to message. I told myself it was the natural closeness of blossoming friendship; that it was always intense at the start. But I knew I was suppressing the depth of my feelings. Jack was never far from my mind.

Dougie stared me out, his eyebrow still arched high. He knew me; could spot the signs a mile off. It was hugely infuriating. There was no hiding from his astuteness.

'OK, fine,' I conceded. 'Maybe a little bit. But maybe he really does just want to help. Maybe, just maybe, he actually likes me. Because God forbid that could happen.'

'Don't get defensive.' He held his hands up in front of him. 'And yes, fine, maybe I am a bit jealous. But H, you know I didn't mean it like that. I spoke to him because if anything does happen, if he upsets you in any way, he'll have me to deal with.'

'Terrifying.'

'Oh shut up.' He threw a cushion at me. 'You trust too easily, H. I just don't want you to get hurt.'

'I appreciate the thought, but it's still not cool, Dougie. You can't just give people pep talks on my behalf. I'm an adult – I'll make my own choices.'

'Point taken.'

However, I noticed he didn't apologise. My anger was still simmering. I tried to ignore it. I'd made my point. I didn't want to have a full-on fight with Dougie, especially when I was about to leave the flat.

'How long until you're back here, anyway?' he asked. I was grateful for the change in topic.

'Eight days,' I replied. 'Hopefully. Not that I'm counting. And you're going back to work soon, right?'

'Next week,' he said. 'Yeah. And then it'll be all systems go with the move. I won't be able to put it off with Hal much longer.' His smile faltered. I reached out to touch his arm.

'Dougie, are you all right?'

'Me? Oh, yeah.' He waved away my sympathy. 'Don't worry yourself about me, H. You just focus on getting yourself back here, OK?'

'OK.'

His grin was back, yet there was something in my best friend's expression that made me hesitate, a cloud behind his eyes. I knew Dougie Oyinola like my own sibling. Just like he'd spotted my feelings for Jack, I could tell that something wasn't right. Still, I decided not to push it. He'd tell me in his own time. There had been enough tension for one day.

We said our goodbyes and I met Jack in the corridor, leaning against the wall on his phone. He looked up as I closed the door behind me.

'Ready?' he asked.

'Yep.' My insides fluttered at the sight of his trademark smile. 'Let's go.'

He buzzed the lift, gesturing for me to go ahead. We stood shoulder to shoulder in companionable silence as it raced down to the ground floor. Catching my gaze in the mirror, Jack placed a hand on my arm. It only lasted for a moment, but his touch, light and hesitant, sent an electric shiver down my body. And this time, it wasn't phantom pain.

Chapter Twenty

It was my turn at Breakfast Club. The idea was that while the other patients had their usual watery porridge courtesy of Fajah, each day two of us would get to practice our cooking and kitchen mobility skills by making breakfast for ourselves and the staff. It was billed as occupational therapy, but it was also slightly like slave labour. This week, my partner was Skye. Naturally, she was fizzing with enthusiasm.

'This is an absolute shit show.'

She stood at the counter and spooned instant coffee into four mugs. Still a few steps behind me in terms of recovery, she was able to stand but remained very wobbly when it came to walking on her prosthesis.

'We need to build your confidence moving around,' Steph said.

'Her confidence is built up enough already,' I said. Skye flicked her middle finger at me.

'Whatever. Seriously, Heidi, do you honestly think this is useful? I've lost my leg, not my fucking brain.'

Steph scowled at her, but I couldn't help but laugh. 'Just go with it,' I replied as impartially as I could. 'It's better than being up there in that dining room, isn't it?'

'You've got a point there.'

Since the drunken incident, Skye and I had formed an unlikely friendship. She'd lowered her guard, telling me about the pressure she felt as the daughter of two geography lecturers to follow a conventional route and go to university. Her brother, Clay (so-called due to the geography link, she reckoned) had just finished his medical degree. She felt like the black sheep of the family. Which she was, to an extent, although she was more of a vibrant rainbow sheep, barging through fences to escape to a fresh patch of grass.

And yet, Skye was more complex than the average rebellious teen. She was fierce, funny, and deeply sensitive, even though she didn't like to show it. I felt privileged that she'd allowed me to see past her protective barrier. In recent weeks, I'd developed a real fondness for her.

I stood at the hob, watching as the transparent egg yolks began to change colour. I simply could not fathom the diabetic gang's collective mindset. They were all so blasé, so unbothered about their life-changing lack of mobility. The worst thing was, it could have been prevented. And for that I could never forgive them.

'So why exactly is your friend here again?' Skye glanced suspiciously at Dougie, who was leaning back against the worktop, flicking through a Spotify playlist.

'I don't know,' Steph and I said together. Dougie gave Skye a silent salute.

'Looks good,' he called to me. On hearing it was scrambled eggs and salmon, he'd invited himself along; any opportunity for free food. 'Can you speed it up a bit though? I'm ravenous.'

'Oh, go away.' I waved my spatula at him. 'This is a therapy session, remember? You're lucky you were even allowed in.'

'It's not the usual protocol,' Steph added. Behind Steph's back, Skye made a face. I stifled a laugh.

'And here at the ARU, we bloody love the rules,' Skye said. 'Do you know I got told off for using crutches the other day, Heidi? Those old men are heaving their fat butts to the corner shop and smoking an entire pack of fags – and I'm not even allowed to hop to the loo. Tell me how that makes sense.'

'You could fall,' Steph said.

'They could get lung cancer and die.'

'Well, I think the two things are quite different . . .'

'Or worse.' Skye waved a teaspoon at her, too high on her horse to stop. 'They'll smoke and eat and drink themselves into a stupor until they lose another limb, and then, guess what, they're back here at the jolly old ARU again – costing the NHS even more money. How is that a good idea?'

'Preach, sister,' Dougie chimed in. I shot him a look – although we both knew Skye was right. For a teenager, she was remarkably clued up.

'Skye, your hair should be tied up in the kitchen,' Steph said.

'There we go again, yet another rule.' She swished her blonde princess locks defiantly. But when Steph passed her an elastic band she conceded, tipping her head upside down and sweeping it up into a big, messy bun. 'This elastic's going to rip my hair like you wouldn't believe.'

'Look, can we just focus on what we're doing?' Steph asked. It was clear the fight had gone out of her. Skye nodded, triumphant.

'Sure.'

It felt good to be cooking again. I'd never been the best chef, and my attempts to condense recipes and skip steps in my impatience for the finished product had led to many a kitchen nightmare, as Dougie had frequently been witness to. However, I'd missed the capability and freedom to at least try, to mix and season and watch a meal come together. I added a knob of butter and a splash of milk to the pan. It was yet another thing I'd taken for granted.

'I've missed our weekend brunches,' Dougie said. It had been a firm part of our routine; an enormous midday fry-up post-night out. 'Still, not long until we can do them again, right?'

'If you haven't moved in with Hal by then.'

'I won't have done,' he replied. His tone was certain. I stopped stirring and looked at him.

'Honestly, Dougie, you don't have to put your life on hold because of me. I don't want to be a burden.'

'I know.'

A small smile passed between us. On the hob, the scrambled eggs were reaching their finished consistency. I added a drop more milk.

'Heidi,' Steph appeared behind me, making me jump. 'Looks like it's going well.'

'Yep.' I turned the heat down. 'All under control.'

'Don't forget the avocado. It's in the fridge – remember your side-stepping.'

'Will do.'

'Bloody side-stepping,' Skye said from across the room. Several strands of long hair had fallen out of her bun and were dangling delicately across her round, rosy face. 'So inefficient.'

'It's a start,' I told her.

I held on to the counter and began to move. I was surprised and pleased to discover that my prosthetic leg wasn't nearly so painful as it had been.

'Skye, watch how Heidi does it,' Steph said. Spurred on by the audience, I stepped a little faster. Across the room, Skye took a tentative step. She winced as the weight went down through her prosthetic leg.

'Fucking hell, that's sore.'

'It will be,' I answered. 'But honestly, power through it. It's the only way to get used to the feeling.'

'Right. OK. God, it's like when I used to do *pointe*. Push through the pain.'

'You did ballet?' I asked.

'Yep. Dad made me do every dance class under the sun growing up. Got me out of his hair I guess. Anyway, let's do this.'

She stepped again, this time with a little more confidence. And then again. Each time, the wincing was less.

'That's it,' Steph said. 'Keep hold of the work surface.' Skye nodded, her cherubic face set with determination.

'You kind of get used to the pain,' she said to me.

'For sure.'

'Can someone do more toast?' Steph called.

'On it,' Dougie replied. He rummaged in the cupboards, pulling out a loaf of brown bread.

'So what did you think about Jack yesterday, then?' I asked him.

He was silent for a while. I watched his face cloud over. I could practically see the words forming in his head.

'If you really want to know, I still can't warm to the man.'

'But why not?' I really didn't understand his hesitance. 'He's just being nice.'

'I know.' Dougie popped two slices of bread into the toaster. 'I just hope my little pep talk made a difference. But honestly, what's in it for him?'

'Nothing, Dougie!' I mashed the avocado more forcefully, wishing I hadn't brought it up. He was being ridiculous. Blobs of green goo sprayed into the air. 'We're friends – is that so wrong?'

Dougie scooped a stray lump of mashed avocado from the work surface and popped it into his mouth. He shrugged.

'You asked what I thought. I've told you.'

I turned away from him, annoyed. I was hoping he'd meet Jack and see the man I saw. I was hoping he'd change his mind. The pop of the toaster broke our silence.

'Toast's up,' I said.

'Heidi . . .'

'Look, let's leave it, Dougie. We can agree to disagree.'

We worked in silence; him buttering the toast, me spreading scrambled eggs and avocado on top. As we did so, I ran through Jack's behaviour once again in my mind. Sure, the challenges had been his idea. But it was all innocent; two friends helping each other out. He hadn't done anything that weird, had he?

I was annoyed with Dougie. He'd always been a one-person friend, the kind of pal who favoured fewer, meaningful friendships over large and noisy groups. My own preference was somewhere in the middle, and my desire for the best of both worlds had been a continual source of disagreement growing up. At primary school, my girlfriends had welcomed Dougie into the fold, but he'd always been too shy to voice opinion or emotion in front of the group, instead lurking in the background, waiting for the chance to spend time with me on his own. One to one, he'd been a different person, thoughtful and expressive, full of ideas for new games. As an adult, he'd got better, but his envious side still occasionally resurfaced. I knew him well enough to realise he felt threatened by Jack. Since the accident, he seemed more protective of me than ever.

In the end, it was Skye who broke the ice. She'd obviously sensed the tension.

'Christ, I'm starving.' She sat down in her wheelchair. 'This is bloody hard work.'

'You've done brilliantly,' I said. Almost as though she'd forgotten her toughness, Skye grinned, the praise lighting up her pale, rosy face. In that moment, she looked a lot younger than her seventeen years.

'Thanks, Heidi.'

'It was very good teamwork,' Steph added.

And then I did something historic. Without thinking, I picked up a plate. I walked over to place it down on the table. There was a collective intake of breath.

'What?' I said. But then I looked back across the kitchen. And I realised. 'Oh my God, did I just . . . ?'

'Yes!' Dougie said. His smile was back with a vengeance, all traces of tension vanished. Even Steph was grinning.

'Completely unaided!'

My stomach flipped as the monumental weight of what had just happened dawned on me. For the first time since my accident, I'd moved without pause or analysis. I had walked on my own.

'I don't . . . I don't quite know how I did that,' I said. 'It just kind of happened.'

'Amazing!' Skye yelled.

'That's the way we want it,' Steph said. 'Your prosthetic should become a natural part of you. And just then, it did, Heidi. That's a massive achievement. You should be very proud.'

'You are one bloody amazing woman, H, you know that?' Dougie's big arms enveloped me. He smelt like toast and dried paint. 'You can do anything now. Seriously. Nothing will stop you.'

I looked from my position at the table to the work surface behind me, where the other three plates stood waiting. It was only five steps – but each one held a deep, resounding significance. Slowly, carefully, I turned on my heel. And then I strode back across the room.

Chapter Twenty-One

I leafed through my tiny chest of drawers, casting aside the sensible loose dresses and endless activewear until my hands clasped upon the black denim skinny jeans. Hands trembling, I held them up to my body. They still had the label on.

'Going somewhere, love?' Maud asked from across the room. It was 5.30 p.m. and she was already in her pyjamas.

'Back to work,' I replied. After months of unemployment, the word felt weird on my lips. 'I'm doing a trial shift.'

'At the bar?'

'Yep.'

The list was on my bedside table. I noted the big ticks beside *Independence* and *Body*; the glaring gap beside *Career*. In recent weeks, the paper had got crumpled, the edges dog-eared, crinkled with possibility. I was getting there.

It had been Jack's idea to phone Conscience. At the time, I'd agreed it was a good idea. But now, I was beginning to wonder. Was I really ready for standing up all night; for making small talk and carrying drinks? I'd been isolated for so long. I was nervous about being back in the public domain. I was equally also nervous about an evening with Jack.

I hoped Maud couldn't see the way I was fumbling with my button and zip. Get a grip, Heidi, I told myself. I was being ridiculous. Jack and I had hung out so much already. And yet, the prospect of an entire evening with him, coupled with seeing my colleagues, had caused a shivering sensation in my stomach. I clamped my teeth together. I needed to chill out.

'New jeans?' Maud asked.

'They sure are.'

Cautiously, I manoeuvred the skinny jeans up my legs. They went on much more easily than I'd expected. I stood up and wiggled, performing a half-jump as I pulled them up to my waist. Maud watched, chuckling.

'The things we do for fashion, eh?'

I blew my fringe from my eyes and straightened up. My nerves were jangling, electric and unstoppable. I felt a shimmer of telltale perspiration forming on my upper lip, and quickly wiped it away. I pulled on a new emerald green blouse. The loose, flowing fabric was nearly the same shade as Jack's eyes. When and how had I become the sort of woman who thought sickening things like that?

'Give us a twirl,' Maud said.

Grabbing a walking stick, I moved over to the tiny half mirror above the sink in our bedroom. I craned my neck, trying to get a good view. Not for the first time, I wished it were full length.

I was surprised to find that I was pleased with my reflection. The skinny jeans hugged my figure like a second skin, and my muscles were toned and defined. Hours outside in the ARU garden meant my cheeks had more colour in them than before. A scattering of summer freckles had appeared around my nose.

'You look lovely, Heidi,' Maud said.

'Thank you.'

I sat back on the bed and stretched my legs out in front of me, admiring the strong curve of my left calf, the defined muscle of my thighs. On the prosthetic side, the bottom of the jeans hung loose. I rolled them up, revealing the metal pole beneath. It didn't look anywhere near as bad as I'd imagined. It actually looked quite cool.

Then my phone buzzed. I jumped. Maud chuckled at my reaction. I took a deep breath, trying to ignore the sudden palpitations in my chest. He was here.

Like everything else in Hackney Wick, Conscience bar had started out as a pop-up. The canalside establishment was minimalist and wooden, with light bulbs in glass milk bottles suspended by wire from the ceiling, and wine bottles as candle-holders, old wax erupting from their tops and drying onto the mismatched, upcycled tables. For those who preferred a less conventional drinking experience, seating areas comprised of numerous bales of straw were grouped in each corner, while pot plants hung from every spare inch of ceiling, giving a jungle vibe.

'Is it how you remember?' Jack asked. Tonight, he'd chosen a silver-grey shirt. It was the colour of moonlight.

'More or less.'

It felt very strange, being back. My surroundings were so familiar, and yet I didn't recognise a single server behind the bar. I knew well enough that shift work and temp jobs meant that there was always a high turnover of staff, but the lack of familiar faces brought a sadness to my heart. It brought back feelings of frustration and confinement. Everyone around me had gone on with their lives, but I was stuck; inching along at a far slower pace as I desperately tried to move forward. A shot of nerve pain ran up the back of my right leg. I shifted my weight and grimaced.

'Are you OK?' Jack frowned.

'I will be in a minute.' I flexed my right knee back and forth. 'My phantom pain's just come on. It's killing me.'

Behind the bar, one of the girls I'd never seen before was rearranging the bamboo straws. She looked hideously young; long false eyelashes overhanging a round baby face.

'Jackson! Long time, mate!' A firm hand on my shoulder.

'Ben!'

I felt a rush of pleasure to see my former colleague standing behind me. Tall and tanned with chipmunk cheeks and a light dusting of stubble, Ben Grady was the embodiment of enthusiasm. An eternal traveller from Melbourne, Ben had started at Conscience on the same day as me, nearly two years before. We were the stalwart staff members, the ones who had stuck around. His natural, easy chat and the laugh that bubbled beneath his every word made him a very charismatic man. While his total incapability to have a serious conversation had rendered him useless boyfriend material, we'd been sleeping together on and off for the best part of a year. The last time had been just two weeks before my accident. It felt weird seeing him again when so much had changed; particularly with Jack standing beside me.

'Jack,' he said now, his hand outstretched.

'Hey mate.' Ben locked him into a firm, hearty grip. 'Listen, thanks for bringing her back to me.' He winked. I cringed. 'Sorry, I mean us.'

'No problem.' Jack answered – but there was a hint of question in his tone.

'So how are you, Jackson? So good to see you.' Ben slapped me on the back. I wobbled but managed to right myself. My stump was throbbing.

'Yeah, good – bit weird being back here though. Are you working tonight?'

'Made sure I was – for you.' His eyes glittered. He held up a green Conscience bumbag and dangled it in front of me. 'Here ya go, mate.'

I clipped it around my waist. The flirtation was so blatant. I hoped Jack hadn't noticed.

'Thanks.' Trying to steer onto safer ground, I took a breath. 'So what else are you doing these days?'

'Same old.' He gestured around the room. 'This, mostly. I thought about moving on, but there's way more flexibility in bar hours. More chance to travel, you know?'

'Yeah.'

I wasn't surprised. Ben was an eternal traveller, a nomad who liked nothing better than turning up in a new place armed with only a rucksack. His natural friendliness and hunger for new experiences meant he had friends all over the world, people he'd met through couch surfing or chance encounters. It also meant he could never decide on a conventional career route. Since he'd left his teaching job in Australia, he'd pretty much just floated around. While I admired his independence, it also frustrated me. He lived in a dream world of restless adventure, a bit of a Peter Pan.

'Anyway, listen, Heidi,' he said, his Australian accent soft and easy. He seldom used my first name, but I had to admit I'd always liked the way the syllables rolled off his tongue. 'We were all so sorry to hear what happened to you.'

He moved closer, brows furrowed as he spoke. It was probably the most serious I'd ever seen him. Beside me, Jack took a small step backwards.

'Thanks, Ben,' I answered. I retreated as subtly as I could. He was one of those people who always stood a little too close.

'Really. I mean it,' Ben said. 'Such a shock. If there's anything I can do, just let me know, OK? It hasn't been the same without you here. Everyone says it.'

'They do?' I felt touched by the knowledge. So they did care.

'Oh, yeah.' He grinned. 'Right, let's get you set up, shall we? Jack, mate – wanna sit at the bar and watch the dream team in action?'

'Er, OK.'

In a swift, smooth motion, Ben linked my arm and steered me away. I cast a quick glance over my shoulder. Jack's eyes locked with mine. Then he looked past me.

'Surprise!'

At first, the chorus of voices startled me. There had been a mistake; they'd confused me with someone else. But as I stood there, Ben's hand on my arm, the faces in the dusky candlelight became clearer. They were my work friends. Well, I say that. None of them actually worked here any more. But we had done, all together over the years. We'd built a group and stayed in touch. Now they were there in front of me; Ally, Caitlin and Laura. The Fab Five, reunited.

'How did you . . . ?' I started.

'Not bad, eh, mate?' Ben grinned. 'Wasn't sure I could pull it off, but I'm not gonna lie, I'm pretty pleased.'

'Heidi Jackson,' Ally boomed. The oldest of the group, she was a large woman with grown-out highlights and a foghorn laugh. She was also the alcohol enabler, the one who never said no to a party. 'The one and only.'

'You're looking great,' Laura said from behind her. An oboe player from Sheffield, she'd moved to London a few years ago seeking to make it big. She hadn't quite found fame; instead, she'd found Conscience. However, she'd left our ranks shortly before my accident having finally secured work in a touring orchestra. I realised with a jolt of emotion that her leaving party had been my final night out with two legs.

'Laura, what are you doing back in London?' I asked, incredulous.

'When Ben sent the message I couldn't not come.' She smiled, revealing the gap between her front teeth. 'I had to see how you were getting on.'

'Bloody bossing it, it seems!' Caitlin added. Caitlin had more tattoos and piercings than I'd ever known. After years bumming around at Bar Conscience claiming she didn't believe in 'The Establishment', she'd now finally caved in and enrolled on a college course in Health and Social Care. Ultimately, she wanted to be a social worker. Despite her tough exterior, she had a good and caring heart.

'It's so good to see you all,' I said.

I felt awkward under their attention. They all wore matching smiles; their voices seemed several decibels too high.

'Well, we couldn't miss your triumphant return, babe,' Ally said. 'Now, I'm bloody gagging for another G&T. What do you have to do to get service around here – sleep with the bar staff?'

She threw back her head and roared with laughter. My insides shrivelled. I couldn't look at Jack. Ben didn't take the bait, a wry smile playing across his lips.

'Coming right up,' I muttered. Ally winked at me.

'I bet it is.'

I chose not to respond. Instead, I lent on the bar and took a moment to compose myself. Jack was disengaged, staring out across the room like a man who'd rather be anywhere else.

'I can do this,' I told myself. I stuck on a smile and turned towards the spirits.

For the first half an hour, I was fine. A lot of it was muscle memory, moving mechanically to retrieve spirits, clean glasses and wedges of lemon and lime. I used the bar itself to help me, leaning on it for support and side-stepping in a way Steph would have been proud to witness. I was a bit slower than normal, but I was managing.

'Nice one, mate,' Ben called from the other end as I threw two pots in the air and successfully caught them. They were plant pots posing as cups, the holes filled in so we could use them as cocktail vessels. It was a Conscience trademark.

'Someone's done that before,' Jack said. He was perched on a stool on the other side of the bar, sipping a raspberry gin and tonic through a paper straw.

'No beer?' Ben remarked. His eyebrows were raised in clear judgement. Jack shrugged.

'Not the biggest fan of it.'

'Oh, leave him alone,' I said. I found it strangely endearing, the way Jack swirled the raspberries around in the glass. 'Not every man has to drink beer.'

'All right, touchy.' Ben gave me a wink. 'I'm just being friendly.'

It didn't feel like it. In fact, it felt like he was marking his territory; us on one side of the bar, Jack marooned with his gin on the other. I knew which side I'd rather be on. Ben's constant flirtation and pointed comments were grating. For someone who hadn't bothered to visit me once in hospital, he had a lot of gall.

Around forty-five minutes into the shift, the first twinge of nerve pain struck. Before that, my leg had been tingling but bearable, my pain threshold noticeably higher these days. Yet as I turned to reach up for the Jack Daniels on the shelf behind me, I was gripped by a sudden, crippling jolt. My knee gave way and I stumbled, almost dropping the bottle.

'Are you OK, Heidi?' Jack shot up and leaned over the bar, reaching out towards me.

'Phantom pain,' I said through gritted teeth. I set the bottle down and rubbed my leg. On the other side of the bar, a half-cut financial type banged his fist.

'Oi! Are you getting my drink or what?'

I realised he couldn't see my prosthetic leg. He clearly just thought I was slacking. I paused for a second, unsure how to react. The pain was fizzing and popping, my nerves alive with agony.

'I'll sort it,' Ben said.

'No, no it's OK.' I straightened up and took a deep breath. It would pass, I told myself. It always passed. Just don't think about it. Carry on.

I poured the rude man's drink and held the card machine out for his payment. Unseen to him, I flexed my knee, hoping it had just stiffened up, that a bit of stretching would sort me out and ease the discomfort. But it didn't.

The next bolt of agony happened as soon as the man walked away. I gripped the bar with both hands, my face screwed up in pain.

'Mate, you can't carry on like this,' Ben said.

'I can.'

But as soon as I replied, I was hit by another wall of pain. I felt suddenly lightheaded. I hadn't been breathing properly.

'Heidi, come and sit down,' Jack said.

'No, I can't. I need to carry on.' I was on the verge of tears; both from the pain and the humiliation. My face felt hot. 'I don't want to fail.'

'You haven't failed.' His green eyes were earnest and reassuring. He looked at Ben. 'Has she?'

'Nah, mate. Course not.'

'See?' Jack's tone was soft and coaxing, as though speaking to a frightened animal. 'You've been standing up for almost an hour, Heidi. When was the last time you did that?'

I sniffed. 'I can't remember.'

'Exactly. So give yourself a break, OK?'

The pain was fiery now, my stump throbbing. I could barely put weight on it without another surge of agony.

'OK,' I said finally.

Swallowing down tears, I unclipped my bumbag. I was defeated.

*

My friends were still there in the corner, loud and merry. One hand on my walking stick, the other arm linking Jack's, I made my way over to join them. He helped me into an upcycled wooden chair.

'Here she is!' Ally bellowed. 'Back from the frontline, are you?'

'How was it?' Laura asked.

Caitlin was moving her lip ring around with her tongue as she looked at me, a sign of concentration. She'd done it when she was making cocktails, too.

'Here you go.' Jack placed the gin down in front of me. It was the raspberry one I'd seen him drinking earlier.

'Thanks.'

'Oh dear, that bad eh?' Ally raised her painted eyebrows. 'Come on, drink up and give us all the gossip.'

'It was harder than I thought,' I admitted.

I glanced back towards the bar, where Ben and the young child-girl were efficiently managing the punters. Their movements were smooth and confident, Ben performing a little jig in time with the background beat as he poured the next pint. I found myself feeling jealous of his confidence.

'You did really well,' Jack said. He'd perched next to me, his moonlight silver shirt incongruous to the rest of the group's very casual attire.

'Mmmm.'

I took a sip of my drink. The gin hit my throat, warm and comforting. The nerve pain was dying down now that I was seated. The occasional residual twinge made my leg twitch without warning, but I was able to conceal it, no longer ruled by the spasms. However, within my relief was a deep well of defeat. If I couldn't manage to go back to the bar, what would I do for money? I was useless.

The lively chatter grew louder as I found my mind drifting, more distant than ever. I watched as people headed back and forth to the bar, my gaze fixated on their legs. Long and skinny, short and muscular, denim clad or bare under short skirts. Some walked with purpose, others with indecision. Large strides, small strides, lurching lollops fuelled by prosecco and cider. But all of them, even the drunkest, were balanced and stable. All of them moved without fear. The injustice, envy and anger overcame me. It manifested itself as sadness.

'Heidi,' Jack said. He touched my good leg and I blinked.

'Oh. Sorry,' I replied quickly. 'Miles away.'

'Such a dreamer,' Laura remarked. 'Nothing's changed there, then.' I tried to smile. I didn't quite manage it.

'So, our Hardcore H is back then,' Caitlin said. She clicked her tongue piercing, another habit I'd forgotten about. I found it quite off-putting. 'Go on then, tell us all about your recovery. Bet you got up to some crazy stuff at rehab, am I right?'

'Well . . .'

'You met a new man, for starters,' Ally added. Next to me, I felt Jack stiffen.

'We're not . . .' I stuttered. 'He's not . . .' My face was warm.

'Ah, like that is it,' Ally said. 'I see.'

'I've been helping Heidi out,' Jack said. Was it me, or was his tone a bit defensive? 'My Nanna's her room-mate.'

'Oh, that's so lovely,' Laura replied. Ally and Caitlin were nudging each other. I ignored them.

Jack's expression was polite and neutral but his body language was awkward, hands clasped in his lap, spine held slightly too rigid. His chair was even pushed further back from the rest of the group; teetering on the edge of the easy chatter.

'Heidi, what was rehab like?' asked Laura. She picked nervously at her short shellac thumbnail, as though worried she'd asked the wrong thing. Her nails were mint green and she wore a ring on almost every finger.

'It's been surreal,' I replied, grateful that the attention had moved on from Jack. 'It's kind of hard to describe, unless you've been there. A lot of old men with missing limbs. And a lot of exercise.'

Laura's small, grey eyes had misted over. She lowered her voice dramatically. 'I can't even imagine.'

I took a large gulp of gin, surveying my friends as if for the first time. They'd always been my fun group, the most sociable people I knew. Yet just like with Ben, it felt weird trying to be even halfway serious. Somehow, the dynamic had shifted. Next to me, Jack had fallen silent. I wondered what he was thinking.

'Mate, I love telling people you were in rehab,' Caitlin grinned. 'You should see the reactions I get.'

'Like Amy bloody Winehouse,' said Ally. I flinched as she let rip with a burst of her foghorn laugh. I'd forgotten how loud it could be.

I tried to laugh along, but my voice sounded fake. These were my friends, so why did I feel like they were mocking me? Sure, they'd sent a card in hospital at the very beginning, but none of them had tried to visit. They were all thrilled to see me now, but their efforts had been lukewarm – where had they been when I needed friends most? Not by my side.

'Evening, gang.' Ben appeared in front of us, still wearing his Conscience bumbag. He set a tray down on the table, and my heart sank as I saw what was on it. 'Seeing as the shift's nearly finished, I thought there's only one way to celebrate Heidi's return. On the house. Sambuca!'

There were riotous cheers as he handed round the glasses. I saw Jack look towards me, concern across his face. He raised his eyebrows questioningly and I responded with a slight shake of my head. The last thing I wanted was to ruin their expectations by making a scene. I'd just have to go along with it.

'Oh my God, remember my leaving do?' Laura said. 'You did five of these in a row! Or was it six?'

'Ugh, I remember,' I replied. 'Well, barely.'

I'd felt on top of the world, one of those heady nights when your heart feels full of love, when you want to go on dancing forever. Life had been so easy, so uncomplicated. Now, the prospect of getting drunk filled me with fear. Because if I was drunk, I was out of control – and that meant I was likely to fall.

'Ha! Absolute classic,' said Ally.

'To Heidi!' Ben raised his shot glass. We all followed suit. 'And to many more nights of crazy shots and dancing on tables. Right, mate?'

He winked at me. Instead of the usual flutter I used to feel when Ben was around, my insides recoiled. Since the accident, it was clear something had shifted. He looked the same; caramel tan, defined muscles and square, Action-Man-like jawline. But I didn't fancy him any more.

'Right,' I smiled back, but the corners of my mouth were twitching.

A creeping dread filled my body as I saw my friends with new, shattering perspective. Drunk in love, we'd hugged in dingy nightclubs and proclaimed we'd be there for each other forever. So why was I hiding my feelings now; why couldn't I be honest? It was two-dimensional, all of it. None of them had made any effort.

'One, two, three, SHOT!' yelled Ben.

I didn't want to, but I did it. The sambuca burned. I coughed as it went down, choked by the ferocity of my shame and resentment.

'Been a while, has it?' Caitlin laughed.

'Knowing you, you'll be back on it in no time,' Laura said. 'Surprised you didn't have a cheeky hip flask in hospital.'

'Oh come on, I'm not that bad,' I replied.

I was annoyed at the inference. Was that really how they saw me? Looking around at their grinning faces, I realised that it was. After all, that was how I'd always projected myself in front of them. It was the only side of myself I'd shown.

'See, Jack,' Ben nudged him in the ribs. 'We don't call her Hardcore H for nothing.'

'Sounds like you've had some wild times,' Jack said. I sensed hesitation in his tone. Compared to the uncomplicated joy of the others, he seemed out of place; serious and intense.

'Oh, the wildest, mate,' Ben said. Surreptitiously, he ran a hand down my spine. I shivered – and not with pleasure. 'The wildest.'

Embarrassed, I turned my attention to the window. Outside, colourful houseboats lined the canal, a warm glow emanating from their circular windows. An old man shuffled past on the footpath, two scruffy little dogs at his feet. A crescent moon lit up the sky. Sitting here, the rehab centre seemed a million miles away. But then again, so did my old life. Jack must be wondering if he knew me at all. I wasn't even sure I knew myself. I was trying too hard to fit their assumptions, to be the carefree party girl they wanted and expected. But too much had changed. I had a smile on my face but fear in my heart. Because that girl was gone. And I had no idea who would replace her.

In the taxi home, we sat in silence. I stared out of the window, watching the city rush by, cars and people with a destination in mind. Meanwhile, I felt lost. The weight of my worry dragged me down; regret about these strangers who once were friends, disappointment that Jack and I hadn't had any time alone, confusion about who I'd become.

Sitting in the front seat due to legroom, I stole glances in the mirror at Jack. His eyes were fixed on the world outside, too, caught up in unreadable thoughts. There was so much I wanted to say. I wanted to apologise, to explain, to laugh like we used to and turn over the page. And yet a strained tension filled the car. It stretched between us, vast and suffocating. I didn't know what to say.

'Miss, where is leg?'

The taxi driver – a man who clearly didn't wear deodorant – pointed at my prosthesis. There was a yellowing stain around his shirt collar. I flinched at the abruptness of the question, as much as at the stench of his breath, which held the distinct smell of cheese and onion crisps.

'What?'

'Leg is where?' He gestured again.

'Sorry, do you mind if we don't talk about it?' I said. I felt tears prick my eyes. I couldn't deal with this. Not tonight.

The sharp, vinegar-like aroma of his sweat was making me feel sick. I wound down the window, gulping in lungfuls of fume-drenched London air.

'She had an accident.' Jack spoke up from the back seat.

'Accident?' The driver made eye contact with Jack in the rear-view mirror. I shrunk in my seat. 'What happened?'

'Please,' I said, my voice choked.

'Leave it, will you, mate?' Jack said. 'She doesn't want to talk about it.'

'But—'

'Just stop!'

I'd never heard Jack shout before. It was sudden and sharp, a complete turnaround from his usual gentle tone. His eyes flashed with anger. Next to me, the driver raised his hands in a surrendering gesture. The car swerved again and my stomach lurched.

'OK, OK,' he said, glancing in the mirror at Jack as though he were a madman. 'No leg. No talk. OK. No get angry, please.'

He turned up the radio, Kiss FM blaring through the car. My eyes met Jack's and he gave a faint, reassuring smile. His kindness made me want to cry even more.

'Thank you,' I croaked.

The buildings rushed by; near-empty office blocks with the lights still on, solitary workers hunched over computers. As we passed through London Bridge, a noticeable buzz filled the streets, couples hand in hand and pub punters spilling out onto the streets. All of life, passing me by.

'Dad's found me a job,' Jack said suddenly.

'What?' I turned to the back-seat to look at him. It should have been good news, but his face had clouded again.

'Yeah. News Editor at a local paper. Dartford – it'd be a bit of a commute.'

'But Jack, it's a job.'

'Heidi, you don't get it.' He brought a hand up to his face. 'It's a job my dad has found. He knows the editor, they go back years. I told you before – I don't want to be living in his shadow. I want to be successful on my own merit.'

'I do get that,' I said emphatically. 'Of course I do. But I also know you need a job. And right now, it doesn't seem like you have a lot of options . . .'

'Don't you think I don't know that?' I recoiled, unused to his brusque tone. Jack ran a hand through his hair and sighed. 'Sorry. I shouldn't have snapped then. It's just . . . oh, forget it.'

'Jack . . .'

I tried to protest, but he was staring out of the window again. I'd lost him.

The road was covered by darkness, no one was awake in the quiet Lambeth hamlet save insomniacs and nurses – and us, of course. As Jack helped me out of the car, the night's calm was absolute, distant traffic sounds the only indication of the nocturnal city's continued buzz.

'Wait there a second, mate, will you? he asked. The driver nodded.

'OK. I wait.'

Jack turned to me. 'I'll probably just take this taxi home,' he said. 'You don't mind if I don't come in, do you?'

I shook my head, suppressing the urge to grab onto him. I did mind really. I didn't want him to leave. But I didn't want to look clingy.

The rehab centre rose up from the shadowed street, blazing industrial lighting incongruous with the homely neighbourhood vibe. My body felt heavy at the sight of it again. For a moment tonight, I'd been normal.

'Home sweet home,' I said bitterly.

I could still taste sambuca. I'd reached that strange, competent level of tipsy. I felt confident and focused, convinced I could pull off appearing sober in front of the nurses if I just concentrated hard enough. It was similar to how I'd felt as a teen, creeping back into my parents' house after alcopops in the park. Jack stood in front of me. He gave a wooden smile.

'It's been fun,' he said.

'Yeah.'

Silence reached out like the darkness, enveloping our words in its grasp. The streetlights glowed orange and yellow. Despite the slight autumn breeze, it was a beautiful night. I looked at Jack, eyes like stars, silver shirt like a slither of moonlight. Fuelled by alcohol, I moved towards him, so close that our noses were touching. My lips brushed his. And then he pushed me away.

'Heidi . . .'

I wobbled backwards, grabbing my stick tightly. I'd almost overbalanced. Jack's face was flushed. He stuttered and stumbled over his sentences.

'Heidi, no. I can't . . .'

My shoulders were tingling, every cell in my body replaying the sudden, brutal rejection. I felt tears in the corners of my eyes. Jack moved awkwardly from foot to foot.

'Look, I'm sorry if I gave the wrong signals,' he said. 'It's just . . .'

'No,' I stopped him. 'I'm sorry.'

I was sorry – for all of it. For subjecting him to spend time with people I'd once seen as best friends. For showing him the side of myself I'd now realised was all an act. For being clingy. For kissing him. For misjudging the situation so terribly. A horrible, nausea-inducing embarrassment rose in my throat. I'd ruined everything.

There was a strange distance in his eyes, a grey mist flecked across the usual startling green. He moved to give me a brief, parting hug. I rested my chin on his shoulder, now both comforted and repelled by his familiar scent; cigarettes and sweet, musky aftershave. He gingerly patted my back.

'See you soon?' I ventured.

I'd been so excited about the evening, built it up so much in my mind. And yet here we were, cutting through waves of awkwardness like ships seeking solid ground. The space between us felt vast; a yawning cavern of doubt and uncertainty. I didn't understand why he wouldn't talk to me.

'Yeah.' He climbed into the front seat of the car. 'Bye, Heidi.'

'Bye, Jack.'

I watched the taxi pull away. As it disappeared around the corner, Jack wound down the window to wave. There was sadness behind his smile; the glimmer of words left unspoken. My eyes brimmed with tears. I stood there in the empty street until a night nurse knocked on the window, beckoning me back inside.

Chapter Twenty-Two

On the day of discharge, I woke up early. In fact, I don't think I'd really slept. The room was already flooded with sunlight. I checked the time on my phone: 5.30 a.m. Why hadn't the centre ever considered curtains?

I yawned. My body felt heavy and my stump was tingling, the sensation exacerbated by stress and lack of rest. Unsurprising, really, given the skittering of my stomach and the never-ending stream of anxious thoughts. I'd wanted this day to arrive for so long. But now that it was here, I was terrified.

I rolled over and picked up my phone. Several excited messages from Mum, Jenny and Dougie. But nothing from Jack. I hadn't heard from him for two days. I couldn't concentrate on physio. I couldn't concentrate on anything. Instead, I kept replaying that night at the bar over and over in my mind. He'd been kind to me and I'd latched onto him. Over the past weeks, my feelings had steadily risen. That night, they'd overflowed – and he had firmly pulled the plug. I'd imagined something between us; something that didn't exist. Now, I'd scared him away.

Maud's deep breathing filled the room. Punctuated by the occasional snort, it was unapologetically heavy, a sleep uncomplicated by worry.

I couldn't lie there any longer. I hauled myself into the wheelchair, grabbing two towels from the shelves by the door. The rehab staff had placed a strict ban on us using our legs first thing in the morning after Shahid had taken a dawn adventure to the corner shop and was found face down on the pavement surrounded by packets of fags and jumbo sausage rolls.

When I returned to the bedroom, Maud had woken up. Her hospital bed was in an upright position, and she grinned at me broadly. She'd already spritzed her Chanel. The familiar sweetness filled the room. I'd always associate that scent with her.

'Well, look who's dressed up to celebrate their escape,' she said. 'Quite right too, love.'

'Is it too much?'

I'd treated myself to a new outfit for D-Day, a fitted khaki maxi-dress. I stood on one leg to tug it down over my body, ignoring the 'stop, think, missing leg' poster.

'Course not,' Maud answered. 'You look beautiful.' She raised her arms, giving an enormous stretch. I could hear things clicking.

'Ah, that's better. So, what's the plan when you're released?'

'Well, I've got hospital transport booked to take me back to the flat – and then I guess just hang out with my flatmate.'

'Lovely.'

By now, Dougie had sent me six messages and a voice note to declare his excitement. I wished I could summon it too.

'Maud . . .'

'What's up, love?' She squinted at me through the brightness. 'Not getting cold feet are we? Or cold foot, should I say . . . ? Sorry.'

'No, no. Well, not exactly.'

I tied the top half of my hair into a mini-bun, leaving the rest of it loose. I wanted to disguise the fact that I still hadn't had my roots done.

'It's just . . . I haven't heard from Jack for a while.' I tried to keep the tremor from my voice. 'I just wondered if everything's OK?'

'Ah.' She hesitated. 'Well, to be honest love, I think he's still in a bit of a muddle.'

'About the job hunt, you mean?' Maud sighed.

'There's a lot going on. I haven't heard from him recently either. Maybe he just needs a bit of space.'

'Maybe.' But something didn't add up. Maud smiled kindly at me.

'Look, it's a big day for you today, love – you're bound to feel a bit worked up. I would come over there and give you a hug, but, well . . .'

She gestured to her leg, which lay on top of the sheets, her large stump encased in its compression sock. I smiled, grateful for her attempt to lighten my mood. But she hadn't really answered the question. Where was Jack?

'OK,' Tara said. 'Are you ready to have a go at walking, Maud?'

'Is the Pope Catholic?' Maud crowed. She was in her wheelchair but wearing her new prosthetic leg, with Velcro flower-patterned trainers. She'd also put her eighties sweatband on for the occasion. She gave it an experimental ping. 'Time to stand on my own two feet, right, Heidi?'

'Definitely.'

Being my last day, I had no scheduled sessions of my own. Instead, I'd decided to watch Maud's big moment; to support her, to kill time, and to detract from my runaway thoughts. I sat awkwardly on a plinth in the physio gym, legs pressed together. After so many weeks spent in gym clothes, I was unused to the feeling of wearing a dress. The stretchy fabric tugged across my thighs, round and bulging with newly acquired muscle. Rather than worrying about their increase in size, I was proud of the definition; a physical indication of my progress.

'Well, here goes nothing,' Maud said.

She wheeled herself over to the parallel bars. Tara crouched in front of her, pointing out the prosthetic's outer casing and inner liner as she checked the fit of the leg. As usual, her uniform strained over her bosom. She was also wearing non-regulation bright pink nail varnish.

'OK, so when you're ready, you can stand up,' Tara said. 'But remember to hold on.'

'Got it.'

For a woman in her eighties, Maud was amazingly agile. She got up without effort, hands on the bars as she adjusted her weight, shunting from side to side. When she took her first step, it was with the most enormous grin spread across her face.

'I'm doing it, Heidi,' she called joyfully. 'I'm actually bloody doing it!" She raised a triumphant fist and wobbled dramatically. 'I'm walking!'

'Careful,' Tara warned. 'Hands on the bars.'

I gave her a thumbs up. After weeks of waiting for her wound to heal, I understood what a big moment this was. My heart swelled with pride. As Maud made her way back to her wheelchair, I saw her look towards the door; a fleeting but definite glance. Her eyes met mine – and I knew exactly what she was thinking.

Even now, I half-expected him to walk into the gym with his distinctive half stride, half lollop. The Jack I knew wouldn't have missed this. He wouldn't have forgotten. I stared at the doorway, willing him to appear. This was a big day for us both. We needed him. But the corridor remained empty. Maud gave a slight shake of her head, her initial joy wavering with her smile. He wasn't coming.

*

Sitting in my room with the balcony doors flung open, I could hear the men outside, chatting animatedly over their post-mealtime cigarette, a necessary precursor to exercise.

'It's here,' George bellowed as the sound of the car engine floated up through the windows. 'Someone go up and tell her.'

'Don't be daft, mate,' Shahid answered. 'That's the nurses' job, innit.'

Sure enough, Sharon soon appeared in the doorway. Her world-weary face lit up with a rare smile when she noticed my bags, piled up on the wheelchair seat.

'You won't be needing that then, I presume?' She pointed at the wheelchair.

'Hopefully not. I thought I'd give it a new purpose,' I replied.

'Well, it's better than stashing snacks under the cushion.' She smoothed down her uniform, which was crisp and ironed as usual. 'Your taxi's outside, Heidi. You head downstairs and I'll sort your things.'

'Thanks, Sharon.'

I retrieved my walking sticks and headed out into the corridor, casting a final glance behind me at the room where I'd learnt to walk. As I did so, I felt strangely nostalgic. Soon, I thought, this would be someone else's temporary home, a continual rotation of limbs.

Downstairs, a gaggle of staff and patients had formed a human alleyway, standing (or sitting) in two lines at either side of the main entrance. As well as the nurses, Tara and Steph were there, plus Fajah in her hairnet, her creased uniform giving off a distinctive smell of lasagne.

"Ere she comes!' yelled George. He was wearing one of his many polo necks and the smart brown shoes he sometimes sported in the gym. His prosthetic leg hung down from his wheelchair, dragging on the lino floor. Next to him, Bessie lent heavily on the wheelchair. She was grinning broadly.

I hesitated in the middle of the room, unsure what to do next. Was this some kind of tradition? My cheeks grew hot. I looked up and down the line-up. My gaze found Maud's.

'Not my idea, love,' she said with a brief, apologetic shrug. She had her fluffy dressing gown pulled over her exercise clothes, the cord pulled tight, high up on her waist.

'We all wanted to say goodbye,' Tara explained. 'Plus the boys thought this might be a fun way for you to leave.'

'Of course they did.' It made sense. 'Kings of the Conga.'

'So embarrassing,' added Skye. She was standing up, rainbow-coloured fingernails gripping her crutches. 'A.K.A. the perfect send-off.'

I tugged my dress further down, suddenly aware of all eyes on me. My skin prickled at the attention. Gingerly, I began to walk.

'That's it,' George bellowed. 'There she goes!'

The men started to clap. Even Shahid gave it a go, his new prosthetic arm banging animatedly against the palm of his other hand.

I felt a rush of fondness for this barmy bunch. For the past six weeks, they'd irritated and entertained me in equal measure. As I passed slowly through the line, they clapped my shoulder and patted my back. I stopped in front of Skye. I hadn't noticed it before, but we were exactly the same height.

'Good luck,' I told her. 'You're going to do amazing things.'

'As long as I don't get pissed, right?' She grinned.

'Time and a place,' I smiled back. 'But seriously, if I've learnt anything at all, it's that you need to do what makes you happy. And if you haven't figured out what that is yet, honestly, that's totally fine. You will.'

'D'you know what, Heidi Jackson? You're actually pretty cool.'

'I have been told that, yes.'

She rolled her eyes. 'Less cool now. But keep in touch, yeah?'

'Of course.'

Both wobbling slightly, we attempted a brief but meaningful hug. When I got to Maud at the end of the line, she leant forward in her chair, beckoning for me to bend down.

'Be happy, love,' she said into my ear.

I wrapped my arms around her, pressing my face into the soft folds of her dressing gown. Her silver bracelets jingled as she hugged me tightly.

Swallowing my tears, I straightened up and she squeezed my hand. With cheers and applause ringing in my ears, I stepped outside into the sunshine.

Part Three

Part Three

Chapter Twenty-Three

I'd never seen so many balloons. They filled our tiny flat, covering every inch of floor space. As Dougie opened the door, my family threw them into the air.

'Welcome home!' they chorused.

I stopped in the doorway. The first thing I noticed was that the cardboard boxes had gone. Without them, the hallway appeared conspicuously wider; even when covered in balloons. Dougie's stray canvasses had been packed away and the walls were visible for the first time in months, light scratch marks in the cream paintwork now the only reminder of the organisational chaos that had once reined. Dougie saw me looking and gave a very slight shake of his head.

'Come on in,' he said.

He led me into the living room. My parents, Jenny, Mark and Evie were all there, their faces lit up with joy. Glittering banners and Evie's home-made drawings adorned every wall. The tinny portable speaker in the corner played Kool and The Gang's 'Celebration'. A bottle of fizz stood on the side in an ice bucket, surrounded by our mismatching glasses. I took in the smiles and the love around me. And then I burst into tears.

'H, are you OK?' Dougie rushed to my side.

'Sorry, yes.' I sniffed. 'It's just . . . it's so lovely to have you all here.'

'Tears of joy, eh?' Dougie grinned. 'I get that a lot.'

They'd all dressed up for the occasion. Mum wore a pale pink pleated skirt and a floaty blouse, her long grey hair coiled up at her neck with her favourite floral print clip. Jenny had opted for a demure but elegant pinafore dress. Both Mark and Dad had jackets on. Even Dougie wore a crisp white shirt, freshly ironed, not a paint stain in sight.

I plastered a smile across my face. Cautiously, I manoeuvred around the balloons to the sofa. I sat down heavily, and Evie jumped onto my lap. She was wearing a turquoise dress with an enormous tutu skirt and a matching glittery bow at the top of her long ponytail.

'Auntie Heidi, Auntie Heidi!' she bounced up and down.

'Gently, Evie,' said Jenny.

I hugged my niece to my chest, burying my nose in her hair. She smelt like talcum powder and strawberry shampoo.

'I'll crack open the bubbly,' said Dougie. 'Time to toast your escape.'

I kept up the high wattage smile. Best to let them think the tears were purely joy. This was too much, all of it. The decorations and the party clothes and the fizz had created an atmosphere of jubilation I simply didn't feel.

In truth, I was terrified. I felt like my comfort blanket had been ripped away. For so long, my life had been a stream of physical obstacles. I'd overcome them all, reached every milestone, crossed the finish line and now what? I was lost. Because what did I do now? What would happen next? The familiar had become the unfamiliar. I didn't know where I belonged.

I tried my best to look happy. Jenny passed the glasses around while my parents fussed with food – mini sausage rolls, quiche slices and fondant fancies. At the sight of the colourful icing,

Evie began to dance around her grandparents, pretending to 'help'. She didn't take her eyes off the pink cakes. Mark, as usual, was reading the newspaper.

Dougie moved to sit next to me. Despite his smart clothes, he still somehow managed to look endearingly scruffy. He was wearing mismatching socks.

'How does it really feel to be back then?' he asked.

'It's . . . odd.'

'I can tell. A bit much, right?'

Dougie cast his eyes around the small living room come kitchen. My parents were bickering about something food-related, Dad pointing furiously at a plate of mini iced buns. Jenny stood between them, hands on hips, the eternal mediator. Evie made her mermaid toy perform elaborate kamikaze jumps and somersaults from the top of the counters and chairs.

'Yeah,' I replied. 'I'm not used to it, I guess. Everything's a bit overwhelming.'

He nodded and curled his big hand around mine. The warmth was comforting.

'H, I need to tell you something. I'm not moving in with Hal.'

'What?' I turned sharply to face him.

'It hasn't been right for a long time.' He was speaking more quietly now, looking down at his trainers. 'I think I was in denial. I'd been pretending things were fine. But the way he's been with me the past few weeks . . . well, I guess it confirmed what I already knew.'

'You mean it's over?' The shock felt like adrenaline through my veins. My heartbeat sped up.

'Yeah.' He nodded. 'I ended it a few days ago. He was getting annoyed that I hadn't seen him enough; that I was putting off the move and spending all my time with you. He said I was using your accident as an excuse. I was so angry with him, H. I basically exploded.'

I saw the remnants of rage sparkle in his eyes. My gentle, thoughtful best friend usually had an abundance of patience. It would have taken a lot to push him over the edge.

'Hal doesn't get it at all,' he continued. 'He just sits up there in his Canary Wharf palace stroking Princess Diana, not a care in the world except for himself.' He laughed bitterly, mirthlessly. 'Honestly, Princess Diana. I mean, what kind of name is that for a cat, anyway?'

I squeezed his hand. 'Dougie, I'm so sorry it didn't work out.'

'Thanks, H.' He sighed deeply, anger evaporating into the sadness he'd been concealing beneath. 'I know it's the best thing, but it's still tough to get used to.'

'Of course.'

Seeing his slumped shoulders and turned-down mouth, I felt heartbroken on his behalf. I hadn't much liked Hal, but Dougie had. In fact, it was the most enamoured I'd seen him for a long time. Then a tiny voice spoke up from inside me – if I hadn't had the accident, they'd definitely still be together. This was my fault.

'What are you two up to?' Jenny asked, shoving herself next to Dougie on the sofa.

'Just chatting,' Dougie said quickly. He smiled at her, replacing his mask. I held his hand more tightly.

'Oh, good.' She wriggled herself into a more comfortable position and turned to face us. 'Listen, Heidi, I've been thinking about the wedding. I was wondering, do you think you could make us a playlist? I'm sorry to ask so soon after your discharge but Mark's had a go and quite frankly, his song choices are diabolical.'

'I heard that.' Mark looked up from the paper. Jenny shot him an exasperated look.

'Honestly, there's only so much Canadian folk music one wedding can endure.'

'I don't know what you're talking about,' Mark said, without a hint of amusement. 'Corb Lund is one of the great musicians of our time.'

'Corb who?' said Dougie.

'Corb Lund. He mostly sings love songs about horses.' Jenny pushed her hair from her face.

'Niche.'

'Please, Heidi?' Jenny asked.

I paused, taking in my sister's tired eyes and pale face. She raised her prosecco glass to her lips and I saw she'd nibbled her nails to the quick. There was too much worry attached to the wedding; I didn't want to even think about it. And yet, I'd let enough of my loved ones down already. I couldn't upset Jenny, too.

'OK. Sure,' I answered.

'Great, thank you so much.' Jenny exhaled. 'Oh, and another thing . . .'

'Right, everyone.' Mum clapped her hands together. 'Come and help yourselves to food.'

She shot a glance at Evie, who already had a mouthful of crisps and a sausage roll in each hand. Sticking a smile on my face, I rose to join my family.

My first night in my old bed wasn't as blissful as I'd hoped. After several more proseccos with Dougie once my family had left, my head was throbbing, my body unused to the effects of alcohol. I lay there, dizzy and nauseous, willing sleep to come. Every time I closed my eyes, it felt like I was on a carousel, whirling and spinning, out of control. And then I was watching a film of my accident; falling down, over and over. I kept jerking awake.

An hour passed. Then two. The numbers flashed by on my digital clock. When I was a little girl worrying about bad dreams and monsters, Dad had taught me that knowing the time when you're stressed about sleep would only make it worse. But it didn't stop me looking.

At 2 a.m., I downed the glass of water by my bed. My mouth was dry. I reached for my phone. There was still nothing from Jack. I had to do something. I needed answers. Of course, his phone rang to voicemail. Anyone who wasn't drunk or an insomniac would be long asleep by this time. And then I heard his voice.

'Hello, you've reached Jack McNally. I'm not around right now. Please leave a message.'

'Jack, it's Heidi.' I paused, collecting my thoughts. 'I'm sorry to ring so late. It's just I'm back home now and I couldn't sleep and . . .' I was gabbling. I took a breath. 'Actually Jack, I'm angry. I'm seriously pissed off. What the hell has got into you?' The rage boiled from within me, exploding down the line. 'I've been patient with you about your job. I've listened, haven't I? Well, now I'm fed up, Jack. You knew what a big day this was for me. And now I'm home. I'm fucking home, and you don't even care. Know what? I've had enough of it. I'm not wasting my time again. Goodbye.'

I threw my phone down. I felt out of breath, my body humming with adrenaline. Had I done the right thing? Or had I just made everything worse?

Outside, it was quiet save for the distant, barely perceptible hum of traffic. No machines beeping. No nurses talking. And yet, anger pulsated within me. The walls of my small bedroom seemed to press inwards, creeping closer in the darkness.

In hospital, a consultant had told me that I'd probably miss being on the ward, that I'd struggle to adapt when I eventually went home. Back then, his comments had felt like insanity. I'd yearned to be back in familiar surroundings, for my soft bed and a world without continual observation, not to mention those grating call buttons. Yet, lying there in my familiar bedroom, I saw that he was right. Normality seemed so out of reach.

There was too much happening in my head. I grabbed one of my grey furry throw cushions and wrapped my arms around it, the fabric soft beneath my fingers. I pulled the duvet over my head and waited for sleep to release me.

Chapter Twenty-Four

Jenny's hen do was an afternoon tea. Arranged by Natasha (pronounced *Na-tarsh-a* and worse, known to her close friends simply as *Tarsha*), her best friend from school, the idea was for us 'chicks' to meet in the St Pancras Hotel and set up the table with banners and bunting ahead of Jenny's 2.30 p.m. arrival. However, my continual reliance on taxis meant I only just made it in time.

I spotted them all immediately. With the exception of me and Tarsha, the small group was predominantly made up of Jenny's school mum pals, the yummy mummies or Prosecco Ladies, as their WhatsApp group was called. Most of their children had been at Evie's party last year, and I remembered a few faces. There was Julie, the GP with very large teeth, who was part of Jenny's NCT group and who once handed out nit combs in the playground. There was Sarah-Louise, the footballer's wife with bright red hair that flowed down her back like Ariel's (Evie's description). There was Karen who'd just got divorced, Aapti the dental hygienist and Lilia the Russian interpreter, who didn't say much but who was known among the parents for banning all TV and iPads in her home in favour of board games and educational colouring.

'Heidi, darling, over here!'

Tarsha beckoned manically as I entered the large, plush dining room. My prosthetic foot sank into the thick, deep blue carpet. I gritted my teeth, trying to ignore her bright, fake smile. After a mammoth strop and argument with Jenny when she wasn't chosen as a bridesmaid, she'd acted oddly around me. She'd since taken on the hen do as her personal project, which to be honest, was fine by me.

The Prosecco Ladies had decorated the big round table with pink and purple flowers and Cath Kidston napkins. It wasn't my kind of vibe, but I was sure Jenny would approve. She'd been typically strict in her instructions: No cardboard cut-outs of Mark, no butlers in the buff, and absolutely no willy straws or genital-themed games of any kind. To my mind, this was a big shame. Willy Hoopla was one of my favourites.

'Hi, everyone.' I sat down next to Sarah-Louise. 'So sorry I'm late.'

'Don't worry about it, hun.' Sarah-Louise gave my arm a friendly pat. Her fake nails were adorned with purple glitter. No wonder Evie and her pals thought she was a Disney princess.

'You're here before Jenny, that's the main thing,' Tarsha said. Her hair seemed to change every time I saw her; from short braids close to her head to a wild afro, to today's straightened black bob. I wasn't sure about her decision to wear a black pencil skirt to a hen do either. Tarsha was a lawyer, and I hadn't seen her dress down since she was around seventeen and wearing tiny denim hot pants to the under-18s night at Strawberry Moons in Maidstone. She checked her Fitbit and stood up.

'Right, everyone, it's 2.26,' she announced. 'I'm going to head outside and meet Jenny. Remember, when she comes in, we're going to shout surprise. She has no idea you're all here – she's only expecting me. Got it?' There were nods and approving noises around the table.

'Can we open the prosecco yet?' Karen mumbled.

I gave her a sympathetic smile. Despite layers of make-up and bright red lipstick, the bags under her eyes were clear. Bringing up Evie's over-competitive friend, Leah, and her nine-year old brother, Max – who was famed at the school for his football-pitch strops – couldn't be easy, particularly as a single mum. Tarsha ignored her, already turning to leave.

As a general rule, Jenny hated surprises. Even as a child, she made comprehensive lists for birthday and Christmas gifts. Our family knew not to stray from them. She always liked to be in control. Yet this time, her reaction was not what I expected.

She strode into the room, moving across the carpet with poise and purpose in her kitten-heeled sandals. She was wearing a summer tea dress I hadn't seen before, white with pink flowers, cinched in at the waist to accentuate her curvaceous figure. She'd even applied pink lipstick to match.

'Surprise!' we chorused. Jenny stopped. Her eyes widened, her hands flew to her mouth, and then, amazingly, she was crying.

'No way,' she stammered. 'No way. How? Tarsh, how did you pull this off?'

Tarsha smiled coyly and fiddled with a strand of her hair, a display of faux modesty that was definitely anything but.

'It was tricky,' she said. 'You're not an easy person to surprise, that's for sure.'

There were guffaws of laughter. Jenny greeted us all in turn, planting kisses on cheeks and sniffing as the tears subsided. When she got to me, she pulled me into an uncharacteristic hug, my face flattened against her bony chest.

'I'm so glad you're here, Heidi,' she said. There was real feeling in her tone.

'I'm glad I'm here too,' I said. My knee was stiff. I straightened my prosthetic leg. 'At least, most of me's here.'

I was still struggling, still unsure of who I was and where

my place was in the world. I was in limbo, no longer institutionalised and yet just as trapped as ever.

Jenny smiled at my comment, but shook her head very slightly, an echo of the big bossy sister I knew. She still thought it was too early for jokes.

'Sisters, eh?' Sarah-Louise said, although it was a well-known fact among the Prosecco Ladies that there was no love lost between her teenage twin girls and their little sister, Evie's friend Isabella.

'Lovely,' Karen nodded, her eyes firmly on the ice bucket in the centre of the table. Tarsha coughed pointedly, clearly annoyed that she'd lost the spotlight.

'OK, so this sister thing is all great, but how about some fizz, girls?' Tarsha said. 'It is a hen do after all!'

'Yes. Alcohol,' Lilia replied. A few heads turned to look at her. It was the first thing she'd said since I'd arrived.

The prosecco was popped. Inevitably, wedding chat was the talk of the hour. I struggled to summon enthusiasm for the 'wedmin' minutiae, amazed at how excited the rest of them got about the smallest of things. Table plan calligraphy caused a passionate discussion, while Jenny's announcement that she'd booked a hog roast whipped them into a frenzy.

I felt myself glazing over. In recent months, Jenny's spreadsheets, charts and general wedding organisation were pretty much the only thing she talked about. It was clear to me that they were her version of my jokes; a way of moving on, of finding new life amid the heartache and worry. I couldn't help wondering how she'd cope when it was over.

'And how are you doing, Heidi?' Tarsha asked. I blinked, unprepared for the question. They all turned to me.

'Er, yes, good,' I replied. An obvious lie.

A very young waitress trembled as she manoeuvred a three-tier cake stand of tiny sandwiches and mini macarons onto our table.

'She's doing brilliantly,' Jenny said. 'Honestly, no one can believe how much she's progressed.'

'That's great.' Tarsha cast me a disingenuous grin. I wasn't convinced she cared. 'Really great to hear.' There was a cannon of nods and smiles. 'Anyway, Jenny, I'm sure your wedding will be the most wonderful day.' She raised her glass. 'Here's to the rest of your life. To Jenny and Mark.'

'Jenny and Mark,' the group responded.

As I lifted my glass to echo the toast, a strange feeling came over me. It was as though someone else was speaking from my mouth, my lips moving without support from my brain. I blinked, forcing myself back into the moment. But the sensation persisted.

No one had noticed. They were all too busy swapping memories of Jenny and Mark; Tarsha regaling a long and over-complicated tale about visiting Jenny at uni, the two of them getting locked out and having to go to Mark's house and all share a bed. She laughed too loud and she spoke too quickly. My own laughter was delayed, fake and shrill and arriving several seconds after everyone else's. I felt like I was miles away. Willing the sensation to disappear, I rose from my seat.

'I'm just popping for some fresh air,' I said, as casually as I could manage. Knee-deep in nostalgia, the Prosecco Ladies largely ignored me.

'Sure,' Tarsha said vaguely.

Outside, I leant against the grand hotel's red brickwork, watching the traffic crawl up the Euston Road. The noise seemed to reverberate through my body, car horns and distant sirens piercing my thoughts. The smell of petrol caught in my throat. My knee was sore from sitting. By the main door, a porter in a top hat and tails eyed me with suspicion. I watched him cast a lingering glance up and down, then saw his gaze settle on my leg. He looked away quickly.

'Heidi?' It was Jenny.

'Jen, why are you out here?'

'I was worried about you.' She leant gingerly next to me, smoothing down the back of her dress, careful it didn't crease. 'Are you OK?'

'Fine, yeah.' I waved away her concern. 'Just needed some air.'

'Heidi,' she fixed me with a big sister look; stern and worried in equal measure. 'It's OK if you're struggling. You can admit it, you know.'

'Not in front of that lot.'

'Well, no. I understand why you wouldn't want that. But generally – don't feel like you have to be a hero.'

'I know.'

'We have to talk about how we feel more. All of us do.'

I gave her a weak but genuine smile. Out here away from the chatter, my sense of surroundings was starting to return. The scent of fast food and car exhausts pricked my nostrils. The blurred, distant feeling finally began to lift.

'Dad's had a breakdown,' Jenny said quietly.

'What?' Her words slammed into me, knocking me off guard. 'When?'

'A couple of weeks ago.'

'What . . . what happened?'

'Stress, they think.' She spoke in a low, concerned voice. 'He's been working so hard. Look, don't tell Mum and Dad I told you. They'll be furious.'

An ambulance sped past, weaving through the traffic with blue lights and siren blaring. I watched it until I couldn't see it anymore. I thought about my dad; strong, capable, untouchable, now crumpled by fatigue and the weight of parental responsibility. I should have insisted he didn't work. I should have seen it coming.

'It's my fault,' I said finally.

'No.' Jenny put a hand on my arm. 'Don't say that.'

'Of course it is, Jen,' I snapped. 'He was only working because of me.'

'They knew you'd feel like that. It's why they didn't want to tell you. But it's too important, Heidi. I thought you needed to know.'

'So what's happening now?' I felt numb with guilt.

'Mum's looking after him. The doctor's signed him off for a couple of weeks, to give him time to get back on his feet.' She glanced down hurriedly, realising what she'd said.

'Sorry, bad choice of expression.'

For once, I didn't make a joke. I couldn't. In that moment, even the black humour had deserted me; my security mechanism stripped away, leaving me open and wounded.

'And the wedding?' I asked. Jenny shook her head dismissively.

'He'll be fine for that, I'm sure. It's stress. He just needs to rest. Look, Heidi, we can't stay out here much longer. Tarsha will wonder where we've got to. And Karen will be inebriated. Promise me you won't blame yourself?'

She said it as a command, a statement rather than a decision to be made. I had no choice but to nod.

'I'll try.'

But it was too late. The guilt had already carved a deep hole inside me. I felt hollow and broken. The damage of my accident extended so far beyond me, a ripple effect of grief and despair that I was unable to stem or control. How many more lives would I be responsible for ruining? Wordlessly, Jenny linked my arm and led me back inside; two damaged souls with a macaron tower to demolish.

Chapter Twenty-Five

Stepping back into the rehab centre was like stepping back in time. From the moment I sat down in the airless, character-less reception area, I could feel old emotions resurfacing – the fears, the anguish and the feeling of a journey as yet incomplete. Above me, I knew, a new patient was sleeping in my bed; pulling the clinical curtains around them each night, travelling a parallel path. The thought provoked a mixed reaction. From a distance, I was relieved and amazed at my progress. I knew objectively how far I'd come. Yet a small part of me felt a poignant nostalgia being back here, like someone else had stolen my home.

'Hello stranger,' a voice called. Maud was walking, yes, walking, down the long corridor towards me. She made slow, doddering progress, both hands clutching a Zimmer frame. The sight of her upright cheered me. I needed something to alleviate my sadness.

'Steady.' Tara walked behind her, hands held out like a deep fielder. 'Remember to concentrate.'

'Oh, rubbish.' She took a hand off the frame and wobbled spectacularly. Tara reached out to grab her. 'Tara, can you give me a breather? I want to talk to Heidi.'

'Of course.' The physio smiled at me. 'You're looking good, Heidi. One stick now, is it?'

'Yep.' I patted the walking stick beside me. I'd gone for an old-fashioned wooden one. It was marginally cooler than the metal hospital issue sticks. 'I'm getting there.'

'That's great to hear.' She guided Maud towards me, helping her plop down into a chair. 'I'll be back shortly to pick you up, Maud. Don't think you're going to get away with slacking.'

'Never, Miss.' Maud winked at her. 'Star pupil, that's me.'

'So, are you walking all the time now?' I asked. Maud was wearing her exercise headband again. It brought back a rush of fond memories.

'Mostly,' she replied. 'I take it off for an hour or so a day, y'know, just to let the old stump settle. And you? What are you doing back here so soon? Couldn't keep away, could you?'

'Nope.' I grinned. She always knew how to cheer me up. 'Actually, I'm back to see Bryony.'

'OK.' She didn't probe, and I was grateful. I didn't really fancy a pre-therapy therapy session.

There was a comfortable silence between us. I was surprised to find I missed the safety and predictability of the rehab routine. I missed Fajah scowling in her hairnet. Bizarrely, I even missed The Diabetics. But most of all, I missed laughing with Maud. She was a key part of my recovery, a dear, if unlikely, friend.

'So guess what, I'm out of here next week,' she said. 'Home at last.'

'That's great!' Just then, an idea struck me. 'Look, Maud, it's Jenny's wedding coming up.' Maud slapped her hands against her thighs.

'Oh, so it is! How's that all going? I hope she's not putting too much pressure on you . . .'

'She's got a bit better,' I replied.

'Well, good. No one likes a bossy boots, so they don't.'

'Exactly.' I took a deep breath. 'Maud, this might be a totally weird idea, but seeing as you're going to be home soon and everything, well, I wondered if you wanted to be my plus one?'

'Your plus what, love?'

'Plus one. Jenny said I'm allowed to bring a guest to the wedding, but seeing as I don't have a boyfriend . . .' I trailed off. But Maud had understood.

'A wedding guest!' she crowed. 'What will I wear? Oh, Heidi, I would love to come! Are you sure it's not odd, you bringing an old lady along?'

'Not at all,' I told her. 'In fact, there's honestly no one else I'd rather invite.' I meant it, too.

'Well then, if that's the case, I would be honoured to be your guest, Heidi Jackson. I might even buy a new hat.'

'Maud,' Tara called. She poked her head out of the physio gym at the end of the corridor. 'Break time's over.'

'Christ, she works me hard, this one,' Maud said. But she was smiling. She heaved herself to standing and took my hands in hers. 'I'll see you soon, Heidi. You've made an old lady very happy.'

'Not as happy as you've made me.' I whispered.

I looked into her kind, crinkled face; moss green eyes filmed with wisdom and fun. They say you find friendship in the most unlikely of places. They couldn't have been more spot on.

The counselling room hadn't changed. Same sickly green walls, same drooping houseplant, same peeling posters of sunrises and ships on the waves. 'Life is a voyage, not a destination,' read one. I sat down on one of the fraying cushioned chairs. My own sea was unpredictable and choppy. I felt like I'd been thrown overboard.

'So, what's on the agenda today?' Bryony asked.

'Guilt,' I said.

It felt strange being back in the rehab centre. My own world was evolving, a future developing despite the fear and doubt. Yet here, the routine ticked onwards, the schedules never-ending as a continual rotation of people and prosthetics moved through the system. I thought about the stranger in what was once my bed. They'd no doubt be wondering how they'd cope, just as I'd done just weeks before. We all had different lives and situations, but the cycle of emotions remained largely the same.

'Guilt?' Bryony folded her arms over her sizeable bosom. 'In what way?'

'It's my fault.' I'd learned now to get straight to the point. There was no use dodging the issue. Bryony could always tell. 'Everyone around me is struggling – and it all comes back to me. How do I deal with that?' Even as I spoke, the emotion bubbled within me. 'How do I stay strong and help my family when I've caused all this in the first place?'

I told her about Dougie, about Jenny and Dad. I told her how they'd hidden their true feelings, attempting to protect me when in fact it only made me feel worse. Bryony listened intently as always, nodding occasionally, but otherwise silent. When my tirade ended, I took in a shuddering breath. I felt like I'd poured my problems out in front of her. I could see her wading through them, almost.

'OK,' she said finally. 'I can see why this is difficult. Remember, though, it's not just you feeling guilty.'

'What do you mean?'

'Well, sometimes, the people closest to the trauma victim harbour unprecedented guilt too.'

Her grey hair seemed even bigger than usual today, sticking up at all angles. I wondered how many people's grief and worry those curls had absorbed over the years.

'But why?' I asked. 'Why would they feel guilty? It was nothing to do with them.'

'They love you. They'd do anything to take your pain away, right?'

'Right . . .'

'So maybe they feel guilty it was you who had the accident. Maybe, on a deeper level, they wish it could have been them instead.'

I thought about Dad. Strong and largely silent throughout my life, he didn't need to voice his love for me to know that his constant reassuring presence was there; that under his watch, nothing bad would ever happen. That was how he'd always wanted us to feel. That protective instinct didn't just vanish as we grew up. Once again, Bryony had a point.

'My Dad would definitely think that,' I told her. 'But what do I do about it?'

'There's an exercise I sometimes like to do. It's about appreciation. I want you to write him a letter.'

'OK . . .' It seemed a bit of an odd idea. I waited for her to explain.

'Write down everything you love and appreciate about him. Often, we take for granted the things we feel about the people we love. We assume they know. As a result, we very seldom tell them. It doesn't need to be long, just a side of A4. But trust me, it works.'

'So then I read it to him?'

'That's the next stage.'

'I . . . I don't know.'

The idea of talking feelings of any kind with Dad was alien. Mum was the emotions expert, the one we went to to discuss school stress, boy dramas or any other internal conflict. I couldn't imagine how it would go down with Dad. It would probably make both of us feel worse. But Bryony was nodding.

'Read it out to him. Don't just post it or hand it over – it won't have the same impact. Watching his face as he takes in the words will benefit both of you.'

'I don't think he'll appreciate it,' I said. 'I mean, it's a nice idea in theory, but my dad he's, well, he's not really like that.'

'Why? Because he's too closed? Too shy? Too awkward with his feelings?'

'All of the above.'

'Oh, Heidi.' A knowing smile played across her lips. 'If you knew how many times people had said that to me. That's the point. The letter of appreciation is often quite an uncomfortable experience, for both parties. But it works. People like to know what their good qualities are. Your dad will remember what you said for a long time.'

'But how will it help?' The idea made me nervous. 'I still don't really understand.'

'He'll know you still have a high opinion of him. He'll know you don't blame him. And in acknowledging that, hopefully he'll then stop blaming himself.'

'That makes sense, I guess.'

'You can take your time with it. I'm not saying you have to go home and do it tonight. But mull it over, OK? I promise it's a useful exercise.'

'OK. I will.' I smiled at her. 'But what about my own guilt?'

'Well, what do you think is the source of it?' I paused, considering.

'I guess, maybe it's because I could have avoided it,' I said. 'Falling, I mean. It's so stupid – who loses their leg by tripping over?' I gave a bitter laugh, more regret than mirth. Bryony didn't smile back.

'Heidi, it happened,' she replied simply. 'No amount of reminiscing will change that.'

'I know, but if Alexander had caught me . . .' I stopped. Alexander. His face appeared suddenly in my mind, as clear a memory as ever. I shuddered.

'The man on the path?' Bryony prompted. I nodded.

'Yeah. Sorry, I was just wondering, well, I was thinking that maybe . . . maybe I need to see him.'

'And that would help?'

'I think so. Well, I don't know. But it's worth a try, right?'

'Heidi, you do what you think you need to do. You're more self-aware than many of my clients. I know you worry that you've changed, that you don't know yourself any more, but honestly? I'd say the opposite's true.'

'Thank you, Bryony.' I felt a rush of fondness. 'Really, that means more than I can say.'

'It's true. You know who you are. The future, the worries about what might happen, they all pale into insignificance in comparison. You have a very strong core. Your coping mechanisms are all there inside you.'

I smiled at her then, a real, genuine smile. Because I knew what I had to do next. Sometimes, we all had to break out of our comfort zones. It was time to step into the unknown.

Chapter Twenty-Six

Waterhouse Taylor was enormous; an imposing structure of concrete and glass, dominating the surrounding landscape. I got out of the Uber and looked up at Alexander Mitchell's office, leaning heavily on my walking stick. My legs were trembling.

Craning my neck, I gazed up at twenty or so rows of identical, shining windows. Behind them, I could see desks and ergonomic chairs, a pale carpet and the odd pot plant. One floor, the second, had table football by the window. I wondered which floor was his.

'Scuse me.' A fierce looking man with a handlebar moustache barged into my shoulder. The brazenness of his movement made me flinch.

'Oh, sorry,' I stammered.

I moved aside. I was right in the centre of the pavement. The man gave a curt nod. As he passed, he swung his briefcase and it hit my prosthetic leg. The unusual 'thunk' noise caused him to look down in confusion. Spotting my leg, he did a brief but obvious double take before hurrying on his way. I felt even more shaken than before.

I had to do this. I took a deep breath and tried to re-summon my certainty. It seemed to be buried by nerves.

The revolving doors were my first problem. Much like the

escalators, it seemed as though they moved more quickly than they ever had before, a trip hazard waiting to happen. I stood and watched as a stream of people, mostly young men, streamed through them without hesitation. Some were on their phones. Some looked hurried and pushed the doors with force as they entered, willing them to go even faster.

To the right was a door marked 'goods entrance.' As I paused, two couriers with large cardboard boxes pressed a buzzer on the side. The door opened. Without thinking about it any more, I followed them in.

Waterhouse Taylor's reception was a grand affair of leather sofas, black marble walls and several giant TV screens depicting the weather and time zones of every country across the world. On the wall behind the main desk, there was a W and a T in giant gold lettering. At least six receptionists sat in a long line, all wearing smart black blazers and phone headsets that reminded me of the Spice Girls. Visitors queued up behind a snaking red rope as though waiting for some sort of tourist attraction. Two security guards, standing with their hands behind their backs, flanked the entrance. Their expressions were somehow attentive yet utterly fed up at the same time.

My heart was thumping. I loitered for a moment, wondering whether to just turn back. Maybe I'd feel better if I didn't see him; if I simply tried to forget. What would I even say? The the nearest guard, called out to me.

'Ma'am? Can we help you?'

'No. I mean yes, maybe,' I stuttered. 'I've come to see someone who works here.'

'Join the line,' he said, pointing.

His face moved promptly back to its resting position, like a waxwork or wind-up toy. Though my legs felt shaky and phantom pain sliced through my prosthetic foot, I had no choice but to obey.

'I've come to see someone,' I told the peroxide blonde receptionist. With her hair scraped back into the highest, tightest ponytail, the woman appeared permanently surprised.

'Who?' the woman said. It was a question, but it sounded like a statement.

'Alexander Mitchell.'

Saying his name out loud induced another wave of nausea. I inhaled. I exhaled. I needed to calm down.

'Right.' The receptionist tapped heavily on her keyboard. Her long, acrylic nails were painted in a garish shade of glittery lilac. 'Is he expecting you.'

Another question-statement. I shook my head. 'No, he's not.'

'Right.' More tapping. 'Well according to his calendar, he has a meeting in thirty-five minutes. How long do you need?'

'Oh, thirty-five minutes is more than enough.'

'Right. Your name?'

'Miss . . . erm . . . Miss Jackson.'

The woman typed some numbers into the phone and adjusted her headset.

'Mr Mitchell?'

So he was here. My hands gripped the walking stick tighter. The handle slid against my palm.

'Yeah, there's a Miss Jackson in reception for you,' the receptionist said. 'No, it's not. Yeah. She says it won't take long. Right. OK.'

She looked up at Heidi. 'Take a seat.'

'Thank you.'

Somehow, I got myself over to a sofa. I pressed my hands between my thighs, willing the shaking to stop.

I scrolled through my phone even though there was nothing to see. I tapped my left foot. I couldn't stop fidgeting.

'Miss Jackson?'

It was as if he'd materialised in front of me. I looked up and jumped. His white-blond hair stood out against the shiny black reception. Like all the other men in the building, he wore a sharp suit; his was navy blue, with a white shirt, brown shoes and a pale blue tie which was close to the colour of his eyes. I noted a plain gold wedding band on his fourth finger. Had that been there before? I couldn't remember.

'Yes, hi,' I said, trying to keep the tremor from my voice.

Alexander held out his hand. He gave off a cool, confident air; this was his territory. His expression was neutral, tinged with confusion. He hadn't worked it out. I took a deep breath and rose from my seat. My leg felt stiff and sore.

'Call me Heidi,' I said.

'Heidi. What can I do for you?'

I remembered that voice, calm with an undertone of ego. For a moment, I was transported back to the path, back to his polite yet panicked tone close to my ear, his rushed apology; his abandonment.

'I'm sorry, have we met before?'

He stood there, head on one side. I forced the memories away. I needed to focus on the present.

'Yes,' I said quietly. If he had been stalking me, he was doing a pretty good job of playing dumb.

'You'll have to forgive me, I don't remember.'

'Forgive you,' I muttered. That very much depended on what happened next. I paused, allowing Alexander another moment of contemplation.

'If I mentioned the canal path near Stratford?' I said. I bent to adjust my trousers, ensuring the pole of my prosthetic leg could be seen.

His pale eyebrows furrowed. His lips tightened. He looked down at my leg and an expression of forced politeness crossed his face.

'I'm very sorry, I don't recall.' His tone was measured, almost as though he was speaking to a child.

'But . . .'

I could feel my emotions spiralling out of control. There was so much I wanted to say. But I could feel his attention waning; he clearly just thought I was mad. My mouth opened and closed. I was desperate to tell him – and yet his blankness kept the words inside me. If he really didn't remember, there was no way he'd believe me. After all, who had their leg amputated after tripping over on a flat path? If I didn't know better, I would have dismissed such a story myself. Alexander shook his head, more decisive now.

'No, I'm sorry. You must have me confused with someone else. Look, it's a busy day. I really should be getting back.'

'Please,' my voice was trembling, almost a whisper. 'Don't leave.'

'Have a good day, Miss Jackson.'

And with a final nod, he was gone.

Across the road was a tiny square. It was the kind of green area that had been planted specifically for the purpose of office workers and their packed lunches, with wooden benches around the outside and a patch of grass in the middle. Balancing my stick beside me, I sat down on a bench. At this time of day, it was empty, save for a young woman walking a French bulldog and a gaggle of pigeons arguing over a discarded bacon roll.

On the other side of the road, Waterhouse Taylor gleamed, rays bouncing off the huge glass windows. I imagined Alexander back at his desk and rage rose up inside me. I felt it charging through my body, pushing and scratching with red-hot claws. Had he really had no idea who I was? The blankness in his expression suggested so. For him, it was a moment in time like any other, a fleeting decision before he'd got on with his day. Maybe I should have pushed him more. Maybe I should have just come out with it. And yet, the shock of his reaction had thrown me, rendered me incapable of rational thought. I felt numb, too stunned to even cry. He simply didn't care.

I raised my face towards the sun. A tiny plane made its smoky trail across the sky. I had a sudden urge to call Jack. He'd know what to say. On instinct, I even pulled out my phone; but then I remembered. He didn't want to know either. But I knew who could make me feel better.

The phone rang for ages. I imagined her scrabbling around in her floral make-up bag where she kept her brick of a mobile, its tinny, piercing ringtone filling the air. When she answered, she was out of breath.

'Hello. This is Maud McNally speaking.'

'Maud, it's Heidi.'

'Heidi!' Her voice was full of fondness. I wished she was in front of me, reaching out with bracelets jangling as she pulled me in for a hug. 'Lord, I'm glad I remembered how to answer this thing, so I am. How are you, my darling? How is it being back out there in the real world?'

'Daunting,' I replied. There was no point trying to sugar-coat for Maud. 'It's hard.'

'Of course it is, love. It was never going to be easy.'

Her soft Irish accent soothed me. In an instant, I was back in that room, laying opposite her with the windows thrown open, her voice lilting and cheerful like a summer's day. I could practically smell her Chanel down the phone. The nostalgia overwhelmed me. I felt choked.

'Heidi?' she said gently. 'You still there, love?'

'Yeah,' I managed. 'Still here.'

'So listen, they say I'll be out of here by the end of next week.'

'That's great.'

'Can't come bloody soon enough, let me tell you.' She gave a little 'ooof' noise. I could tell she was shifting her position in bed. 'Honestly, Heidi, the old woman I'm sharing with now is deathly boring. The other day, she asked if I wanted to sit in the dining room and listen to Andrew Lloyd Webber's *Greatest Hits*. I mean, come on. I may be eighty-two but I'm not bloody dead yet.'

I found myself smiling. 'Well, at least she's trying.'

'Trying my patience, is what she is. Really, it's not the same here now. I miss you, gal.'

'I miss you too.' I took a deep breath. 'Have you seen Jack recently?'

'Oh he's been here a bit, yeah.' Nerves flickered in my stomach. 'Still agonising over that job my Billy found him. Honestly, I don't know why – he needs a job. If he doesn't decide soon they'll need to recruit someone else.'

'I did try to tell him that,' I answered. But it had been the last time I saw him.

'I dunno, Heidi. He's a funny boy sometimes, that one.' Maud gave a chesty sigh. 'Honestly, there's no wonder Lara gets fed up.'

'Lara?'

I thought back through my conversations with Jack. I was sure he'd never mentioned a family member with that name. Unless . . . no. I must be wrong.

'Mind you,' Maud continued, oblivious to the tightening noose of her words, 'I'm not sure that's all rosy since she kissed that bloke from her work. So awful, being betrayed like that.'

Betrayed. The word brought a heavy realisation. I felt sick. In the café that day, Jack had spoken about betrayal. In a moment, it all made sense. My emotions whirled; sympathy and sorrow hand in hand, the reality horribly, bitterly clear.

So that was why he hadn't wanted to kiss me. I couldn't trust myself to speak.

'Heidi?' Maud ventured.

'He never told me he had a girlfriend.' I spoke in a whisper, fearful my voice would crack. On the grass, a sunbathing girl was laughing with her friends. The piercing sound penetrated my skull.

'Oh, love . . .' Maud's voice wavered.

'I don't understand.' The words tripped from my mouth, pulling me down, further down, a swirling vortex of questions. 'Why didn't he tell me?'

'Maybe he thought you knew?'

'No.' I shook my head, the tears falling now. 'He didn't.'

'Jack's a good lad, love, really,' Maud said. 'He doesn't always think. He's been that way ever since he was little. Head in the clouds, you know . . .'

She sounded like she was on the verge of crying, too. Her voice was so faint. I imagined her then, her tiny figure propped up against the pillows of her hospital bed. I shouldn't take it out on her.

'Look, Maud,' I managed, 'this is a lot to process.'

'I'm sure.' She exhaled deeply. 'Oh, Heidi. I thought he could be a friend to you – someone the same age to help you move on with life, you know? I had no idea you didn't know about Lara. Ah Christ, I'm so sorry . . .'

'It's fine,' I interrupted. I took a big, shuddering breath as another sob caught in my throat. 'Maud, I'm going to have to go.'

'Of course,' she said softly. 'But call me again soon, won't you?'

We said goodbye and the sobs wracked my body. The sunbathing girls looked up in alarm. I no longer cared who saw me; I'd lost control. My arms were prickled with goose-bumps and I pulled my denim jacket closer. I felt numb with betrayal, as though my newly grown self-confidence had been snatched and tossed away like confetti. Of course Jack wouldn't ever fall for someone like me. He was just being kind, he'd felt sorry for me all along. I was damaged goods; a figure to be pitied, not loved. I was a fool.

'Heidi?'

The voice was familiar. Wearily, I looked up. Every muscle in my body ached. When I saw the face, I rubbed my eyes, raw and blurred with tears. Alexander Mitchell was standing in front of me. He had his hands in his pockets and a sheepish look on his face. He looked me straight in the eye as he spoke.

'Heidi, I remember.'

His words were quiet but sincere. He adjusted his weight from side to side as he spoke. But he never broke eye contact. I sniffed, struggling to regain composure. This was too much; all of it.

'You . . . you what?'

'That day on the canal path.' He sat down heavily next to me. 'I remember, at least I think I do. You were jogging. You fell. That was you, right?'

I nodded, too exhausted from my conversation with Maud to formulate a response. Around me, the familiar noises of the park seemed incongruous to the weight of the space between us; the casual lunchtime chatter and rustling breeze in the trees.

'I tried to catch you.' Alexander's voice wavered. He'd lost all the bravado he'd shown in his office reception. His guard was down. 'I tried, but I couldn't. I didn't reach out in time. And I had no idea that . . . that . . .' He gestured at my leg. 'Oh, God. It's so awful.'

'Where did you go?' I asked. My voice was a whisper. He had to lean in to hear me. 'Why did you leave?'

'Oh jeez, I don't know.' He sighed heavily. 'I was going to the station. I was running late. But if I'd known that you . . . I never would have . . .'

'You left me,' I said. The tears still ran down my cheeks. I didn't bother wiping them away. Let him see the emotion. Let him see the devastating struggle. 'I was in so much pain. I was screaming. You left me on my own.'

'What?' His piercing eyes widened. Their intense pale blue frightened me. 'No! A girl came along. She stayed. She helped.'

'A girl?' He must be lying. It had been the two of us on the path. No one else was around.

'Yes.' Alexander spoke with certainty. 'Look, I know I probably shouldn't have left. That was a mistake – and it will haunt me forever. But Heidi, you must know that you were never alone. You can't think that I . . .' He put his head in his hands. 'Oh, Christ. You passed out before she came. You think I abandoned you there.'

'You did . . .' I said. But I was less certain now.

'No, Heidi.' He was gentle but firm. 'I didn't. I left, yes. But you were never alone.'

I tried to think back. I remembered him on the phone to the ambulance, his face bending over me, his concerned expression. I remembered footsteps in the dirt, a flash of pink and black. Had that been the girl he'd mentioned? I searched deep through my memories, desperate for verification. But there was only blackness; a yawning memory gap.

'Did you – were you in the hospital a few days later?' I asked. My mind clung to fragmented strands of memory. 'The Royal London in Whitechapel, in the café. I saw a man who looked just like you.'

Alexander shook his head. 'No. I'm afraid not. I've never been to that hospital.'

'Then. . . the Tube? Euston station – on the escalator?' I could tell I was gabbling, tripping over my words in my desperate search for truth. 'It would have been two months after that day. I'm so sure I saw you. . .'

'I'm really sorry, but it couldn't have been me.' There was finality in his tone. 'I've been away, you see. I went to Thailand for two weeks with Kate – my wife. And anyway, I try to avoid the Tube whenever I can. I much prefer to walk.'

I looked at him, noticing then the dusting of faded, flaky sunburn across his pale cheeks. My face flushed with hot emotion and the noise of the traffic grew louder, racing like my heart in my ears. Confusion reigned as I tried frantically to realign my thoughts. Because I could tell that he was telling the truth. Alexander Mitchell had never been following me. I had imagined it all.

Chapter Twenty-Seven

When I got home, I shut myself in my room. There were too many thoughts in my head. Alexander and I had parted on amicable, if strained, terms. He'd wished me well and I'd apologised again, trying hard to hide the tears of embarrassment that had crept behind my eyes. After so long looking out and wondering, it felt like something of a relief; an exorcised demon laid to rest, leaving an exhausting clarity in its wake. We hadn't said we'd keep in touch. To be honest, I didn't want to either. Maybe now, I'd stop seeing him in other people's faces, or snatched glimpses in crowds. Maybe now, I could move on.

But Jack was another story. I sat on my bed and pulled my blanket over my prosthetic leg. I couldn't even look at it. I didn't want to go out that night. Like, *really* didn't want to. I'd been invited to Caitlin's birthday with the Conscience crew, and the last thing I wanted was to see them again. It meant another night of pretending, of building a wall of fake confidence and forcing myself into another performance of Old Heidi, arguably the best acting I'd ever done. I knew they'd ask about Jack, and I wasn't ready to answer. I felt cheated, foolish and irrationally heartbroken. He'd never promised me anything more than friendship – so why did I feel so bereft?

In the end, it was Dougie who forced me out. He'd hugged me, handed me a tissue and told me gently but firmly to go and put some make-up on. That's how I ended up in Euphoria bar in Soho, wearing a long black maxi-dress and a bright pink lipstick that didn't match my mood. I plastered a smile on my face, wondering how much chit-chat I could realistically get away with until I ordered a taxi home.

'There we are. Another G&T.'

Dougie lurched over and placed my third – or was it fourth? – drink in front of me. He wore an Adidas polo and his hair was loose for once, dreads spilling across his face as he drunkenly gesticulated.

'Obviously I got a double. You need it.'

'Thanks.'

I swung my legs out of the booth, allowing him to squeeze in next to me. I needed to be on the end so I could stretch out. It hurt to sit with my knee bent for too long. Dougie patted my arm and raised his glass to mine.

'To new starts,' he said. 'And to freedom from idiot men.'

We clinked our glasses together. But I didn't feel like celebrating. Each time he referenced Hal, it was like a knife to my stomach. I knew Dougie didn't blame me, but I also knew he was wrong. His loyalty to me had broken his relationship. I'd never get away from that.

'Honestly, it'll do you good to be out, H,' he said, slurring. 'I knew there was something weird about Jack.' He couldn't keep the hint of smugness from his voice. 'I sensed it from the start.'

'Don't.' I didn't want to dissect his behaviour. I'd done enough of that in my own head. 'Let's just not talk about it.'

'Sure. If that's what you want,' he said. 'Distraction is the best cure for heartbreak anyway. Look, remember when Rich broke up with me?'

'How could I forget?'

It was scarred into my memories forever. Dougie's previous relationship – the one before Hal – had come to a dramatic end. It had resulted in him telling a hen party that he was a professional rapper, demonstrating said rapping and finishing the evening by snogging the mother of the bride in a car park. I allowed myself a small smile. Dougie pounced on it immediately.

'That's more like it,' he said. 'How old was that woman again?'

'Fifty-three.'

'Christ. But the point is, you need one of those nights you'll look back on and laugh at. A healing hangover.'

'There is no such thing,' I said.

I swigged my drink. It was like dousing a raging fire with petrol; the hurt and the emotion still burning deep inside me, refusing to be quelled. I felt light and heavy at the same time. My body still wasn't used to alcohol.

'Course there is,' Dougie answered. As I looked at him, his face blurred slightly at the edges. 'Friends always help. Wait there, I need a wee.'

Nursing my drink, I glanced around the booth. Several rounds of sambuca down, it was that time of the evening where emotions surfaced; emboldened by alcohol and hiding behind bottles. Ally and Laura were deep in what seemed to be a highly amusing conversation, Ally's laugh even louder than ever, a high-pitched cackle that seemed to echo around the bar. Meanwhile, Caitlin had her arm looped around a broad-shouldered girl I didn't recognise, stroking her arm clumsily as she whispered into her ear.

'This is Donna,' she slurred at me. The girl smiled. She was plump and plain, with large tortoiseshell glasses that covered her round face. Skinny Caitlin looked tiny beside her.

'Nice to meet you,' I replied. But they clearly weren't interested in conversation. The next time I looked, they were kissing.

'All right, Jackson?' Ben slid into the booth. He reached out to hug me, his muscular forearms tanned and flecked with pale blond hair.

'Hey, Ben.'

'Billy no-mates, are you?' He gave me a relaxed smile, oozing confidence and sunshine. When alcohol was involved, Ben became even more Aussie, his accent noticeably pronounced.

'I'm waiting for Dougie,' I said, or at least tried to say. My words didn't seem to be working properly.

'Fancy a dance?'

'What?' I couldn't hear. He leaned in, speaking loudly and pointedly.

'A dance!' He pointed to the small dance floor, already thick with swaying crowds.

'No, I don't think . . .'

'Ahh, c'mon mate!' He stood up suddenly, pulling at my arm. 'What ya gonna do, sit here on your own all night? It'll be fun!'

I looked around the table. Ally and Laura were having an intense heart to heart. Caitlin and Donna continued to snog, their hands everywhere, oblivious to the world around them. I could see Dougie by the bar, chatting away to a tall Latino-looking man. He'd clearly forgotten to come back.

'I'll look after you, promise.' Ben tugged my arm again. 'Let's go.'

Too drunk to argue, I downed the rest of my gin and allowed myself to be led onto the crowded dance floor. There, a bald DJ inexplicably wearing rosary beads nodded his head in time to the music. The nondescript beat jarred through my skull. I tried to concentrate on where I was putting my feet. I felt short of breath and panicky. One wrong step and I knew I'd fall.

'Just relax,' Ben said into my ear. He slid his hands around my waist. We began to move.

The music was loud. It shot through my body, my stump twinging as I struggled to remain upright. It brought buzzing, painful relief; it drowned out my thoughts. The dance floor smelt of warm bodies and sweet dry ice. A smoky haze filled the air. I tried to adjust my footing, shifting my weight onto my good side. The number of people around was making me increasingly claustrophobic. The gin swirled in my stomach.

When Ben moved in to kiss me, I let it happen, closing my eyes as multi-coloured lights flashed and faded around us. He was hungry with desire, his tongue in my mouth, hands in my hair, roaming fingers leaving scratchmarks on my neck. I didn't have the energy to refuse him. Instead, I slumped against him, giving in. Ben pulled me closer, kissed me harder. I didn't resist.

When I opened my eyes again, the room wouldn't stay still. The music was throbbing and distant; the bass jarred my skull. I felt woozy but powerful, as though I could conquer the world. I raised my face to the lights, the colours flashing and dancing. I held my hands up and started to sway. My body took over my mind. There was no fear, no worry. There was only the music.

'Heidi.'

I was aware of someone calling my name, a faint voice, a familiar outline. Dougie.

'This is Mateo,' he was saying. 'He's a dancer.'

The man next to him had coffee hair and caramel skin. His spine was straight and poised, his shoulders thrust backwards, chest out. He took my hand in a firm handshake. Ben wound his arm around my waist more tightly.

'So, you want to learn to dance,' Mateo said. 'Your friend, he tell me.'

'N-no . . .'

I didn't want to think about the list. I didn't want to think about anything. I closed my eyes and lurched sideways, almost losing my balance.

'Woah there.' Ben grabbed me. 'Steady, girl.'

'No dancing?' Mateo asked.

'She does.' Dougie nodded eagerly. 'It's on this list she wrote – stuff she wants to achieve. H, I've found you a teacher.'

I looked down. In a rush of nausea, I remembered. My prosthetic leg was hidden beneath the folds of my maxi-dress, ungainly, and ugly. As suddenly as it had started, my euphoria crashed. The lights were too bright, the music too loud. The beat felt like punches. My eyelids flickered open and shut. I was struggling to maintain my focus.

'I don't want to dance,' I slurred. 'I don't want to do anything.' My words weren't coming out properly. I repeated them again, unsure if I'd made my point.

'Babe, you're drunk. Come home with me,' Ben said. His face was close to mine, his beer breath hot on my neck. 'Let's have some fun.' He ran a hand down my back, coming to rest on my bum. 'It can be a first for both of us. I've never had sex with an amputee. But I'm into it. Is there a release button on that leg?'

'No.' I jerked my head away. The thought of taking my leg off, of him seeing my stump, invoked a terror greater than any other. I couldn't imagine ever showing it to anyone. I would never be sexy again.

'Mate, leave her,' Dougie warned.

'I'm going to the toilet,' I said. I could feel tears coming. I wanted to be alone.

'Need help?' Ben asked. He stroked my shoulder. This time, my reaction wasn't submission. It was revulsion. Clumsily, I pushed his arm away.

'Get off me.'

I took one step forwards, then another. My vision had somehow cracked. I blinked, trying to right the world again. Coloured lights and swirling faces blurred in front of me. There was a fizzing sensation in my head. It seemed to tingle all the way down my body, my stump still pulsing with pain.

I told myself to breathe. Halfway to the toilets, a passing man's flailing elbow bashed into my shoulder.

'Whoops, sorry,' he shouted.

I tried to regain my balance, but my legs buckled beneath me. And then I was on the floor, beer and tears running into my hair.

Chapter Twenty-Eight

The next day was Evie's birthday party. I didn't want to go, my hangover and my embarrassment raw, the darkness in my head thicker than ever. My head was throbbing as I dutifully rang the bell of Jenny and Mark's Kent home. Just ten minutes down the road from the house where I'd grown up, the new estate was populated with near-identical square brick houses. Unlike their next-door neighbour who seemed to be breeding stone animals, they'd opted for a clean, simple front garden. Instead of squirrels, hedgehogs and bizarrely, a large concrete cow, my sister's plain gravel path led across a manicured front lawn. There was a pink glittery banner taped across the front door.

Standing on the doorstep, the sound of little girls shrieking from within made me wince. Mark answered the door, his expression strained behind his tortoiseshell glasses.

'Hey, Heidi,' he said. 'Thanks for coming.'

'No worries.' I forced a smile.

I was still feeling overwhelmed by the night before, the hangover taking its toll on my emotional state. A fog of sadness permeated my thoughts. It felt like I was standing on the top of a mountain, looking down into the valleys beyond. Sometimes, the horizon was clear, a lush green countryside stretching out in front of me. Yet often, I couldn't see my hand in front of me. Today was one of those days.

'As you can hear, it's a bit manic in there,' Mark said. 'I landed from Frankfurt this morning and I must admit I'm slightly struggling.'

He did look tired. I wondered what Jenny thought about him having had yet another business trip. He'd almost missed his only daughter's birthday.

There was a sudden squeal from the living room. Mark blinked several times; a nervous habit he'd had ever since I'd known him.

'Sounds like it's going well,' I said, trying to keep my tone bright. In truth, my insides were churning at the thought of all those curious little girls and their unpredictable comments.

'Yes, well, they're all very excited that's for sure . . .'

'Darling!' Mum rushed forward to embrace me. She had glitter on her cheeks and dusted across her chest. 'Welcome to the party!'

Dad lurked behind her. At the sight of him, my stomach dropped. His face was sallow, the skin around his jawline thin and drooping. His kindly eyes were outlined with purple shadow. But when his gaze locked on mine, he smiled.

'There's my Heidi.' He held out his arms and I crashed into them, breathing in his familiar scent; sweet sawdust and Fairy washing powder.

'Dad.'

He kissed the top of my head. 'I know Jenny told you,' he said. Over his shoulder, I saw Mum strategically disappear into the living room, dragging Mark with her. I hugged Dad more tightly.

'Oh, Dad, I'm so sorry,' I said into his shirt. My tears sank into the fabric. 'This is my fault.'

'Shhh. It's not.' He stroked my head. 'Not at all. I'm doing much better now.'

'Really?'

I released myself from the hug and faced him. His haggard frame and unshaven face suggested he hadn't told me everything.

'Really.'

Jenny appeared in the hallway. She had a child's plastic tiara on her head. The sound of Taylor Swift pumped from the living room behind her.

'Heidi, I wondered if you could be party games DJ . . . Oh.' She raised her hands when she saw us and started to reverse. 'Sorry.'

'Come here, Jenny,' Dad said. Hesitantly, she obeyed.

'I don't want to interrupt—'

'I know that Heidi knows, and I know that you told her,' he explained. I shot Jenny an apologetic glance.

'Nothing to do with me,' I said. I adjusted my grip on my walking stick. Being tired or run down – or in this case, hungover – always made my phantom pain worse. 'Must have been Mum.'

'I'm sorry, Dad.' Jenny folded her arms across her pastel pink blouse. 'I thought it was important. She had just as much right as me to know.'

'You're right, love.' He sighed deeply, leaning back against the hallway wall. In the past few months, he seemed to have shrunk, a shell of his former self.

'She's always right,' I quipped. He smiled wearily.

'God forbid our Jenny ever lost a board game.'

Growing up, Jenny had had a terrible habit of stropping off to her bedroom. It was why I'd developed the strange desire to lose; my natural competitiveness tempered by my desire to keep the peace. It was a trait Dad and I had always shared; anything for an easy life. Jenny shook her head in mock-annoyance.

'I wasn't that bad . . .'

'You were,' Dad and I answered in unison. We smiled at each other.

'Oh, my girls,' Dad said. He moved to put an arm around each of us. 'You're both wonderful, do you know that?'

'Dad,' Jenny squirmed. Unlike Dad and I, she really wasn't a hugger. 'Anyway, speaking of games, we should probably go and get the kids started. Evie will be getting impatient.'

'Takes after her Mum,' I replied.

'You'll hold me up if things get bad, won't you?' Dad asked suddenly.

He glanced at each of us, both now almost as tall as him. I had a vivid flashback then of being a child at waist height, my head cuddled into his stomach. I used to wonder what it would be like at eye level. Now, I could see the fear and the pain for myself. I could sense the need for reassurance. Jenny and I looked at each other and shared a brief, understanding smile.

'Always,' I said. We were a team.

The living room was a pink paradise, complete with balloons, sparkly banners and a mermaid piñata, which had already been mangled in the children's enthusiasm (desperation) for sweets. All around, small princesses and fairies jumped and danced. Evie waved wildly as we came in.

'Auntie Heidi!' she shrieked. 'I'm going to win!'

Jenny beckoned me over to the speaker system.

'Come and do the music, will you, Heidi? I can't judge and be DJ at the same time. I mean, bloody hell, where is that fiancé of mine?'

'He told me he's been in Frankfurt.'

She sighed heavily. 'Yep. To be honest, I think he's doing it on purpose, Heidi. He's been very clear what he thinks about the wedding. It's obviously avoidance.'

'Jenny . . .'

But Evie interrupted us. 'You have to wear wings,' she announced, pointing to a purple pair left out on the carpet. 'I saved them for you!'

I exchanged a weary look with Jenny before dutifully shrugging on the fairy wings. Made for a little girl, the elastic cut into my armpits. Dad was wearing some too – I hadn't noticed before.

'What do you reckon?' he asked.

'Lovely.' I mustered a smile, then closed my eyes as a surge of nausea hit. I waited for it to subside, willing myself not to be sick.

'Is everything OK, Heidi?' Dad asked.

'Mmmhmm.'

Dad, Mark, a houseful of little girls and a hangover – it was simply all too much. I sat on a pouffe in the corner and began to start and stop the music. A dozen girls jumped up and down to the Disney playlist, while Mum and Jenny decided who was out at the end of each round. They appeared to have made a wordless pact to leave Evie in until the end. They knew what was good for them. Jenny had learnt from her own childhood strops.

'I think that was you, Carys,' Mum said as a red-haired girl in a *Frozen* Elsa dress wobbled dangerously mid-kick.

'OK.' She sat down without a fuss.

Three children now remained – competitive Leah who was always top of the class, Evie in her new purple mermaid costume, and Isabella, who was wrestling against the enormous hoops of her *Cinderella* dress and sparkly plastic heels. She was also adorned with blue eyeshadow and garish pink lip gloss, apparently done for her beforehand by her two teenage sisters.

'Highly inappropriate for a five-year-old,' Jenny muttered in my ear.

Between songs, I checked my phone. Still nothing from Jack. Not that I expected anything, but I couldn't help my disappointment. Against the backdrop of my hangover, every emotion seemed to burn brighter, flaring in blinding technicolour. Jack's silence was a physical ache.

For the past few nights, I'd struggled to sleep. The videotape sensation of my accident had returned again, and I lay restless in the dark as the disturbing images flashed across my mind. Each time, the blueness of the sky and the light on the canal became brighter and more vivid than ever, like someone had turned the colour and sound up on the TV screen in front of me. When it happened, I always tried desperately to stop the film from playing, but just as it had been immediately after the accident, it was like the pause button wasn't working.

'Evie, what's the matter with your auntie?' Leah demanded, hands on hips. 'Her leg is weird.'

'Yeah, it's like a robot,' Carys lisped. Already out and sitting on the sofa, she spoke with her thumb in her mouth.

'I think it's scary,' Isabella added.

They were harmless enough comments, observations more than malice. I knew they were only children. And yet, each one sliced through me, wrenching at my heart. I wanted to disappear.

'She had an accident,' Evie said, chest puffed out with new-found wisdom. 'It was really, really bad. So the doctor took her real leg away.'

'Woahhhh,' said Leah. There were a series of fleeting gasps. But they didn't linger.

'Can we keep playing?' asked Isabella. The game was their focus again.

'Auntie Heidi?' Evie said.

I didn't hear. I felt disconnected, the shouts of the girls muffled by my thoughts.

'Hey, Auntie Heidi, are you gonna stop the music or not?' Evie marched over, hands on hips. She really was a mini version of Jenny.

'Oh, yes, sorry.' I said. 'I was just testing you.' I waited a few more seconds before pressing pause on the music. The three little girls froze, arms quivering with the effort of keeping still.

After a few heated final rounds – to the tense soundtrack of the *Lion King*'s 'Circle of Life' – it was eventually announced that Leah had won. She held her colouring book prize aloft, as though it were an Olympic trophy. Fortunately, Evie had already moved on and was showing off her new mermaid knickers.

'Evie,' Jenny said sharply. 'Pull your skirt down, now!'

Evie screeched delightedly, but she did as she was told. The girls embarked on an elaborate make-believe game involving mermaids and a werewolf. I was envious of their simple joy. In their make-believe world, anything could happen – and there was always a happy ending.

A few times, Evie tried to assign me a role in the game.

'You're a mermaid,' she instructed. 'You can't walk on the ground because you have a tail,' she pointed at my leg, 'but that cushion is your special rock you sit on.'

'Right.'

I sat on the cushion as instructed, trying my best to take part. However, I found their innocent positivity hard to fathom. I was there in body, but my mind had drifted far away, as though I was existing in a different reality.

After a while, I got up from my mermaid rock and headed to the kitchen. I hoped a change of surroundings would shake off the gathering fog.

'Everything OK in there?' Dad asked.

He was distributing paper plates and plastic cups (mermaid-themed, of course) around the kitchen table. He was even wearing a pink apron – one of Jenny's, a Mother's Day present from Evie.

'Yep, think so. Another game finished without too much drama.' I leant against the kitchen work surface and stretched my leg.

'That's a relief. We don't want any tears – especially not on our little one's birthday.'

I smiled while Mum had taken charge of discipline, Dad had always been the softer touch, only raising his voice if we did something truly serious. Since becoming a granddad to Evie, he seemed to have become even more placid. Evie could wrap her granddad around her little finger. He'd do anything for her.

'So Dad, how are you?' I asked.

'Oh, fine, love.' He didn't look up.

'No, really.' I leaned against the kitchen worktop. My nausea had faded, but the headache and emptiness remained. 'Please talk to me. Properly.'

'Heidi, I told you. I don't want you to worry about me.' Placing the final cup into position, he sat down heavily at the kitchen table. Somehow, he looked even more haggard in the pink apron. 'It's why we didn't tell you to begin with.'

'I know.' I limped across to sit next to him. 'But I want to know what happened. This isn't like you, Dad.'

He sighed, a world-weary noise that seemed to come from deep inside. I knew that feeling.

'I was working all hours,' he said. 'So many new builds out there now, it's not hard to occupy yourself.'

'But why?' I pressed. I needed to understand. 'You're retired.'

'Well, yes.' He shrugged. 'I told your Mum it was extra funds for the family, but well, I suppose I was using it as a distraction, too. You know me, love, I'm not very good with all that emotional stuff.'

I smiled sadly. In a house with two hormonal teenage girls, poor Dad had often been out of his depth. He tended to leave the mood management to Mum, favouring a long solo walk or some quiet time in the garden.

'I suppose, well, I suppose in the end, it just got on top of me. Trying to be the strong one all the time – I just couldn't do it.'

'I know how you feel,' I said.

Looking at my worn-out, broken dad, I felt a sadness more acute than any worries about Jack. My family were my lifeline, the ones who stuck by me, no matter what. I realised how similar we really were; both trying to fit into our assigned boxes, hiding from the truth of our feelings. But sometimes, the boxes crumpled. Sometimes, the true person inside was revealed.

'Two weeks, they've given me,' Dad said. 'They were really very good about it. I'm doing a phased return after that. I might not go back full-time.'

'Dad, you shouldn't be going back at all.'

'I know.' He ran a hand through his thinning grey hair. 'But I can't give up just yet. Not until things are, you know, more settled. Anyway, what about you, love? You've been a bit quiet today.'

His intuition startled me. I'd thought I was covering it well. And yet, I was still locked in my own world of worries; present but not truly there. It took an enormous effort to drag myself back.

'OK, yeah, so I'm not great,' I said. I stared at the kitchen wall, hung with Evie's artwork next to a framed print of Van Gogh's *Sunflowers*. I wasn't sure where to start.

'I've seen a counsellor.'

'Well, that's good, isn't it?' Dad gave me a reassuring smile.

'I think so. But going back to the real world, well, it's hard.' I'd decided not to tell them about finding Alexander. They had enough to think about – and besides, I'd found my closure there. I didn't need to rake it up again.

'Of course it is,' Dad said.

'I've been trying to manage my emotions,' I continued. 'Some days, I think I can. I feel like I'm on top of it all. But other times, I just . . . well . . . want it all to go away.'

The tears took me by surprise. Dad squeezed my hand, his big fingers curled around mine, warm and comforting.

'Sounds like we're in the same boat there, love. I must say though, you seemed so on top of things at rehab. Your mum and I – we stepped back a bit to let you recover. I wish we'd realised.'

'But you were so happy with my progress,' I admitted. 'I didn't want to let you down.'

'Heidi, you would never let us down.'

Devoid of all energy – and still wearing fairy wings – I slumped against his shoulder. He stroked my head, the way he had done when I was a child struggling to sleep. Calm passed over me; pressure let out like a pinhole in a balloon.

Dad slid one of the bowls of party food across the table towards me.

'Cherry tomato?' he asked. I smiled.

'Thanks.'

It was the closest we'd ever been to a true heart to heart.

The rest of the party went without a hitch – minus a bit of carpet burn from musical bumps and mild hysteria from Isabella when she eventually and inevitably tripped over her hooped *Cinderella* dress, spilling Ribena down the front of it. When the last of the girls was picked up and the last of the party bags handed out, Jenny collapsed onto the sofa. She – like the rest of us – was covered in glitter. There were toys and pieces of piñata strewn everywhere.

'The house . . .' she said.

Well-versed at children's parties, Mum already had a dustpan and brush in her hand. 'Don't worry, Jenny. We'll sort it.'

'You did well, Jenny.' Mark sat delicately next to his almost-wife, one hand on her knee. 'The girls loved it.' She pushed his hand away.

'No thanks to you.'

'Now, Jenny,' Mum warned.

'No, I'm sorry, Mum, but it needs to be said. He's been absolutely no help at all. Swanning off to Frankfurt or Lord knows where else.'

'Jenny, that's not very fair,' Mark said. Jenny's eyes flashed with anger.

'Not fair? I'll tell you what's not fair. Planning a wedding on your own, that's not fair. Organising your daughter's party single-handedly – that's not fair. Doing absolutely everything while your husband-to-be continually runs away and leaves you. That, Mark, *that* is not fair.'

There was a stunned silence. Mark looked as though he'd been slapped. He straightened up, gathered himself.

'Jenny,' he said, his voice quiet. 'You know how I feel about this wedding.'

'And you know how I feel too,' she retorted. 'I've tried to explain how much it means to me, Mark – but you're just not listening. I'm sick of you sticking your head in the sand.'

I stared at the carpet. I couldn't meet anyone's eyes. When I looked up, Mark's cheeks had flushed red with anger. His usually soft voice had a hard, unrecognisable edge.

'You're not listening to me. I'm not listening to you. So maybe, Jenny, maybe we should just call the whole thing off.'

'What?' Jenny's mouth opened and closed. I felt a sharp stab of shock in my gut when I saw Mark's face. He was serious.

'Yeah.' He spoke passionately, the red flush on his cheeks now spreading down his neck. 'I mean it, Jenny. It's changed us. It's spiralled out of control. And to be honest, I'm fed up with your selfishness.'

'Selfishness?'

She stood up suddenly and stormed across the room. Mum and I both recoiled. For a terrifying moment, I thought she was going to hit him.

'Jenny . . .' Mum said.

'This isn't to do with you, Mum,' she snapped. She towered over Mark, hands on hips. Even from the sofa, I could see her whole body was shaking. 'Selfishness?' she said again. The veins in her neck were prominent and straining.

'Even now – after all the times I've tried to explain to you that I'm doing this for my family – even now you use that word. Well, do you know what, Mark? Fine. Cancel it. Cancel the biggest, most important day of my life. See if I care.' She stuck her chin in the air, but I could see that her eyes were shining.

A terrible silence filled the room. Shell-shocked, I looked to Mum, who bit her lip and wrung her hands in her lap, holding back her own torrent of emotion. Jenny stood in front of Mark like a freeze-frame, holding her exact position the way we used to in improv games at drama school. But this was no game; this was happening.

At that moment, Evie zoomed into the room, an enormous smile on her face. Her hair, initially carefully curled by Jenny, was now matted and messy. Dad followed close behind; he was still wearing his wings.

'Grandpa's chasing me!' Evie yelled. 'He's the tickle fairy!'

Dad stopped in the doorway, taking in the scene. I watched him glance from face to face. When he looked at me, his eyes were questioning. I gave a tiny shrug. There was no way I could explain in front of Evie.

'Evie, darling, calm down,' Dad said quietly. 'I think Mummy's tired.'

'No she's not!' Evie ran over to Jenny and began jumping up and down in front of her. 'Are you, Mummy? You want to play with me!'

'Don't,' Jenny said. Evie backed off, pouting.

'Maybe we should all go to the park,' Mum suggested. 'Let Jenny and Mark have a bit of time to talk.'

Mark's brows dropped behind his newspaper, but he nodded.

'Perhaps for the best.'

Evie's face lit up. 'Oh, yes! I can show you how I go down the big slide backwards!'

Coats, forced smiles and a missing Barbie trainer later, we were ready. As Evie skipped along the street in front of us, I clung to my walking stick and turned to look behind me, unable to shift the horrible, strained expressions of my sister and Mark, the finality of the slammed front door. My headache was back, skull throbbing beneath the weight of my worry as terrible revelation took hold. Again, my family was suffering. Again, it was my fault.

Chapter Twenty-Nine

Bryony was running late. I sat on one of the sturdy high-backed chairs in the waiting room, watching the woefully mistranslated subtitles of *Rip Off Britain* roll along the silent TV screen. Wheelchairs were scattered all around the room, most of them occupied by dozing fat men. A few came complete with long-suffering wives, who sipped sweet coffee from the 50p vending machine or pored over out-of-date TV mags and ancient copies of the *People's Friend*. The youngish man opposite me had tattoos on his two short stumps. He gave a yellow, toothy smile.

'Afghanistan,' he said, I assumed by way of introduction. 'You?'

'Accident,' I said. I looked away, but he persisted.

'Car?' He casually scratched his crotch. He was wearing what looked like swimming shorts. Nothing was left to the imagination.

'Yeah.' It was easier than explaining.

'Shit, man. That's rough.'

I needed this counselling session more than ever. Even after our strategic walk with Evie on the day of her party, nothing had been resolved. Mark remained stalwart in his conviction that cancelling the wedding, even as last-minute as a month before was for the best, but encouraged by Jenny, they'd reached a middle ground of postponing. That said, she hadn't yet noti-fied the guests. This small act of defiance gave me hope. I clung to it with every fibre of my being. Because Jenny loved Mark and Mark loved Jenny. Surely that was enough?

'Heidi?'

Bryony stood in front of me. Today, she wore a large magenta flower in her hair, the same shade as the tiny spots on her black and pink skirt.

'Sorry I'm late,' she said.

'That's OK.' I shut the laptop and stood up to follow her.

'Counselling is it, love?' the man with the uncomfortable genitals called as I left. 'Got issues, have yer?'

'Not as many as you,' Bryony muttered. I couldn't help but smile.

Inside the therapy room, two steaming mugs were waiting on the table.

'I hope you drink tea,' Bryony said. 'I was making myself one and I thought it was the least I could do.'

'That's really kind, thanks.'

She handed me a mug with Eeyore on the side. '*I am too tired for this*,' it said beneath the donkey's forlorn expression. I was inclined to agree. Bryony saw me looking.

'You should see my kitchen,' she said with a smile. 'Organised chaos.'

I could imagine. There were folders and papers strewn every-where in the sparse green room and novelty pens scattered across the desk; fluffy, neon and a giant glittery flamingo. Bryony settled back in her chair.

'So, how have you been since our last session?' Bryony smoothed down her skirt. Pale grey cat hairs were visible against the black material.

'It's not been easy,' I admitted.

'No. It won't be.' She waited for me to continue.

'This time it's my sister. She's postponing her wedding – and it's because of me.'

'What do you mean?"

I told her about Mark; about his lack of understanding when it came to Jenny's manic organisation.

'I get that it's annoying for him, but she's repeatedly tried to explain.' I felt choked recounting the story. 'And it's not even really about their relationship. They've always been so strong as a couple. It can all be traced back to me.'

'Heidi, what did we say about guilt before?' Bryony cast her eyes over me, an intensity I was now used to.

'We said . . . what's done is done,' I answered. Not that I believed it.

'Exactly. You need to stop blaming yourself for everyone else's actions. It's hard, I know. But your sister's relationship is about more than your accident. That's not the only variable here.'

'But—'

'No.' She held up a hand. 'I'm being firm here, Heidi, because you need it. You need to remember that you're not responsible for others around you. You don't force the decisions they make. I appreciate you're worried about your sister, of course I do. But it's not your fault.'

She said these last few words slowly and firmly, as though etching them into my brain. I hesitated, allowing them to sink in.

'OK,' I said finally, though the guilt still gnawed at me. I'd just have to keep reminding myself – not my problem. 'I guess you're right.'

'I usually am.' She smiled. 'It's what they pay me for. Now, what else has been happening?'

I thought back. So much had happened; it was hard to trawl back through the memories. Then I remembered something else. Something crucial I needed to tell her.

'I saw Alexander,' I said. 'The man – the one who was on the path. I tracked him down. I went to his office.'

What with everything else that had happened since then, that day seemed a million years ago now. Bryony's eyes widened.

'You did? And what happened?'

'He didn't remember. Well, not at first. And then he did – but the thing is, I got it wrong.' I felt stupid admitting the truth. 'After I fell, someone else turned up. A girl, who stayed with me when he had to go, apparently. He didn't leave me on my own. But Bryony, I don't remember it like that. Why can't I picture her?'

'Well, trauma can skew our perceptions.' She took a gulp of tea. 'That's normal. But the key question now is, have your feelings towards this man changed?'

I thought about it. For so long, I'd harboured hatred and resentment. Now, I just felt foolish. Alexander Mitchell's actions hadn't been cruel or calculated. Caught up in his own time schedule, he had made a split-second decision. He wouldn't have realised the seriousness of my injury. He hadn't known it would change my life.

'I don't blame him any more,' I told Bryony. She nodded. The look in her eyes told me she'd already known my answer.

'Closure is a very powerful thing, Heidi. It was brave of you to find him.'

'Or stupid,' I smiled. 'I think he was quite surprised.'

'I'm sure.' She laughed. 'But the important thing is, it was what you needed to do. Now you can move on.'

'How?'

'However you want. You can live your life, plan your future. You could have died, Heidi, but you didn't. You're here.'

I found I couldn't answer her. I'd never thought about death. Even in intensive care, wild on ketamine, burning with fever, I

266

hadn't considered the fact that I might not recover. That was why my family had been so worried, so attentive. I reached for my mug. The tea was lukewarm now, and while I didn't normally take sugar, I was grateful for its comforting sweetness.

'The question you need to think about is: what do you want to do next?' Bryony asked.

'I don't know.'

'Acting?'

'I'm not sure I can handle it, Bryony. All those eyes on me.' I shuddered at the thought. I still struggled to look at my stump, let alone show it to others. 'And anyway, my career wasn't exactly working out how I wanted before. I was lucky to get ad campaigns, let alone proper theatre roles.'

'Right.' She took a sip of tea, a thoughtful expression on her face. 'Disabled theatre companies? There are lots of those around.'

'And put myself in that box forever? I don't think so.' Being labelled was the last thing I wanted.

'OK, OK,' Bryony said. 'I understand. I know it's a tough time for you, Heidi. And from what you're saying, the road ahead wasn't clear even before this happened.'

I nodded. 'You can say that again.'

'So,' she licked her lips and tried again. 'Let's rewind a bit. Start small, build your confidence and a new path or direction will follow. Sometimes, it's good to set pen to paper to work out what you want to achieve. Maybe try writing a list?'

'I've done that,' I said quietly.

'You have? That's great! And how did you get on?'

'It was good. Well, to start with. But then I kind of stopped.'

'Why was that?'

I paused. It was still painful to think about Jack. There was a link there with Alexander Mitchell which only emphasised and deepened the betrayal. They'd both left me when I needed them most.

'Someone was helping me,' I said vaguely. 'But then they couldn't any more.'

'OK.' Bryony adjusted her flower and fixed me with a look so acute I felt she could see straight into my head. 'So this . . . person. Would you say you relied on them to help you?'

'Yes.' My voice came out so small that she had to lean in to hear me.

'And you don't feel like you can carry on without them?'

'No.' I swallowed. I didn't want to cry.

'I see.' She sat back in her chair. 'Heidi, were you an independent person before your accident?'

I nodded wordlessly, still attempting to control my emotions.

'I thought so. And you've told me that you want to go back to how things were.'

'I just want to be normal,' I croaked. Bryony made no direct reference to my impending tears. Instead, she slid a box of tissues towards me. I took one and scrubbed at my eyes.

'So, how about finishing the list?' Bryony said. I'd known where her questioning was leading, but it still felt like a stab in my gut. Fear overtook my sadness.

'On my own?'

'Why not?' Bryony locked her gaze with mine. She wouldn't let it go. 'Finding that sense of purpose and achievement is the best way to move forward.'

'But what if I fall?'

'Then you get up again.'

I thought about my list. I'd done public transport. I'd been to my flat. I'd even been back to the bar, as awful as the night had turned out. Each time, I'd completed something I never imagined I could do. And each time, yes, a ray of happiness had burst through the clouds.

'Heidi?' Bryony prompted. 'What do you think?'

Her tone was coaxing yet gentle, like she was addressing a frightened puppy. She was clearly being careful not to send me into another anxious fit.

'Dance,' I said quietly. 'That was one of the ideas I had.'

'That sounds amazing.' A smile crept across Bryony's face. Her eyes gleamed with genuine enthusiasm.

'I did want to learn . . .' I trailed off.

'You still could.'

I thought about my list; the certainty of the written words, black ink against the cream, lined paper, I hesitated.

'Maybe you're right,' I said slowly. The beginning of an idea was taking shape in my mind. If I could track down Alexander, I could do this, too.

'You can, I'm sure of it.' Bryony waved the fluffy flamingo pen aloft. 'Heidi, you can do anything you set your mind to.'

'Do you think so?'

'I know so.'

Her words felt like the sun on my heart. I didn't need Alexander. I didn't need Jack. I didn't need anyone. I could do this on my own.

Chapter Thirty

Somewhat ironically, the studio space was called FootWorks. The morning I arrived, I was greeted by a young, over-enthusiastic man with diamond studs twinkling in both ears.

'Welcome!' He stood up from his seat behind the reception desk and threw out his arms theatrically. 'And how can I help you, Madam?'

'I'm here for a dance lesson.'

'Lovely. And which teacher is that with?'

'He's called Mateo?'

At this, his eyebrows shot to the top of his forehead. His smile grew bigger.

'Mateo DeSilvas?'

'Er, yes.'

'Wow. I mean, lucky you.' He looked utterly star-struck. 'If you don't mind me asking, how did you manage that? Mateo's like, kind of a big deal around here. His private classes are booked up for months!'

'Oh, through a friend,' I replied vaguely. The man behind the desk blinked a few times, recovering himself.

'Well, you are going to have the best time,' he said. 'I'll let him know you're here. Do take a seat.'

'Thanks.'

I moved over to the waiting area, where four squashy sofas flanked a glass coffee table. On the far wall was a large mural, the word '*FootWorks*' painted in looping calligraphy. All around it were doodled images of pairs of feet, pointing and posing in ballet shoes, tap shoes and heels. Just a few weeks ago, I would have struggled to see the funny side. But today, I found myself smiling.

'Heidi?'

Mateo stood in front of me. He was tall and graceful with glowing olive skin and defined muscles rippling beneath a tight black T-shirt. He had bare feet and his chin-length hair was pushed back from his forehead with an eighties style headband – not dissimilar to Maud's. Most people would have looked ridiculous. He looked gorgeous.

'Mateo, hi.'

I rose and held out my hand, feeling a flush of embarrassment at the memory of our previous meeting in the bar. I say *memory* – to be honest, I barely remembered it. But Mateo didn't seem fazed. He pulled me into a hug.

'It is good to see you again,' he said warmly. 'This is going to be fun.'

'I hope so.'

I couldn't avoid the nerves. They twirled and tapped in my stomach like a dozen pairs of dance shoes.

'Come on, follow me,' Mateo beckoned. Even the way he turned seemed rehearsed, as though every movement was part of a professional performance. I turned to follow him. The man at reception gawped.

The studio was even more luxurious than I'd imagined. Floor-to-ceiling mirrors covered three full walls, with a shining ballet barre and sprung floor dotted with silver glitter. There were large, high-tech speakers and a full lighting rig in the ceiling. There was even a mini-kitchen area in the corner, complete with table and chairs, microwave and coffee machine. On the far side, a set of sliding patio doors were flung open to reveal a large strip of decking overlooking the studio's central courtyard beyond. I let out a low whistle.

'Is impressive, right?'

'Very.'

I stood in the centre of the room, taking it all in. I'd been in my fair share of rehearsal spaces over the years, but many of them were makeshift, often too small with old bits of coloured tape on the floor and old unused props or hastily stacked chairs providing a constant trip hazard. It was an accepted state of affairs, the price any unknown performer in any small show had to pay at the start of their career. But this was unlike any studio I'd been in before. This was the real deal.

Mateo was fiddling with the sound system. A few moments later, the sound of Basement Jaxx's 'Do Your Thing' filled the room.

'OK, so we do a quick warm up and stretch first,' he said. He flexed his neck and rolled his shoulders, limbering up.

'OK.'

I draped my jacket over a coat stand and dumped my backpack on the floor. I double-checked the fit of my prosthetic leg and moved over to where he was standing. I was thankful that I had no nerve pain – although there was never any way of predicting its onset. I swiftly pushed the thought from my mind. There was no way I was going to let my brain ruin this.

'You do what you can, OK?' Mateo said. I caught him tentatively eying my leg. 'There is no pressure here.'

'Got it.'

We began with a series of simple stretches, touching our toes and stretching our arms to the beat. Following his lead, I felt comforted, the process of copying his movements reminiscent of my drama school classes. I was pleased to discover that my muscles were more supple than I expected. Sitting with my legs out in front of me, I could almost reach my head to my knees. Mateo looked suitably impressed.

'Have you been practicing?' he asked. I shrugged.

'Double-jointed. I'm just pleased I've still got it.'

'Ah, a dancer's gift.' He looked up at me from a seemingly impossible position, legs open and torso flat on the floor. 'But you need to be careful.'

'Tell me about it,' I answered. 'When I was a child my doctor told me not to climb trees. My thumbs are too bendy, apparently.'

Mateo smiled. I noticed that one side of his mouth curled up higher than the other.

'Your friend,' he said suddenly. 'Dougie. You live with him?'

'That's right, yeah.'

'He's cool.'

Mateo's dark eyes glinted wickedly. Catching on to his thoughts, I smiled.

'Yes, he is.'

The song finished. Mateo gave me a quick wink before leaping up, conversation clearly over.

'So, what dance do you want to try?' he asked.

Slowly, I rolled onto my knees. My rise to standing resembled a giant toddler getting up after a fall, the complete opposite of his swift, graceful movements.

'I'm not sure,' I said.

The nerves had started up again now. The warm-up was one thing, but actual dancing – well, that was different. Doubt invaded my thoughts. Was this really a good idea? Mateo frowned, considering.

'We can do anything you want. Jive? Foxtrot? Quickstep?'

'Definitely no to the quickstep. Maybe something a bit slower?' A light-bulb smile played across his lips.

'Aha, OK. I've got it.'

'What?'

In three gazelle-like bounces, he was at the sound system again. I blinked, taken aback by the speed. He began to scroll through his phone.

When the next track started, a very different vibe filled the room. I recognised the song immediately – Adele's *Make You Feel My Love*. The soft, soulful piano brought an instant chill to my skin. My stump tingled.

'Rumba,' Mateo said. He took my hands and faced me. My palms were damp. I hoped he hadn't noticed. 'One of my favourite dances. Three steps in four counts. You do the opposite to me – like you're looking in a mirror.'

He began to move, stepping forwards on his right leg. Gingerly, I moved my left one backwards. Unused to balancing on my prosthetic side, I lurched and wobbled. Mateo grabbed me.

'OK?'

'Y-yeah,' I stammered. 'I think so.'

'Just follow my feet.'

I inhaled deeply and tried again. This time, I successfully managed one step.

'That's it,' Mateo said. He gave me a wide smile.

I felt suddenly lightheaded. I whistled air out through my teeth, realising I'd been holding my breath.

'Now, for the rumba walk, you need to walk with your toes first.' He demonstrated. I'd never seen a man with such swaying hips. I looked down at the floor and felt a jolt of concern.

'But my toes . . .' I gestured.

'Ah, yes.' Mateo's cheeks coloured slightly. 'So sorry.' He fiddled anxiously with his headband.

'No, it's OK.' I exhaled deeply, composing myself. Don't be oversensitive, Heidi. I couldn't let my lack of toes stop me. 'I'll just do it on the other leg.'

'OK, yes.' Mateo still looked uncomfortable. 'Good idea.'

The song finished and then began again, set on a repeating loop. He took my hands.

'OK. So, when you hold out your hands, keep them at belly level. Never below your hips. It should be a soft touch, imagine each finger clipping against the thumb and then relax them. Hold them delicately.'

I copied his stance, allowing my hands to go floppy. It reminded me of childhood ballet classes.

'That's it,' Mateo nodded approvingly. 'Now, when you turn, it's like you've forgotten something. You twist back to get it.'

He swirled me around. But I wasn't ready. My leg went in one direction, my body in another. My foot slipped from under me. And then I was on the floor.

'Heidi!' Mateo gasped.

I was in an ungainly position on the studio floor, legs splayed, my stump and my cheeks burning with pain and embarrassment. Mateo looked down at me, his eyes wide.

'Are you OK?' he asked.

'I think so.' My heart was thumping.

Mateo held out a hand. 'Come on. We try again.'

The music continued to play. Resisting the urge to flee, I allowed him to pull me to my feet. I was shaking. I could feel the tightness in my chest, the warning sign of impending panic. I tried to fight it.

'There's too much to think about,' I said.

'Close your eyes,' Mateo replied. I obeyed. 'Now, just listen to the music.'

He held my hands. I clung to him, trying to regain control of my breathing. I felt a cool breeze from the terrace flutter in and stroke my face, washing over me like the gentle, soothing piano. Slowly, I began to feel calmer.

'The most important thing is to relax,' Mateo said. 'Free your mind. You just have to be lost in the music. Remember this feeling, OK? Now, open your eyes.'

We started again. This time, I imagined the journey of the song, the story we were telling with our movements. I trod on his feet. I stumbled. I wobbled. Yet thankfully, this time I didn't fall. I was scared, I was wavering, and it was nowhere near the perfect scene I'd imagined in my head. My heart was still pounding. My palms were hot and clammy. But I was dancing. And when I caught a glimpse of myself in the studio mirror, I realised I was smiling, too.

Chapter Thirty-One

During the day, Bar Conscience was a café. The vibe was completely different, light streaming into the bright white room, the hanging plants and trailing foliage bathed in sunshine. A few punters were scattered around, some solo with coffee and laptops, others chattering in groups, girls tucking into veggie brunches and couples sharing pastries, lovingly dropping flaky crumbs across each other's laps.

Ben was there that morning; of course he was. Living in a box room in a giant house-share and constantly desperate for funds, I used to tease him that he lived in the bar, taking on as many shifts as possible as though determined to set some kind of record. When I arrived, he was sprinkling chocolate onto two cappuccinos, shaking the cocoa powder through a stencil of Conscience's trademark leaf pattern. His hair was carefully messy and he wore his bumbag across his body, tanned biceps bulging from the sleeves of his deliberately too-tight T-shirt. The old me would have soaked up this meticulous casualness. The new me saw how ridiculous it really was.

'Hey, Jackson,' he called breezily.

'Hi.'

I used to love the way he used my surname. It had felt matey and easy and intimate all at the same time, inducing electric sparks through my stomach every time I heard his voice. Now, I couldn't believe how much had changed. It was as though I was seeing him for who he really was; a shameless flirt with very little real empathy beneath that Aussie charm. The flames of desire had been well and truly doused.

'So, to what do I owe this pleasure?' Ben finished the coffee decorations with a flourish and leant across the bar. 'Bit early for shots, even for you, isn't it?'

'Probably.'

I perched on a stool. I knew he wanted me to go along with the banter, to fall into the back and forth routine we were both so used to. It would be so easy to flirt, to retain his curiosity and ignite his lust. Strangely, this knowledge gave me confidence. It reminded me I could still be attractive. I also held the power of rejection.

'Two cappuccinos, table sixty-six,' Ben called. He slid the drinks onto a wooden tray. A nervous-looking couple who were definitely on a date waved at him from the corner sofa. 'Coming right up. Hold that thought, Jackson.'

I watched him prance, peacock-like, across the room. I did feel nervous today, but for once, the source of the butterflies wasn't Ben. I felt for the piece of paper in my back pocket. I was wearing my skinny jeans again, a reminder of challenges completed, of a future now in reach. Bryony's words zoomed around my head – small steps. One thing at a time.

'Right, I'm all yours.' Ben said with a wink. 'What's up?'

With trembling hands, I held out the folded piece of paper to him.

'I'm handing in my notice.'

'Yeah, right, good one.' Ben lent back against the bar and patted my shoulder.

'No, really.' I shrugged him off and swivelled the stool to face him. 'With immediate effect. I mean it. I can't work here any more, Ben.'

'What?' His brows dipped, a flicker of confusion covering his usually impenetrable joy. 'But why? You've only just come out of that rehab place. Don't think that one duff shift means you can't do it at all. You'll get there, Jackson.'

He was trying to be nice, and yet to me his tone just sounded patronising. I shook my head.

'It's not even about that shift. I just don't want to work here any more. I don't want to spend my days pulling pints and drinking shots and sprinkling chocolate into the shape of fucking leaves.'

'C'mon, Jackson, you don't mean that. We're the ones who stayed. We're the team.'

'I do mean it, Ben. The accident, it changed things. It changed me.'

'Ah, bullshit,' he said breezily, waving away my explanation. 'You're the same fun-loving gal you always were.' He wound an arm around my waist. 'I don't see you any differently, anyway.'

'Well, thanks, but—'

'And I don't see why anyone else should either. Stay at the bar, Heidi. Carry on how things were.'

He gave me a squeeze and pulled me towards him. My head was against his chest, breathing in the woody aftershave smell that had once drawn me into a state of instant arousal. Now, I was surprised to find it was nothing more than vaguely comforting, a mere whiff of lust and nostalgia.

'It was good, wasn't it?' he asked. 'We're cool, right?'

I broke away from his embrace. 'Ben, you're not getting it.' His intentions were good, but he still wasn't listening. 'I feel different now. About everything. Including whatever this whole thing is . . . was. It has to end. All of it.'

'You sure, Heidi?' He'd dropped the carefree tone now. I was surprised to see he actually looked disappointed. Perhaps even sad.

279

'I'm sure, Ben,' I said softly. 'I need to move on.'

'OK, yeah.' He spoke slowly, as though collecting himself. 'Fine. I get it, Jackson. I understand.' Then he gave me a wide smile. Almost as soon as the façade had lifted, it was back.

'So, what are you gonna do instead then?' he asked.

I shrugged. 'I don't know yet. I'll work it out.'

'But you'll keep in touch, right?'

'Course,' I answered. Truth be told, I wasn't sure – but I didn't quite have the heart to admit it.

I stood up. Somehow, I felt taller than before, my body lighter with the relief of my decision. I glanced around Conscience, years of memories and laughter soaked into the chipped white walls. Ben pulled me into a hug and I hugged him back, exhaling the worry and the fear.

'Go easy, Jackson,' he said as he let go.

I gave him a smile and then I turned to leave. I knew I'd done the right thing.

That night, Jenny came over for dinner. Dougie was at the pub with friends and Mark had stayed with Evie, so it was just the two of us in the flat, sharing an oven pizza and a half-hearted Caesar salad. Since the argument at Evie's birthday party, Jen had been uncharacteristically quiet, no wedding demands or even photos of Evie on the family WhatsApp group. Now, she sat across from me at the tiny kitchen table, picking pepperoni off her pizza, her plate already full of discarded crusts. It wasn't like her to be such a fussy eater. Usually, she'd be the first to criticise such behaviour.

'Jenny, we have to talk about this,' I said. I'd already tried to broach the subject of the wedding several times, each one unsuccessful.

She looked up and sighed heavily. From the outside, she was the same Jenny; smart pinafore dress and carefully ironed shirt selected for school that day. Yet looking closer, her turmoil was clear. Her hair was greasy and pulled back into a low ponytail, her blusher too pink, her lipstick too severe.

'OK. Fine,' she said finally. She nibbled at a slice of pizza. 'What do you want to know?'

'Well . . . what's going on?' Her silence meant I was completely in the dark. She hadn't even spoken to Mum. 'How are things with Mark?'

'The wedding's happening, if that's what you're asking.'

'OK. So that's good news, isn't it?' Relief flooded through me – but Jenny wasn't smiling.

'I suppose.' She pushed her plate away. 'The thing is, Heidi, he thinks I'm just putting on a show. He doesn't understand that I'm doing this for all of us. After all our family's been through, I just want it to be a perfect day.. I don't think anyone gets it.'

A flush of emotion had spread across her face and neck. Jenny never cried. I reached across the table and took her hand.

'Jenny, I do,' I told her. I looked into her graphite grey eyes, the mirror image of my own. So different in some ways and yet so many similarities in others, the blood of sisterhood forever holding strong. 'I get it.'

She squeezed my hand. 'Thank you.'

'And listen, it's not exactly my specialist subject as we both know, but this wedding isn't about the details, Jen. It's not about the catering or the decorations or any of that stuff. It's about you guys. It's about your family. It's about love.'

'You're right.' She smiled weakly. 'When did you get so wise, little sis?'

'It's always been there,' I replied with a grin. 'You just never listen.'

'Oi!' She made a face. 'I do, too.'

'Do not.' I stuck out my tongue. Jenny laughed at me.

'You seem happier these days, anyway,' she said.

I nodded. 'Yeah. I guess I am. I don't know Jen, something's shifted in the past few days. It's an emotional whirlwind, this recovery journey – I never know quite how I'm going to feel. But recently, I do think I've turned a corner.'

I really did. I felt buoyant, on top of my emotions; floating rather than drowning. I was riding on them, rising above the hurt and the worry, seeing the blue sky beyond. Finally, there was hope.

'Heidi, that's great.'

Now that our worries had been aired, the atmosphere in the flat had altered; peace overriding the previous tension. Jenny's expression had relaxed, her tight-knit brows released, her smile genuine rather than forced. I had to remember I wasn't the only one with problems.

'You know what would go well with this pizza?' I said. 'A glass of cold white wine.'

'That's the best idea I've heard all day..'

She moved to get up but I stopped her. 'No, don't. I'll get it.'

I stood up and walked, unaided, to the fridge. The feeling of putting one foot in front of the other was still a novelty. I relished being upright, spine straight and shoulders back, lungs filled, stomach no longer crunched into a seated position. I reminded myself never to forget the joy of this feeling. There was nothing better than freedom.

Chapter Thirty-Two

The next morning, I headed back to rehab. This time, it wasn't for Bryony. There was another visit I needed to make.

Skye was sitting on the high-backed chair beside her bed, prosthetic leg crossed over her left thigh. She wore a heavy-knit high-necked jumper over leggings. Her cloud of pale blonde hair fell across her face and shoulders like a halo. Beneath it, her blue eyes shone in a way that was anything but angelic.

'Look who's come crawling back,' she said. 'Took your bloody time, didn't you?'

'Nice to see you too, Skye.'

She was still in the side room. Just as before, it was a tip, clothes thrown over the floor and a mound of sweet wrappers on the bedside table, jumbled up with tubes of mascara and lip-gloss. Her collection of knick-knacks had grown since I was last here, notebooks, novelty pens, DVDs and three phone chargers.

'Good of you to show your face here again,' she said, but her sarcasm was tinged with fondness. The corners of her mouth tilted upwards into a smile as she spoke. 'I thought you'd forgotten me.'

'Easier said than done with you.' I dumped a pile of jumpers and leggings on the floor and took the plastic chair across from her. 'I brought you something, by the way.'

'It better not be a fucking fruit punnet. Christ, I swear, if I see another bunch of grapes . . .'

'No.'

I handed her the silver gift bag. Unused to the company of seventeen-year-olds, I had to admit I'd struggled. Besides, with her wry humour and wisdom beyond her years, Skye was no ordinary teenager. But when the idea had come to me, I was pleased with my flash of inspiration. I just hoped Skye was, too. She held up the package, eyeing it with suspicion.

'It's heavy.'

'Just open it,' I replied. 'I've kept the receipt if you don't like it.'

'You sound like my grandma at Christmas.'

She pulled the bag open and took out its contents; a silver box containing a set of ten nail varnishes in ridiculously named rainbow colours: *Girls' Night In* pink, *Catch the Lightning* yellow and *Paint the Town* red. I watched as her smile grew wider.

'Heidi, these are great.' The cool girl act had gone and her grin was pure pleasure. I felt faintly relieved. 'Thank you so much!'

'You're welcome. How are you doing, anyway? How long have you got left here?'

'Two and a bit weeks now.' She wrinkled her nose. 'Counting down.'

'I bet.' I remembered that feeling well. I pointed at her leg. 'Looks like you're getting there, though.'

'Yeah. Thank God. I was beginning to go stark raving mad in that wheelchair.'

'Only in the wheelchair?' I raised my eyebrows. She flicked two fingers up at me.

'Whatever. But yeah, I can't wait to get out. The physio and stuff's OK, it's the free time that gets me. It's just so mind-numbingly dull – if you don't like *Homes Under the Hammer*, you're pretty much screwed.'

She was spot on. I snorted with laughter. 'Oh God, I know what you mean.'

Skye nibbled thoughtfully at her chipped blue glittery thumbnail. The sleeve of her jumper slipped down, exposing the cloud and sun tattoo on her wrist. Seeing it there always made me smile, a symbol of hope inked in a moment of rebellion that had since become so apt for both of us. Eventually, a brighter day would always come.

'Like, I know they have that half-hearted gardening club, but the place isn't exactly teeming with activities,' she said, now carried away on her train of thought as usual. She spoke faster, addressing herself as much as me. I listened. I was thinking.

'There needs to be some more entertainment, a better choice of stuff to do, y'know? We don't all like dirt down our freshly painted fingernails and watering fucking mint plants . . .'

I stopped her. 'Hang on, Skye. You know what, you might have a point there.'

'Well, yeah.' She rolled her eyes. 'Obviously.'

Her talk of gardening had planted a sudden, crazy seed of an idea in my mind. It was germinating, roots forming, tendrils of thought digging deeper, exploring further. Maybe, just maybe I could make it sprout and grow. Skye waved her hand back and forth in front of me.

'Paging Heidi Jackson. Earth to Heidi . . .'

'Sorry.' I blinked back into the present moment. 'I was just thinking. What about dance?'

'Sorry, what?' Skye stared at me. 'As in, ballet and shit? OK, so it's happened. You've finally lost the plot. Imagine that old George bloke in a leotard . . . no thank you.'

'No, wait.' I tried to reorder my thoughts. They were running faster and faster. I really felt like I was on to something. 'Listen. I mean like specialised classes, for exercise. We do all that physio work in the gym, but how about something a bit different?'

I thought about my session with Mateo; the elation I'd experienced when I began to master the steps. It was a feeling like nothing I'd had before. If I trained up enough, if I practiced and found the drive and motivation to make it work, then maybe I could share that feeling with others. Maybe it could become my new purpose, the focus I'd been searching for. Skye stared at me, wide-eyed.

'It would be optional, of course,' I added quickly, seeing her face. 'You're right, not everyone would be keen to try it. But then not everyone wants to pot plants, either.'

'You can say that again.' Skye bit her lip, considering. 'I guess maybe it could work. If you advertised it enough. Built up a buzz kind of thing.'

'And that's where you come in.'

'Sorry, what?' She frowned. 'Are you serious?'

'Yep. You used to dance, didn't you?'

'Well, yeah. Back when I was a kid. But that was ages ago. Way before all . . . this.' She gestured at her leg. 'You wouldn't catch me *en pointe* these days. In case you haven't noticed, I can barely bloody walk.'

'But the point is Skye, you have rhythm. You can help me. Come on. You're lost, I'm lost. Let's do this together.'

She paused for a moment, considering. Then she pushed her mane of hair back and leant forward, her expression now sharp and focused.

'I think you're fucking insane, Heidi Jackson. But you know what? I've got nothing better to do when I get out of here. So, I can't believe I'm saying this . . . but I'm in.'

She leant forward and held out her hand, the one with the tattoo. We shook. It was only an idea, but I felt a sense of purpose more acute than I had done in months; stronger even than when I'd decided to pursue acting in the first place. I was certain I could make this work; that Skye and I could find a new focus. We'd help other people – and in doing so, help ourselves too. Together, we'd bring the sun out from behind the clouds.

Chapter Thirty-Three

The morning of the wedding, I woke up beneath a *Sabrina the Teenage Witch* duvet cover. For a moment, I wasn't sure where I was, blinking myself back to reality after the deepest, most peaceful sleep I'd had in weeks. My childhood bedroom was largely unchanged; lilac walls and glow-in-the-dark-stars on the ceiling, cuddly toys gathering dust in a hammock on the wall. A chink of light glowed from the edges of the blackout blind. I reached to pull it upwards, flooding the room with daylight and possibility.

I hadn't been awake long when Jenny knocked on my door. That in itself was quite unusual – as children she'd very much expected the reverse to occur.

'Come in,' I said croakily. My throat felt clogged with sleep. 'Morning.'

Her hair was wet from the shower. Over her pyjamas she wore a white towelling dressing gown with 'Bride' on the back in silver letters. I glanced wearily at the pale pink 'Bridesmaid' one hanging on the back of my door. It wasn't my thing. I pulled back the duvet of my single bed and she squeezed in beside me. There wasn't as much room as there used to be.

'You're up early,' I said. She smelt clean and fresh, like mint shower gel. I reached up to crank my window open, conscious of my fusty, unaired bedroom.

'I couldn't sleep.'

'Excitement?'

'Nerves, more like.' She pulled the large polar bear teddy who lived on my bed into her arms and hugged him to her chest. His name was Polo and I'd had him since I was ten.

'You're going to be fine,' I told her. 'It'll be great, promise.'

'I hope so.' She stroked Polo, holding onto him like driftwood on a raging sea. 'I can't quite believe the day has finally come. It feels like yesterday we first met.'

'Snogging in the students' union to the romantic sound of "Don't Stop Believing".'

'Heidi,' she warned – but she was smiling. I put my head on her shoulder. Amazingly, she didn't try and shrug me off.

'I'm so glad it's worked out, Jenny. You're a brilliant couple. I mean that. And you're the best parents Evie could wish for.'

'Thanks, sis.' She rested her head on top of mine.

For a while, we lay like that, heads together, each engrossed in our own thoughts. It was a beautiful crisp day outside, the kind of transitional weather where jackets are optional and cold sunshine lights the sky. Nerves about walking up the aisle still flickered and danced inside me, and yet cuddled up with my sister, I was gradually beginning to feel calmer. If I couldn't do it, I couldn't do it. There was no use worrying about things I was unable to change.

On the landing, I heard the thundering of running feet. Seconds later, Evie burst into the room, still in her pyjamas, hair tousled and sticking in all directions.

'Mummy, Auntie Heidi,' she cried. She pounced on us. I gave a low moan as she landed on my stump.

'Careful,' Jenny said.

'Can I play with Polo?'

Jenny handed the cuddly toy over and Evie snatched at it, sticking her thumb in her mouth.

'He's so soft,' she lisped.

'Evie, why haven't you had your bath yet?' Jenny asked. 'I thought Grandma was helping you?'

'Well, she was, but then the thing with Grandpa happened.'

'What thing?' I asked. I slid my stump out from under her, adjusting to a more comfortable position. Three in a single bed was not the most practical of situations.

'He won't come out of the bathroom,' she said. It was the matter-of-fact tone only a child could use. 'He went in there and he locked the door. Grandma's been knocking for *ages*.'

Jenny and I locked eyes. I thought back to Dad's vulnerability, his volatile thoughts and darkened moods. He'd said he was doing OK, but I knew better than anyone how easy it was to put up a front. A sickening fear crept into my stomach. None of us knew how he was really feeling. In that moment, I knew what I had to do. Reaching into my bedside drawer, I pulled out the letter.

'Dad, are you in there? Dad, it's Heidi.' I banged on the door, the noise of my palm echoing across the landing. 'There's no one else here now. It's only me.'

Knowing a full audience would make him even less likely to appear, I'd sent the others downstairs. I could hear them having breakfast in the kitchen, plates clattering and Evie singing, my gorgeous, innocent niece completely unaware of the potential chaos going on above.

'Dad,' I said again, my mouth close to the door. 'Please let me in.'

Silence. I sank down onto the brown carpet, my back against the bathroom door. My whole body felt heavy with worry, my stump twinging and tingling in the prosthetic socket. My head was full of horrific scenarios – what if Dad had passed out? What if he couldn't move? What if he was hurt? And worse, much worse, what if he'd caused that hurt himself?

The smells of toast and frying bacon wafted upstairs. Although I'd woken up ravenous, the aroma now caught in my throat, instead inducing panic and nausea. Because I knew what it felt like to be in that black hole of misery, that dark place where no light can penetrate, no joy can override the pain. When it feels like the hurt will never end.

'Dad . . .'

I was on the verge of tears, the solidity of the bathroom door against my back the only thing stopping me from collapse. And then I heard his voice. It was so low, so soft, that I had to put my ear against the crack. But it was him.

'Heidi.'

'Dad, please open the door.'

A pause. A shuffling sound, the bolt sliding across. I moved away and heaved myself to standing. And then the door swung open.

He was slumped against the side of the bath. He looked horrendous. His face was haggard and lined, dark with grey and black stubble. His shoulders were stooped, his grey pyjama T-shirt hanging of his skeletal frame. His body language told of misery and defeat; a man who'd fully given in to his emotions.

'I can't do it, Heidi,' he said. His voice was gruff and quiet, a tone I'd never heard before. It tore at my heart.

'Oh, Dad.' I bent down and sat next to him, our legs stretched out side by side. 'The wedding?'

'How will I face them all today? It's too much.'

'You're the father of the bride,' I said. 'You have to be there.'

'I know.' He sighed heavily. 'I want to snap out of this for Jenny. It should be such a happy day. Oh, Heidi, I hate that you're seeing this. You shouldn't be seeing this.'

I put a hand on his shoulder, hard and bony beneath my touch. I hadn't realised he'd lost so much weight.

'Dad, it's OK. I get it,' I said. 'I've been there, remember?'

'But how did you get out of it? I feel so weak. It's pathetic.'

'It's not,' I replied. 'Look, Dad, I need to read you something.' With trembling hands, I unfolded the letter. 'You might find this strange, but it's part of my therapy, and I think it'll help you too. Just, hear me out here, OK?'

'OK . . .' He sounded hesitant.

Trying to push down the nerves that had risen in my stomach, I began to read.

Dad,

Remember when I was four, or maybe five, and you took me to the farm park? It was just the two of us, quality time on our own. I was so excited to see the animals, I remember singing in the car all the way there. Anyway, you know what happened next. We got to the gate and I got stung on my finger by a wasp. I was so upset, so scared, so totally traumatised that suddenly, all my excitement vanished. I didn't want to go in. I just wanted to go home.

And what did you do? You picked me up, carried me through the entrance and showed me the baby goats. It was such a small thing, but I learnt an important lesson from you that day. Never let a setback stop you from doing what you want to do.

I've remembered that, Dad. I've remembered it for all these years – and I still remember it now. I know we don't talk about our feelings, but I want you to know I love you. I appreciate every single thing you do. And while it may not be easy, while this time in our lives is quite frankly shit, none of this is your fault. You need to remember that. Because I need you to stay strong, Dad. I need you to pick me up and carry me into that farm park. I need you to show me that it's OK when bad things happen. There will always be those baby goats; those reasons for us to smile.

Love always,

Heidi

By the time I finished, there were tears rolling down my face. Dad turned to me, his eyes glazed with emotion. I'd never thought of my dad as old before. But now I saw the passing of time, sixty-six years of graft and memories written across his face.

'Oh, Heidi,' he said. 'What have I done to deserve such beautiful daughters?'

There on the bathroom floor, I snuggled into his chest, wrapping my arms around him. We were a father-and-daughter team. And we would face this day together.

Chapter Thirty-Four

I'd walked up the cobbled path to St James the Great hundreds of times. I'd held the Brownie flag, sung carols at midnight beneath the light of the stars and haggled for second-hand toys, books and CDs at Christmas and summer markets. But I'd never walked up it with a prosthetic leg. As Mum, Evie and I made our way through the throng, I took care to lift up the folds of my bridesmaid dress. The flowing fabric nipped in at my waist, little lace sleeves falling daintily from my shoulders. After all the trauma at my fitting, I was surprised and thrilled at how good I felt. And I knew it wasn't the dress that had changed. It was me.

A dusting of cloud fell across the mid-morning sun. It was bright and warm, a cooling breeze rustling the leaves of the ancient oak trees that lined the path. Guests were already gathering, milling outside the church in their suits and fascinators. They looked up as we approached, nudging each other and smiling. Beyond the crowd, an elderly woman wearing an enormous cream hat and sunglasses was sitting on a long wooden bench. As we approached, she reached for her crutches to stand. I saw the silver bangles on both arms and my nerves were replaced by a surge of happiness.

'Heidi!' she cried joyfully. 'Well, don't you just look a picture.'

'Maud!'

Leaning heavily on her crutches, Maud tentatively took one step, then another towards me. Watching her brought sudden tears to my eyes. I'd never seen her walk properly before. It was wonderful.

'Surprise!' She grinned. 'Bet you thought I'd turn up in the wheelchair.'

'Well, yeah!'

Her wrinkled face was pink with blusher and pride.

'You're shorter than I thought,' I told her.

'And you're taller than I thought.' She chuckled. 'Amazing what a wheelchair hides.'

'How did you get here?' I paused. 'Did someone drop you off?' I wondered if it was Jack.

'My Billy's doing door-to-door service,' she smiled. I nodded. Of course. Jack wouldn't come anywhere near me. I pushed the thought from my mind. I wasn't going to let him infiltrate my happiness. Not now – and not ever.

'Maud, honestly, thank you so much for coming,' I said. She leaned in to kiss my cheek and I caught a familiar whiff of Chanel.

'Any excuse to get dolled up, that's what I say.' She winked. 'I'm absolutely thrilled you invited me, so I am, love. I feel honoured. Oh, it's been a long time since I went to a wedding. Such special days. They always make me think about my marriage to Pete.'

'Really?'

'Oh, yes.' A mist of nostalgia crossed her face. 'Such a silly darling, he was. Head permanently in the clouds. He somehow managed to go to the wrong church – turned out there were two Virgin Marys in Killarney.' She chuckled at the memory. 'The humour of that sentence didn't escape us neither, so it didn't.'

'So what happened?' I asked. Maud adjusted her grip on her walking sticks.

'Well, in the end, we turned up at the same time. I was supposed to be traditionally late, but we walked down the aisle together. My mother was not happy, let me tell you. Good Catholic woman, she was. Hated anything that didn't follow tradition. Still, me and my Pete, we laughed till his dying day at that memory. I'll never forget it.'

'Daddy!' Evie shouted suddenly.

We turned to see Mark coming out of the church. Evie ran to him, the layers of lace beneath her baby-blue tutu dress bouncing as she ran.

He was chatting to my Great-Auntie Carol and her husband Nige, fiddling with his corsage as he spoke. His suit was immaculate and his hair was gelled to one side, not a loose strand in sight. Evie launched herself at him and he scooped her into a hug.

'Am I like a real princess?' she asked.

'You look beautiful, darling,' he replied, his voice thick.

Mum came over and linked my arm. For the first time since the accident, I wasn't wearing trainers. Instead, I'd opted for silver brogues in soft leather. Getting them on to the prosthetic foot hadn't been easy. It had involved a giant shoehorn and a lot of cursing. But they looked great.

'All OK, Mark?' Mum asked. She adjusted her coral jacket. It matched her shoes and the flowers on her cream and navy dress.

'Yes, well, I think so.' Releasing Evie, Mark bent to brush a speck of dust from his gleaming shoes. He straightened up and smiled nervously. 'You know how it is.'

'Of course,' Mum soothed. 'Nerves are only natural.'

'Mummy looks so beautiful,' Evie said. 'She looks the most beautiful ever. But Grandma says you can't see her yet. You have to wait until it's time to get married.'

'That's right,' he answered. 'And I can't wait.'

'What's up, Jacksons?' Father John, the vicar, joined us. Though a middle-aged man with a paunch and a receding hairline, he had a disconcerting habit of speaking like one of the kids. John was known for cracking jokes during sermons, treating the pulpit like a religious comedy club. Jenny had warned him to keep the jokes to a minimum during the wedding ceremony. I wondered if he'd manage.

'It shouldn't be too long now,' Mum said.

Father John checked his watch. I noticed with amusement that the leather strap was decorated with the letters WWJD (What Would Jesus Do?).

'You know Jenny, traditional though she might be, she wouldn't want to be more than ten minutes late for her wedding.'

'Get her to the church on time, eh?' Father John grinned. Mum gave him a tight smile.

'Something like that, vic,' Dougie said. My best friend had scrubbed up well. He wore a striking bright blue suit and had tied half his dreadlocked hair into a bun on top of his head.

Mark was moving from foot to foot. 'I think we should probably go in,' he said.

'Of course, yes.' Father John made a sweeping gesture. 'Heidi can wait here. I'll herd the flock, as it were. Herd the flock . . . get it?'

'Very good,' Mum answered dryly.

'Good luck,' I whispered to Mark as he passed. 'It's going to be great.'

'Thank you.'

The last stragglers ducked inside. Dougie squeezed my shoulder as he moved past me. Father John gave me a double thumbs up. And then I was on my own. I leant against the ancient stonework and the familiar sound of church bells tolled high above me. I gathered my thoughts.

I'd been waiting about five minutes when the car pulled up outside. It was a Ford Galaxy with blacked-out windows and a white ribbon on the front – Jenny had insisted upon keeping the transport simple. A chauffeur in a black hat jumped out to open the back doors. I saw my dad first, dark navy suit and coat-tails, the corsage on his jacket the same shade of pale purple as my dress. He smiled at me before bending down to offer his arm to Jenny, a silent pact between us; time to put on the mask. I sent him silent, positive vibes.

I'd seen the dress before of course. It had been hanging from the door frame that very morning. And yet, the sight of my big sister getting out of that car still took my breath away. Her hair was swept up with a few escaping strands and tiny white gypsophila sprigs were pinned into the sides, an intricate lace veil clipped into her bun. The boat neck looked stunning, exposing her defined collarbone, the style a simple, classic cut which nipped in at her waist before falling to the floor. It was sophisticated and elegant, no show or extraneous detail. It was perfect.

She walked slowly, cautious of her train. She wasn't partial to stilettos either. Instead, she'd gone for a pearly kitten heel, her favourite type of smart shoe.

'Jenny, you look absolutely beautiful,' I said. I felt like a little girl again, full of awe as I watched my sister getting ready for her school prom.

'Doesn't she?' Dad was teary too. 'And so do you, Heidi.'

'We need to start soon,' Jenny said. 'Are you OK, Heidi?' She turned to me, her expression serious. 'Are you sure you'll be able to walk down the aisle?'

'I'm sure,' I replied. 'I want to do this, Jen.'

'Okay. Great.' She smoothed her dress. 'Now, where's that vicar?'

Right on cue, Father John appeared in the doorway. Evie was by his side. She was jumping up and down with her basketful of petals, a devoted little flower girl.

'Mother Mary, don't you look fabulous?' he exclaimed, catching sight of Jenny. Despite her controlled manner, she blushed.

We followed him into the porch. He gave Ethel the organist a thumbs up and she moved to press play on the sound system, in charge of all things music, both live and recorded. The gentle, recognisable notes of Pachelbel's *Canon* filled the church. It was time.

'Are you OK, Dad?' I asked. He turned around. Our eyes connected, an understanding passing between us.

'I think so, love. Are you ready?'

'As I'll ever be.'

Evie went first, scattering petals across the red carpet, the biggest smile on her round, rosy face. I saw Jenny squeeze Dad's hand. Then they began to walk, arm in arm, the faces of our family and friends turned towards the procession in rapt attention. Jenny was guiding Dad, his legs visibly trembling. They were holding each other up.

And then it was my turn. I was at the back, the dress train lifted out in front of me. I sought out Maud and she gave an encouraging nod.

'Go, girl,' she mouthed.

I pulled my shoulders back and straightened up, trying to relax the tension that had seized every muscle in my body. I heard Tara's voice in my ear, her instructions to look ahead, to keep my head high and my hips level. One step at a time.

I felt like all the months of rehab had been leading to this moment. And I made it. I didn't stumble. I didn't fall. The elation was overwhelming. I felt the urge to cheer. As I sat down in the front row, I gave Maud the biggest grin. She was dabbing at her eyes with a tissue.

Father John held out his arms. His bald head shone red and green beneath the dappled light from the stained-glass windows.

'Welcome, everyone,' he began in a booming voice, as though addressing a crowd at Wembley. 'God made Adam, and he rested. Then he made Eve. Since then, well, let's be honest . . . no one's rested. Definitely not me, anyway!'

There were low groans and chuckles. I thought about the vicar's wife, Maggie, a tiny, insipid woman who made a cracking ploughman's lunch. It was hard to imagine her as the type to boss her husband around. I stole a glance at Jenny, standing to attention at the altar. Her expression was impassive.

'Right, let the proceedings begin,' Father John said. He took a breath and closed his eyes, slipping into professionalism. 'Dearly beloved, we are gathered here today in the presence of God – and in the face of this company – to join together this man and this woman in holy matrimony.'

It was a beautiful ceremony. I couldn't deny it, Jenny's planning had paid off. The hymns went without a hitch, despite a slight discrepancy with the number of verses to 'All Things Bright and Beautiful' and the occasional duff note from Ethel. Mum delivered her reading with the reverence and projection of a truly experienced churchgoer. Evie only danced in the aisle twice.

The way Mark looked at Jenny was an expression of pure devotion, an outpouring of love. Of course he loved her. Of course she should never have doubted it. Surrounded by my family and friends, my heart was full of gratitude. There was a joyful future out there – for all of us. As my sister and her husband signed the register, I had tears in my eyes. Next to me, Evie tugged at my dress.

'Don't cry, Auntie Heidi,' she said in that incongruously wise way that only children have. 'Everything will be happy now.'

She had no idea of the gravitas of her words, but they made me cry more. Because finally, I realised that she was right.

*

After the service, there were photos in the churchyard. I was shuffled and bustled from one picture to the next, Jenny leading the
operation with military precision. She grouped the gaggles into
families and friendship groups, barking instructions at the poor
young photographer. He consented and nodded to her demands,
his black skinny jeans soon brown with mud from kneeling.

The atmosphere was lively. Dougie was playing hide-and-
seek with Evie as she ducked behind the gravestones. Mum
and Dad were in full host and hostess mode, chatting animatedly with expansive hand gestures. I was relieved to see Dad
looking happy. Dougie bunched in for a photo and backed into
a gravestone, exclaiming 'Christ!' at the top of his voice as he
very nearly overbalanced. Even Father John laughed.

Soon, my leg was twinging from the effort of remaining
upright. The bone rubbed against my prosthesis. I needed to
sit down. On the other side of the churchyard, Jenny was still
directing the crowds, lining up the Prosecco Ladies so that
their dresses didn't clash. No one noticed as I slipped around
the corner, towards the back entrance of the church. Just a
quick breather; then I'd be back.

I'd always loved the churchyard's ancient oak tree. I remembered how we weren't allowed to climb it as children, understanding from a young age that it was protected, that we needed
to be careful and gentle. In our young minds it was magic, full
of stories and secrets waiting to be unearthed.

Slowly, I lowered myself to the ground, not easy in a full-
length bridesmaid dress. I rested against the tree trunk. In the
distance, I could hear the noisy chatter of my family. I stretched
my prosthetic leg out in front of me, grateful that the nerve
pain was fading. Five minutes, that was all I needed. Just a
little pause before returning to the throng. I leaned my head
back and closed my eyes briefly. When I opened them, there
was a figure coming towards me.

He walked with his head down, shoulders drooping as though embarrassed by his shadow. Then I saw the shirt. It was a kind of shimmering violet, pink at the collar and fading down to purple, the bottom a deep midnight blue. I blinked, not trusting my own perception. But as his advance continued, the more certain I became. My heartbeat sped up. I felt short of breath. Because it wasn't a trick of the light. It really was him. Jack McNally was walking through the churchyard towards me.

A few metres from the tree, he paused. We stared at each other. His features were so familiar to me; the imprint of dimples on his round cheeks, his sticking-out ears, scorching red hair like a sunset. He squinted in the sunlight and I noticed the deepening creases on his forehead. There were greenish rings beneath his eyes. He looked exhausted.

'Heidi,' he said. A small smile flickered uncertainly on his lips. Fury rose up inside me.

'What the hell are you doing here?'

My hands were shaking with rage. He came closer. His tall shadow brushed my face. He fiddled with the contents of his pockets.

'I – I came to pick up Nanna. Dad sent me.'

'Well, you're too early,' I snapped. 'She's coming for the wedding breakfast. You'll have to come back later.'

'Oh, really? I'm sure Dad said that—'

'I know the schedule of my own sister's wedding, Jack.'

'Right. Yes. Of course.' He ran a hand through his hair. 'Sorry.'

'Why didn't you call?' The words burst out of me. How dare he just turn up?

'I wanted to.' He sighed then, a sound that seemed to ricochet off the trees. 'It was . . . difficult.'

'Because of your girlfriend?' He took a step back, as though I'd slapped him.

'Well, yeah, I guess.' He was visibly floundering now, shuffling from one foot to the other. 'Look, it's not that I kept it from you on purpose, Heidi. I promise that wasn't how it was.' My rage burned brighter.

'Really? Because do you know what, Jack? From where I am, that's exactly how it seems.'

Jack blinked furiously. He looked like he might cry. Good, I thought, the extent of my venom surprising me. Give him a taste of what I've been through.

'I started those challenges because I wanted to help you,' he said feebly. 'Honestly, that was my only intention. I guess . . . I guess I didn't expect us to become such good friends.'

I met his eyes; olive green flecked with gold, now filmed with sadness. Let him be sad. Let him suffer like I did.

'I trusted you more than anyone,' I said. My anger was charred with his betrayal.

'I know.'

He moved to sit beside me, leaning back against the oak tree. He drew his legs towards him and hugged his knees. I shifted further away from him.

'I'm sorry,' he said.

He reached into his pocket for his lighter and a cigarette. I turned to see the side profile of his face, his brow contorted with worry.

'Still smoking?' I asked flatly.

'When I feel I need it.'

He took a deep drag, pursing his lips and turning his head to blow the smoke away from me. I watched as it dissipated into the air. I was fuming.

Just then, I heard distant footsteps crunching on the gravel path that led into the graveyard. I looked up to see Jenny rounding the corner, Mark holding up her dress train. Jenny looked flustered. Her kitten heels stuck in the grass as she advanced.

'Heidi, where have you been?' she called, slightly out of breath. 'The taxis will be here any minute and you've just disappeared and . . . Oh!' She spotted Jack and her face broke into a smile. 'How romantic!'

'What?' Jack and I said together. Ever so subtly, he stubbed out the cigarette in his hand behind him.

'Coming to surprise Heidi like this.' Jenny threw her arms in the air and giggled, the sound of her laughter jarring and unexpected. Buoyed by marital bliss, she'd clearly overlooked the fact that Jack had disappeared from my life. 'Isn't that just lovely, Mark?'

'Lovely,' he agreed.

'It's not . . . I didn't . . .' Jack stuttered.

Then Mark turned to Jenny. His eyes glinted behind his glasses.

'You know how Great-Uncle Terry's plantar fasciitis is playing up?' he said. She nodded.

'Yeah . . .'

'And he couldn't make it today . . .'

Jenny cottoned on. She threw an arm around her new husband.

'Oh, yes! Lovely idea, Mark!' She kissed him on the cheek. 'Looks like Jack's not the only romantic here.'

'So, Jack, how do you feel about joining us for the reception?' Mark asked.

I did a double take. Surely he was joking. But they both stood there, smiles wide, waiting. Jack's face grew paler than ever.

'I don't know if I should,' he said.

'Nonsense!' Jenny answered. 'It'll be a chance for you two to catch up properly.'

'And we've already paid for the meal,' Mark added.

'Really, I don't want to intrude . . .' Jack floundered. I could see beads of sweat on the side of his face. 'I was only here to pick up Nanna – but I'm early. I – I got confused.'

303

'Oh, well, that works out perfectly then,' Mark replied. 'You can take her home at the end. Look, Jack, after everything you've done for Heidi, it would be our pleasure to have you there.'

Jenny smiled her agreement. 'Exactly. Plus I'm sure Heidi would love you to come, wouldn't you?'

She turned her attention to me. When I saw the joy in her eyes, I knew I didn't have a choice. I didn't want to temper her happiness. I couldn't fill her wedding day with drama. Very slowly, I nodded. I felt Jack's eyes on me. I couldn't look at him.

'Excellent!' Mark said. 'That's all sorted.'

'We really do need to go though,' Jenny added. 'The cars have been waiting for ages.' She linked Mark's arm and began to pull him back across the grass. 'Come on, *husband*.' She spoke the word with relish. 'Let's go.'

I watched them go, open-mouthed. Wordlessly, Jack held out a hand to help me stand. Shell-shocked, I allowed him to pull me up, though my anger burned brighter than ever. What the hell had just happened? And more to the point, why hadn't he said no?

The barn looked beautiful. It was decked out with fairy lights and flowers, round tables with white cloths, each with a lavender and verbena centrepiece. Next to each guest's place name were different books, tied up with purple ribbon. They'd been chosen from charity shops by Jenny and Mark and signed with a personalised message.

I tried to be normal. I nibbled at my smoked salmon and my lamb, although I wasn't really hungry. I immersed myself in the speeches, clapping and laughing at my dad's terrible anecdotes of our childhood. I jiggled Evie up and down on my lap as she clamoured for a cuddle. I cried and wiped my eyes along with the rest of the room as the usually unemotional Mark professed the depth of his love for my sister. I drank my coffee and I chatted. I kept up my smile.

However, I'd begun to feel distant from the buzz around me, all too aware of Jack's presence. To an outsider, he appeared to be the picture of confidence, sitting behind his 'Terry' place name and chatting animatedly to Maud. To me, it seemed like he was over-compensating with enthusiasm. His body language was tense. His shoulders were hunched, his gestures quick and frantic. At one point, our eyes connected. A laser beam of complicated emotion shot across the room between us. I quickly looked away. But I couldn't help but wonder what he was thinking.

As evening came, everyone headed outside. The courtyard was strung with tiny lanterns that twinkled in the dusky light. I stood on the patio with Dougie, watching as Evie and the other younger children practiced handstands on the grass.

'I wish I had their energy,' I commented.

'We used to.' He grinned at me. 'Remember our treasure hunts in the woods? We'd be out there for bloody hours.'

'Until it got dark.'

'Until we got told off.'

I looked around the courtyard. Most of the guests were milling and chatting on the patio. The Prosecco Ladies were playing giant Jenga. The elderly contingent had gathered by the gaggle of chairs and tables to take the weight off their new knees and hips, the warmth of wine visible on their cheeks.

'It's been a lovely day, hasn't it?' Dougie said. 'So full of happiness.'

'It's beautiful.' I rested my cheek on his shoulder. A head taller than me, he was the perfect leaning height. 'Dougie . . .'

'Mmm?'

'Are you sad about Hal?'

'I knew you felt guilty about that.' He straightened up and turned to face me. '*I was* sad, yes. But I also know it wasn't right. If it was, there's no way he would have reacted in such a selfish way about you.'

'But I don't want it to be about me, Dougie,' I said. 'That's the whole point. This is about what you want.'

He smiled then, his white teeth gleaming in the evening light.

'What I want is to live with my best pal. And what I certainly don't want is to be with anyone who owns a cat named Princess Diana.'

I let out a snort of laughter. 'OK. Just as long as you're doing what's right for you. I don't want you to build your world around me.'

'I know. Trust me, H. I'm secure in my decision. In fact . . .' he put a hand on my shoulder and whispered conspiratorially. 'I've got a date next week – with Mateo.'

'Dougie!' I slapped his arm in mock-annoyance – but I was thrilled. 'You kept that one quiet!'

'Ha, I know, sorry.' He winked. 'We've been texting a bit. But I didn't want you to think I was stealing your dance teacher.'

'Course not. I think it's great! You need to move on.' I paused. 'We all do.'

'Exactly. Speaking of which, I'm also thinking of showing some of my art to a gallery in Shoreditch. They're looking for up-and-coming artists for some new exhibition thing.'

'Dougie, that's amazing!' I felt choked with pride. 'I'm sure they'll love your stuff.'

'Let's hope so.'

'You have to promise me though, you will tell me if living with me gets too much? You know, with the leg and every-thing. The last thing I want is to be a burden.'

His black-brown eyes glittered with amusement.

'Mate, you've been a burden to me for thirty-two years. Why should it stop now?' I rolled my eyes at him.

'Whatever.'

He put an arm around me and held up his glass.

'Here's to new starts.'

'To new starts,' I answered. I drained the remainder of my drink. Just then, Evie ran up to us.

'Mummy's throwing her flowers!' she yelled, tugging at both our hands. 'Come and see!'

Dougie and I allowed ourselves to be pulled into the throng of guests. Everyone had gathered on the lawn in front of Jenny, who held her bouquet up above her head. I glanced around. I couldn't see Jack. And I didn't care.

'What are your chances then, H?' Dougie asked as the sound of encouraging cheers around us grew louder.

'Not great. I think I have a handicap,' I said, pointing downwards. He grinned.

'Brilliant. Out of my way then, love.' He elbowed me gently in the stomach. 'This one's for Mateo.'

'You are ridiculous . . .'

'Three, two, one!' Jenny called.

The crowd surged forwards, jostling and jumping. I saw the flowers soar above my head. Dougie leapt towards them. Half-heartedly, I reached up, but I was too late. They flew past us both and behind to the back of the excitable group.

When I turned around, I saw an amazing sight. Maud, resplendent in her giant hat, had thrown her walking sticks to the ground. Arms aloft, the flowers sailed straight into her grasp. For a moment, she stared at them, stunned. Without her sticks, she stumbled – and Dougie and I rushed towards her. But she righted herself, her expression transforming into an enormous, wicked smile.

'Bloody hell, would you look at that!' she exclaimed. 'Life in the old girl yet!'

Everyone was cheering now, the sound of applause ringing around the courtyard. Dougie handed Maud her sticks back and she tucked the flowers under her armpit, inhaling deeply.

'Well done,' I told her. The joy on her face made me feel strangely emotional.

'Oh, they smell lovely,' she told me happily. 'Now, I wonder who my new beau might be, eh?'

'That's the spirit,' Dougie grinned.

It was then that I noticed Jack. He was walking towards us, two glasses of prosecco in his hands.

'Er, Dougie?' I gestured with my eyes.

He clocked on immediately. 'Come on, Maud, let's get you a seat,' he said, taking her arm.

The old lady looked over towards her grandson then back at me. She nodded, understanding.

'Ah, yes, good idea,' she said loudly and pointedly. 'I really do feel quite tired after all that excitement. Must be my age, eh, Dougie?'

'Never,' he replied. 'You're in your prime, Maud McNally.'

He began to guide her to the tables and chairs at the far end of the courtyard. She looked back at me and winked.

'Maybe I've found my new man already, Heidi,' she remarked.

'Yeah. Good luck with that,' I laughed.

'Can we chat?' Jack asked as he reached me. He held out one of the glasses and I took it wordlessly. 'Maybe somewhere slightly less public?'

I nodded. 'Follow me.'

I took him around to the far side of the barn, where a stretch of grass and a wavy gravel path led off to the bridal quarters. We sat on one of the wooden benches by the back door of the barn. *'For Freda and Michael,'* an old bronze plague on it read. *'A love story to last forever.'*

'Do you think it did?' Jack asked, pointing. 'Last forever, I mean?'

'I'd like to think so,' I said. 'But I guess it's not always that simple.'

'No.' He bit his lip, cleared his throat to change the subject. 'So look, Heidi, I said no to the job my dad found.'

'Right.' I didn't want to engage, didn't want to pretend. How could he speak to me like this, as though everything was normal?

'Yeah. I thought about it, I really did – but I don't want to live in his shadow. So I've decided to go freelance. It's a big move, quite daunting and I'll have to build up contacts, but it's my choice, my career. And at least I'm in charge of it.'

'That's great, Jack,' I said, without enthusiasm.

I couldn't be nice. I couldn't be normal. At that moment, I felt completely out of control. There was so much I wanted to say. We sat there, the unanswered questions between us shining and floating like stars. They burnt brighter beneath our silence. They couldn't be ignored.

'Look,' Jack said, 'I need you to understand.' I put a hand up to stop him. His mystery was making me angry again.

'Shouldn't you tell your girlfriend you're here?' I snapped.

'Heidi . . .'

'Well, she'll probably be wondering, won't she? After all, we wouldn't want her to think you've vanished without explanation. She'd be heartbroken if you disappeared. What kind of person would do that? Oh, wait . . .' I downed the rest of my drink in a triumphant rage. Jack looked pained.

'Heidi, please, just listen for a moment.' He angled his body towards me. I folded my arms.

'Spit it out then.'

'Lara and I broke up.'

'What?'

'Yeah. It's over.' His green eyes held mine with their intensity. 'And look, OK, maybe I should have told you about her. But it wasn't right, Heidi. It hasn't been good for months.'

'Because she kissed some bloke from work?' I snapped. He reeled for a moment, wide-eyed.

309

'Wait, how did you . . . ? Oh. Right. Nanna. And yeah, since you asked. That is why.' His expression darkened, sadness overtaking his defensiveness. 'I tried to move on from it. I wanted to. But every time I looked at her, every time she tried to overcompensate, I just couldn't stop thinking about it – about him.'

'That must have been tough.' In spite of my anger, I felt a stab of sympathy for him. No one deserved that betrayal.

'Yeah.' Jack ran a hand through his sunset red hair. 'I mean, stuff wasn't right between us before that. But I think we were both pretending. I had to stay away for a while, get my head in order. I'm sorry, I just . . . I needed time. And then something else happened that put everything into perspective.' He paused, leaning in closer. 'I met you, Heidi.'

The breath constricted in my chest. I stared at him. I didn't know what to say. Gently, he put a hand on my shoulder, his fingers warm and hesitant against my skin. Despite the warm evening, I felt a shiver pass down my spine.

'I'm sorry,' Jack said. He pulled his hand away. Pink blotches had appeared across his cheeks and neck. 'That was an unfair thing to say. You've had so much to deal with already. The last thing you need is some man professing his feelings when you're trying to rebuild yourself.'

'Jack,' I interrupted. I couldn't listen to any more. 'Don't.'

'But Heidi, I—'

From inside the barn, the speaker system crackled into life.

'Ladies and gentlemen,' the DJ's deep voice proclaimed. 'It's time for the first dance.'

'Already?' I pulled myself to standing, suddenly panicked. 'We need to go back inside,' I told Jack. 'Right now.'

For a moment, he continued to sit there. His expression was torn. He licked his lips then shuffled his feet in the gravel. He looked like he was about to say something.

'Jack,' I urged. At that moment, the only thought in my head was my sister. If I missed her first dance, I'd never forgive myself. 'Seriously. Let's go.'

Almost mechanically, he got up and followed me into the barn, where a large circle had formed around the dance floor. I spotted Dougie on the far side, Evie clinging like a monkey to his back. He raised his eyebrows at me questioningly and I shrugged. There was really nothing I could say.

The sound of Ed Sheeran's 'Perfect' filled the room. It was an obvious wedding choice, but somehow it suited Jenny and Mark perfectly, the safe yet romantic melody creeping straight into everyone's hearts. Mark held a hand out to my sister and pulled her into his arms. She rested her chin on his shoulder and they began to sway, like teenagers at a school disco. It was as though no one else was in the room but them.

When the second verse began, Mark beckoned Evie and she ran to her parents on the dance floor. Sandwiched between their legs, she gazed up at them in joy and wonder. Soon after, other couples began to join them; tentatively at first but then with growing conviction. Even my parents were dancing, Dad spinning Mum in circles and bending her backwards theatrically. As the crowd of observers thinned out, I felt increasingly isolated. My leg began to throb. I was halfway to a chair when I felt a hand on my arm.

'Shall we dance?' Jack said from behind me. I turned to face him, my vision blurred from crying. It was an impossible ask. I resented him for putting me in this position. The injustice of it boiled up inside me.

'Why, Jack?' I asked through my tears. 'Because I'm the disabled girl you feel sorry for?'

'Never.' He moved closer. I could smell cigarettes and mint on his breath. 'I have never thought that, Heidi.'

Sincerity glimmered with the frosting of gold in his eyes, his pupils large and earnest. I felt my face flushing.

'Jack, look, I don't want anything. Not right now.'

'Why?' His face was close to mine, brows creased. 'I thought . . . I thought you felt the same.'

'I thought so too,' I replied. The disappointment shone in his eyes. I couldn't bear it. And yet, my gut instinct drove me onwards, filling me with certainty through the pain.

'For a long time, I thought you were what I needed,' I continued. 'But in a way, by leaving you did me a favour. I need to focus on myself. Until that happens, I can't be open to love. The answer isn't you, Jack. It's always been me.'

The song had reached its bridge, swelling to a crescendo. My pulse was racing. But as the words tumbled out, I realised I'd never felt more certain. I was independent. I was powerful. I was in control.

Jack paused. He bit his lip, taking in what I'd said. After what felt like forever, he nodded.

'OK. I get it,' he said finally. 'So look, let me rephrase my question. Heidi Jackson. As my friend, as one of the most determined, sometimes frustrating and downright remarkable people I've ever met – will you dance with me?'

My stomach felt jittery. The fears of falling, of embarrassment and abandonment were heightened and raw. But then I looked up at Jack, standing in front of me in his purple shirt. His dimples deepened as he smiled. He held out a questioning hand. Slowly, I nodded.

'Go on, then.'

His fingers were warm against mine as he led me to the dancefloor, our palms clammy with possibility. And then I was in his arms beneath the twinkling barn lights, clumsily stepping and swaying. Jack winced when I stepped on his toes.

'Ouch!' But he was smiling.

'I've got one leg, mate,' I retorted. 'Give me a break, will you?'

As the song played on and my family twirled around us, the nerves in my stump fizzed and popped like fireworks. Yet for the first time, I stopped worrying about falling. Instead, I closed my eyes and let the music carry me away. I could feel both my feet.

ONE YEAR ON

ONE YEAR ON

29/05/17

The canal path hasn't changed. It's bathed in spring sunshine, the overgrown trees and distant city skyline reflected on the slowly moving water. I look down at my feet as I walk, my new white trainers pristine against the dusty ground.

'Are you OK?' Jack asks. He's a few steps behind me, keeping a respectful distance. I feel glad that he's with me, a reassuring presence to combat any wobbles, emotional or physical. It's equally likely there'll be both.

'I think so.' The nerves are dancing in my stomach. But my determination overcomes them. I know now that it always will.

I check my watch, conscious that I can't let time slip away. In just over two hours, I have another day of dance training with Mateo and Skye. The rehab centre loved my idea of dance workshops – they've even agreed to pay for my services. Long term, I'm going even bigger than that. Eventually, I'm going to teach inclusive drama and dance full-time; performing arts for all ages and abilities. Performance that shows ability, not disability. I haven't felt this motivated in years. But right now, nerves are overshadowing determination. Jack taps my arm lightly. He can sense it, too.

'If you want to turn back, we can,' he says.

'No,' I reply firmly. 'I have to do this.'

It has to be today. I carry on. I'm concentrating on my gait, hips level and abs tensed, maintaining a rhythm to my steps. I'm definitely walking better these days; my balance and my confidence both greatly improved.

When I reach the spot, I stop. There's nothing remarkable about this patch of ground, and yet I remember it exactly. The accident happened just over halfway along, where the trees hang thicker, casting floating shadows across the narrow path. I run my hand along the cracked railings, remembering how I clung to them that day, the scratched paint against my fingertips as I clamoured for solidity within the chaos.

'Here?' Jack asks. I nod.

'Yeah.'

'The last challenge.'

We smile at each other. It often feels like so long ago that I wrote that list; back when nothing seemed achievable, when the world had shrunk around me. Now, the future stretches ahead, tantalising in its possibility. I can use escalators, I can board a Tube alone, and I can live independently without worry. I can even wear skinny jeans. The things I once thought impossible have become my everyday.

We sit down and Jack hands me the bag that's on his shoulder. I prop it up by the bench. I can still picture the exact angle of my body as I lay here, the way I bent my left knee and curled it upwards, my hands scrabbling in the gravel as I tried to fight the blackness. Seeing it again for the first time, I feel a strange sort of sadness; not grief but a darkened nostalgia creeping into my heart.

'Thank you for bringing me here,' Jack says. The morning sunlight bounces off his red-gold hair. 'Really, it means a lot.'

'I wanted you to see it.'

'One whole year.' Jack exhales through pursed lips. 'The final chapter, eh?'

We smile at each other. He's right; it's the last challenge, but there's finality in this moment for us both. Jack's freelance career has really taken off and he's writing a book about my journey, a ghosted memoir that will hopefully help other amputees to weather the storm. This day marks the beginning of the ending – and we're both hoping for happiness.

'The book will be great,' I tell him.

He's very self-critical. He's agonised over every word of every sentence, determined to do my story justice. But he's a beautiful writer – I trust him implicitly with my story. After all, he's lived it, too. He looks at me now, sincerity shining in his jewel green eyes.

'I'm so proud of you,' he says.

The words light my heart. I still can't quite believe how far I've come. I've walked here without sticks or help, putting one foot in front of the other, thankful with each step that I still can.

Out on the water, a man prepares breakfast on his barge, sitting on the deck spreading jam onto thick slabs of toast. A pair of swans float by. Just another day in the place where everything changed. I notice our silhouettes side by side, the pole of my prosthetic leg casting a long, stretched shadow across the path.

I unzip the black bag and remove its contents, then I take off my prosthetic leg. I slide my stump into the running blade and stand up, bouncing experimentally as it clicks into place.

'Ready?' Jack asks.

'Ready,' I say. Jack reaches out to take my hand.

'No,' I tell him. 'I'm OK on my own.'

He smiles at me and we start to run. And this time, I'm not looking back.

Acknowledgments

I was sitting on a square in Seville when I first discovered I had a book deal. I immediately ordered a sangria to celebrate - and that overwhelming feeling of disbelief, joy, excitement and a whole lot of gratitude has stayed with me ever since. That's why my first huge thank you must go to you, lovely reader, for picking up my debut novel. It still hasn't quite sunk in yet!

Heartfelt thanks to super agent and pal Richard Pike at Conville and Walsh, and to the entire Orion team – Virginia Woolstencroft for being a publicity guru and my incredible editor Sam Eades, who listened, encouraged and didn't run a mile when I cornered her in her kitchen and tipsily pitched this book.

I'd like to extend huge thanks to Curtis Brown Creative – to Anna Davies and the 2015 three month novel writing course contingent, whose advice, laughter and monthly gatherings have been invaluable. To all my colleagues at *Good Housekeeping*, *Prima* and *Red* for being unwavering in their support – especially to Gaby Huddart, Jackie Brown and to writing powerhouse, Lindsay Nicholson.

To Rebecca Smith at Southampton University for believing in me when I was a fresh-faced student with a big writing dream. To Sue Pilkington and Sue Thomas, my 'journalism mummies' who taught me so much. I'd also like to extend an enormous thank you to Victoria Hislop for her friendship, guidance and for the most beautiful writing retreat imaginable.

I can't write a book so close to my own story without mentioning our wonderful NHS, and the amazing care I received – and receive – at the Royal London Hospital, Lambeth Amputee Rehabilitation Centre, Harold Wood Long Term Conditions Centre and the London Prosthetics Centre, particularly genius prosthetist Abdo Haidar. Thank you, all of you, for putting me back together, physically and mentally. Thank you to the Limbless Association and Barts' Charity – two wonderful organisations – for giving me new opportunities and restored confidence.

Five Steps To Happy is dedicated to my sister, Althea, who was with me on the morning my life changed forever. But not a single day went by during my recovery without my family and friends by my side. To my parents, Richard and Sara, Auntie (and personal physio) Clare, Uncle Andy, Granny, Nana, Auntie Connie and to everyone who wrote me letters, made me laugh through the pain and tears and helped me to feel like me again – thank you. I couldn't have done this without you.